CLOUD

ALSO BY ERIC McCORMACK

CLOUD

a Novel

ERIC

McCORMACK

PENGUIN

an imprint of Penguin Canada Books Inc., a Penguin Random House Company

Published by the Penguin Group

Penguin Canada Books Inc., 90 Eglinton Avenue East, Suite 700, Toronto, Ontario, Canada M4P 2Y3

Penguin Group (USA) LLC, 375 Hudson Street, New York, New York 10014, U.S.A.
Penguin Books Ltd, 80 Strand, London WC2R 0RL, England
Penguin Ireland, 25 St Stephen's Green, Dublin 2, Ireland (a division of Penguin Books Ltd)
Penguin Group (Australia), 707 Collins Street, Melbourne, Victoria 3008, Australia
(a division of Pearson Australia Group Pty Ltd)
Penguin Books India Pvt Ltd, 11 Community Centre, Panchsheel Park, New Delhi – 110 017, India
Penguin Group (NZ), 67 Apollo Drive, Rosedale, Auckland 0632, New Zealand
(a division of Pearson New Zealand Ltd)
Penguin Books (South Africa) (Pty) Ltd, 24 Sturdee Avenue, Rosebank, Johannesburg 2196, South Africa

Penguin Books Ltd, Registered Offices: 80 Strand, London WC2R 0RL, England

First published 2014

1 2 3 4 5 6 7 8 9 10 (WEB)

Manufactured in Canada.

LIBRARY AND ARCHIVES CANADA CATALOGUING IN PUBLICATION

McCormack, Eric, author
Cloud / Eric McCormack.

ISBN 978-0-14-319128-5 (pbk.)

I. Title.

PS8575.C665C56 2014   C813'.54   C2014-901283-7

eBook ISBN 978-0-14-319293-0

Visit the Penguin Canada website at www.penguin.ca

Special and corporate bulk purchase rates available; please see
www.penguin.ca/corporatesales or call 1-800-810-3104.

FOR NANCY

If all the skies were parchment,
and all the seas were ink,
and all the feathers of all the birds were pens,
and all the men and all the women were scribes—even then
it would be impossible
to describe this marvel.

GAMALIEL

PROLOGUE

It was in La Verdad that I came across the book.

I'd flown down there from Canada for a mining conference and had just attended a meeting that finished around midday. My walk back to the hotel, along the Avenida del Sol, wasn't too pleasant. July's a steamy time of the year, especially in an inland city like La Verdad, built where there used to be nothing but jungle. The sidewalks were almost empty, for by this time of day even natives of the city look for shade. My northern body was unused to the sticky heat, making it all the worse.

The sky turned suddenly black and a drenching tropical downpour began. I ducked under the awning of a used bookstore I'd noticed on my way to the meeting. According to its stencilled, fly-by-night sign, it was called the Bookstore de Mexico. From the hybrid name, I thought it might have some books in English, though in the window I saw only worn-looking paperbacks with Spanish titles.

Since I couldn't really go anywhere else till the lashing rain let up, I went through the open door for a look around.

No one else was in there except for an old Mayan woman in her traditional dress with its geometric patterns. She was sitting near the front at a table with a blue metal cash box on it. The store behind her was narrow, not much wider than a corridor, with warped, pressed-board bookcases along the walls and filling the space between. The only lighting came from some dangling electric bulbs without shades. A number of small lizards, as still as gargoyles, were clinging to the ceiling. In spite of everything, the smell of old books made the atmosphere not unpleasant.

As I strolled through, I could see that the books were indeed nearly all paperbacks. I glanced through the pages of a few of them, trying to figure out, from my smattering of Spanish, what they might be about. Some of the books were in poor condition and contained nests of silverfish. Others looked as though they'd been nibbled by rodents of one kind or another.

From experience, I handled them all gingerly. Years before, browsing through an old book in a store in northern Australia, I felt something soft moving under my fingers. I dropped the book and from it a scorpion the size of my hand scuttled away into the shadows.

I'D BEEN IN THE Bookstore de Mexico for maybe five minutes when I noticed the sky outside was lightening and the rain was letting up—it was now barely pattering down on the awning. I started to move towards the front door.

That was when I saw some hardcover books low on a shelf. One of them in particular caught my eye. It was a thin, oversized volume that didn't fit properly amongst the other books, and it was lying flat on top of them. I leaned over for a closer look. It seemed to have an English title, so I lifted it out for a quick inspection.

The book gave off a musty smell. The print on the spine was of faded gold, so even close up all I could read was part of the title: *The —dian Cloud*. The cover was made of brown leather and the pages were so big and thick it was hard to separate them. There weren't many of them—maybe a hundred, blotched with mildew and dampness. But I did manage to pry them apart at the title page:

THE OBSIDIAN CLOUD

෬෧

*An account of a singular occurrence
within living memory over the skies of the town
of Duncairn
in the County of Ayrshire*

By

Rev. K. Macbane

The Old Ayr Press
Printer and Bookbinder
Scotland
18—

Duncairn!

Seeing that name again so unexpectedly here, in another hemisphere, took my breath away. Duncairn was a little town in the Uplands of Scotland where I'd stayed for a brief time when I was a young man. Something had happened to me there that changed the whole trajectory of my life. It was a thing I'd never been able to forget. Or understand.

WITHOUT TRYING TO pry open any more of the pages of the old book, I took it over to the Mayan woman at her table. I wasn't all that interested in what this "singular occurrence" might be that had taken place in Duncairn. But that familiar name made me want to have the book. I asked the woman for a price.

Her long hair, streaked with grey, was tied back. Her eyes were brown and unreadable.

"*Dos mil pesos,*" she said without blinking.

The price was ridiculous and probably meant for haggling over. But I paid her what she asked and she put the money in her metal box. She slid the book into a plastic bag and handed it to me in silence.

I thanked her for the shelter.

She nodded slightly, though I'm not sure she'd any idea what I'd said.

I LEFT THE Bookstore de Mexico and picked my way amongst the steaming puddles along the Avenida Del Sol. When I eventually got back to my hotel room, I settled down on the vinyl armchair with the book. Even the air conditioning couldn't quite conquer the stink of mildew that arose from it. I lingered again over the title page, marvelling at the coincidence of seeing that name,

Duncairn, and thinking back with a mixture of sadness and bitterness to my time there.

Then, carefully separating the thick, oversized pages, I began reading.

THE OBSIDIAN CLOUD seemed to be a factual account of what we'd nowadays call a "weather event."

It began on a windy July morning. Just after ten o'clock, the wind shunted a wedge of low, dark clouds from over the North Sea onto the Scottish mainland. By the time the clouds reached the hills of the Southern Uplands, it was early afternoon and a particular grouping of them had melded together so smoothly that it had become just one very big cloud with a black underbelly.

At two o'clock, the wind died completely and the black cloud stalled directly over the high valley where the little town of Duncairn sits. The sky above the town, from hilltop to hilltop, north, south, east, and west, was so black and so smooth it resembled a mirror of polished obsidian, reflecting all the countryside beneath. Astonishingly, Duncairn itself was visible up there, with everything inverted: its streets and square, church and spire, surrounding fields and cottages, even the streams that would become the River Ayr worming their way down the hillsides and valleys.

Numerous reliable eyewitness accounts of the occurrence were given by those who lived in and around Duncairn, amongst them a greengrocer, the town clerk, a kiln operator, a tailor, a brewer, an apothecary's assistant, the town constable, the lawyer, and even an itinerant dentist who was in the town on his quarterly visit. They all signed their names on affidavits.

The black cloud was so low-lying that some of those with

acute eyesight swore they could make out their own tiny reflections up there, looking back down at them. "I could see my goodman rounding up the sheep in the east pasture," the wife of a local farmer reported. "I could even see myself at the door of the cottage, and my cat Puddock sitting on my shoulder."

Two lovers lying in a bracken-filled cranny high amongst the hills got quite a shock at seeing their activities reflected in the sky above them. They were willing to state what they'd seen but, understandably, since they were each married to someone else, asked not to be named.

One of the eyewitnesses, Dr. Thracy de Ware, a well-known naturalist and astronomer, added scientific weight to the testimony. He happened to be travelling in the Uplands that day, engaged in research. When the black mass approached overhead, he saw squadrons of panic-stricken birds darting for cover in the hedgerows and woodlots: they perched in the thousands in the boughs, motionless and silent. The mirroring effect of the cloud itself inspired de Ware to a rather poetic-sounding comment: "Through that vision I comprehended that our tiny, rotund earth, the merest particle in the great silent reel of the firmament, is also a garden of the most profound beauty."

After an hour or so, the inhabitants of Duncairn were already getting so used to the phenomenon overhead that they returned to doing what they'd been doing before the cloud arrived. The lawyer went back to writing his writs, the kiln operator to baking his clay pottery, the brewer to stirring his vats of frothy, strong-smelling Upland beer, the various farmers to hoeing their rows of beets and potatoes, and the housewives to preparing the thick, chewy kale soup, as usual, for dinner. The children "resumed their childish games, playing peever and ring-around-the-rosy, with scarcely a glance at the strange sight above them, as though it were an everyday event."

As it turned out, the phenomenon was about to end. The account concludes in this way: "The kirk belfry chimed the hour of three, the wind began to gust with unwonted violence, black hailstones crashed down on Duncairn, and on the faces of the few brave souls who looked up. Others, from the shelter of their abodes, witnessed the final dissolution of that obsidian mirror in the skies. The black hail turned to black rain that ran like ink down the gutters of Duncairn then turned into plain water. By five minutes after three, the rain had ceased and the Upland sky had returned to its wonted grey aspect."

A mottled blank page was followed by a section entitled "Appendix." It was only a few pages long.

AS I SAT THERE in that uncomfortable chair in my hotel room in La Verdad, I felt puzzled by what I'd read. I knew *The Obsidian Cloud* must surely be fiction. Yet it was all done in that factual way, with not the slightest hint of irony, or parody, or any of the usual signs to indicate it was made up. Since the author was a clergyman—the Rev. K. Macbane—I wondered if it was meant to be some kind of spiritual or religious parable. If so, its meaning wasn't at all clear to me.

I got up out of my chair for a moment to clear my head and went over to the window to check the aftermath of the rainstorm. The Mexican sky was now a clear, killing blue, not a cloud to be seen. The streets and sidewalks below my window already looked bone-dry. If I hadn't been out in it an hour ago, I'd never have known there'd even been a storm.

Such a transformation in a subtropical climate wasn't miraculous. It was a daily, commonplace phenomenon in the rainy season and easy to understand. Certainly, it was quite unlike the book's "obsidian cloud."

So I went back to my chair and began reading again. Maybe the Appendix would give me some indication of what was going on.

MACBANE OPENS THE Appendix with a significant confession: he himself did not see the phenomenon. He was "acting only as an historian," relying exclusively on the eyewitness accounts: "I have faithfully recorded those things that were told to me and leave the reader to pass judgment on their credibility." In fact this Appendix was needed because of "two new testimonies" about the phenomenon that had only come to his notice some weeks after the main text had gone to the printer. Like any historian, he felt "an obligation to the complete truth" and was passing along this latest information.

The first testimony had come from the provost of the little mining village of Glenmuir, a few miles east of Duncairn. There, the four children of the Mitchell family—two boys and two girls—were staring up at the black cloud. All at once, so their horrified mother told the provost, their eyes burst, making little popping noises that she likened to "soup bubbling on the hob." A moment after that, each child vomited forth a stream of blood and fell down, quite dead. The provost himself could attest to the emptiness of the eye sockets of the four children where they had been laid out on the floor of the woman's house.

Gruesome though that first testimony was, the second really caught my attention. It was an extract from the journal of a local poet, Meg Millar, about her various inspirational rambles in the Uplands. She records that on the day of the phenomenon, she was halfway up the Cairn Table, the highest hill in the region, collecting the little yellow saxifrages which grow only on the southwest side. She was thus a thousand feet higher than anyone down in the valley when the cloud stopped overhead, and thus had the closest view. "I at first believed the cloud was reflecting the earth beneath. But then my own eyes revealed something other. What I beheld was not this world but another planet slowly whirling its way past. The inhabitants were staring right at me, their eyes glittering red in such a way as I have never before seen and never wish to see again. Their arms were stretched out as if to seize me if only they could come near enough. I left my precious saxifrages where they were and scrambled like a mountain goat down the Cairn Table into Duncairn."

Meg Millar's observations, if true, were certainly astonishing enough. But for me, the very sight of her name stirred up other memories of Duncairn. When I was there, I'd been given one of her books. The gift of it would turn out to be an ill omen, though I was too innocent to understand that at the time.

After these final testimonies, the Appendix concludes with a personal reflection by Macbane himself. His response to everything he'd heard about the strange matter of the obsidian cloud seemed to me so full of common sense, I quote it here in full:

> As a rational man, my first inclination is to dismiss the story of the obsidian cloud over Duncairn as yet another instance of mass delusion, such as the many Apparitions of the Virgin, or bleeding trees, which the more superstitious of human beings have allowed to be imposed upon them, or have imposed upon themselves, from the Dark Ages up to this very day.
>
> Yet, as to this black cloud, I cannot help but wonder

at the many reports from persons still living, with no trace of any mischievous collaboration or apparent motive for perpetrating a deception upon the gullible.

I have, in consequence, thought it best in this book merely to compile their attestations, without passing judgment. For it is a truism that we who live now in a changeable and perplexing world are like ancient Archimedes: we lack any stable ground from which to wedge apart the illusory and the real. Perhaps some future scholar looking upon this history of the obsidian cloud may be able, with a more justified confidence than I now possess, to distinguish the one from the other.

A FEW DAYS FOLLOWING the discovery of *The Obsidian Cloud*, my business was over and I flew back to Ontario with the book in my bag. I was going to find out what I could about it when I got home to Camberloo.

And indeed, once I'd settled back into my routine, I spent a few hours in the local university library leafing through encyclopedias and literary histories, thinking I was bound to come across some reference to such an extraordinary piece of work. But I could find absolutely nothing on *The Obsidian Cloud*, or on any comparable natural phenomenon, or on the author, Macbane.

I soon realized I didn't really know what I was doing, and that this kind of research would be much better carried out by an expert.

Someone knowledgeable in these matters was even more logical.

"Don't ask just any old expert," he said to me. "Why not a Scottish expert? After all, Scotland was where the incident was supposed to have happened and where the book was published."

So I ended up phoning the National Cultural Centre in Glasgow and managed to talk to the rare books curator. After listening to my request for help (I hinted I'd be sending a substantial cheque to support the centre's efforts), he asked me a few brief questions about myself and about how I came into possession of the book. He then asked me to mail it to him so that he could examine it and see whether it merited any kind of serious research. He'd be in touch with me when and if he found anything of note to report.

It would be fair to say he didn't sound very enthusiastic.

THAT WAS THAT—for the moment—so far as my own efforts at trying to find out something about *The Obsidian Cloud* were concerned. Coming across it in the Bookstore de Mexico was the highlight of that trip. Like any book lover, I was curious to know whether there was even a grain of factuality behind it.

If I'd been a credulous man, I might almost have believed that *The Obsidian Cloud* had singled me out, lured me into that bookstore to seek shelter from the tropical downpour, so that I might discover it and attempt to resolve its mysteries.

I wasn't that credulous. But my heart really did leap at the unexpected sight, in such an alien setting, of that familiar name— Duncairn—and with it, the recollection, for the thousandth time, of a thing that happened to me in that little Upland town when I was barely twenty-one. Comparing that boy with the man I've since become is always disorienting for me—as it must be for most people thinking back to when they were young—like watching two movies overlap in some dizzying way. But I still feel a great sympathy for that earlier version of myself, who spent only a few ecstatic months in the little town, then slipped away on the train at dawn one foggy morning, broken-hearted and mystified.

I'd told the curator that after graduating from Glasgow University I'd lived in Duncairn a short time and that I'd travelled quite a bit around the world since. I didn't confess to him that I sometimes felt the ups and downs of my life were just about as baffling as the connection between dreams and reality. That may have been what caused me to react to this particular book in such an intimate way—as though the book and I were, somehow, intertwined. Isn't that the way it is for all readers, when it comes to certain books? But I certainly hadn't the slightest notion that in attempting to solve the riddles *The Obsidian Cloud* presented, I'd find the answer to the great mystery in my own life.

The burden of memory seemed to me then as a great boulder to be carried over an endless quicksand.

Tancrede Arnold

PART ONE

THE TOLLGATE

1

Where I was born it was the custom, when a baby was nine months old, for the mother to rub vinegar on her breasts. That was the tried and tested method for weaning babies away from breastfeeding, and I've often wondered if my mother used it on me. Not that I'd have dreamt of asking her. But I've always disliked the smell of vinegar.

I often wonder, too, if an experience like that might lead someone to expect even the purest love to end in bitterness.

THE CIRCUMSTANCES of my birth were, no doubt, peculiar: I was born outdoors, into a chilly night and a fog, in an area of Glasgow called the Tollgate, a slum even the police tried to avoid going into.

The month was December and the fog was caused mainly by smoke from the steelworks and shipyards that lined the banks of the River Clyde. The river itself was polluted from their poisonous drainage. Some of the old people claimed that one winter night long ago it actually caught fire and looked just like lava flowing out of a volcano, the way it does in movies. In summer, children who went into the river for a swim (as they sometimes did in the rare spells of warm weather) would lose a layer of skin a few days after.

On that December night, the foggy night of my birth, my parents left their apartment in the row of tenements they lived in and set out for the doctor's surgery. They wanted their first child, at least, to be born in a clean place with a doctor and a nurse present, and they'd saved up the money needed. Mainly, children in the Tollgate were born in metal bathtubs in their apartments. If the mother received any assistance, it would be from an experienced family member.

But my parents had decided on another method, especially since they had no family member to rely on. So they were walking to the surgery two miles away, as fast as they could, for my mother had felt stirrings and was afraid something was going wrong.

Of course, they didn't make it. My birth took place right there on the grime of the sidewalk, with my inexperienced father acting as midwife. There were one or two spectators who'd no experience either, so they couldn't help. It seems I wasn't keen on coming out and nearly killed my mother by my struggle to stay inside her. At last I did make my exit into the colder womb of the fog.

I discovered these bare facts from my parents years later. Naturally, I've no memory of the event myself, though I often think it must have had some effect on me.

IN MANY WAYS we weren't a typical Tollgate family: I was an only child, for example, whereas most of the other families around were big. My mother would have liked a lot of children, too. Again, it wasn't till I was much older when I realized that the damage I'd done to her by my struggles on the sidewalk had probably made her incapable.

She was a short, solid woman, and she didn't have a job outside the house—few women at that time did. She had jet-black hair which was usually tied up in a bun, but at night when she let it down, it was the most exotic, beautiful sight. I loved to touch it, and when my father would compliment her on it, her face would turn pink with pleasure.

She was one of those people whose eye colours don't match. Her right eye was blue, her left was green. Depending on which eye you looked at, it was as though two different people were in there. The woman behind the blue eye looked dreamy and happy, the one behind the green one often seemed worried and sad. When I grew older and pointed this out to her, she said there might be something to it: that often, for her, the world was a place of beauty and hope, but at other times, everything seemed black and desolate. She'd never told this to anyone else in the world except my father, and now me.

AS FOR MY FATHER, he was a thin man with thin hair, a hollow chest, and slightly tremulous hands. Even when he was only in his mid-thirties—I was ten years old by then—he looked older than most men of his age. He had a natural gift for numbers and was a bookkeeper at the offices of Random Mill, where steel plates were made for the shipyards. The mill's huge chimneys belched smoke day and night.

He himself was a heavy smoker. Because of his quivering hands, he often had trouble guiding the cigarette to his mouth. Once he got it in he'd leave it dangling there till it was almost smoked out and the tip was a fraction away from his thin lips. Then he'd spit it onto the floor and stamp on it with his shoe.

"Gotcha!" he'd say, as though it was one of the cockroaches that infested these tenements.

From living with him, I learned young, without anyone ever saying it outright, that it's foolish to read too much into people's appearances. Sometimes, the most unprepossessing of faces—like his, for example—belong to the kindest, smartest people. And vice versa.

He coughed a lot, even when he talked—which was usually to make wisecracks or disagree with what most people believed in. He also loved sitting by the fire, reading, as did my mother. They couldn't afford to buy books, but borrowed them by the dozen from the public library. Long before I went to school they taught me the alphabet and showed me how magical combinations of these little marks could create in my mind the most fascinating images and people and events.

It was through my parents, then, that I too came to love reading.

LIKE MOST TENEMENT dwellers, we had a cat to keep control of the rats, mice, and cockroaches that lurked everywhere in the building. Penny, our ginger cat, was a stray with the tip of her right paw missing. That didn't seem to affect the way she'd leap onto the window ledge to check out what was happening on the street below, or onto my mother's shoulder when she was at the stove, making dinner.

When I was very young, we also had a black half-Labrador dog named Rex, a stray who'd lost his right eye somehow in the streets. My father coaxed him home one day and he settled in. Rex's main job was to bark when someone came to the door, and he was very good at it. His other job, on winter nights, was to sleep on top of the sack of potatoes in the back room, keeping them warm so they wouldn't rot. Penny would lie on top of him, purring noisily.

We called him Rex but he was actually a female. It was my father's idea to give him the masculine name. He felt it was easier for males, whether human or animal, to survive in the Tollgate. He was wrong in this case. One day Rex rushed through the half-open door and down the stairs into the street to greet my father coming home from work. He went under the wheels of a passing coal cart and his back was broken.

We never had another dog.

FOR ME, MAYBE the oddest thing about our family was the fact that both my parents were orphans.

All my father knew about his parents was that they'd been refugees from somewhere. They'd been on an immigrant ship from Amsterdam to New York and, along with dozens of other passengers, they'd been stricken with the Great Influenza. They both died while the ship was anchored off Glasgow. Their only child, my father, who was then six months old, was deemed a Scottish national—his parents' name, Steen, sounded quite Scottish. He was put in an orphanage ashore and stayed there till he was fourteen.

My mother's story was more typical. When she was a baby she was found outside another orphanage one cold morning wrapped in a blanket. Nothing was ever known about her parents so a name was selected for her by the administration. After fifteen years, she left the orphanage and became an office cleaner at Random Mill. When she was eighteen she met my father there, they married, and in due course I was born.

In the Tollgate slum, families of ten or twelve children were common. We three, having no other living relatives, were obliged to be everything to each other. Even as a child, I was aware of that burden.

I was also aware that they loved me and each other, though love wasn't a word you heard much in the Tollgate. Once in a while, my father, puffing at his cigarette and trying not to sound complacent, would say: "There are people born in palaces who don't have what we have."

AS I GOT OLDER, my parents asked me to call them by their first names: Joseph and Nora. They hoped I wouldn't find that objectionable. My mother explained it was because, in the orphanages, children were mainly called only by their last names. My parents were trying to make up for that now.

I said I didn't object at all.

But secretly I didn't like being deprived of the use of those powerful words, "mother" and "father." So, for my own sake, even though I did as they asked, in my mind that's what I always called them.

I WAS NAMED HARRY. That was in memory of my father's best friend in the orphanage, a boy who'd died of pneumonia shortly before his tenth birthday and so had never experienced freedom. My parents hoped I'd have a chance to live the kind of life Harry had been denied.

IN THE TOLLGATE, rows of tenements stretched as far as the eye could see. Our apartment was on the fourth floor of one of them. The worn stone stairs that ran up to the various floors were a daily obstacle course of broken bottles and tin cans and also served as latrines for passing drunks.

The apartment, like all the others, had one large living-room-kitchen-bedroom, with an inset bed where my parents slept. There was also a small unheated bedroom at the back, which was mine. The whitewashed ceilings of both rooms were permanently stained with damp.

Aside from the usual ravages of typhus and consumption, almost every row of tenements had something unpleasant in its history. Beatings and stabbings and domestic murders were commonplace. The Tollgate slum was particularly well known for its hereditary razor-wielding gangs, with fathers passing the mantle on to sons. Frequent battles took place over territorial rights.

Even during the war the gang violence continued. Some gang members did join the army, but many preferred to prowl the streets looking for trouble. My father wasn't surprised.

"What's the fun in having to shoot people from a distance when you could be slashing their throats from close up?" he said.

He himself had been rejected from military service because of his thin chest and his cough.

"They don't know what a great warrior they've turned down," he'd complain. Even my mother couldn't help laughing at that, and he'd dissolve into a fit of laughing mixed with coughing.

AS THE WAR WENT ON, there were frequent air raids on the steel-works and shipyards near the Tollgate, so public shelters with concrete domes were built to give people a place to be safer. But pets weren't allowed and the shelters leaked so much they were even damper than the tenements. After a while, most people just stayed at home during air raids and took their chances.

We stayed home, too.

"At least if we're here, nobody can steal our things," my father once said to me and my mother as he puffed on a cigarette. "That's the kind of thing people do when too many of them are bunched together. Cities make human beings unnatural. During the outbreaks of bubonic plague in London, people who were infected would deliberately spread it amongst their neighbours. I just read that in a book."

"But that was hundreds of years ago," my mother said. "It can't be the same now. Our neighbours wouldn't steal from us." She was looking very anxious.

"Well, maybe it's not the same in London anymore," he said. "But I wouldn't be too sure about the Tollgate."

She looked even more upset when he said that, and he noticed. He puffed on his cigarette for a while, then said, "On the other hand, maybe you're right, Nora. You never know. Maybe you're right."

DURING THE ENTIRE WAR, none of the rows of tenements in our part of the Tollgate were actually hit by bombs. In the final air raids, though, a really big one didn't miss by much. We all heard the thud of its impact into a piece of waste ground behind our building. But it didn't explode.

Later, a group of soldiers came along and disarmed it, and then covered it up with a load of dirt. They put a barbed-wire fence around it along with a warning notice to keep away.

Not long after that, the radio and newspapers announced that the war was over. Soon men who'd been in the army came back, searching for work. My father met some of the job seekers at the offices of Random Mill.

"You can see from the look in their eyes they've had to kill people," he told me one night when my mother was over by the stove out of hearing range. He didn't follow up with one of his wisecracks, but just puffed at his cigarette. "Don't tell Nora about that," he said quietly.

2

The war hadn't really affected me much—I had complete faith my parents would protect me from any of the physical dangers around us. But I was prone to other terrors much more frightening than a mere war—for example, I would have awful dreams, though I couldn't remember most of them when I awoke.

My father tried to make a joke of them.

"Nightmares are very good training for life in the Tollgate," he'd say.

My mother would look at me anxiously when I mentioned my bad dreams. She wouldn't say anything, but I suspected she had her own share of nightmares.

The Tollgate was also full of superstitions. When my mother would go to wash our clothes at the communal laundry, she'd sometimes hear women from other tenements talk about such things as sightings of ghostly figures, or loud groans and banging sounds coming from empty rooms. One woman even claimed to have seen a pot of stew from her stove float through the open window and drop with a crash into the street.

"Old wives' tales," my father used to say, snorting and puffing, when my mother would tell us about them. It was clear he enjoyed hearing them, however, and so did I, though they too gave me nightmares. I kept quiet about that, for I didn't want my mother's stories to stop.

THEN, WHEN I WAS FIFTEEN, I discovered that one of these frightening things had happened in a tenement near our own. Often, on my way to school, I passed a square, paved area the size of a little garden plot, full of broken beer bottles and litter. In the middle of the square, a stone marker stuck up—it was about three feet high with a greenish bronze plaque screwed onto it. Some words were engraved on it that were hard to make out. They were covered in grime with the usual obscenities and street-gang symbols scratched over them.

One overcast November morning, I was passing the marker when no one else was around. I took out my handkerchief and quickly wiped the plaque clear enough to see the words:

IN MEMORY
OF
—CAMERON ROSS—
WHO ONCE LIVED HERE
—MAY HIS SOUL FIND REST—

On my way home from school that afternoon I called in at the public library and, after some searching, found what I was after: a heavy, worn-looking book called *A Miscellany of Authentic Characters, Scenes, and Incidents from the History of Old Glasgow*. It was laid out like an encyclopedia and consisted of brief entries in small print on numerous topics. One of the entries was headed "The Tollgate: The Exsanguination of Cameron Ross."

I took the book to a reading table, opened it at the page indicated, and was immediately on my guard: right in the middle of the page, an X shape had been slashed, maybe with a razor.

A dark blotch on top of the cut had seeped into the page underneath. I bent over and sniffed, just in case, but there was only the usual book smell. Under the entry-title, a warning was printed:

Readers of a delicate sensibility might do well
to avoid this section.

I'd never come across that in a book before. It made me even more curious and I began reading.

Little is known about Cameron Ross's early life except that he lived in the Tollgate, was married to a local woman, and was thirty years old at the time of the incident that made him, for a short time, infamous.

On a January morning of the Glasgow winter of 1810 his wife discovered that the side of the bed on which Ross lay was soaked in blood. Indeed, the blood was still in the process of seeping through the blankets, oozing down to the floor where it coagulated on the cold wooden planks. Ross was not asleep but lay staring up at her in silence.

A physician was called and examined Ross but could find no source for the blood on his body. He was suspicious, for he well knew about the violence in these slums. He could elicit no satisfactory answers to his questions, so he merely left a bottle of cordial for Ross.

All was well for six days. On the morning of the seventh day just before dawn Ross felt the blood again and this time awakened his wife. She lit a lamp and brought it over to the bed, and so was able to witness what happened. The blanket at his chest had turned dark and blood was welling through it. She lifted it away and saw that the tip of something sharp, like a knitting needle, was protruding from inside his body through the flesh of Ross.

The physician was again sent for and examined Ross, but though there was much blood it had ceased to flow, and he could detect no sign of any cut, or trace of any scar. He advised that at the first premonitory sign of any recurrence of the exsanguination Ross's wife should fetch him, so that he might see for himself the cause of the blood.

Seven days later, in the early morning, Ross's groans alerted his wife. She went immediately for the physician and they both hurried back, arriving at the bedside no more than a half hour after the commencement of the onslaught. But Ross was dead, his eyes staring up at them. The blood was of a lesser quantity than before and there was no sign of a wound. Though Ross had been dead only a short time, his body was so cold that the sheen of blood was as brittle as wax.

The Glasgow Royal Infirmary, later that day, was requested by the physician to conduct a post-mortem on the body in hopes of discovering the cause of this strange exsanguination of Cameron Ross. The request was denied on the grounds that no useful medical purpose would be served thereby.

On the day of Ross's burial, a large crowd such as might have attended the funeral of some dignitary followed the coffin along the streets of the Tollgate to the city Necropolis. Some claimed Ross's death was a miraculous event. When his body was lowered into the earth at the paupers' area, many wept.

An editorial next day in the *East Side Tribune* noted the unexpectedly large crowd of spectators at the funeral of such an obscure man as Ross and made mention of the exsanguination said to have afflicted him. The editor expressed skepticism about the reality of the illness and conjectured that Ross had deliberately wounded himself, and eventually killed himself, as a means of garnering posthumous attention. In the view of the editor, the gullible masses were ever prey to such fraudulent practices.

Ross's wife disappeared shortly after the funeral, and it was rumoured she had drowned herself in the Clyde or found employment in a brothel. Later reports alleged that the supposedly dead Ross and his wife had recently been spotted walking together, laughing, on a street in London.

Whilst the exact site of Cameron Ross's grave is no longer known, a plaque in his memory placed near his former home in the Tollgate may still be seen.

Sitting there in the library, the hair on the back of my neck stood up. I wondered if there was more of this kind of frightening stuff in the old book and skimmed through it, but no more warnings appeared at the tops of pages.

WHEN I LEFT the library and headed home that day, my mind was still full of the image of Cameron Ross, bleeding to death. After dinner, I must have been quieter than usual.

"Are you all right?" my mother said. She was sitting by the fire with Penny on her lap. The cat blinked at me in a friendly way. My father, in his armchair, glanced at me over the top of the newspaper, eyes narrowed against the smoke rising from his cigarette.

I knew what they were worried about now that I was fifteen. Any time I was a little late getting home from school, they thought I might be meeting a girl, that I might end up like some boys who weren't much older than I was, marrying girls they'd got pregnant. These boys and girls were thereby condemned to live in the tenements, like their parents before them, doing the most unskilled work in the steel mills or the shipyards—if they were lucky enough to find jobs.

So, I immediately put my parents' minds at ease. I told them I'd been at the library and was preoccupied thinking about a book I'd read there. It was about Cameron Ross, the man whose name I'd seen on a plaque down the street. They'd never heard of him, so I told them what I'd read and they listened with great interest.

I also mentioned that somebody had slashed the book, maybe with a razor.

"Well, that's somebody I wouldn't like to bump into on a dark night," said my father.

I didn't laugh and neither did my mother. I was curious about the people at the funeral who claimed that the way Ross died involved some kind of miracle. Maybe they were right?

My father spluttered, looking like a gargoyle with smoke belching out of its nose.

"Miracle?" he said. "If you ask me, the only miracle in this world is that so many people believe in miracles." He liked that. "Am I not right, Nora?" he said, the way he often used to call for her approval when he thought he'd said something astute.

My mother didn't answer him. She sat there, petting Penny and looking more worried than usual. So, my father left it at that and just puffed on the ever-shortening cigarette dangling from his lips till an inch of ash fell off. It slowly settled over his shirtfront, mingling with the evening's already accumulated ash.

THAT NIGHT I LAY in bed staring up at the damp stains on the ceiling. Many nights I'd imagined they were tropical islands, like those I read about in adventure books. The sky was always blue there and the people were carefree and suntanned. Someday, when I was old enough, I intended to live in one of those idyllic places. I'd bring my parents with me and all three of us would stay in an airy bungalow overlooking the sky-blue ocean, far from these grim tenements.

But on that particular night the stains refused to be anything but Tollgate stains, pulsating in the dark like some kind of deadly fungus. In the end, I had to turn on my side, clench my eyes tight shut, and force myself to fall asleep.

3

At the age of eighteen, I became a student at the university— no fees were required of qualified applicants. It was in the west side of the city, a half-hour bus ride from the Tollgate. The massive, Gothic-looking structure, full of arched windows, dark stairwells, cold corridors, and drafty lecture halls, dominated the landscape.

I especially loved the library, with its spiral staircases and labyrinthine passageways between bookshelves. Some of the librarians were pale and otherworldly enough to be the ghosts of earlier librarians who'd lost their way amongst those passageways centuries ago.

In the middle of the library was a study hall completely hemmed in by ancient bookshelves full of the very oldest books. That study hall became my favourite place. It seemed almost to welcome visitors, breathing softly on them like some huge kindly animal. After morning lectures, I'd install myself at a table there and work happily all afternoon.

Then at six o'clock each night I'd squeeze onto a crowded bus for my journey home. Soon enough the elegant villas around the university, then the bustling, well-lit streets of the city centre, would be left behind and we would enter the canyons of grimy warehouses and tenements that constituted the Tollgate.

IN SOME OF THE STREETS we now passed along, murders and acts of violence were so commonplace they barely rated a mention in the newspapers. Even a glimpse through the bus window of the top floor of a certain tenement on Sheldon Street always made me shudder.

A thing had happened there before I went to university, but it had stuck in my memory, for my father had known the man involved. The man had lived in this tenement and was, by trade, a master carpenter. He'd built some cabinets and desks at the Random Mill offices where my father worked.

This master carpenter had been forced to retire from practising his trade because of chronic depression. Soon afterwards he'd brought some supplies of lumber into his apartment and spent most of his time in there, sawing and hammering. Some neighbours complained about the noise. He politely assured them that he'd been making some new furniture and was almost finished.

One day, the sawing and hammering ceased. After a week, a bad smell came from inside his apartment. The neighbours got no response when they knocked at the door.

The police were called, broke in, and discovered the true nature of the master carpenter's work in his apartment. He'd been building an elaborate small-scale gallows in the living room, working from a complicated-looking set of blueprints.

The master carpenter himself was hanging from the gallows beam, quite dead. It seems he'd put the noose round his neck and used a broom handle to spring the latch of the trap door. His workmanship was precise: his toes dangled exactly three inches above the floor, ensuring that the fully extended rope would strangle him successfully.

A note was found on the floor beside him:

On this, my fiftieth birthday, I hereby find myself guilty on all counts and sentence myself to be hanged by the neck until I am dead. Sentence to be carried out immediately.

Exactly what he'd adjudged himself to be guilty of, no one was ever able to discover. My father, who'd spoken to the master carpenter only a few times and had found him a quiet, courteous man, was shocked at his death. But he couldn't resist joking about it to my mother.

"If all the depressed people in the Tollgate start hanging themselves, there'll soon be a national shortage of rope. Right, Nora?" he said.

She, as usual, looked anxious but didn't answer.

A WIDELY REPORTED incident happened in another of the tenements during my first year at university.

The building in question was just a mile or so before my bus stop and was completely boarded up. Such a sight was not at all common. Despite the Tollgate's reputation, its population kept growing and the demand for housing was always strong.

In one of the apartments in this particular tenement, a young woman, assisted only by her husband, had given birth to her first child in the traditional way—in a portable metal laundry tub on the floor of the back bedroom. But then, after the baby was born, the mother's heart stopped and she died within minutes.

Once he understood what had happened, the husband proceeded to cut the baby's throat. He then sat in a chair, drank a large glass of scotch, slit his own wrists, and bled to death.

At least, that was what the police and the neighbours concluded. The couple had been looking forward to the baby and the husband had seemed fond of his wife. All in all, his decision was understandable: he didn't want to live without her and he didn't want to leave an hours-old baby to the mercy of strangers.

But it wasn't the tragic deaths of the three of them in that single apartment that emptied the entire tenement. No, the people of the Tollgate weren't that sentimental. In fact, within a week of the deaths, after the apartment had been cleaned up, it was advertised for rent.

A young couple from a nearby tenement were first in line to look the apartment over. They'd checked the main living area and found it quite satisfactory. They were about to open the door of the back bedroom where the deaths occurred when they heard a strange noise. It sounded like a man's voice coming from inside, sobbing and groaning. They quickly called some of the neighbours to come in, and when they did, they thought they heard the sound too. No one wanted to open the bedroom door.

In the following days, the apartment was examined by the city authorities and nothing was found or heard. But rumours spread and the exodus of the neighbouring tenants began. Within months the entire building was empty and boarded up. Whatever the people of the Tollgate may have lacked in sentimentality they made up for in superstition.

When this behaviour was duly reported in the newspapers, some of my fellow students laughed at it as the product of ignorance and illiteracy. I'd often heard them talking about the Tollgate, marvelling that civilized modern cities still contained such brutal slums. I, of course, didn't advertise the fact that I lived there. I'd nod my head in agreement with their views. But I hadn't forgotten my own reaction, as a boy, to the story of Cameron Ross, whose memorial wasn't far from the haunted tenement. Even now, the thought of it gave me a chill.

Indeed, one day in the university library I was passing the Anthropology and Folklore area. Out of curiosity, I went in and found a large section devoted to the history of Scottish superstitions. The titles were scholarly enough, but some of the chapter headings contained such alarming terms as "the Evil Eye," "maledictions," "propitiatory sacrifices," and "demoniac possession."

A quick glance through some of these chapters led me to conclude that while the culture of the Tollgate might be inbred and violent, its proneness to superstition was as ancient as humanity itself.

ON MY NIGHTLY journeys home, by the time I arrived at my stop I was the only university student left aboard the bus. The stop was about a half-mile walk from our tenement. If the streetlamps were unbroken, I'd enjoy the way my shadow raced from one lamppost to the next, catching up on itself only to be outstripped again. I was also glad of the unbroken lamps for another reason—and it wasn't for fear of ghosts. It meant I could keep an eye out for street gangs. Whenever I saw a group of men on a corner, I'd make sure to keep well away from them. The fact that I was carrying books would have been a good enough reason, in the Tollgate, for being beaten up.

4

During my years at university, when I'd get home my father would want to know what I was studying. After dinner we'd spend hours discussing the various ideas I'd picked up, especially in philosophy and psychology. I must admit I was more easily impressed than he was. I remember telling him one night that when ordinary people say "Life's full of contradictions," they actually mean "Life's full of subcontraries." And that to say "It's not not raining" means exactly the same as "It's raining."

He puffed furiously on his cigarette.

"Ordinary people never say 'Life's full of contradictions' anyway," he said. "But if they did, you'd know what they meant. If you told them it was 'full of subcontraries,' they wouldn't know what you were talking about. In fact, they'd think you were mad. Or should I say, 'They'd not not think you were not not mad.'" He found that hilarious and turned to my mother. "Right, Nora?"

But I could see she didn't find it funny. She didn't much like the idea that language might be full of such snares. I'd tried to convince her of that once before by using some of the examples I'd learned in philosophy lectures. For instance: How many pieces of straw have to be heaped on top of one another before they become a haystack?

She just shrugged her shoulders in despair.

Once, she did laugh, though. I asked her: How much hair does a man have to lose before his wife considers him bald and not just thinning on top?

She glanced over at my father's thinning hair, and they both began laughing. He was really enjoying her laughter at his expense. They were clearly so fond of each other, I might have gone on and asked: How much liking do two people need to have for each other before you'd say they were in love?

Of course, that would only have embarrassed them.

ONE NIGHT AFTER DINNER I told my father how we'd had a discussion in a philosophy seminar on the Theory of Intelligent Design: the theory was based on the notion that this world is so marvellously structured and contains so many wonderful things that there must be a great Mind at the root of it.

He snuffled and snorted.

"Only someone who'd never lived in the Tollgate could come up with an idea like that," he said. He shuffled over to the fireplace and brought back a book he'd been reading from amongst the pile of library books on the mantelpiece. He found a page in it and handed the book to me. It was called *The Aphorisms of Pablo Renowski.*

"Here, read out that section to us," he said. So I did.

"*Look at the world, with its thousands upon thousands of years of wars, plagues, famines, murders, public and private brutalities, injustices, parricides, genocides. One would have to be a supreme cynic not to believe there must be some great pattern, some great plan behind it all.*"

When I finished, my father was puffing away at his cigarette, very pleased with himself.

"What would your professors think of that?" he said. "The world only sounds great, depending on how you look at it. If you're from the Tollgate, *The Theory of the Big Blunder* would fit better." He laughed and turned to my mother. "A good one, eh Nora?"

She didn't look happy. I think, for her, unpleasant ideas were bad enough without having to hear them put into words.

IN FACT, most of what I learned at the university seemed to upset my mother. On another night, I was talking about a lecture on the effects of psychological stress on soldiers returning from the war.

My father heard me out, choking and coughing on the smoke from his cigarette, and seemed impressed, which surprised me. He made what amounted to a little speech, punctuated with coughs and throat clearings.

"For once, your professor may be right," he said. "In fact, I wouldn't be surprised if all the civilians in Glasgow during the war are suffering from psychological stress, too. I mean, the planes dropped bombs on us, trying to kill us day and night, didn't they? The same goes for all the civilians in Europe and Russia and the other countries that were bombed too, right?

"In fact, when you come to think of it, it's not just war that causes the psychological stress. If you consider the Black Death and all those other horrible things that have terrified people for centuries, your professor could include nearly everybody who's ever lived—they've all suffered from psychological stress, including the kings and the prime ministers and the politicians and that whole gang.

"So, that would explain why everything's such a mess. Psychologically stressed, every one of us! What hope is there for the world?" He turned to my mother. "And it's even worse for us, eh Nora? On top of the war and everything else, you and I were brought up in orphanages and then had to live in these slums. I wonder what kind of mess the two of us must be in—just psychologically, of course."

My mother looked so worried, he immediately backed off and laughed.

"Oh, Nora," he said. "I'm only kidding. Harry and I are just having a bit of fun."

INDEED, THOSE NIGHTLY discussions with him were fun, but they often opened my eyes. He had so many astute things to say— things I'd never have thought of. Talking to him was sometimes like opening an old shoebox and finding jewels inside.

5

My mother was much more interested in my social life at university, especially how I got along with the female students. I'd gone for coffee with a few girls from my various classes, nothing serious. So I was happy to tell her about those.

I didn't tell her I had my eye on one girl in particular.

It was at the beginning of my second year when I became aware of her. She would come to the study hall only once or twice a month and, even though there might be vacant chairs at tables all around, she'd make a point of sitting opposite me at my favourite table. Without looking up I'd know, from the faint smell of lilac that accompanied her, that she'd arrived.

Once she settled down and was concentrated on her work, I'd sneak a glance at her. She had long brown hair and green eyes. Her handwriting, though I couldn't make out the words upside down, looked elegant, unlike my own choppy scrawl. Whenever she rose to go to the bookshelves, my heart would beat at her graceful walk, the way her skirt swirled round her thighs and calves.

Again and again I made up my mind to speak to her but kept putting the moment off. It was clear to me she was from that privileged world that had nothing in common with the sordid streets of the Tollgate, or with me. Yet, for some reason, she'd pick my table in the study hall.

At home, in my bed each night, I used to imagine a thousand scenarios in which she lay in my arms—two lovers brought together by destiny. Under the damp stains of the ceiling, she was the focus of all my sensual fantasies.

ONE AFTERNOON near the end of that second year, I decided to say something to her. She'd come to the study hall, sat opposite me as usual, and had been reading and making notes for at least two hours.

I'd rehearsed over and over what I was going to say and was in the process of taking a few deep breaths before introducing myself. Just then the main doors at the end of the study hall swung open noisily and a man came in. He was a plump man of maybe thirty-five; he wore a formal dark suit and had a shiny face, his scalp showing through his thin, combed-back hair. He must have been a professor. He walked over to our table and put his hand on the shoulder of the girl opposite.

"Deirdre," he said, "I'm sorry I'm late." His voice was a bit loud for the study hall.

She smiled up at him and touched his hand with hers.

"I'll just get my things together," she said, barely above a whisper.

I kept my eyes on my book but heard her gathering her books and notes, putting them into her leather satchel. She stood up and he helped her on with her coat, which had been draped over a nearby chair.

I still kept my eyes on my book.

"Goodbye," I heard her say.

I looked up and saw she was looking right at me, that it was me she was talking to.

"Good luck with your studies," she said.

I mumbled a thank you.

She and the plump man then walked hand in hand to the main doors, which swung shut after them.

I WAS SO ELATED by her speaking to me that I didn't at first realize what her goodbye might mean. In the weeks following, I went to the study hall every day as usual, looking for her—I thought of her now as "Deirdre"—but there was no sign of her. Then I began to worry.

In fact, the weeks became months, the months years—two whole years went by and she didn't reappear. Even when I got to my fourth and final year, I still couldn't quite accept the reality that I'd never see her again.

Over and over, I cursed myself for not having spoken to her during all the months she'd sat at my table.

Even though I'd only heard her voice on that one occasion, only heard her name once, barely knew her, I was sure I must be in love with her. I tried not to contaminate that love by wondering too much what her relationship to the plump man might be. For a long time, her exit from my life seemed to me the worst thing that could ever happen.

6

But something much worse did happen, at the end of March in my last year at university. It was on one of those early spring days when snow sometimes fell briefly on the city. It would even beautify the streets of the Tollgate for a short time before melting and laying bare their grim reality once more.

On the snowy morning in question, a Friday, my father had

a day off work. As I was about to go out the door to catch the bus, he was standing at the window, smoking one of his morning quota of cigarettes and watching the snow fall.

"You'd better wear a cap," he said. "It's NOT NOT snowing outside." He snorted this through a cloud of cigarette smoke— he'd adopted the double negative as one of his favourite jokes. "Right, Nora?" My mother was clearing up the remnants of breakfast. "Did you hear that? It's NOT NOT snowing?"

My mother frowned, as ever, at these word games. Our latest cat, long-haired Milly, was clinging to Mother's neck as she worked, loudly purring her love. She was a cat with so little faith in language she rarely responded even to her own name.

My mother came over to see me off.

"Do you have to go on such an awful day?" she said.

I nodded my head, though I wouldn't have minded staying home. But today we'd have the last lectures of the term and there might be some hints of what would appear in the final exams.

I put on a wool cap to please them. When I got down the stairs into the chill wind and snow, I was tempted to climb back up into the warmth and comfort of home. But I didn't.

AT THE UNIVERSITY, I attended final lectures. As usual, around one o'clock—by then, the snow had turned into a heavy, cold rain—I went to the study hall and prepared myself for an afternoon's work.

I'd barely opened my book when the entire building trembled, ever so slightly, for three or four seconds. The students at other tables looked around, puzzled. The trembling stopped and we heard a rumble outside, perhaps a clap of thunder in the freakish winter weather. Everything became quiet again and we got on with our work.

At four o'clock, since it was the last day of term, I decided

take an earlier bus home. All traces of the snow had been washed away and the rain was now only a cold drizzle. The bus made good time, for the traffic was fairly light. I got off at my usual stop and began walking the last half mile home. My mind was so full of the upcoming exams that I wasn't at all ready for what was in store for me when I went round the last corner into our street and saw a crowd of spectators gathered there.

They were looking at the tenement I lived in. The middle part of it—where our apartment as well as a dozen others ought to have been—was now only a ragged gap, as though a tooth had been ripped out of a huge jaw. All that was left was a deep crater and smouldering rubble. Fire trucks and soldiers and policemen were milling around. The crowd of spectators was watching the scene from behind a wooden barrier.

In a state of shock, I pushed my way through to the barrier and told a policeman standing there that this was where I lived. Did he know if my parents were all right?

All he knew was that a crew of city engineers had arrived in the morning to try and remove the unexploded bomb that had been buried behind our tenement since the war. Something had gone wrong and the bomb had exploded. The policeman took my arm and guided me to an emergency trailer parked along the street where I could inquire about survivors.

The soldier in charge of the trailer gave me the blunt facts: the crew of city engineers, along with all living persons in the affected apartments, had either been blown to pieces or incinerated in the resulting inferno. He was very sorry if my parents were in there. Soldiers and policemen were in the process, right now, of gathering whatever body parts they could find. They'd been at it since the explosion had occurred at one o'clock—the noise was so loud it had been heard all over the city.

That was just the time when I was settling down in the study hall, felt the trembling, and heard the rumble.

LONG INTO THAT EVENING I waited, hoping my mother or father might have gone for a long walk and were miraculously unscathed. Of course, I didn't really believe it—they never went for long walks. They didn't appear.

Near midnight, all work on the crater stopped. I was taken, along with the other remnants of families who for one reason or another weren't at home when the explosion occurred, to a charity hostel where we were allocated rooms.

There, for two days, I spent most of my time sitting alone in the tiny room they gave me. My life seemed empty and pointless. At times, I could hardly breathe for sobbing. The two people whose love I'd taken for granted as the foundation of my existence had been obliterated. Yet I couldn't quite grasp the absoluteness of their deaths. I particularly hoped my mother had managed to get to the end of the book she'd been reading. Nothing used to annoy her more than having to leave a book unfinished.

From time to time during those two days, I'd fall asleep from exhaustion in spite of my efforts to stay awake. I didn't want to sleep because, in my dreams, my parents were still as alive as ever. Each time I'd wake I'd have to confront afresh the awful realization of their deaths. Like them, I was now an orphan.

On the third day after the explosion, a funeral service for all those who'd died was held in an area of the Necropolis called the columbarium. There, niches in the walls held urns containing the ashes of the dead. Only one urn was needed for the ashes of the bits and pieces of those who'd died in the explosion, for there was no way of knowing who was who. The service was attended by more than two hundred inhabitants of the Tollgate wearing their best suits and dresses. The names of the dead—there were seventeen in all—were read out to the accompaniment of weeping, mainly from the women and children.

I tried to be stoic, but when I heard "Joseph Steen and Nora Steen," I lost control of myself and gratefully joined the chorus of weepers. In a way, I was glad my father and mother were included in this communal mourning, for we had no relatives or close friends. If my parents had been the only ones killed in the explosion, I would surely have been the sole mourner.

The way they died justified their beliefs about the world. My mother's unspoken dread about the precariousness of everything had certainly been borne out. As for my father, he'd at least have taken some satisfaction from this unassailable evidence that his views were correct. I imagined him sitting at the bottom of the smouldering crater, his cigarette smoke mingling with the smoke of the bomb, calling up to me: "Well, Harry, wasn't I right about The Big Blunder?"

7

After two weeks of mourning and moping in the hostel, I made up my mind to do what would have pleased my parents most: start preparing for my final exams. Using the allowance given to the survivors of the explosion, I bought some spare clothes and looked for a room near the university where I could hole up for a month till the exams.

I had trouble finding anything available for so short a period. Then I saw, in the window of a sprawling three-storey house, the sign:

Furnished Room for Rent—Student Only

A flagstone pathway took me past a scrap of lawn to the front door, which was badly in need of paint. The brass nameplate read *J. & D. Nelson*. I knocked several times, but there was no response. Just as I was about to leave I heard the click of an inside bolt and the door opened.

For the first time in weeks, an emotion stronger than grief took charge of me. Standing in the doorway was Deirdre— Deirdre, the girl I'd adored in the study hall, the girl who'd disappeared from my life two years before. She was wearing a grey skirt and sweater and I could smell the faint scent of lilac. Her green eyes were looking at me quite coolly.

"Yes?" she said.

I waited for her to remember me but she gave no sign of recognition.

"Are you here about the room?"

I almost blurted out something about her sitting across from me in the study hall. Instead, I told her I needed a place to study for my finals. Would the room advertised be available for rent for just the next month?

"Yes, it would," she said. "Come in." She opened the door wide into an enclosed hallway. Lying around were various pairs of boots and shoes. She herself had no shoes on.

"There's something you ought to know," she said. "We have a number of cats and they have the full run of the house— except the room for rent. If you don't like cats you should look elsewhere."

I assured her I did indeed like cats. I was thinking fondly of poor old Milly, how she used to sit in the evenings on my knee, or Mother's, purring as we read.

Deirdre's green eyes seemed to soften.

"I'm relieved to hear that," she said. "Take your shoes off and leave them here. There are tails and paws underfoot."

I took my shoes off and put them beside the others in the hall.

"Follow me."

She opened another door from the enclosed hallway into the house and we went inside.

THAT FIRST INSPECTION of Deirdre's house was memorable. The pleasant shock at seeing her again was only slightly negated by the fact that she didn't seem to recognize me. Her lilac perfume made my head spin.

I quickly understood that "a number of" cats was an understatement. There were at least twenty of them of differing shades and shapes all around us, greeting us as we went through the inner door. I placed my feet carefully, tiptoeing through them as though we were crossing a stream with occasional stepping stones.

As we progressed through the house, she talked expertly about the cats, using terms for them I'd never heard: this one was a "patched tabby," that one a "stripy mackerel," the other a "torby." Some were "blotched," some were "ticked," some were "bobtailed," the biggest one was a "barn." All the cats in the house were female. She called them her "girls."

Because of the cats everywhere, but principally because Deirdre was my guide, I had trouble concentrating totally on the house itself. Yet one thing was certain: this was the biggest house I'd ever been in. The kitchen alone seemed to me to be the size of the entire apartment I'd been brought up in. The surface of its huge stove and its various counters were adorned with basking cats.

"Of course the kitchen will be at your disposal," said Deirdre.

She then led me up to the second floor by a staircase that seemed as wide as some at the university. Off the landing she pointed out the main bedroom. Its door was shut but several other doors were ajar, with cats wandering in and out.

We climbed on up to the third-floor landing. The nearest door was open and led into a large room.

"This is the music room," she said. "My husband practises here."

Inside I could see several old bookcases full of books, an armchair, and a tattered leather couch. A number of cats lay around, some on the closed lid of a grand piano. By the window that looked out onto adjacent roofs, an upright wooden chair and a music stand were situated.

I was still thinking about that "husband" as Deirdre led me along the hallway beyond the music room to a door that was closed.

"This is the room for rent," she said. "We try to keep it cat-free."

She opened the door, led me inside, and then closed the door to keep our accompanying group of cats out.

The room seemed as large as the music room, but more dramatic. The entire wall on the south side was built with opaque glass blocks that let in daylight. A bed, a wardrobe, and a big mahogany desk with a lamp and leather chair were the main pieces of furniture. Near the bed, three steps led up to a little bathroom and a shower.

"The previous owner's hobby was oil painting and this was his studio. That's why the light's so good," Deirdre said. "What do you think? Would it serve your purposes?" I thought she sounded a little anxious.

Of course, I told her I really liked it. I'd have enthused over any old rat hole just to be near her again.

"Good! Then that's settled." She looked pleased.

My worry was that the price might be too much for me, but when I asked her about that she shook her head.

"Don't concern yourself," she said. "Since you're a student, whatever you can afford will be just fine. The room's available immediately, so you can move in whenever you wish."

I took her at her word, went back to the hostel, picked up my things, and moved in that very night.

I BEGAN TO STUDY HARD, making much use of the university library. But when I did work in my room in Deirdre's house, I was always aware of her presence. Any conversations I had with her were brief, and mainly in passing, when I was leaving for the university or for a nearby café where I'd sustain myself on bread rolls and coffee (the kitchen cats were rarely disturbed by me).

I kept wondering if I should remind her of our days together in the study hall. Maybe what I'd been through had changed my appearance and she just didn't recognize me. Or maybe I'd made no lasting impression on her at all. Rather than discover that, I preferred not to ask.

I met her husband for a few minutes on my first morning. He was, indeed, the same plump man I'd seen in the study hall.

"Jacob Nelson," he said, holding out his hand. His face was shiny, as though he'd just applied polish to it. He had a confident, grown-up way about him. "I hope your room's all right. As you can see, the house needs a lot of work but we haven't got round to fixing it up yet. I inherited it a few years ago from my uncle, who was an artist. Deirdre probably mentioned that your room was once his studio."

The idea of inheriting such a place—it would have held six families from a tenement—was almost incomprehensible to me.

"Students usually aren't too fussy about little things like decor. That's why we like to rent to them," he said. "Deirdre was a student for a while, too. After we married she decided she'd rather stay home and look after me and the girls." He laughed indulgently. "I play violin in the orchestra so I spend most afternoons rehearsing at Symphony Hall for weekend performances. But I'm afraid I have to practise here in the mornings. I trust that won't disturb your studies too much."

I assured him I'd be at the university in the mornings, so his practising certainly wouldn't bother me. Nor did it. Some mornings, in fact, I'd linger for an hour or more, just to listen to him play. How he could extract such intricacies of sound from one instrument amazed me.

Indeed, most things about this new world I'd stumbled into amazed me. It was so different from the Tollgate it might have been another planet, what with inherited mansions and virtuoso musicians and beautiful women free to devote their lives to the care of a legion of cats. I realized that a woman like Deirdre had always been unattainable for the likes of me. She was a goddess to be adored, not an ordinary woman with everyday human needs.

DURING MY FIRST WEEK in my new room, a curious thing happened. It was around midnight on Saturday.

I'd just climbed into bed after several hours of studying the Anglo-Saxon poem *The Wanderer*, a thousand-year-old meditation by a solitary exile who'd lost everything. Some lines were stuck in my mind as I lay there:

There is now none living
To whom I dare
Clearly speak
Of my innermost thoughts.

Those words had stirred up once again the grief that overwhelmed me the day the explosion wiped out my parents, my home, and everything in it. I felt quite as miserable as that ancient exile.

Just then, a great screeching of cats from outside the room shattered my mood. I lay for a moment, then got out of bed and opened my door a crack to see what was causing the racket.

A crowd of about twenty cats, led by the big barn cat, was gathered outside the music room howling like a mad choir. Their tails were all upright, fluffed out like banners. Unusually, the music-room door was closed, though a sliver of light was visible along the bottom.

During momentary lulls in the howling, I thought I could hear other sounds coming from inside the room. It might possibly be Jacob, going over his music for the next day. Or maybe not. I was wide awake now so I decided to check for myself.

I edged my way out into the hall, closing my own door softly behind me. I waded through the electric bodies of the cats till I reached the music room. Even above the howling, I could definitely hear sounds now from inside. As quietly as I could I turned the door handle and pushed the door open ever so slightly to make sure there wasn't enough space for the cats to slip through.

I put my eye to the narrow opening.

Jacob was lying on top of Deirdre on the leather couch. Their pyjamas and housecoats were scattered on the floor. Unclothed, he looked plumper than ever. She, on the other hand, was much thinner than I'd imagined, the bones of her arms, legs, and ribs quite prominent.

They were making love rhythmically. Deirdre looked up at him, making little squealing noises. At times, her eyes would widen and her squeal would become an outright scream, whereupon the cats' howling would rise to a crescendo.

Since the door was now slightly ajar, I was afraid the howling of the cats must surely sound louder to the lovers. But they seemed not to notice. So for quite a few minutes I maintained my position at the crack, watching their activities. When their efforts began to wind down, I very carefully closed the door, negotiated my path through the cats back to my own room, and got into bed.

Sometime later in the night, the cats woke me with their howling. This time I stayed in bed. The howling went on and on, then, at a certain moment, the cats shrieked in unison. After that, all noise stopped and I managed to fall asleep again.

THE NIGHT HOWLING occurred on some weekdays and on all Saturdays while I stayed with the Nelsons. I must admit that most times I took the opportunity to reassure myself as to the cause, holding the music room door slightly ajar, watching and listening while the lovers and the cats performed.

On mornings after, I'd often meet them before I left for the university and they'd invite me to have coffee with them in the kitchen amongst the cats. They called me by my first name now and insisted I call them Deirdre and Jacob.

I was almost certain they were aware of my being a spectator at their nighttime activities in the music room. But no mention was ever made of it.

Perhaps nothing needed to be said. There was something quite pleasant in it for all three of us, as well as for the cats. But Deirdre was no longer a goddess to me—if anything, she was more human than I'd ever have believed. The sight of her emaciated body and the sound of her amorous screaming were responsible for that.

DUNCAIRN. I heard that name for the first time from the lips of Jacob. It was on one of those mornings over coffee, and we'd been talking about my plans after I graduated. I told him and Deirdre that I hadn't really anything concrete in mind. The truth was, I'd been seriously considering the prospect of leaving Scotland entirely—perhaps heading for one of those warm, exotic places I used to visit in my imagination. But I didn't feel inclined to confess that to anyone, yet.

"Have you given any thought to teaching?" said Jacob. "The reason I mention it is that a few weeks back I ran into an old friend who was at university with me years ago. He's principal of the high school in a little mining town in the Uplands, and he happened to say he was on the lookout for a one-year replacement teacher to start in September. Duncairn, the place is called. Seemingly it's hard to get an experienced teacher to go to these out-of-the-way towns, never mind just for a temporary job."

I could see that he and Deirdre had come up with a plan, for she was nodding her approval as he talked.

"Look," Jacob said. "We were wondering if I should send my friend a note suggesting you as a possibility—that is, if he's still looking for someone. What do you think? I mean, probably nothing will come of it anyway."

I was, of course, interested. The idea of being a teacher in a little country school sounded very attractive, but I couldn't imagine why anyone would want to hire someone so utterly unqualified as I was. Still, I told Jacob to go ahead, if he thought it was worth a try. I didn't give much more thought to the possibility than that.

MY STUDIES WENT very well during the rest of that month I stayed with the Nelsons—partly because my mind was no longer full of Deirdre. My romantic image of her had moderated sufficiently that I was able to concentrate on preparing for the finals.

In due course, the exams were taken and passed. A week after the results were announced, an official-looking letter came for me. I opened it and read the typed single page.

Principal's Office
Duncairn High School

Dear Mr. Steen: On the strong recommendation of Mr. Jacob Nelson, you are herewith offered the position of interim teacher at Duncairn High School, conditional on the successful completion of your degree. Since school commences two months from now, I require an immediate response.

In the event of your acceptance, I suggest you come to Duncairn without delay and arrange accommodation here for the upcoming term. The most convenient way of travelling from Glasgow is by the daily two o'clock train for Carlisle, which has request stops at Duncairn station.

On your arrival, go straight to the school where you will receive travel reimbursement and a partial advance in salary. I will be in touch with you on the matter of your teaching duties.

In anticipation of your favourable response, I remain,

Sincerely, etc.
Samuel Mackay, Principal

I was surprised and delighted. I immediately mailed my acceptance. I thanked Jacob for persuading the principal to offer me the job—he and Deirdre were very happy at the news, too, but sorry I'd be leaving them. For me, the idea of going beyond the boundaries of the city for the first time in my life—of actually living in the countryside—was exciting. I wanted Jacob and Deirdre to tell me more about Duncairn. But they knew no more about it than I'd already discovered from a map. Namely, that it was one of the many small mining towns amongst the hills of the Southern Uplands.

I'd made up my mind to follow the principal's advice and go there immediately. If I found accommodation, I'd just stay on and get to know the town and its surroundings better over the two months before the term began. I told Jacob my intention and that I'd like to settle up the matter of my rent for the month I'd stayed with them.

He wouldn't hear of it.

"The money will be useful to you," he said. "Consider it a little gift from us."

I was very touched and couldn't think of anything to say.

ON THE FRIDAY of that week, they took me in a taxi to Central Station where I was to catch the two o'clock train for Carlisle. My bag contained all my belongings.

On the platform, Deirdre wished me good luck.

"Come and stay with us if you're ever back in Glasgow," she

said. "We'll miss you, and so will the girls." Her eyes were a little moist.

Jacob put his hand on my shoulder and squeezed.

"You're the best boarder we've ever had," he said. "You've been so understanding of … our little habits."

They both smiled at me knowingly.

"All aboard!" shouted the porter.

Jacob shook my hand warmly and said goodbye. Deirdre gave me a hug and whispered in my ear: "I knew you'd be a special friend—even in the study hall."

At least I *thought* that's what she said. But her whisper had to compete with the increased hissing of the engine.

The porter ushered me aboard and slammed the door behind me. I lowered the window, and as the train pulled slowly away I waved to Deirdre and Jacob. They waved to me till a long bend in the track obliterated them completely.

I found an empty compartment and sat down, still thinking about the implications of Deirdre's final words—if in fact I'd even heard them correctly. Was her pretending not to have recognized me part of some game that thrilled her? Did she assume I was complicit in the game, and that was part of the thrill? Was that what Jacob believed too?

What a strange pair they were—but they'd been kind to me when I needed kindness. As to how my idolatry of Deirdre had declined, I didn't dwell on that—though perhaps I should have. It wasn't her fault if my fevered imaginings and distant adoration of her had diminished so much on contact with the reality of her as a woman of flesh and blood. But I was still too young to give up entirely on the belief that ideal love must exist somewhere in this world and that I would, in time, find it.

Now, as I watched the landscape whiz past the compartment

window, I began to think of other things. Here I was with complete freedom to follow whatever path I chose, with no one else's expectations to be taken into account now that my parents were dead.

Dead.

Coming to grips with their fate was still hard for me. Every so often the grief would spring at me from nowhere, like a cat pouncing on a mouse that had let its guard down.

NO MATTER, here I was, by a chance series of events, on a train to this little Upland town of Duncairn. The prospect thrilled me. Though perhaps after what I'd been through, I should have been more apprehensive. I certainly hadn't the slightest suspicion that what was about to happen to me in Duncairn would complicate the entire course of my life thereafter.

DUNCAIRN

1

Around four-thirty in the afternoon, the train pulled into the station of a small mining town in a high valley surrounded by hills whose tops disappeared into slate-coloured skies. *DUNCAIRN* said the sign on the platform. I got off, asked the station porter for directions to the school, and headed there immediately.

As I walked, I noticed that the wind was cooler up here and that the air was the freshest I'd ever breathed.

I was on what looked to be the town's one major street, consisting mainly of single-storey brick rowhouses interspersed with a few bigger granite buildings. After ten minutes or so I came to the school, which was built entirely of grey granite. There was no sign of students around; it was closed for the summer. The caretaker who answered my knock on the main door had with him an envelope that had been left for me by Principal Mackay—he was, unfortunately, out of town at the moment. In the envelope, I was heartened to see the promised salary advance as well as a note from the principal advising me that above Kirk's Pharmacy was a furnished room for rent that might suit my needs.

Kirk's Pharmacy turned out to be a short walk away, in the town square. It was the lower part of a two-storeyed granite building and looked quite old-fashioned. The window contained a dusty display, according to the little cards in faded ink beside them, of some traditional tools of the medical trade—wooden mortar bowls and pestles, test tubes, and coloured bottles of all shapes and sizes. Other items were more ominous—trepanning saws, forceps, speculums, kidney basins, and lancets.

I pushed the door open and went in.

The chemical aura was as bracing as the air outside. A dour elderly woman in a white coat greeted me from behind a polished wooden counter as though she'd been expecting me. She introduced herself as Mrs. Kirk and presumed I was the new teacher. Principal Mackay had warned her I might be along to inquire about the room upstairs. Yes, it was indeed available for immediate occupancy, if I wished. She gave me the key to go up and inspect it.

Access was through a twin door beside the entrance to the pharmacy, then up a creaky stairway. The room itself was plain but clean, with faint traces of that chemical smell leaking through from the pharmacy below. A curtained window looked out onto the square. The furniture was fairly basic, but all in all, the room seemed fine.

When I went back downstairs, I told Mrs. Kirk that I didn't intend to go back to Glasgow, so I'd take the room right away.

"Of course you will," she said without a smile. "You'd have trouble finding another room to rent in Duncairn. There's the hotel, of course, but it's very expensive."

OVER THE NEXT DAYS, I got to know Duncairn quite well, especially the square, which I learned was typical of town squares in any number of places in the Uplands. It was fifty yards by fifty yards with a grassy area in the middle, a few shrubs, and some scrawny trees. The focal point was a war memorial consisting of three bronze soldiers holding bayonets, staring with blank eyes up at the hills; many of the names carved into the plinth came from families with the same name, killed in various wars. On the far side of the square was an old-fashioned police station with a blue lamp outside. Next to it was a church with a low steeple. Its windows and door were boarded up as though it hadn't been in use for a long time. Also noteworthy in the square were Mackenzie's Café, where I would eat most of my meals, and a pub-cum-hotel called the Bracken Inn. And of course, Kirk's Pharmacy.

With the help of a Baedeker lent to me by Mrs. Kirk, I explored the town's surroundings. There really was only the one main paved road, which was fairly flat while it ran through Duncairn but then descended through many miles of moorland, east and west, to the two opposing coastlines. Another much narrower road ran south past the railway station and stopped at the entrance of the coal mine, its elevator looming up like a grimy Ferris wheel.

Along this road, at regular intervals each day, I'd see groups of men coming from or going to the mine. They all seemed to live in those rows of brick houses I'd passed when I first arrived. The miners on their way to work and those returning from it were indistinguishable in the matter of clothing: they all wore the same dark jackets and trousers, with worn-out boots. But the men on their way to the mine had clean, pink faces, and they talked and joked together. The men returning were hunched and quiet, their faces black with coal dust.

I TOOK MY EXPLORATORY walks into the rolling hills in no matter what weather. In Duncairn, even though it was summer, the sun rarely shone and rain fell a good part of most days. The slopes of the hills were relatively gentle, but the Baedeker noted that eons ago they'd been jagged mountain ranges whose edges time had since smoothed out. They were covered in heather and bracken and little blue and yellow flowers. There were various grey fungi that looked so revolting I kept well clear of them, though the book said they weren't at all dangerous.

Other real dangers lurked in these hills, however. Quite innocent-looking areas of bracken were in fact bogs known to have sucked down the unwary, and to have done so for a long time. The Baedeker recorded that the body of a man wearing strange, tattered clothing had been burped up in recent years by a bog just south of Duncairn. Scientists estimated he'd been swallowed by the bog and stayed in there for three or even four thousand years. I myself saw a few carcasses of sheep unlucky enough to have wandered into the wrong areas. Their coats were slick and black.

On my walks I was also startled by creatures that never visited the Tollgate—deer of every size, and hares. There were also squadrons of small black birds whose wings were streaked with white feathers. They would fly at my head, squawking angrily, with greedy eyes I didn't much like the look of.

A SECTION OF THE Baedeker that dealt with the Roman attempt to colonize this part of the world drew attention to the barely visible remains of an old road that ran from the southeast edge of Duncairn into the hills. Archaeologists had found pot shards, denarii, and a variety of mallets and nails near it. They'd also dug up several ancient skulls with nail holes bored into them. Whether this was a horrific form of execution inflicted by the Romans on the original inhabitants or vice versa, the experts hadn't as yet established.

I only managed to find the outline of that old road because of the occasional moss-covered cobblestones that protruded from it. I followed its traces for about two miles to the foot of the Cairn Table—the highest hill in the area. The road came to a dead stop at the remains of a ten-foot-high wall made of stones and earth mixed. The wall itself stretched intermittently for many miles, so I came across parts of it on other walks.

As for the purpose of the road and the wall, my Baedeker noted only that hostile tribes hadn't existed in sufficient numbers in the area to warrant such elaborate engineering. The book speculated vaguely that the Romans might have been afraid of something else and that the wall had been built for protection against it.

Certainly, on an overcast day up in these hills, a citified hiker with an imagination couldn't help glancing nervously over his shoulder sometimes. It was easy to believe that up here there might be something so primitive and unpleasant that neither ramparts nor centuries could keep it at bay.

2

On my fourth morning at Duncairn I found a scribbled note that had been slipped under my door at the bottom of the stairs.

Please come and see me at the school any time after nine
this morning.
Sam Mackay.

Accordingly, after a roll and coffee at Mackenzie's, I made my way to the school. The inside was gloomy and smelled stale. The caretaker directed me to an office on the other side of an assembly area, and there I went, my shoes echoing loudly on the plank flooring. I knocked on the door.

A high-pitched voice called to me to come in.

The man who got up from behind the desk to greet me was one of the widest human beings I'd ever seen. Not fat, but wide. He almost seemed the width of two men, with everything— head, arms, legs—in proportion. Each of his big brown shoes could have accommodated my two feet.

"I'm Sam Mackay," he said. "Welcome to Duncairn." That reedy voice was a surprise coming from such a big man.

He reached out his huge hand and shook mine warmly. He looked about forty, with receding red hair. His face was freckled, his green eyes far apart, his smile wide and friendly.

"Mrs. Kirk told me you'd moved in," he said when we were seated. "I'm very glad of this chance to talk to you. I was afraid I might miss you, since I'm back in Duncairn for only a couple of days. Then I'll be on the road till just before the term starts— I'm with a travelling committee of the Board of Education." He made a face as though he wasn't too thrilled about that prospect. "It was a real stroke of luck for me to run across Jacob last time I was in the city. As I told him then, it's so hard to get competent people to come and work in these country schools, especially on a temporary basis. So I was delighted when he recommended you and you agreed to come here."

I wasn't so sure the word "competent" would apply to me.

"Oh, I know you've never done any teaching, but don't worry about it," he said. "You won't have to perform in front of a class. You'll just be giving extra writing instruction to pupils with problems. It's mainly done on an individual basis."

I was relieved to hear that.

"I hadn't seen Jacob in years," he said. "From his letter, I could tell he thinks very highly of you. He and I were in a music history class together when we were at university. Of course, he was a *real* musician—a wonderful violinist—and I was just picking up an optional course. He was quite a ladies' man in those days. So now he's with the symphony—and has a wife, as well? Isn't it funny, I never thought of him as the type who'd settle down to the boring, domestic life. His wife must be quite exceptional, I suppose?"

I assured him that Deirdre was indeed quite something—and was especially fond of cats.

He now began asking me questions about myself. I told him everything he wanted to know, even about the shocking deaths of my parents.

He listened to that with great sympathy. Some years before, apparently, his own father and his only brother, both coal miners, had been killed in a cave-in at the Duncairn mine. His mother had died, heartbroken, just a year after their deaths. He himself still lived in the family rowhouse, which was full of reminders of them.

"You won't meet too many people in Duncairn who haven't had a family member killed in the mines," he said. "That's the story in a nutshell of these towns in the Uplands. I'd have been sent down the mines myself, but I was just a bit too big." He spread his arms, indicating his bulk. "So, I stayed at the books and here I am, principal of the school where I used to be a pupil."

After that, we talked a while longer about what my teaching responsibilities would entail. He handed me a copy of an elementary grammar and composition book my pupils would be using.

"Take this along with you," he said. "You've lots of time to get to know the contents. There's nothing to it."

AS I WAS LEAVING, I thanked him for all his reassurance.

"I have a feeling you'll enjoy it here," he said.

He lumbered along beside me to the door of the school.

"When I get back from this Board of Education assignment, we'll get together," he said. "I often go to the Bracken for a pint in the evenings, if you'd like that. I'm getting married in October so I'll be trying to make the most of my freedom while it lasts. Did I say a pint? Maybe we'll have more than one." He laughed—a reedy but pleasant sound.

He was so massive I guessed he could put away a fair number of pints without much trouble.

3

On most of the days following, I'd head up into the hills with a bag holding a waterproof shell in case of rain, the textbook Sam had given me, and a sandwich from Mackenzie's, where everyone seemed to know I was the new teacher. I'd walk for a few miles and find myself a clear spot amongst the gorse bushes to sit down. After an hour or two of reading, I'd get out my sandwich. Invariably, at that point, a swarm of those small black birds with the white streaks on their wings would appear, shrieking and swooping. They were so bold I'd have to swat at them with my book to stop them from snatching the bread out of my hand.

Often, on those days, I'd make for a big rock I'd noticed on my first walk. It was an oddity up in the high moors—a lone, twenty-foot-high boulder, just sitting there with no other noticeable rocks around. Its northern side was smooth and mossy. But some indentations for climbing had been sculpted into its south face, and I made use of them. I discovered that the top of the rock was concave—a mossy depression four feet in width and three feet in depth at its lowest.

Sitting up there, I could see farther across the entire landscape below. A mile or two north lay the cluster of Duncairn itself, then nothing but isolated shepherds' cottages, dots of sheep widely scattered, then more hills rolling away behind. To the south were just hills upon hills, except for one lone house about a mile away amongst a windbreak of trees.

The top of the rock became my favourite place for reading. Some days, when the wind moaning over the edge sounded like a great lullaby, I'd even stretch out in the mossy basin and nap.

AFTER LUNCH ONE overcast afternoon—it was well into my second week in Duncairn—I walked to the rock with my book. I climbed to the top and settled down to some syntactical problem. I must have dozed off, for I was startled to hear a voice over my head.

"Am I disturbing you?"

I looked up at a pair of cynical eyes, like a cat's, staring down at me.

I was immediately wide awake.

The cat's eyes were actually the inverted eyes of a woman, leaning over the parapet above me. When I sat upright, I realized that her eyes were most uncynical—in fact, they were blue and pleasing to look at. Indeed, her entire face was pleasing. She seemed around my own age, with fair hair and a fair complexion a little flushed from the moorland air.

"I'm sorry if I startled you," she said. "I just wanted to let you know it isn't always wise to fall asleep outdoors. Even on top of the rock."

Her quiet voice, too, was pleasing.

"Have you noticed those little black birds with the white wing feathers?" she said. "The locals call them 'eye-pickers.' Someone should have told you about them. They sometimes peck the eyes out of sheep, but they've been known to go for the eyes of people who're asleep."

I was shocked to hear that, for the birds looked so pretty.

"Even pretty things can be dangerous," she said.

I thanked her for warning me. She was still on the outside of the rock and looked as though she was about to climb back down. So I quickly introduced myself and told her I'd be filling in at the school for a while.

"So I heard," she said. "I've seen you climbing up here a few times. I thought I'd come up and say hello."

I invited her, in that case, to visit with me for a while, as though this oval on top of the rock was my parlour. I reached out my hand and she took it, climbed over the edge, and sat down opposite me.

She wore hiking boots and a dark-blue wool sweater over jeans. She had the sturdy build of someone active.

"My name's Miriam Galt," she said.

I really liked the look of her. The oval wasn't much larger than a bathtub, so our limbs couldn't help touching quite intimately.

I was mystified at how she could have got to the rock without my seeing her when I first climbed up. I'd looked around the moorlands from the top before sitting down and could have sworn there was no human being for miles—just a few dozen sheep. I'd been asleep for only a few minutes. I'd already noticed, though, how distances in this area were somehow distorted. On my walks, the landscape would seem to me deserted, then a shepherd and his dog might suddenly appear so near I could hardly believe my eyes.

The mystery was solved for me by Miriam Galt.

"Do you see that gully?" She pointed at what looked like a narrow ditch a hundred yards or so from the rock, running to the southeast through the moors. "It doesn't seem like much from here, but it's six feet deep in most parts and easy for walking in. It goes past where I live—up there." She indicated the lone house I'd noticed before, with the windbreak of trees. "I was walking in the gully when I saw you climbing up here today. And here I am." She smiled.

I really liked her smile.

4

That was the first time I saw Miriam Galt. Before we parted, I told her I usually came to the rock each day, if she ever felt like company. She turned up the next day and we talked again for a while.

After that, we began to meet almost daily at the foot of the rock, and from there we'd go for long walks through the moorlands. She assured me that while the Baedeker was correct about the dangers of bogs that might suck an innocent wanderer down, there were other local dangers, too. Not far from the rock, in an area I'd walked through several times on my own, she showed me a hole wide enough for a man to fall into, so overgrown with bracken you wouldn't have noticed it.

"Listen," she said, and dropped a pebble. She counted slowly to twenty before we heard the clink when it hit bottom. "It's an old mine shaft," she said. "Some of the mines in this part of the world are centuries old and there are disused shafts all over the place, so you have to be very careful." She paused. "You must have noticed how few trees there are around here. But in the past this whole region was a huge forest of evergreens, with herds of deer and wolf packs everywhere. When mining began, thousands of the best trees were cut down and used underground as props for the tunnels. So the forest's underneath us now."

She was surprised at my general ignorance of the natural world—that I didn't even know the difference, for instance, between heather and bracken and gorse. I told her people like me from the Tollgate were experts at other things—for example, identifying different types of beer bottles even when they'd been smashed to pieces. I said this jokingly, but it was near to the truth and she was shocked.

So she took pains to introduce me to the wildlife. She identi-fied the various birds—hawks and eagles, as well as others with such local names as "lady quaints," "slit hens," and those nasty little "eye-pickers." With her guidance, I was soon able to spot foxes, wild cats, weasels, and even swamp rats from just the briefest glimpses of them amongst the bracken. She once took me into a deep, narrow cavern where, amongst the stalactites in the ceiling, hundreds of sleeping bats were hanging.

All of this was astonishing to me. I couldn't get over how, in a landscape that looked so empty—just rolling bare hills and sheep—there were so many other living things you'd barely notice.

"They tend not to make a big display of their presence," said Miriam Galt. "That's because most of them eat each other."

I'd never heard it put that way before.

"Yes," she said. "Nature up here's very beautiful from one point of view. But once you get to know it, it can also be quite a nightmare. For example, the ground animals eat the nesting birds and their eggs. Those very same birds eat pups and kittens and fish and any other animal young they can find. That's why the wisest creatures camouflage their babies and teach them to keep quiet when they're not around to protect them. So existence isn't necessarily so great for the animals. Then there's the whole horrific life cycle of the insects. Thank goodness they're so small we scarcely notice the carnage that goes on amongst them."

I was taken aback at this unsentimental description of nature.

"From what you've told me about the Tollgate, you ought to understand it quite well," she said.

MIRIAM GALT soon got me to tell her all about my life before Duncairn, but she seemed reluctant to talk much about herself. From what she did say, I knew that her background was quite unlike my own.

She'd been born in Leith, the seaport of Edinburgh, and her mother had died not long after giving birth to her. Her father had been a partner in a small merchant-shipping line. When she was sixteen, he'd sold his share in the company, left Leith for Duncairn, and moved into the house out on the moors. It was called Duncairn Manor.

When she told me this we were sitting in the high heather, looking down over the great sweep of moorland, and could see her house in the distance. The landscape here was quite a contrast to the romantic pictures I'd seen of Edinburgh, with its castle and the sparkling sea as its backdrop. I wondered why her father had decided to bring her to such a remote place.

"It was for his health," she said. "Maybe he wanted to get as far from the sea as he could. This is midway between the two coasts, after all."

I didn't get much more out of her except that she herself enjoyed the relative isolation. Her main occupation was to look after her father, so she'd received the bulk of her education through correspondence courses. A part-time maid-and-cook did the housework.

I tried to pin down what exactly was wrong with her father.

"Maybe someday you'll see for yourself" was all she would say.

ON ANOTHER GREY afternoon as we sat in the bowl of the rock, I mentioned that, according to the Baedeker, many of the big rocks found in the Uplands were deposited there during the Ice Age that scoured the world two million years ago.

"Well, that may be the geological explanation," said Miriam. "But there's a local legend that's a bit more colourful. According to it, this rock we're on was hurled at Duncairn thousands of years ago by a demon. Fortunately, he just missed his target." She told me how the same legend claimed that the indentations in the side of our rock had been gouged out by the Romans, who used it as a lookout. What they were looking out for was apparently something more than ordinarily fearful.

My Baedeker, I remembered, had made a mysterious allusion to the old Roman road and the remnants of the great wall—that it was built to keep out something terrible.

Miriam knew about that, too.

"The Uplands are full of that kind of mixture of fact and fantasy," she said. "I don't suppose it's like that in cities?"

I assured her that even in the Tollgate occasional weird things happened. For example, there was Cameron Ross, and the thing that cut him open from the inside. And then there was the apartment that was haunted after the violent deaths of the family who lived there.

She listened attentively to these accounts.

"How awful," she said. She was curious about the supernatural elements in the stories. She wondered if I actually *believed* in them.

I tried to explain that I found her question difficult to answer, though I'd often thought about it. Perhaps rather than belief, my attitude towards such things was a kind of wishful thinking. If you come from a grim, cruel place like the Tollgate, at times it's hard to convince yourself that there can be any real point to human existence. But I suppose most of us *want* our lives to mean something—in spite of what reason tells us. So, even though they're not pleasant, the cases of Cameron Ross and the haunted tenement, and eerie things in general, seem like welcome proof that at least there's more to the world than meets the eye.

She kept nodding as I babbled on, as though she agreed with what I said.

"Maybe that's what fascinates me about a lot of the curious things that happen in the Uplands, too," she said. "They may not be supernatural, but they're weird enough to make you wonder. For instance, you must know about the goings-on at Carrick?"

I assured her I'd never even heard of Carrick and encouraged her to tell me more.

"Well, in the case of Carrick, no one's managed to come up with a scientific explanation of what happened," she said.

CARRICK WAS JUST another little town, thirty-nine hilly miles north of Duncairn. No one lived there anymore, but the town and all the buildings in it were still perfectly intact. Sightseeing was completely forbidden, and few were tempted to break the prohibition.

Ten years ago, the entire population of Carrick had been evacuated and the town itself quarantined. The cause of this was the so-called Carrick Plague, and the fear that, even today, it might still be in the air. The plague had manifested itself in a most unusual symptom: the need to talk. As the townspeople one after another were stricken, they wouldn't stop talking. They'd talk and talk and talk themselves to exhaustion, many of them still trying to squeeze out a few more words as they died.

Investigators looking into the pathology of the plague were completely stumped. They recorded as much as they could of the sufferers' endless monologues. They hoped that amongst the heaps of verbiage, certain patterns might emerge; certain words, certain names might recur. But as far as they could ascertain, there was nothing at all unusual—just the mundane, common-place chatter of small mining-town life.

Some investigators refused to give up on that line of inquiry. They even conducted studies comparing what they called "Carrick Speech" with the everyday utterances of other parts of the country, especially cities. Even after all these years the inquiry was still underway, but nothing definitive, so far, had emerged.

Other investigators now suspected that the spreading of the plague was actually a case of mass murder—probably an act of revenge—rather than a natural phenomenon. Support was growing for this attempt at a rational explanation, though no evidence of method or motive had yet been found.

"YOU SEE WHAT I MEAN?" said Miriam when she'd finished. "What happened at Carrick isn't supernatural, like your Cameron Ross story—it's just weird and out of the ordinary. But when so many such instances occur in one region, you do start to wonder, don't you?"

I agreed, of course, and asked her to tell me about more of these "out-of-the-ordinary" things, if that's what she wanted to call them.

"You probably know about Stroven?" she said.

THE LITTLE TOWN OF Stroven was thirteen miles to the south of Duncairn over a few ranges of hills. It had for generations been the most prosperous of all the towns in the region. But now the access roads to it had been closed.

That was because, several years ago, a sinkhole had appeared right in the middle of the town square. It was small to begin with, but over a period of months the hole grew so wide and so deep that it took up the entire square. Within a year all the important buildings around the square, including the town hall and the church, began toppling into it. The hole became wider still, swallowing the inner parts of the town and moving on, insatiably it seemed, to the outlying areas. Then its monstrous appetite seemed satisfied.

By that time, of course, all the inhabitants of Stroven had long abandoned the town.

To government geologists, the cause was evident: the surface of the earth had gradually been weakened in the district by centuries of mining for coal and tin. This vast sinkhole, said the geologists, was the inevitable result.

But the local inhabitants had a quite different theory. They believed the town had been gobbled up as some kind of punishment; even the etymology of its name—"strove in vain"—was a prophecy.

"SERIOUSLY?" said Miriam Galt, when I assured her I'd never heard of the Stroven sinkhole. "You've led a very sheltered life in that Tollgate place." Her expression was serious as she said this.

I'd never thought of it that way, but perhaps she was right.

"Then it's possible you don't even know about the Muirton disaster—it was just recently all over the news," she said.

THIS MUIRTON, she informed me, was a little town only twenty-one miles east of Duncairn. It still attracted sightseers because of a horrific mine accident and its effect on many of the town's male population.

What happened was this. One morning the mine elevator cage, full of coal miners, both men and boys, was on its way down the thousand-foot shaft for the early shift. Halfway down, the elevator cable snapped and the cage plunged on downwards. The miners immediately put into effect the traditional safety method they'd been taught for just this situation. Each of them grabbed one of the leather straps attached to the cage ceiling for the purpose, then lifted one of their legs so that most of their body weight was on the other leg. They'd barely time to take a deep breath when the cage crashed into the bottom of the mine shaft. Many of the miners survived the impact, but the legs that supported their weight were smashed to a pulp. Most had sacrificed their left leg.

Since that day Muirton had become notorious as the town of the one-legged men. Sightseers wanted to know what a place looked like that had had such bad luck. In fact it looked much the same as any other Uplands town. Except for the number of men and boys you'd see hobbling along the main street on crutches or on wooden legs.

I WAS SHOCKED to hear about Muirton, and indignant at these heartless sightseers.

"You can't really blame them," said Miriam. "They'd all read about it in the newspapers. It was made to sound sort of bizarre—even charming, in a way. Though for the miners and their families it was devastating."

I agreed with that, at least.

"If you want, I can give you an example of the same kind of thing, right here in Duncairn," she said. "What happened could almost be out of a book—except that it's true and awful."

Of course, I did want to hear all about it.

"Then come with me," she said.

WE DESCENDED FROM the rock and walked a mile or so into the hills till we arrived at a deep gorge with a rushing stream in it. An old stone bridge linked the two sides of the gorge.

We walked out onto the bridge and looked down cautiously over its crumbling parapet. The stream must have been fifty feet below, with rocks jutting out of it. Miriam explained that it was from this bridge that a man named Tam Halfnight had jumped, after he'd killed his newborn baby daughter.

Since that time the shepherds had called it Tam's Brig.

"The suicide happened a long time before I came to live here," said Miriam. "People who knew him said Tam was a good man and didn't mean to kill his daughter. I don't know all the details, except that he'd something wrong with his right arm and it was in a cast. He was at home, holding the baby in his arms, and she began to slip. He tried to stop her from falling, but because of the cast he held on to her too tight and broke her neck. After that, he came up here and killed himself. Everyone thought he'd done the right thing."

From the way she said this, I knew she agreed with them.

"I've heard that when they found his body, it was face-upwards on the rocks down there," said Miriam Galt. "His back was broken and the little eye-pickers had already taken his eyes."

I was horrified. Together we stared down into the gorge.

"They say he really loved his wife and that baby," she said. "Isn't it strange what love can lead to?"

I'd no answer for that.

I ADORED Miriam Galt and, at first, talking to her and listening to her talk was enough. We'd been seeing each other almost every day for more than two weeks when all of that changed. We met at the foot of the rock one day as usual. She took my hand and without a word we began walking fast up into the hills, half-running, in fact so out of breath we couldn't have talked even if we'd wanted to. We reached a sheltered hollow amongst the grasses and the high heather where we'd sat on occasion before, talking. But this time we threw ourselves desperately at each other. We feasted on each other, sank into each other, tried to become one new creature.

At last, exhausted, we lay back, breathing deeply and watching the passing clouds with their impenetrable dark gulfs. When occasional streaks of gold broke through, the sun would tantalize us with glimpses of hidden treasures. Then the clouds thickened again and all the colours in the surrounding hills fell an octave. The heather and even the little moor flowers seemed almost black.

Then for a few more seconds the sun burst completely through and I turned to Miriam Galt lying there beside me. She was like some ancient priestess, her face, her whole body sheathed in molten gold.

When the clouds blotted out the sun again, she was human. At that moment I felt brave enough to tell her I loved her. I hoped she'd tell me she loved me, too.

After a while she did speak, but it wasn't to say what I wanted so much to hear. With a sigh she invited me to come next day, for the very first time, to her home—the house amongst the windbreak of evergreens.

5

The rows of evergreens that offered the house protection against the weather also helped safeguard the only deciduous tree—a wide but not very tall oak which stood in the middle of a sizable front lawn. The house was of a traditional two-storey rectangular structure, built with granite blocks. On either side of the front door were two symmetrical windows with dark curtains. The second floor had three curtained windows, one of them above the door. Ivy clung to the walls around them. Engraved on the lintel of the door was the formal name of the house:

> ### DUNCAIRN MANOR
> #### 1885

Miriam Galt, who'd walked with me from our usual meeting place at the rock, had been unusually quiet. She now opened the heavy wooden door, we went inside, and she closed it gently behind us. From the hallway, she took me into a living room with the high wainscoting of the previous century and a lot of solid-looking mahogany furniture. A stone fireplace with no fire lit in it took up almost one wall. The room seemed unchanged since the house was built.

"He'll be in the library," Miriam said. We approached another door which matched the wainscoting so well that it was scarcely noticeable. Just before we entered, she said softly, "Now remember, he's not well."

She tapped the door three times and opened it.

We went into a very gloomy room. It had just one window in the southern wall with green stained glass in place of curtains, so not much daylight got through. The walls were lined with bookcases, and on a table in the middle of the room lay what looked like a brass telescope. There was a floor lamp and a sofa near a fireplace in which a low fire had been lit—no doubt to ward off the high moorland dampness. The only ornament on the walls was a dim photograph over the mantel. Pervading the air was a smell like incense.

At first, no one else seemed to be in the room.

Then Miriam spoke.

"Father," she said. "I want you to meet my friend, Harry."

My eyes were now becoming accustomed to the gloom. What had seemed at first like a pile of clothing on the sofa by the fireplace took on the shape of a flimsy-looking man in black pyjamas. He had thin grey hair, a thin face, and sad eyes. The thing I'd taken for a floor lamp beside the sofa was actually a metal pole on wheels with a bottle of some transparent liquid hanging from a hook. A tube from the bottle was connected to his left arm. I could also see now that he had a striped cat beside him.

I went forward to shake his hand. The cat arched its back and hissed at me.

Miriam's father got slowly to his feet but didn't shake my hand. In fact, he even drew his hand back from mine. I didn't really mind. In the poor light, the fingers protruding from the pyjama sleeve looked shrivelled and dark, as though charred by fire—or, worse, they might have been the legs of a big spider.

From what Miriam had told me of his past, I'd associated her father with a life of action, exploring mighty oceans and exotic lands with his fleet of ships. Instead he looked more like a wreck being swept helplessly towards the reef.

"We won't disturb your rest," Miriam said to him. "I just wanted you to meet Harry."

He nodded his head to me and shrank back into the sofa beside his cat.

"Let's go," Miriam said.

As we were leaving, I noticed that the photograph over the mantel was of Miriam Galt herself.

"I'M SORRY," she said when we were outside the room again. "Sometimes he's more sociable. Today, he wasn't in the mood."

Now that I'd seen her father and the state he was in, she was less reluctant to talk about him. Apparently, she herself would often sit with him for hours without his noticing her. Sometimes he'd spend all day on that sofa dozing, only nibbling at the meals brought to him. He even slept there most nights rather than go to his bedroom upstairs. On some of those nights, if the sky was cloudless, he'd disconnect himself from his pole and go into the garden. There, with his old ship's telescope, he'd spend hours studying the heavens.

Miriam seemed to find this behaviour disturbing. But I thought it was, to an extent, understandable from someone who'd spent a lot of time at sea and might be familiar with celestial navigation.

"Yes, and it's true I've learned a lot from him about the positions and motion of the stars," Miriam said. "But now the main reason he watches them is that he believes a message might be written there—something especially for him. He often tells me so."

That certainly made him sound a little mad, in addition to his physical illness, whatever that was. Out of politeness, I said maybe he'd recover and things would turn out all right in the end.

"There's no chance of that," she said.

Her reply made me think Miriam Galt wasn't an optimist.

"I'll show you some of his treasures, if you like," she said.

We went up the staircase to a large room on the second floor. The ceiling light wasn't very strong, so Miriam drew back the window curtain. The floor was of plain wooden planks and clear of all furniture except for a number of glass display boxes you might find in a museum. A bookcase stood against the far wall. There was also a stand with some sort of ship's clock on it. Apparently its bell rang every half hour, day and night—I'd heard its high-pitched sound through the ceiling when we were with her father.

"Some of the collection's worth a look," Miriam said. "His officers used to pick things up for him on their voyages."

Indeed, a number of the items were out of the ordinary. One box held two shrunken human heads, male and female, with long grey hair, their eyelids and lips stitched up. A longer box near the window held a collection of stilettos, machetes, and parangs with brown stains on the blades that didn't look like rust. Another box was full of a variety of scrimshaws made of whalebone and narwhal tusks. They were skilfully incised with the usual kinds of romantic seafaring images, but also with scenes of hangings from yardarms and knifings in taverns.

In the bookcase against the back wall, most of the books were in poor condition, their covers warped, the print almost illegible. Some of them were just the kinds of things you'd expect to find on a ship: *A Young Sailor's Introduction to Seafaring*, and *Tides and Currents in the Straits of Malacca*, and *A Guide to Knot Making*, and *Travels in the Melanesian Islands*. The others were an assortment of mildewed books such as you might find in any library on shore.

"All of them are from ships that foundered without survivors," said Miriam Galt. "He doesn't read them, he just likes to have them. For him the important thing is the idea that the last person to read them had drowned."

What a grisly principle, I thought. This bookcase reminded me a little of the columbarium where my parents' ashes were preserved. The neatly organized, outmoded books were the only memorials to their dead readers—and writers too, for that matter.

I said so to Miriam.

"In the end, that's the fate of the contents of most bookcases," Miriam Galt said to me.

6

Six weeks of bliss had passed and now only a few days were left till school opened. Miriam knew I was becoming a little anxious.

"Come for dinner tonight," she said one day. "It'll be a special treat before school starts."

Accordingly, around seven-thirty that night, I headed up over the moors and arrived at the manor just before eight o'clock. It was late summer but still daylight. For once, the only clouds in the Uplands sky consisted of millions of midges. Miriam welcomed me at the door and told me her father wouldn't be joining us—he preferred to eat alone in the library.

I didn't mind that at all.

"He told me to choose a gift for you—one of those books saved from a wreck," she said. "I'm thinking of one in partic-ular—I'll give it to you before you leave."

She'd cooked the meal herself: a roast beef that smelled and tasted delicious. We ate at the plain deal table in the kitchen then adjourned to the living room with a bottle of red wine. I was very aware of the presence of her father next door in the library, so I tried to talk quietly. Miriam assured me that the walls were thick and that our voices wouldn't disturb him.

The curtains of the living-room window were open and it was dark outside now. We went over for a minute to look out. I could see that the night sky over the evergreens was clear and full of stars.

"They look so brilliant," Miriam said. "But it takes so many eons for their light to reach us, the fact is they're actually dead by the time we see them."

People didn't want to think about anything so sad when they were overwhelmed by beauty, I suggested.

"Truth's truth," she said. "Even on this earth, by the time we see anything it's no longer the same as it was, and neither are we. Any scientist will tell you that's so."

I didn't know what to make of that. So I took her hand and

we went and sat on a couch before the big fireplace. A fire had been lit in it earlier to fend off the night chills. I had my arm around her and the wine gave me courage. I told her once again, as I had many times in the last weeks, that I loved her. Again I hoped she'd tell me she loved me too, and again she didn't. But she looked me in the eye.

"Words are so easily mistaken for the real thing," she said.

I denied that passionately. I wasn't making any mistake. I knew I loved her and it had nothing to do with words. Anyway, my love was above words; it was an intuition. I just knew, from the very core of my being, that I loved her.

For the first time in all the weeks I'd known her, she laughed outright.

"You're incorrigible, Harry," she said. "Intuitions aren't any more right about love than they are about stars. I mean, look at us. We think we're sitting here quite securely talking, when we're actually whirling around the sun at thousands of miles an hour. Our intuition lets us down all the time—what looks like a cat lying in a corner turns out to be a pair of socks, and vice versa."

I could tell that the wine had affected her, too. At one point she deliberately leaned her body in against me.

"How do you know that what you think is love isn't actually lust?" she said.

Even though the feel of her was enough to make me wonder if she might be right, I wouldn't concede. So she became serious again.

"If you did love me, it would have to be on the basis of knowing the true me," she said. "But there are many things you don't know about me. If you knew them, they'd tip the scales and outweigh what you think is love. They'd turn it into something not quite so elevated."

This wasn't the first time she'd hinted that she might have secrets I wouldn't like. But I just kept repeating I loved her as though it was an incantation. As though repeating the words would somehow make up for the lack of her saying them to me in return.

And she kept on looking into my eyes, her brow furrowed as though she couldn't make up her mind about me.

"I wonder," she said eventually.

IT WAS AROUND midnight and I was about to pour us another glass of wine when the bell on the ship's clock upstairs began to sound.

"Listen," she said. The bell rang eight times.

"The Middle Watch is about to begin," she said. "My father told me that's what the sailors call the watch between midnight and eight in the morning. I'll go and settle him in for the night. Come with me—there's something you need to see, and now's as good a time as any."

So I followed her through the door in the wainscoting and into the library.

Her father was lying on the couch by the fireplace, as before. That faint smell of incense was in the air. On a little table beside him were the remnants of his dinner. The striped cat was sitting beside one of the plates, cleaning its whiskers. It growled at me and slithered back onto the couch beside him.

"Ready for your medicine?" Miriam said to her father.

He smiled, showing uneven, yellowish teeth. His eyes looked feverish.

She went to a low cupboard near the fireplace and rummaged in a drawer while I thanked him for allowing her to give me one of his books. He paid no attention whatever to me, just watched

Miriam intently as she came back to the couch. She was holding what looked like a jewellery box and some kind of old-fashioned smoking pipe—a thin tube about two feet long with a tiny bowl on the end.

Now she opened the box and took out a pouch of tobacco and carefully packed the pipe, which had what looked like oriental lettering engraved along its stem. She lit a match, put the pipe to her lips, and puffed on it several times till it was glowing. Her father now lay on his side on the couch, his head on a cushion, staring up at her. She handed the pipe to him and he held it with tremulous fingers and puffed on it.

From the jewellery box, she now took a little medicine bottle full of a black liquid. She tilted the bottle over the bowl and poured a slow, heavy drop of the liquid into it. The smoke immediately thickened and that incense smell became much more noticeable.

He sucked steadily on the pipe for a minute or two, sighing from time to time between puffs. We watched without speaking.

Over a period of about ten minutes, this procedure of filling the pipe was repeated twice more. The feverish look in his eyes began to dim so that now when he looked at Miriam and me, he seemed quite human. Even the cat, curled up beside him, was blinking contentedly.

Miriam at last took the pipe from his loose fingers.

"We'll leave you now," she said to him. "Rest well."

He sighed and closed his eyes. She put the pipe and the box back in the drawer. We gathered together his used dinner things and took them to the kitchen. Once there, she answered my unasked question.

"Opium," she said. "He got into the habit when he used to trade in the Far East. He has stock enough to last him a lifetime.

His hands are too shaky now to deal with delicate things like his pipe, so I have to do it for him."

I'd read about the perils of opium and was quite shocked. I was going to ask her more about his habit, and whether she ought not to try somehow to cure him of it. But just as I about to speak she put her hand on my arm and looked into my eyes.

"It's a bit late now for you to be crossing the moors," she said. "I'd really like it if you just stayed here with me tonight."

My heart leaped.

Miriam then switched off the kitchen and living-room lights, and arm in arm we climbed the stairs to her bedroom.

EVENTUALLY, we fell asleep, despite the intermittent ringing of the ship's bell next door.

But with the three a.m. ringing, I woke because of another noise coming from outside the house. Miriam was fast asleep, so I carefully disentangled myself from her and slipped out of bed onto the bare wooden floor. I tiptoed to the window and looked down into the garden. It was a moonlit night so I could see very clearly.

Her father, wrapped in a blanket, was sitting there on a garden bench peering up at the night sky through the brass telescope. I'd only been looking at him for a moment when he suddenly took the telescope away from his eye and stared right up at me before I could duck out of sight. He waved his thin hand and smiled. His face was hideous in the moonlight.

I quickly retreated to the bed. Miriam noticed and snuggled against me.

"You're cold," she said.

"I heard a noise outside," I said. "It was your father out watching the stars. He saw me—he knows I'm here with you."

"Of course he does. Don't worry about it," she said. "Here, let me warm you up."

IN THE MORNING, I sat in the kitchen drinking coffee. Miriam had gone to see to her father—apparently he'd slept in the library after his star-spotting was done. She came back after a while with the smell of incense on her clothing.

"He needed his medicine," she said. "That'll keep him happy for a few hours. I'm going upstairs to get you that book I mentioned."

She climbed the stairs and was back in a moment with a small volume.

"Here you are." She handed it to me.

The covers were warped and many of the pages were crinkled and salt-stained—I could smell the ocean in them. The book was called *An Upland Tale*.

"It's one of those traditional stories from the Uplands," she said. "Some of the pages are lost, but the main section's there and it's still quite legible for the most part, considering what it's been through. I wonder what you'll think of it."

I thanked her for it and assured her I'd tell her next time we met.

She sipped her coffee, watching me.

"So, now you know all about my father and his problem. Some families seem to be cursed with just one awful thing after another—I fear mine may be one of them. You say you love me, but how much more could you put up with? Wouldn't there be a limit to your tolerance?"

We were sitting on chairs opposite each other at the kitchen table. From the way the light came in through the window, I could see miniature reflections of myself in her eyes, as though I was already a part of her. So I assured her I didn't care about her father's addiction, or anything else about her family, for that matter. I loved her and I always would. I thought, surely this time she'll say she loves me too.

But she didn't.

So I surprised myself and went even further. I asked her to marry me. I liked the sound of that so much, I asked her again.

If I'd surprised myself, Miriam certainly didn't look surprised. Her eyes became almost as enigmatic as that first time I'd seen them upside down on the rock. I begged her for an answer.

"Let's not talk about it any more for now," she said. "I have a lot to think about." Soon after that, rain began to patter against the window and it was time for me to leave. Miriam put the book she'd chosen in a plastic bag.

"It's already had more than its fair share of water," she said.

I WAS CONSCIOUS of the weight of the book in my pocket all the way down to Duncairn. I kept thinking of that weird old man, her father—I now understood Miriam's fascination with those "bizarre," "out-of-the-ordinary" events that took place in the Uplands. She herself was right at the centre of one of them.

I also kept replaying, as I walked, the last moments of our conversation. She knew I loved her and she hadn't laughed outright at my marriage proposal—that was the main thing. I had great hopes. My heart was light even as the rain came down heavier and heavier.

7

For the remainder of that day the rain didn't let up and the wind strengthened. From my window I could see the faces of the three soldiers on the war memorial being battered without mercy. My mind should have been fully occupied, going over yet again the lessons in the book Sam Mackay had given me. Despite his words of comfort, I couldn't help being anxious about the school term about to begin.

Yet at the same time I was thinking about how I'd blurted out that proposal of marriage to Miriam. Not that I was having second thoughts. It was just that I'd begun to consider realistically what marriage to her might mean. She was wonderful, but we'd have to live in that isolated house with her hideous, addicted father. Wasn't it possible that in time I'd become bitter and resentful about restricting myself to such a life in a small town like Duncairn—even with Miriam—just when the whole, exotic world I used to dream of was now available?

But I put such thoughts out of my mind. I was in love—that was all that counted! Meeting Miriam Galt was like a great romantic story from an old book. In the next chapter she'd admit she loved me and would marry me and we'd be happy forever.

ONE TASK I settled down to that evening was the reading of the book Miriam had chosen for me from her father's library.

The book was in very poor condition, as I'd noticed when she gave it to me. Embossed on the inside cover were the words "Property of the SS *Derevaun*." I pictured some poor ship of that name, shattered perhaps on a coral reef, the books from its library drifting like butterflies amongst the eddies.

The title page was certainly legible, the typeface old-fashioned and big:

An Upland Tale

BY MEG MILLAR

with an
Addition of Ten Sonnets

There were no dates or any other information. I flicked through the pages and found they were in reasonably good condition, but not a single one of the ten sonnets had survived their ordeal under water. The pages where they had appeared were blank, the words all dissolved into the ocean where the ship had met its fate.

I began reading:

Gentle Reader: This is an old story of which there are many versions. I record here that which has been known to me since childhood.

It was mid-winter in an Uplands village which was not much more than a group of hovels. Johnny Reed lived in one of these hovels with his wife. They were very poor and not very happy, and lived mainly on kale soup. They had six children.

On one of these winter mornings, Johnny awoke and told his wife of a strange dream:

"I saw myself walking through the hills, along the path to the old Roman bridge. It was snowing, and I was carrying my long-handled shovel in my right hand. When I got near the bridge, I saw a withered alder bush in the bog fifty yards off the path. I felt compelled to go there and I began to dig. My shovel struck something with a clang. It was a big iron cauldron. I lifted it out of the hole and opened it. It was full of gold coins."

The dream was so lifelike, Johnny was sure he knew the very spot where it happened. He told his wife he would go there right now and have a look, just out of curiosity.

So he took his long-handled shovel with him and headed up into the moors.

The day was cold with a winter fog thick enough to stop him from seeing more than fifty yards around him. Still, when he got to the path to the old Roman bridge, he could see the outline of the alder bush in the middle of a dangerous bog—just as in the dream. He stepped off the path and onto the soft earth of the bog, which was bare of snow.

He had to go carefully, testing one step at a time, so it took him a while to reach a little island of solid ground where the alder bush grew. It had almost no leaves now except for a few wilted survivors clinging on, as though it were summer still.

Johnny Reed got to work. He dug and dug, and after a while his shovel struck something with a clang. He kept digging and eventually uncovered the object. It was entangled in the roots of the alder, so it must have been there a long time. With his hands he brushed more dirt away from its top and saw that it was a cauldron with a lid on it. He tried to lift the lid off by its arched handle, but it seemed to be stuck and he did not have enough space to grasp it. So with his long-handled shovel he levered the entire cauldron out of the hole, noting how heavy it was.

He looked the cauldron over and saw that it was made of dark red cast iron with an intricate pattern around the top rim. Again he tried to lift off the lid, without success. He thought it might be screwed on to the top of the cauldron, so he thrust the handle of his shovel through the arch of the cauldron's handle and turned it with all his strength. At last, the lid began very slowly to turn and eventually popped off, causing Johnny to fall backwards. He got back up and looked into the cauldron. Nothing. There was nothing in it.

Johnny told his wife when he got back to the hovel, "See, not a gold coin, not any gold of any kind." For he had brought the cauldron down from the moors so that she could see for herself. All she could see was the smooth dark red inside of a dark red cauldron the size of an ordinary kale pot.

So Johnny and his wife returned to living their normal lives. Time passed and their six children all grew up and married and went to live in other nearby hovels.

Twenty dull years went by, then something out of the ordinary happened again to Johnny Reed.

On a winter's morning, there was a loud knock at the hovel door. Johnny opened it to behold a man in a bearskin riding coat and a tricorn hat, his horse haltered a few yards away. The man apologized for the intrusion. He was a traveller from England, a scholar studying the local customs and traditions of the Uplands. He had been trying to find the main road and had wandered astray in the bad weather. He was now hungry and cold.

Johnny's wife invited him in and sat him down on a three-legged stool at the table near the hearth. She ladled him a bowl of kale soup out of the dark red cauldron on the peat fire.

The soup warmed the traveller's insides and soon he was ready to continue his journey. But before he left, he asked if he might examine the cauldron containing the soup. In all his travels, he had never beheld a dark red cauldron of this type. Johnny Reed's wife, with some old dish rags, moved the hot cauldron off the peat fire and onto the flagstone border of the hearth. Neither she nor Johnny told the traveller about the dream that had led to its discovery.

The traveller perched a pair of wire-rimmed glasses on his nose and looked the cauldron over. He was especially interested in a pattern he discovered around the outer rim, sooty from decades of peat smoke. He rubbed it clean with his kerchief.

"Well, well," he said. "A Latin inscription. It's very possible your cauldron is from the period when Romans were here. Let me see: *Sub hoc alia jacet*. How very curious. It means *Beneath this, lies another*."

The English traveller congratulated Johnny Reed and his wife on their unique cauldron. It might not be worth much in terms of money, but it was an archaeological treasure and he hoped they'd look after it. He thanked them for the food and warmth, got on his horse, and headed for the main road as they'd directed him.

As soon as he'd gone, Johnny took his shovel and set off once more to the place where he'd found the cauldron twenty years before. He was in a state of excitement as he picked his way across the dangerous bog to where the skeletal alder bush still grew. He began digging again deeper, much deeper than before.

CLANG!!

Sure enough, Johnny uncovered another dark red cauldron, and levered it to the surface. He inserted the handle of his long-handled shovel into the arch of the lid. The lid turned slowly, metal screeching on metal. With the final twist, Johnny again fell backwards. He rose to his feet and stared into the cauldron.

Gentle Reader: As of this point of the story, a variety of versions exist. Out of an obligation to truth, I shall include them here for your delectation.

In the version I heard in my childhood, the second cauldron did contain a fortune in ancient gold. But when Johnny, exulting, tried to carry it back to dry land, his foot slipped. His coat snared in the handle of the cauldron and it pulled him down into the bog, where he slowly sank and choked to death. Many springtimes later, the bog heaved up his remains with his arms still encircling the cauldron, which was now quite empty.

In another version, when Johnny unearthed the second cauldron, he found nothing in it, just as before. But although he could neither read nor write, he recognized the Latin words on its brim: *Sub hoc alia jacet.* So he dug again and he found another cauldron, again empty, with the same inscription. He dug once more and found another, also empty, with that inscription. He dug up another, then another. He is still digging, still finding cauldrons, all of them empty, all of them inscribed.

In another version, a very different outcome is presented. Johnny did indeed, after the English traveller left, go back up to the bog; he found the second cauldron with nothing in it. But that very night, after coming home disappointed, he dreamt once more about a cauldron. This time, however, it was not buried by the alder bush in the bog. Instead, it was buried deep below the kale patch directly outside his hovel.

When he awoke, he considered his dream for a long time and discussed it with his wife. They decided to do nothing. A dream was, after all, only a dream, and they had no desire to ruin the little patch of ground where their kale, the food that sustained them, grew to ripeness each summer.

But if only Johnny Reed had taken his long-handled shovel and begun digging in that kale patch, he would certainly have heard that CLANG again. His shovel would have struck yet another dark red cauldron, and this one would have been full of gold. With all that, Johnny Reed would have built a palace for his wife and himself, and for his children and his children's children. He would have planted tall forests again all through the Uplands, and filled them with birds of paradise and orangutans and other animals and birds from around the world. He would have hired a team of wise men to look for the secret of universal happiness. They would not have disappointed him. He would have instructed them to publish their findings for the benefit of all mankind. Everyone in the world would have lived and loved happily ever after.

When I'd finished reading the story, I wondered why Miriam had chosen it for me. It was certainly ingenious enough, but those variant endings were quite pessimistic: whether a man follows his dream or doesn't, the outcome isn't going to be all that great. For me, the additional thought that this little book had last been opened by some poor sailor whose bones were now scattered at the bottom of the sea wasn't very cheering either.

All in all, aside from entertainment value, *An Upland Tale* seemed just as depressing in its way as the story of the Tollgate's Cameron Ross, though definitely without the element of terror. When I saw Miriam tomorrow, we'd have a good discussion about it.

It was now past midnight and the rain was still lashing down. In the square the three soldiers, glistening in the street lights, stared off into the darkness of the hills. Their image remained in my head when I got into bed and switched off the lamp. I tossed and turned for a while and tried to think about Miriam and our future happiness. But tiny waves of uncertainty and even dread occasionally swept over me and it was a long time before I fell asleep.

8

I slept late, dreaming as usual about the Tollgate, with my parents alive and well. I was grief-stricken on awakening into a reality without them till I remembered Miriam and felt good again. I'd barely got out of bed and into my clothes when there was a knock at the door.

"Who's there?" I called, buttoning my shirt.

"It's me. I hope I'm not bothering you." The high, reedy voice was unmistakable. I opened the door to Sam Mackay, massive and a little out of breath from climbing the stairs. He didn't waste words.

"I just got back to Duncairn yesterday," he said. "I'd like to talk to you. Let's go over to Mackenzie's for coffee."

WE WALKED ACROSS the square to Mackenzie's Café. The three soldiers were dry, for now. But it was another gloomy day and the sky was laden with dark clouds getting ready to disgorge themselves. The wind was chilly for the time of year.

Mackenzie's dozen tables were mostly unoccupied. I usually sat at a small table by the window where I could look out onto the square, but Sam's bulk would never have fitted there, so we took a roomier table near the back.

He'd been strangely quiet on our walk over, so I was feeling nervous and talked too much. Between sips of coffee, I told him I couldn't believe the months had passed so quickly. I assured him that I'd gone over the grammar and composition book a few times and knew its contents quite well now. I assumed this was the kind of thing he wanted to talk to me about.

Sam nodded his head, letting me talk, his coffee cup like a miniature in his huge hand.

"That's good," he said.

Since I'd no one else to tell, I also decided to confide in him that something wonderful had happened to me in Duncairn while he was off on his Board of Education business. I'd met a girl and fallen in love with her. In fact, I'd asked her to marry me. She hadn't said yes, yet, but I knew she would.

Sam wasn't reacting, so I just kept on talking. I told him her name was Miriam Galt and that he probably knew her. She lived up at Duncairn Manor with her father, a strange old man.

Something in the way Sam was looking at me with those big green eyes was already beginning to worry me. But I kept babbling on about love and how it had transformed me. Without saying it outright, I implied that the love between Miriam and me was the rarest of things and how awful it must be for others not to have such a love as ours—a special, magical kind of love that would last forever.

In the midst of this torrent, Sam placed his toy cup down carefully on its toy saucer.

"You can't marry Miriam Galt," he said. "You can't marry her because she's my fiancée. Yesterday when I came home, I went up to the manor to see her and we finalized the date of our wedding.

That's really why I'm here. She made me promise to come and tell you about it this morning."

9

I left him in Mackenzie's Café and headed straight for the manor. I needed to talk to Miriam, to hear her contradict this absurdity.

As I half-ran across the moors, rain began pouring down so that by the time I reached the manor, I was soaked through. I knocked at the door and waited. No answer. I knocked again, louder. No answer. I pounded on the door and shouted, "Miriam! Miriam!" over and over. No answer. I stood back and roared her name at the house itself.

The curtains of the window just above the door were slowly drawn apart by Miriam Galt. With her arms still extended she stared down at me for a time, her face expressionless. Then she drew the curtains together again, as though at the end of a performance.

I stood for a while in a state of shock. I felt like one of those ancient warriors I'd read about, pierced by a spear and knowing that if he pulls it out, he'll die. Then I began to make my way back down through the lashing rain towards Duncairn, which now seemed to me the most inhospitable of places. A few hours ago, I'd almost convinced myself I was as happy as a man could ever be. Now I was sure I'd never be happy again.

AT DAWN THE next morning, after a dismal night, I furtively slipped down the stairs into the street. A thick fog that made the world insubstantial suited my mood. I hurried to Duncairn Station with my meagre possessions stuffed in a canvas bag. I bought a ticket for the first train to arrive and found an empty compartment aboard. As it steamed away from the station, headed south, I could see almost nothing of Duncairn through the window for the swirling fog.

Thus, broken-hearted, I left Miriam Galt and Scotland behind me forever.

Time is what prevents everything from happening at once.

John Archibald Wheeler

PART TWO

A LETTER FROM THE CURATOR

So, all these years later, imagine my astonishment, in the seedy Bookstore de Mexico in La Verdad, at the sight of that name Duncairn on the title page of *The Obsidian Cloud*. How could I not acquire the book? A full month had passed since I'd sent it to the National Cultural Centre in Glasgow, and I'd heard nothing from the rare books curator. I was beginning to get impatient. Surely he'd have read it by now and either been impressed or not. Was the book of consuming interest only because of the spell that name had cast on me? Not that I really believed in magic, but if there were such things as a black magic and a white magic, the name of that little town represented both for me— there, I'd both fallen completely in love and been devastatingly rejected.

Then one morning before breakfast the mailman delivered a letter with the heading National Cultural Centre of Scotland embossed on the envelope. I quickly read the typed note inside.

Dear Mr. Steen:
Re. The Obsidian Cloud.

I'm afraid it has taken us even longer than I'd expected to deal with this item. You'll be gratified to know, however, that we have made a number of most interesting discoveries about the book. When we have completed the remainder of our inquiries, I will, of course, send the results to you.

I can already say this: we at the Rare Books department already consider The Obsidian Cloud *to be a Scottish literary curiosity of some distinction. I, personally, am delighted you entrusted the search for its provenance to us. I dare to hope you will ultimately consider donating this unique book to our collection.*

As for your financial gift of some months ago to our centre: on behalf of our Board of Trustees, I should like to convey to you our deepest appreciation.

Yours, etc.
Doctor Neale Soulis, Ph.D. (Bibliophagy)
Curator of Rare Books
National Cultural Centre of Scotland

Of course, I was elated that my judgment of the book's interest hadn't been entirely subjective. But this Dr. Soulis, the curator, hadn't given much away in his letter, so I couldn't restrain myself and decided to phone him. In spite of the time difference, I managed to catch the man himself at his desk.

"Mr. Steen," he said when he realized who I was. "How good of you to call."

He had quite a loud voice and sounded much more

enthusiastic than when I'd first phoned him about the book. I told him how excited I was about his letter.

"Believe me, we're excited too," he said. "Let me say again, I'm so glad you sent the book to us. I assure you, we get dozens of requests from people every month to examine literary works that turn out to be quite worthless, at least from the standpoint of rare books. I've got to the stage where I often tell them we're too busy to accept any more items at the moment. In your case, that would have been a real blunder."

I was pleased to hear that and pressed him for information. What were these "interesting discoveries" he'd made? For instance, did that visitation of the weird mirror cloud really happen?

But Curator Soulis obviously had different priorities.

"Oh, we haven't even begun that kind of research yet," he said. "I'm afraid you'll have to be patient with our methods. What's really attracting our attention at the moment is the format of the book."

Format? I suppose my disappointment came through over the phone, for he laughed.

"Of course, only a specialist in the history of printing could be expected to appreciate how interesting and unusual its format is," he said. "*The Obsidian Cloud* has several characteristics that in themselves make it a noteworthy piece of work from the period. We're not familiar with its printer, so we're in the midst right now of attempting to trace the firm and any possible records of the printing."

So he hadn't found out anything about whether the incident actually happened?

"Not as yet," said the curator. "But we will get to it eventually, Mr. Steen—please don't worry. For now we have a number of other avenues we need to explore before we dig into the matter of the book's actual contents."

At that point the most awful noise was coming from the phone, so much so that I thought something had gone wrong with the line. I couldn't hear what Soulis was saying and was about to hang up and redial when the background noise stopped. Soulis's voice was quite clear again, though he was shouting so loudly I had to hold the receiver away from my ear.

"I just want to assure you I'll keep you apprised of all our findings in due course," he shouted. "By the way, when you first phoned you told me you'd been in Duncairn years ago. Out of curiosity, may I ask what exactly you were doing there?"

I gave him a brief account of how I'd stayed only a few months, theoretically preparing to teach school. In the end, it hadn't worked out and I'd moved on. Naturally, I didn't mention Miriam Galt.

"I see, and now you're in Canada." His voice was back to normal. "I must confess I know very little about Camberloo except that its university has a very good reputation. After Duncairn, it must have been quite a change for you."

After that, we exchanged a few pleasantries. He thanked me profusely for my donation—it would be put to very good use. We said goodbye, and that was that.

But he was right about the gulf between Duncairn and Camberloo. And that got me to thinking about what a circuitous route I'd taken to get here. I'd seen my quota of wonders and mysteries—as we all do in the course of a life, I suppose. But a believer in fate, or destiny, or some other obscure force might well have argued that it all led inevitably to the discovery of *The Obsidian Cloud*. And, at last, to the resolution of the most persistent mystery in my life.

DUPONT

1

The train I'd boarded that foggy morning I fled from Duncairn happened to be headed for London. It arrived at Euston Station in late afternoon in a thick fog, this one as dirty as anything the Tollgate could produce. In the course of the eight-hour train journey, I'd made my mind up that in London I'd look for any kind of work on a ship going to parts of the world that I didn't know and didn't know me. Perhaps the very act of travelling might counter the despair I felt at Miriam Galt's rejection.

So when I got off the train, I found out that the docks were at Wapping and took a bus straight to them. At the Port of London Office, I was told that under normal circumstances my total inexperience as a sailor would have disqualified me from even applying for a position. But a problem had just arisen. The SS *Otago*, a freighter preparing to weigh anchor next morning with machinery bound for the port of Racca in West Africa, reported it was short of the legally required number of deckhands—the lowest ranking on board. Without a full crew, the ship would not be permitted to depart.

The Port Office was willing to issue me the appropriate certificate, no questions asked, if I agreed to sign on right away for the voyage out and back.

I didn't hesitate.

At dawn next day when the *Otago* cast off and headed downriver, I was already on deck with a bucket and mop, swabbing dirt and oil stains from around the cargo bays.

DURING THE NEXT three weeks, any romantic notions I'd got from books about life at sea were dispelled. The *Otago* was reality. It was a rusty old freighter with a noisy coal-fed engine, the food in the below-decks' mess was greasy and bland, and the sleeping quarters were cramped, smelly, and full of lice. Hence the *Otago*'s difficulty in finding crew and the Port Office's willingness to let me, an admitted landlubber, sign on. Certainly, my crewmates could see that and made it clear they wanted nothing to do with me.

The sea itself, at first, appeared to mirror my sorrow over what had happened to me in Duncairn. The Atlantic Ocean with its vast grey emptiness was the perfect setting for a broken heart. Working alone out on deck, hour after hour, permitted me the luxury of wallowing in self-pity at Miriam's betrayal. At times I allowed myself to believe she'd been playing me for a fool all along. Every detail of her behaviour could be seen in that light. Even that book she'd given me—about the man looking in vain for a pot of gold—was probably meant as a mockery of my gullibility.

But even my sense that the grey ocean sympathized with me turned out to be one more illusion. After two days a vicious storm hit and lasted for a week. The *Otago* plunged headlong into steep seas whipped up by gales that outdid anything I'd experienced on hilltops in the windy Uplands. The blinding squalls and bolts of lightning that seemed to roll along the deck didn't excuse the crew from work—the Third Officer showed me how to rope a lifeline to nearby stanchions and continue scrubbing at those ingrained oil stains. Anxiety over the flimsiness of that lifeline did help put my broken heart out of my mind for long stretches.

Things got even worse when a queasiness in my gut developed into a full-blown seasickness. After a while even drowning seemed preferable to vomiting yet once more. Nonetheless, I had to keep working every day till the storm eventually passed.

My seasickness didn't pass, however. Which led to my meeting with a Canadian medical doctor, Charles Dupont.

THE SS OTAGO, like many freighters, always tried to carry a few passengers to help defray the costs of a voyage. Dr. Dupont was one of only four passengers on board, the other three being businessmen. Since the *Otago* had no ship's doctor, the purser had mentioned my chronic seasickness to Dupont, who volunteered to come out onto the deck one morning and see how I was.

This Dr. Dupont didn't exactly match my idea of how a physician should look. He was quite young—in his mid-thirties, perhaps—with green eyes that always seemed to have a gleam in them as though everything in the world was amusing. He had long, thin brown hair that hung to his shoulders. More noticeable was his beard: it was quite short and was combed into two symmetrical parts that hung from his jaw like those stalactites I'd seen in the bat caves at Duncairn. Even more curious: the two points were tipped with green beads the same colour as his eyes. Woven into the hairy tufts were little silver bells that would tinkle when he talked, especially when he used words that required any amount of chin wagging.

My first conversation with him was memorable.

He asked a few questions about the symptoms of my seasickness. Then he gave me a little brown bottle he'd brought with him onto the deck, containing a half-dozen pills: I was to take one each night.

"It's a pity you have to keep on working," he said. "The pills are more effective if you're lying down."

I noticed he spoke with a slight accent and didn't seem in any rush to leave. He began asking me sociable, non-medical questions about how I came to be a member of the *Otago's* crew. I didn't go into much detail, only that I was from Scotland, that I'd just finished university, and that I wanted to see more of the world.

"Ah," said Dupont. "Another man trying to flee from his past." He said this in a humorous way and seemed to be including himself in the category. He himself was on his way back to Africa where he was in his second two-year term at a remote hospital inland, at the meeting place of jungle and desert. He certainly didn't seem like a man cut out for too much sun. He had light skin and his face was permanently rusted with freckles.

When he'd come out on deck, he'd been carrying a paperback book which he laid on an awning. I glanced at its cover while we talked—on it a young woman wearing a very short skirt was being stabbed in shocking colours by a man in a mask.

"It's a whodunit," Dupont said when he saw me looking at it. "I used to be embarrassed at being caught reading them. The truth is I enjoy them. They're a pleasant break from the medical literature I normally have to read—and they're not half so graphic. And, according to my good friend Clara, what genre could be more appropriate than mysteries for shedding light on the great mystery that is humanity?" He laughed and his beard tinkled.

I hadn't yet taken one of his pills, but just having someone on the ship talk to me was already making me feel much better. I asked him about his accent—he didn't sound quite like the North Americans in the movies.

"That's because I'm from Quebec," he said. "French is my first language and I spoke it almost all the time when I was young. Whenever I used English, I felt a bit like a squirrel obliged to walk on the sidewalk."

I didn't know much about Canada or Quebec, for that matter, except that they had always seemed to be very pleasant places compared to the Tollgate. Why would anyone choose to leave them and work in such a backwards and dangerous region as I'd heard Africa was?

He rolled his eyes.

"Ah, that's a long story," he said.

Just then the gong for lunch sounded from the passenger area.

"I'm afraid my story will just have to wait till another time," he said. "Meanwhile, I hope those pills help. It's been nice talking to you. I'll come back tomorrow and see how you're feeling." Then he headed towards the companionway door and disappeared inside.

2

Dupont did come back to see me the next day and indeed every day of the voyage thereafter. He gave me the impression, without ever saying so, that his fellow passengers weren't interesting companions and had as little in common with him as my crewmates had with me. We'd talk sometimes for as long as an hour, and the deck foreman never seemed to mind—there was an unwritten ship's policy that paying passengers should have as much leeway as they wished.

Some nights after my duties were over we'd go to his cabin for a drink. The cabin was small but luxurious compared to my space in the crew's quarters. Aside from his bed and desk, there were two chairs and even a little bookcase with some paperback novels alongside more austere-looking medical journals. We'd sit on the chairs at either end of the desk and he'd pour us each a hefty glass of scotch.

I hadn't had much acquaintance with scotch, so on the first of these occasions, it opened me up and I told him a good deal about myself—about the deaths of my parents, about Jacob and Deirdre and their cats and how that had led me to Duncairn. My heart had been broken there by Miriam Galt. I suppose I must have gone on about that quite a bit, but he listened patiently.

"The place and that girl obviously left their mark on you," he said after a while. "I'm afraid doctors don't have any pills for a broken heart. I can't even offer you some good advice. All I can say is, I know how you feel."

Naturally I didn't believe that. No one could have gone through what I'd gone through.

But it was now Dupont's turn to talk, and talk he did.

"The other day you asked me why I chose to work in Africa," he said. "I've met people who think it must be a saintly quality that would drive a person to give up the luxuries of Canada and go work in some dangerous backwater. But believe me, there isn't a bit of the saint in me. No, the fact is, I actually enjoy working in dangerous places. Maybe that's partly because they take my mind off something that happened to me twelve years ago. As in your own case, it was a matter of the heart."

He poured us another scotch and explained what he meant.

DUPONT HAD ATTENDED medical school in Montreal with the aim of becoming a surgeon-cum-anthropologist. There he met and married the woman he loved. She was tall and delicate, with long black hair, a student in fine arts who worked during the summers in a little jewellery boutique. Between them, they'd very little money but were able to get along because of her part-time job.

One day when she came home from work she told him that the owner of the boutique, who had several others across the country, wanted her to forget about finishing her degree and come and work full time for his business. He'd heard from some of his wealthy clients that she had an eye for just the kind of items that appealed to them. So he wanted her to represent the chain at the big jewellery markets in New York, Boston, and Los Angeles, where he bought his stock. The increase in her salary would be more than enough to make their lives very comfortable while Dupont went through medical school.

She and Dupont talked the offer over and eventually agreed that she should accept it. It was understood that, after Dupont completed his degree and established himself, she'd go back and finish her own studies.

So when the fall term began, instead of heading for the university together each morning as they once did, she began her new job. It involved spending a lot of time on planes and living in hotels. She'd be gone sometimes for a whole week, but whenever she was home they couldn't get enough of each other and would spend every spare minute together. They'd bought a car by now, rented a big new fifth-floor apartment looking onto the mountain, and ate at the very best restaurants in town. She was able to buy expensive clothes, suitable to her new position. Indeed, as a form of advertising, she wore some of the firm's costliest necklaces, rings, and brooches when they were out together. A little safe had to be installed in the apartment especially for these jewels.

In early December of that first year in her new position, she had to go to a dealers' market in Boston. She'd already done a lot of flying and thought it might be a pleasant change just to drive the new car this time. Boston wasn't that far from Montreal—just four or five hours on the highway.

Dupont was a little concerned because, even though there had been no sign of snow as yet, the weather at that time of year could turn bad very quickly. She assured him she'd be careful.

Around seven on the morning of the trip, he walked her to the elevator, kissed her, and told her how much he loved her.

"I wish I were staying here with you," she said, hugging him tightly. "Always remember, I'm only doing this because I love you more than anything in the world." Just before the elevator door closed, she promised she'd call him that night from her hotel in Boston.

Dupont's phone did indeed ring at nine o'clock that night. But it wasn't a call from his wife. It was a Massachusetts police officer, who informed him that his wife had been killed in a collision with a truck during a snow squall on the turnpike an hour out of Boston. The police had found his address in her wallet. The passenger in the car with her was killed, too. The officer gave Dupont the passenger's name: it was the owner of the business. They'd both died instantly.

Dupont wondered why his wife hadn't mentioned that her employer would be travelling with her. But he was too grief-stricken to dwell on it.

Grief or not, along with her sorrowing family he managed to get through the funeral. Then he had to deal with the sad business of winding up her affairs. An insurance company representative assured him that all the funeral expenses would be taken care of, but wondered if he wished to continue the coverage on her jewels.

Dupont was surprised to hear that. The only expensive jewels she ever wore belonged to her employer, so she wouldn't have insured them.

The insurance agent assured him that yes, they were her property and she'd had them expertly evaluated at half a million dollars a month ago. She'd gone ahead and insured them for that sum and they were now Dupont's, as her only beneficiary.

Over the following weeks, with grim determination to know everything, Dupont established the facts. Records showed that his wife had indeed been given the jewels as outright gifts by the owner. In addition, he discovered that the owner had accompanied her on several of her business trips—hotel clerks remembered especially the striking woman with the long black hair. The two shared planes and meals—and hotel rooms.

Dupont couldn't believe what a fool he'd been not to have suspected. Now her sudden elevation within the firm made sense. His first instinct was to take those jewels of hers and throw them into the deepest part of the St. Lawrence.

Then he thought better of it and instead went to a dealer in jewels and sold them for half of what they were worth. But he couldn't bear to be in Montreal anymore, so he transferred to the medical school at the University of Camberloo in the province of Ontario. There he was able to live very well on the money from the jewels.

He graduated as a physician and put in his years of surgical residency, but he couldn't find a cure for himself. The wound caused by his wife's treachery was now compounded by a deep sense of self-loathing at having allowed himself to live comfortably on its benefits. He'd left Montreal because of the one, and could no longer endure Camberloo because of the other. In the desperate hope of somehow cleansing himself, he volunteered to work as a medical generalist in whatever remote corners of the world could use his services.

DUPONT TOOK a big gulp of his whisky.

"So, here I am, headed for Africa again," he said. "Not that I expect any longer that my service in such places will resolve my personal problems. I'm afraid it's true that you always take yourself with you, no matter where you go.

"But things are much better for me now with the passing of time. For years, I tormented myself over what happened. Did she really love that other man? Was it the jewels she loved? Or did she really love me? Or maybe she thought it would be nicer for us to live in comfort while I finished my medical studies, and that what I didn't know wouldn't harm me? After all, the last words she said to me were *I'm only doing this because I love you more than anything in the world.* I couldn't get them out of my head."

He shrugged his shoulders.

"In the end, I came to believe she did love me and that everything she did—even giving herself occasionally to her boss—really was for me." He looked at me sympathetically.

"Of course, after what you've been through, it's hard for you to understand. When I was young, I felt the same. But now, what she did no longer seems so awful to me."

I honestly couldn't see any similarity between our situations. His wife's infidelities, if she'd done them out of love, weren't really all that treacherous. To forgive her didn't require great generosity. But Miriam's rejection of me was quite another matter. She'd let me fall in love with her, didn't love me in return, and had all along intended to marry another man. It was my misfortune that I still loved her. In the matter of forgiveness, I was too mixed up to know where to begin.

Dupont, as I was contemplating these things, was fingering the two little green beads on the tips of his beard.

"I didn't sell all her jewels," he said. "These are sapphires from one of her rings. I've been told they're the stones for remembrance. Whenever I touch them, I think of her."

3

At night in the crew's quarters, some of the men would lie on their bunks smoking what they called "kief." They'd stuff little ornate pipes with a brownish substance, inhale it for a few seconds, then slowly exhale. The entire area would be filled with a sweet smell, for this kief was a mixture of rose petals and marijuana—naturally, I'd never heard of it in the Tollgate, where beer and whisky reigned supreme. Some of the crew, when they were smoking, became a little friendlier towards me. One of them even offered me his pipe.

But the whole scene brought to mind that horrible old man lying on his couch in Duncairn.

"No thanks," I said.

My shipmate was in too good a mood to be offended.

I ASKED DUPONT about kief one night in his cabin over a glass of scotch.

"I occasionally smoke it myself," said Dupont. "I'm one of those travellers who believe that participating in such local customs can be an important aspect of understanding other parts of the world."

He saw I was interested in hearing about that.

"I'll give you a useful illustration," he said.

ONCE, HE WAS posted to a group of islands in the Pacific. He'd been sent there by a philanthropic agency to set up a clinic to treat the islanders' ailments. But when the clinic was ready, they stayed away from it. Dupont discovered the reason in a round-about way.

At some distant point in their history, it seems, the islanders had realized that the skin of little fish from certain mountain streams stored a type of narcotic. This fish soon became an integral part of various rituals. The men of the tribe would assemble at some holy place where the women would serve them the fish. The men would lick the skins of the fish and go into a state of religious ecstasy. The women could only watch as it was taboo for them to lick the fish.

Dupont, when he heard about the fish-licking, wanted to try it out. For him, it was his professional obligation as an anthropologist as well as a medical doctor. Fish-licking seemed to be intimately related to island culture. For a researcher not to try it out would be as foolish as a confirmed teetotaller attempting to grasp the essence of many Western forms of celebration.

One of the islanders he'd come to know told Dupont he'd introduce him to the drug itself. But since he was a stranger, the islander certainly couldn't allow him into the secret religious rituals associated with the fish-licking—the drumming, the chanting, the costumes, the ceremonial trappings, and so on. So, for the demonstration, he brought Dupont to his own home and took him out onto the balcony after sunset.

The scene was quite domestic. The man's wife had caught a fresh fish—a very small one, since Dupont wasn't experienced with the drug—and she now brought it out on a saucer, along with a glass of water for cleansing the palate after the licking.

The fish was about six inches long, light green in colour, and plump for its size.

Following the islander's example, Dupont slowly ran his tongue from the head to the tail of the fish, twice. Then they sat back in their chairs and let the drug do its work.

Dupont was almost instantly transformed into a swimming creature. He felt the chill of the highland stream as he patrolled its pebbled beds in search of food. His heart thudded at the sight of monstrous rats, eels, frogs, and even slit-eyed crocodiles prowling the water around him. Once, a huge bird swooped down from above and tried to grasp him in its claws. Not long afterwards, Dupont became a thing that crawled on its belly on the mossy shore, burrowing and eating, turning the earth into compost, tasting its world. Language by now had slipped away and his mind was filled with images so harrowing he feared he'd go mad.

Fortunately the effects of the drug were already beginning to ebb. Dupont was relieved but at the same time regretful as his perceptions shrank once more to those of a human being.

When his eyes were able to focus again, he saw that the

islander had long returned from what, for him, had been a mild experience. Dupont wanted to talk about what he'd seen—what he'd been—but could barely find the words. The islander assured him that even if he were a master of language, it would be no more possible to reconstruct the fish-licking experience in words than to turn the bungalow in which they sat back into the *vesi* trees from which it was built.

After that introductory experience, Dupont spent two years on the island and participated in the fish-licking a number of times. He noticed that each time he came out of his ecstasy, he was equally speechless. But he also now began to feel a keen fellowship with the islanders and intuitively grasped something of their world view.

The reason they wouldn't come to his clinic, for example, was that they believed in a form of reincarnation that completely negated Western ideas of medicine. Fish-licking had taught them that human life was only one of the innumerable life forms each spirit would inhabit and that nothing must be allowed to interfere with that continuity. Likewise, all afflictions of the physical sort must be endured. Indeed, if any attempt were made to moderate them, they'd have to be undergone again in subsequent lives in even more virulent forms.

Obviously, then, no islander with any sense had the slightest use for Dupont's services. If the international agency that had sent him to build the clinic had first done the groundwork to grasp this basic tenet of island culture, they'd have saved themselves both time and money.

NOW, IN HIS CABIN aboard the SS *Otago*, Dupont concluded his story.

"I think if I'd stayed on that island a little longer, I might have become a total convert," he said. "I just needed a few more fish-licking sessions to clarify my thinking."

He laughed, and I laughed, too. I couldn't always be sure what to make of him. He'd admitted before that his desire to work in various exotic parts of the world satisfied his love of risk and danger as much as any humanitarian impulse. No doubt, that conflicted with my idealistic notions about the kind of man a doctor ought to be.

"Well, Harry," he said, "all this talk about the good old days makes me feel like having a smoke." Then, in a stage whisper: "I just happen to have some kief handy."

He went to his desk and returned with one of those pipes I'd seen the crew use. He filled it, lit it up, and sucked on it. Then, holding his breath, he offered it to me.

Not wanting to offend him, I took the pipe and inhaled. The smoke smelled fine, but the taste was awful. I choked and coughed until my lungs were clear.

Dupont's beard jingled from laughing.

"Kief's just like life," he said. "Sometimes it takes your breath away."

4

The *Otago* had been at sea more than two weeks now. The skies were still overcast for the most part, but the water was much smoother and the air was becoming so steamy that the crew worked on deck without shirts. My seasickness, if that's what it was, hadn't abated even with the pills Dupont had given me. One day on deck when he was talking about its persistence he made a suggestion.

"Look, why don't you disembark at Racca," he said. "You could travel with me to the hospital and see a bit of the country while you're at it. If it's just seasickness you're suffering from, being on land for a while should get rid of it. If it's something else, I can treat it properly when we get to the hospital."

The hospital was a hundred miles inland from the port of Racca. Dupont had worked there for the last few years and brought it up to date. It had been built to cater to the needs of scattered tribal peoples on the fringes of the desert, mainly women with complications from childbirth.

"Clara's the head nurse—you'd meet her if you come with me," he said. His eyes softened at the mention of her name. He'd referred to her often, so I guessed he was very fond of her. "What do you think? It might be fun."

The idea of leaving the ship appealed to me, as I was still an outcast amongst the crew. But there was the matter of my contract: I'd signed on for the return voyage, too.

"That shouldn't be a problem," Dupont said. "I'll speak to the captain right away."

HE WAS AS GOOD as his word. He advised the captain that it would be wise to release me from the contract because of my health problems.

The captain was quite agreeable.

"He'll have no trouble replacing you," Dupont told me. "It seems there's no shortage of sailors in Racca looking for ships. They don't like being stuck there, so they'll sign on with any ship that's leaving."

I found that hard to believe, for by then I'd had more than enough of ships. Terra firma couldn't possibly be worse.

THE DAWN AIR was stifling when the SS *Otago* arrived at the port city of Racca. Or, at least, near the port, which was on the northern outskirts of the city. Ships of our tonnage had to anchor in the deep water just beyond the breakers, a half mile out from the shoreline. The water inshore was too shallow for them.

The *Otago* came to a halt and the engine was cut. A welcoming party of a million mosquitoes and stinging flies came rushing aboard to greet us.

THE PERILOUS operation of unloading the cargo soon began. Everything had to be transferred into shallower draft rowboats that came out from the port and surrounded the *Otago* like kittens suckling on a restless mother cat. My shipmates disliked this transferring of cargo. There was a grisly history of mutilations and drownings that had occurred during the process.

As it turned out, my last job as a member of the crew was a good deal less dangerous. Instead of unloading the mute and uncooperative cargo, I was to help ferry Dupont and the other three passengers ashore in the ship's boat.

Nonetheless, even that task was nerve-racking. The boat was lowered by a pulley to the sea thirty feet below. An experienced sailor climbed down the hull on a swaying rope ladder and jumped into the bow of the boat. He then fended it off the hull and kept it as steady as possible in the swell while I assisted the passengers and their luggage down. Last, I managed to lower myself successfully.

With the passengers all safely aboard and the luggage stowed, the veteran sailor took charge of the oars and rowed the boat through massive breakers, which were being patrolled by squadrons of sharks. Only Dupont, who'd been ferried this way several times before, didn't seem too worried that we might breach and spill into the jaws of the sharks. To everyone else's relief, we eventually reached the shore. Obeying my last order as a crew member, I jumped into the shallows and pulled the boat the last few feet onto the beach.

Standing at last on solid ground wasn't quite what I'd expected. The sandy beach seemed to roll just as unpredictably as the ocean and I'd trouble keeping my balance. For a while I felt like an alien creature, at home neither on land nor sea.

THOUGH I'D HEARD from the crew that Racca was smelly and overcrowded, I wouldn't have minded exploring it for a while. But Dupont already knew the city well and had no desire to linger. Instead, from the port he arranged places for us as passengers in the bed of an open truck that had wooden sides and rear. It was ready to leave and would transport us from the coast into the dense bush of the hinterland.

"Not that we have any choice, but a truck's really the only way to travel if you want to get a sense of this country—it'll be an education for you," Dupont said as we squatted behind the truck's cabin. "This one will take us right to the hospital door." These trucks acted as buses, going from village to village along the way, picking up and dropping off passengers. With any luck, we'd arrive at the hospital before sundown.

Some other passengers boarded, the truck's engine roared, the gears crashed, and we lurched on our way. At first we had to stop and start frequently as we traversed the messy sprawl of the suburbs around the port. Then we left modern life behind and entered the band of primeval jungle that separated us from the grasslands and the desert.

5

The roads had now become trails that were potholed and deeply fissured from lack of repair. Sudden violent rainstorms would turn them into rushing torrents with steep, muddy banks. The truck would have to clamber out of them and stop till the rains let up, which usually took only a few minutes. Then the water level would sink enough to make travel possible once more.

As we proceeded farther into the jungle, I sometimes felt slightly feverish. The huge trees leaning over the trail became an endless library with bookcase after bookcase full of the same tattered book, or a monotonous canyon of slums in an oddly sweltering Tollgate.

But in spite or because of my stupor, I was generally at ease. The jungle's dark embrace, limiting our horizon to only a few yards in all directions, was at this point more comforting to me than the sea's endless vistas.

I WAS FASCINATED by the passengers who got on and off at their villages along the way. Their smooth, dark complexions were noticeably free of the pimples, boils, and pockmarks of slum dwellers. The women, in their vivid floral dresses, were especially beautiful. When they spoke and laughed, their words sounded like a strange poetry.

The layout of most of the villages, aside from the fact that they were built in clearings in the middle of a vast forest, wasn't all that different from the little Upland towns. In the centre of each village was the market where the spear makers, bakers, potters, and meat sellers displayed their wares. Also in this main area was a sort of high street with the compounds of chiefs and various members of their council. The less important people lived in smaller huts at the edges of the village where the jungle began, so, according to Dupont, they were easier prey for lions, wild boars, black mambas, and a host of other creatures much more deadly than those in the Uplands.

The flimsiness of the buildings surprised me at first—their walls were made of bamboo with slats you could see right through. Dupont pointed out that the climate here required that houses have as much ventilation as possible. Still, those slats in the walls didn't allow them much in the way of privacy, in our Western sense.

"Maybe they have fewer secrets than those of us brought up in brick dwellings," Dupont said. "Or maybe they have different kinds of secrets from us. Wouldn't it be interesting to know what those might be?"

Around noon, while I drowsed on, the truck halted for a while and a fire was built to enable our fellow passengers to cook their lunches. When I smelled roasted meat, I began to feel hungry and looked over the edge of the truck. The passengers and drivers were sitting around the fire holding individual bamboo skewers.

Impaled on each skewer was the roasted body of a tiny baby, complete with all its limbs.

Dupont saw I was aghast.

"They're not what you think," he said. "They're actually little tree monkeys. They do look quite human though, don't they? They're supposed to be very tasty."

The sight of the others stripping the meat from the tiny bodies as though they were chickens, together with the crunching noise of teeth on the little finger bones—these things became too much for me. I climbed out of the truck and, in a bush nearby, allowed myself to be sick. When I came back, Dupont gave me a little talk on the proper attitude of a wise traveller.

"You must understand, Harry, that these people aren't violating some universal code of ethics by eating different foods from us," he said. "Some travellers refuse to accept the basic dietary fact that, like it or not, we all have to eat other living organisms to survive. It's pure chance whether you're born in a place that eats pigs or one that prefers monkeys—rather than kale and porridge, as I suppose you did in Scotland."

I didn't like being lumped in with narrow-minded travellers. So although the idea of eating little monkeys was nauseating, I didn't argue with him.

6

We now emerged from that area of heavy jungle onto a red dirt road that led us into a much more open landscape. It consisted of head-high thorn bushes and clusters of narrow-leaved gum trees on endless stretches of grass.

"We're getting nearer the desert," said Dupont.

Even in these less confined spaces, however, things were not always as they seemed.

For example, several times, what appeared to be carpets of fallen leaves on the road ahead would leap into life as the truck approached—the leaves were actually huge swarms of locusts, basking in the sun after their ravages.

The most remarkable instance occurred when the road—which was really just the ghostly trace left by previous vehicles on the red dirt—was taking us through an area full of blackened gum-tree stumps, the remnants of some past inferno. Dupont pointed out what looked like boulders standing precariously on top of some of the stumps.

These boulders matched the surroundings so well that I hadn't even noticed them. But now that he'd brought them to my attention, I assumed they must have been put there by local tribes for some ritualistic purpose.

Dupont shook his head.

"Watch this," he said, and asked the driver to stop the truck for a moment.

He got out, picked up a pebble at the roadside, and threw it in the direction of one of those stumps. Immediately, the boulder on top metamorphosed into a bird, sprouting heavy brown wings and taking off into the air with furious squawks.

Dupont then threw stones at other boulders, all of which turned out to be perching birds. They milled around in the air, protesting angrily.

Dupont got back in the truck.

"They're called nightjars," he told me.

The truck had barely got underway again when the birds settled back on their stumps, becoming inconspicuous once more.

"During the daytime, they're so immobile against their background you'd never know they were living things," said Dupont.

Even then, for some reason, witnessing these transformations filled me with a sense of foreboding. I told Dupont so.

"Probably there are human beings with the same talent," he said.

Neither of us could have had any inkling of the ominous significance those words would have in a far-off day, in a distant hemisphere.

DUPONT WAS well known in some of the villages, having visited them on his previous trips. He was able to get by in pidgin and in several of the native languages. The chief or the shaman would sometimes come to greet him, having heard by means of the drum-telegraph that he was passing through. They'd fawn over him and beg him to use his alien magic on their behalf.

We stopped for a brief clinic at one of these grasslands villages. Dupont had told me I'd see someone of interest there, but wouldn't say more.

"It's a surprise," he said.

From a hut near where the truck stopped, a man and several women came to greet us. The man was tall and thin, with big sad eyes. But what astonished me about him was this: he had a wispy grey beard divided in two parts, adorned at the points with green beads and little silver bells.

"I wanted you to see where I got the idea," said Dupont, smiling and fingering his own beard. "This man's the tribe's shaman—their medicine man—and I'm our medicine man, so why not?"

He went to the tall man and shook his hand. They chatted in a strange language for a moment, their bells jingling as they talked. Dupont turned to me.

"Apparently almost everyone's out harvesting crops, so there won't be any need for a clinic this visit," he said. "But there's a woman who's just given birth to her first baby in this hut—it's the maternity hut—and he's about to perform the initiatory rite. I'm going in to watch. Do you want to come along? I guarantee it'll be quite educational."

Knowing Dupont as I did by now, I tended to be cautious when he said something like that. He saw what I was thinking.

"Don't worry," he said. "It's not as if they're going to offer us anything weird to eat."

Though I was feeling a little dizzy, I agreed to go with him. We all proceeded—the shaman, the women, Dupont, and I—into the hut.

THE MATERNITY hut was large and airy. Some other female villagers were already there, standing around a rattan mat on the floor. They made room for the shaman. One of them tied an elaborate multicoloured cloak around him.

On the rattan mat lay a naked woman with swollen breasts. The baby she'd just delivered was being held by an onlooker, who rocked it gently in her arms and crooned to it. The little body was streaked in blood and slime.

After Dupont and I took up our places watching, the sad-eyed shaman knelt down and bent over the woman who'd given birth. He then spread his arms dramatically and shook his multicoloured cloak. It immediately burst into a clamour of screeching and chirping. I saw that it wasn't really a cloak at all, but a piece of netting with dozens of little birds of different colours attached to it by their legs in some ingenious way. The sound they made reminded me of those noisy flocks of starlings that would nest in the infrequent, skeletal trees of the Tollgate.

Soon the birds became silent. The shaman grasped the woman's breasts in his hands and began to suck, taking a few minutes at each. Then he straightened up and looked with his sad eyes at all of us gathered there. His mouth was open wide, milk dripping from his chin. I could see he had no teeth, only bare, pink gums.

The birds again began their shrieking and the baby, perhaps sensing the milk, howled even louder than the birds. The child was handed down to the mother. She put it to her breast and it sucked furiously.

ON OUR WAY back to the truck, Dupont asked whether the experience had been as educational for me as he'd hoped.

In fact, I'd felt queasy even from the first sight of the baby—especially that horrible slime and blood.

"All human beings enter this world covered in slime and blood—even if they're born in palaces," Dupont said. Then he explained the meaning of the ceremony. "In this tribe, the cloak of little birds is supposed to prevent the baby's soul from leaving its body. But what's particularly interesting is that mother's milk is the only food a shaman is ever allowed. So, for him, women are the most important members of the tribe—he depends on them completely for his survival. This is very good for the women and elevates their status. For new mothers, it also has a practical benefit: the shaman makes sure the breast milk flows for their babies. Contrary to what most men think, that's not always a simple matter."

It was certainly news to me. What with that and the sight of the revoltingly slime-covered baby, I was curious as to why any woman in her right mind would ever want to have one.

"All it takes is the right man to talk her into it," said Dupont with a laugh that set his beard tinkling merrily.

I was too queasy to laugh. Anyway, I couldn't help thinking: surely it was just as important for a man to find the right woman? But hadn't I already done that, and she'd broken my heart?

7

At a certain point in the journey, the truck became our private taxi. There were no other passengers and we stopped at no other villages. Trees of any kind were now rare as we drove hour after hour through great expanses of undulating grasslands. The wind was steady, bending the tall grasses before it. Then the truck crested a hill and the grasslands abruptly ended. Before us lay the desert, like an ocean that had been miraculously turned into sand, with huge waves in suspended motion.

A final check had to be done on the truck's engine before entering a place so hostile to machinery, so Dupont proposed that we take advantage of the break.

"Let's go for a short walk," he said. "Your first time on foot in the desert will be something to remember."

I didn't at all mind getting out of the truck bed for a while, though the air was like the blast from a hot oven. We walked about half a mile, navigating sand dunes, our feet sinking deep at every step. With Dupont's help I was able to scramble to the top of one of the highest dunes.

"Let's sit here for a while," he said.

We could see for miles around us.

"The hospital's only about an hour that way," he said, pointing to the northeast where the desert seemed to stretch to infinity. A fine powder of sand fell on us, carried by a wind that howled eerily.

"It's called the *harmattan*," said Dupont. "Before I came here, I used to think winds made a noise only because they were blowing through trees and wires and buildings. But there are no such things in the desert, so you almost feel it's the voice of the wind itself you hear."

We were silent, listening to it. It had such an unsettling, mournful quality that it raised the hairs on the back of my neck. I thought back to those Upland winds Miriam and I used to listen to when we wandered the moors around Duncairn. They were bracing and often chilly, but I loved their voice because I myself

9

I dozed most of that day and got up around five. I wasn't at all hungry, but I was feeling much stronger, so I shaved and put on my freshly laundered clothes.

At just before six o'clock, darkness, as usual, fell like a stone, and not long after that a nurse appeared at the door of my room to lead me to wherever I was to dine. She took me along dimly lit corridors, past rooms with open doors in which I could vaguely see patients settling down for the evening.

One door we passed bore the sign *Delivery Room*. The door was ajar and we could hear a bustle of activity and the sound of moaning from inside.

"One of our patients is having some difficulties," said the nurse.

SHE BROUGHT ME to another well-lit room with a dining table set for two. A ceiling fan whirled silently as the nurse set off back down the hall. I had barely seated myself when Clara came in.

"I'm so glad you felt well enough to join me," she said. "I'm hungry. Let's eat."

The meal consisted of a spicy stew made from some kind of desert deer, followed by figs and various fruits. Clara encouraged me to try a little of each, so I did.

While we were at the table, aside from brief comments on the food, the state of my health, and the expected progress of my recovery, we didn't talk much. Afterwards, we moved to a side room that had more comfortable chairs and drank some hot tea.

As she sipped her tea, Clara relaxed and became much more talkative. I discovered, amongst other things, the reason Dupont had been on the *Otago* in the first place. He'd been returning

was in love. Up here on the dune, the wind's lamentation again seemed to reflect the state of my own mind.

In my feverish condition, even this amount of thinking tired me out. I could hardly get to my feet again when, after a while, Dupont said we'd better walk back to the truck.

8

We advanced into the desert along the vaguest hint of a road. It was now four in the afternoon. We had to swath our heads in our shirts to keep from breathing in the sand, so I felt more ill than ever.

Dupont eventually nudged my arm.

"Look," he said. "We're almost there."

Over the edge of the truck I could see a compound consisting of three white-painted, modern-looking buildings glimmering and floating on the far shore of a lake of the bluest colour. I blinked several times. I'd no idea there were lakes in the desert.

"The lake's just a mirage," Dupont said. "You get used to them. But the buildings are real. When the hospital was built this whole area was grasslands. The desert's been encroaching for years now. That's one of the big problems here, but not the worst. Some of the human beings around this area are determined to outdo the havoc caused by nature."

Feeling so ill, I was intent only on finding a less painful position in our bumpy, mobile oven. So I didn't ask him what he meant by that last comment.

SOON WE WERE coasting along a much smoother surface—an occasional landing strip for small planes—and came to a halt in a courtyard in the midst of the three buildings we'd seen. The middle block ran east to west and was larger than the other two, which were like prongs in a fork, pointing north. All three buildings had long, shaded verandahs facing onto the central courtyard. Some beds had been pulled out onto the verandahs, and patients were propped up in them, watching our arrival. The sheltered area contained a number of garden plots full of vegetables and flowers—a welcome sight in this arid landscape.

As Dupont helped me down from the truck, a straggle of house cats that had been lying in the shade wandered out to meet us, their tails erect—for a moment, in my fever, I thought of Deirdre's herd of cats in her house in Glasgow, and I half expected to see her here, too.

But these desert cats were accompanied by several white-uniformed female nurses. The welcoming party, cats and nurses, appeared as delighted to see Dupont as he was to see them. He greeted each of the nurses by name and stooped to pet each cat.

The last of the nurses, the only European, was a tall, thin woman with cropped black hair that was greying a little. Her face was lined from the sun. She wore thick, wire-rimmed glasses that gave her the huge stare of an owl.

She and Dupont hugged each other for quite a few moments while the others looked on, smiling.

Dupont, holding her hand, introduced us.

"Clara, this is Harry," he said. "He has a persistent fever, so he'll be with us for a while till he feels better."

"It's a pleasure to meet you," she said to me. "I do hope you'll enjoy your stay with us." She sounded like an Englishwoman.

Dupont wasted no time in assigning me to a little guest room at the back of the staff quarters in the main building.

The window had no glass, only a fly screen, and the bed was protected by a tented mosquito net. He immediately injected me with something and ordered me to rest.

FOR THE NEXT forty-eight hours I lay in bed, sleeping off and on, nibbling on snacks of fruit and bread. Occasionally I'd awake to a soothing noise, like a machine running quietly. It turned out to be a little black and brown cat that had found a way under the mosquito net and would lie near me, purring happily. I was comforted by its presence when I drifted in and out of sleep.

Early on the third morning, Dupont came into the room a few minutes after I awoke. He lifted the net and felt my forehead.

"Your temperature's very high," he said. "The fever should break any time now."

The little cat was at the bottom of the bed, watching and purring. Dupont stroked its fur.

"I see you have little Sadie looking after you," he said. "The hospital's cats were Clara's idea. We got them at first just to keep down rodents and insects, but then we discovered that some of patients recovered faster with them around."

I assured him that Sadie was the best of company.

"Speaking of which, I'm here with a dinner invitation for you," said Dupont. "If, and only if, you feel a bit better tonight, Clara would like you to dine with her at six. Normally I'd be there too, but I'm afraid I'll be gone till at least tomorrow. A village a hundred miles east is reporting an outbreak of yellow fever. I'll go over and see what I can do. Clara will keep an eye on you till I get back."

from a short visit to London where he'd been called to advise the ministry on the political situation here in the desert. Apparently it was worsening, daily.

"We can sometimes hear artillery in the distance at night," said Clara. "It's frightening for us all. The patients and the staff have to be prepared for instant evacuation if the hospital comes under threat."

Now I understood what Dupont had been hinting at as we were approaching the hospital.

"We hope we won't actually have to leave," said Clara. "But we have to be realistic and acknowledge that an attack on the hospital isn't out of the question." She then gave me a brief history lesson.

Vicious intertribal wars had been going on in these regions for centuries. When the various colonial powers took over, they enforced an artificial peace amongst the tribes and put them together in equally artificial countries. The borders of the new countries were strictly for the foreigners' administrative convenience and often lumped together peoples of the jungle, the savannah, and the desert—traditional enemies who didn't share the same languages or world views. Naturally, when the colonial powers left, or were thrown out, the benefits of the peace and order they'd imposed were quickly replaced by instinctive, traditional animosities. Violence flared up over and over, usually aimed at not-quite-legitimate governments.

"Hence the artillery fire at night," said Clara. "We try to carry on as best we can, but who knows how it will all end?"

NOW, AS THOUGH to signal a change of subject, she took off her glasses. Her huge owl eyes were restored to normal size, green and lively.

"I hope you don't mind that Charles has told me all about you and your unhappy love affair," she said. "I must say—and he agrees with me—that it's to your credit how deeply you were affected. But you're young and have the whole world before you. Rest assured, in time, you'll find happiness."

Here we go again, I thought: Dupont's told her to give me some advice.

"The main thing is not to retreat, not to fear getting involved again in future," she said. "Some of us swear off any entanglements after we've been hurt. But that isn't a virtue. It's just a form of cowardice—a fear of being wounded again."

That comment hurt a little.

"Of course, in your case I don't mean right now," she said, to make me feel better. "You're still in your period of mourning. But you must never become a cynic about love. If you do, the very women who are worth loving will sense an emptiness in you and will stay away. They'll understand you can't take root in their hearts, nor they in yours."

She was enjoying very much having someone new to tell her theories to, I suspected. I wondered if advice to a novice like myself would culminate in some revelations about her own life and experiences in the matter of love.

I couldn't have been more right.

"As a matter of fact, I myself know exactly what you've been through," she said. "Yes, I married a man two decades ago, now. Just one week after our wedding in England, my new husband and I came to Africa. We were both twenty-one and quite a pair of innocents. I'd barely finished my nursing training and he was an adventurous, idealistic schoolteacher—that's why he wanted to work in a part of the world that was most in need."

I did my addition: twenty-one, twenty years ago would

make her now forty-one. Her skin was so wrinkled by the sun I'd thought she was much older. Yet in other ways she might still have been twenty-one: her green eyes were so youthful and lively and there was an energy about her that seemed somehow out of place in that worn face.

"My husband died unexpectedly just four years ago," she said. "Physically he wasn't a strong man, so the climate and various tropical diseases killed him though he was quite young. He was the first District Education Officer in the region of the Basio people, five hundred miles south of here. I was in charge of nursing at the local hospital. I was very much in love with him when we came here—I wouldn't have left England otherwise. But the man I loved turned out not to be the same as the man I married. I don't suppose that's too uncommon."

Clara sipped her tea and I waited to hear more.

"You see," she said, putting down her cup, "during that period of almost twenty years when he was on his various official education tours—they lasted for weeks, sometimes months—he'd been intimate with a variety of Basio women. I'd never have known if he hadn't confessed it to me just six months before he died. I'd have been in blissful ignorance and broken-hearted at his death."

She'd caught my interest now and wanted to make the situation quite clear.

"The way he behaved wasn't entirely his fault," she said. "It was one of those cultural things neither of us had been aware of when he took the position. In much of the Basio region there's no such concept as fidelity in marriage. Everything's communal. Property belongs to the people as a whole and all children are raised communally. Aside from those specific occasions when husband and wife get together for the purposes of propagation, sexual activities are communal too, based on what the Basio regard as the quite normal desire of a husband or wife for a variety of partners.

"The fact that my husband was a handsome man, as well as a stranger from another race and a guest in their territory, made him very much in demand. If he'd refused the advances of their women, not only would it have been a huge insult to the Basio culture, it would have made his work as Education Officer quite impossible. So he didn't refuse.

"When he eventually confessed to me, I understood his predicament on an intellectual level, and I didn't really blame him. He insisted he still loved me and had loved me all along— that his activities with the Basio women had nothing whatsoever to do with love. But inwardly I was very disappointed in him."

It was so silent in the room now that we could hear the cicadas in the flower beds outside. Clara sipped her tea, choosing her words carefully.

"The fact was, after he confessed, I just couldn't find it in myself to love him anymore," she said. "Still, we made a decision never to raise the subject of his extramarital activities again. During his final months—of course, we didn't know that's what they were—whenever he came back from one of his trips, we'd pretend nothing questionable had gone on while he was on the road."

I thought that must have been a very hard act to keep up.

"You're right," she said. "The time came when I couldn't bear it anymore and I'd made up my mind to leave him and go back to England. But before I could tell him my decision, news came that he'd died of a heart attack in one of the villages he was visiting. After his death, I wanted to get away from the Basio region as quickly as possible and applied for the position here."

I nodded sympathetically and she again sipped her tea.

"I was sure I'd had quite enough of men," she said. "Then Charles appeared. Funnily enough, he reminded me of my husband in some ways—certainly with his adventurous spirit. Probably these are always the kinds of men who're willing to come to such dangerous, out-of-the-way places. A woman can fall in love with them but she can't fully trust them, as I've learned from experience. I'm sure Charles isn't faithful either, but somehow that's not as important to me as it once was. Which tells me something about myself I hadn't quite understood before."

She could see I looked puzzled.

"You see, the main thing is I love him, and he loves me, too," she said. "He'd never lie to me about that. It's what counts most of all between a man and a woman." She nodded her head in satisfaction at the idea.

I was beginning to feel unwell again, but I wanted to ask her how she could be so sure her conclusion was valid. Before I could ask her anything, however, she returned to my own love problem.

"From what I gather," she said, "you fled from Scotland before you really had a chance to find out why that girl rejected you."

Again, I didn't like to hear someone else use the word "fled" to describe my action, no matter how accurate it might be. Also, I was feeling really unwell.

Clara hadn't noticed and kept talking.

"You don't really know what was going through the girl's mind," she said. "Maybe she had very sound reasons for what she did. But, of course, you're still at the stage in life when you think that if the world lets down a good person like you, you can never trust it again. When you get older, you'll see that's not the way it is."

My head was so befuddled by that stage, I wasn't really sure what she meant.

JUST THEN THERE was a knock at the door, followed by the entrance of the nurse who'd brought me to the dining room. She was carrying a newly born baby wrapped in a little shawl. She didn't say anything, but looked worried. Clara put her glasses on again, got up, and took the baby from her. She opened the top of the shawl and looked inside for a moment.

"How's the mother?" she said.

"She's not wide awake yet," the nurse said.

"Did she see it?"

"No, I kept it away from her."

"That's good," Clara said. She looked over at me.

"This is the kind of thing that can happen because of malnutrition, or genetics, or any number of causes," she said.

I was feeling really dreadful, but she wasn't to know that and brought the baby over. She opened the shawl a little more so that I could see clearly.

The baby, if it could be called a baby, had no head, only shoulders and a neck. From a plateau on top of the neck a little pink tongue protruded through a narrow opening, and two little brown eyes stared up at me alertly.

I was now sweating heavily and feeling so queasy I thought I was going to vomit.

"I have to go," I said, and quickly made my way back to my room.

I'D BEEN IN BED no more than five minutes when there was a brief knocking at the door and someone came in. I'd left the bedside light on and saw Clara through the mosquito net.

She came over to the bed and looked down at me.

"I'm sorry I showed you the baby," she said. "I didn't realize you were feeling so sick."

I wished she would just go away and let me sleep.

She reached under the net and put a cool hand on my brow.

"Your fever's ready to break," she said. She then picked up my scattered clothes from the floor and put them on the chair. "Never leave clothes or shoes on the floor," she said. "Scorpions and other creepy-crawlies can get into them during the night."

Through the veil of the mosquito net I saw she had begun to undress. She put each piece of clothing, then her shoes, on the chair on top of mine.

My heart was beating very fast, both from the fever and from the sight of her through the net. Her brown, wizened face didn't seem to belong to her body. Its startling white smoothness took my breath quite away.

She now put her glasses on the bedside cabinet, switched off the lamp, lifted the mosquito net, and slid in beside me. Very deliberately, she leaned into me and put her arms around me. The coolness of her against me was a wonderful sensation. In spite of my fever, I became aroused.

She moved my hand away gently.

"I'm here for medicinal purposes only—this is a local custom to help cool down a fever, and it's generally quite effective," she said, pressing her body once more against me. "Now try and sleep."

AND I MUST have slept deeply, for when I opened my eyes again it was morning. Clara and her clothes were gone. I was feeling much better and was very hungry, so I got myself ready and went along to the nurses' dining room for breakfast. On the way, I passed the nurse who'd brought in the little headless baby the night before.

I now wondered if the whole incident, together with Clara's visit to my bed, hadn't been figments of my delirious imagination. But I asked tentatively about the baby.

The nurse shook her head sadly.

"It was a little girl," she said. "She died during the night. It was the best thing for all concerned."

I couldn't help but agree with that.

Clara was leaving the dining room as I came in. The owl eyes blinked at the sight of me and she reached her hand out to mine.

"Don't worry," she said dryly. "I only want to take your pulse." She encircled my wrist with her fingers and after a few moments, nodded with satisfaction. "Near normal," she said.

I told her I was feeling much better.

"There you are then," she said. "Sometimes these traditional cures do seem to work."

DUPONT CAME BACK sometime during that day. He dropped by my room after doing his round of the wards.

"I'm glad your fever's down," he said. "I was afraid I'd have to take my own clothes off and lie down beside you for a while." He laughed at my embarrassment. "I hear from Clara you got a little overexcited last night. Maybe it's a sign you're recovering from your broken heart, too."

I couldn't think of anything to say.

"We all *wish* love would be eternal and exclusive," he said. "But it rarely seems to be the case. We lose one love, find another, and we're sure this time it'll last forever. And so on and so on. Lovers are supreme optimists at heart."

But I refused to feel optimistic. Though my fever had definitely receded, I was certain a cure for my broken heart was just as remote as before.

10

Some weeks went by and all signs of my fever were completely gone. To pass the time, I'd begun helping out the nurses around the hospital, changing beds, polishing floors, working in the little garden, and trying to be useful generally. Dupont and Clara were busy during the days, but we'd usually get together for dinner at night. We all got along well. Sometimes we talked about the Tollgate and Duncairn. I didn't even mind talking about Miriam, and they were careful to be respectful of my broken heart.

One morning as I was watering the garden, two military jeeps came hurtling into the compound, clouds of sand trailing behind them. They carried six soldiers and an officer. Dupont came out to see what was going on, and I heard the officer ask if he'd go with the patrol to a nearby place where a rebel group had recently attacked a platoon of government soldiers. Apparently Dupont often accompanied these patrols in case medical help was needed.

He came back into the hospital for his medical kit, saw me, and wondered if I'd keep him company.

"It's bound to be interesting," he said. "These rebels have a reputation for doing odd things with their victims."

That should have been enough to make me hesitate. But I was so full of pent-up energy now that my fever had disappeared I said I'd really like to go.

ROOM WAS MADE for me in the jeep beside Dupont and we sped away, generating our own sandstorm. After five or six miles, the jeeps slowed down for a moment. The officer, who was in the front passenger seat, pointed ahead.

A few hundred yards off to the north, thick black columns of smoke were rising from the ground.

Before I had a chance to say anything, Dupont shook his head.

"Not smoke," he said. "Flies."

Oh no, I thought.

WE GOT OUT of the jeeps at the edge of what looked like a volcanic crater, fifty yards or so wide. This was the area where the battle had occurred. Now that the jeeps' engines were switched off, the noise from the seething black pillars of flies was as loud as an express train hurtling past. The columns towered over heaps on the ground that weren't yet identifiable, though it was easy to guess. The soldiers threw rocks and the flies scattered, buzzing angrily. Then the soldiers, Dupont, and I scrambled down into the crater.

The withdrawal of the flies revealed an awful sight: not just dead body after dead body but each of the bodies eviscerated, their intestines draped around them like carnival decorations. A few had been dismembered and their various parts then grotesquely reassembled. Some had been given four legs, or four arms. In one case, a bloody head protruded from a split stomach, as though in an agonizing birth. Desert plants had been stuck in mouths and eyeholes.

The body parts weren't all human. A herd of goats had been cut up, too. Goats' heads and limbs had been put on human torsos. Human heads and limbs were attached to goats' bodies.

Some of these hybrids had been propped up with sticks so that from a distance they looked alive.

Dupont didn't have to spend too much time on his examination. The victims, twenty in all, were quite dead and the flies were aggressively reassembling around their banquet.

The officer ordered us all back into the jeeps. He feared the rebels might be hiding nearby watching our movements, ready to attack if we lingered. So we quickly drove away from that awful place.

After a mile or so, the jeeps paused on top of a hill and we looked back. We could see no movement, only the faint outline of the columns of flies again.

"Just as well no one lived," Dupont told me. "Sometimes we find survivors in such a state the only humane medical treatment is to shoot them." He looked at me. "That may sound like a violation of ethics, but in my view it would be a crime to keep them alive."

BACK AT THE hospital, we sat together over a cup of coffee.

"I used to wonder why they mutilated the bodies that way," said Dupont. "Then last year I had a chance to talk to one of the rebel leaders. He'd been shot in the stomach during an ambush and captured by government troops. They were taking him to the capital for a show trial and were afraid he'd die of his wound on the way. They stopped in at the hospital and asked me to give him a shot of morphine to keep him alive.

"That's when I asked him why his men treated the bodies of soldiers this way. His dialect was hard to follow, but I understood him to say that people of the region had been doing this to their enemies, and vice versa, since time immemorial. Yes, there was an element of pure terror in it, but it was more than that. The combining of parts of animals, humans, and plants was to show off the superior creativity of the rebels—that they could come up with forms even the gods hadn't thought of." Dupont hesitated. "That's if I understood him properly. He was in a great deal of pain and I didn't know the language well. Anyhow, I gave him the morphine and it kept him alive long enough to be taken to the capital, where they hanged him in the city square a few days later before a big crowd."

I was shocked at how cruelly human beings could behave. I said so to Dupont and he thought for a while.

"It's true we do inflict a lot of pain on each other," he said. "But it's nothing compared to the suffering in this world that we're not responsible for. As a physician, I've seen decent, kindly people in agony from cancers, snakebites, diseases, malarial fevers, and so on. Not to mention schizophrenia and a host of mental torments that make life unbearable for the sufferers and their families. Even children who haven't had time to do anything wrong aren't spared. What about that little baby born without a head? Who's to blame for that? Clara says you were a bit upset over it." He frowned. "If there is indeed a Creator, it's easy to understand why some people think He's either the torturer-in-chief or has a very sadistic sense of humour."

Those words reminded me of my father scoffing at the Theory of Intelligent Design, and of Miriam Galt describing the cruelty of nature. Dupont would have seen eye to eye with each of them on that matter.

EARLY ON THE morning after the massacre, Dupont knocked at the door of my room and came in, looking upset.

"All foreign nationals have been ordered out of the country immediately," he said. "The government can't guarantee our safety any longer."

Apparently this official decision had been brought on by a rash of rebel attacks not far from the hospital. It would have to be evacuated. Dupont and Clara, along with the rest of the staff, would be permitted to stay on for another week to wrap up affairs and ensure that all the patients were transported back to their villages. Dupont had tried to persuade the authorities to let me stay on, too, and help with the evacuation. They wouldn't hear of it since I wasn't a medical professional.

"So I've just radioed the coast and arranged a plane to come for you," he said. "It would be too dangerous for you in a truck, on your own. The plane should be here around noon and will take you directly to Racca. After that, I'm afraid you'll be left to your own devices. With any luck, you should be able to get on a ship to some place that's safe. I'm so sorry now for bringing you into this mess in the first place."

I came here of my own free will, I assured him. And the fact that I was healthy again was thanks to him. Anyway, he had enough problems without dragging me around. I was much more concerned about his own fate, and Clara's. Would they be all right?

"We'll be fine," he said. "This is just another of the hazards of working in these places."

I looked at little Sadie, the cat, lying as usual at the foot of my bed. I stroked her fur and she purred. Dupont read my mind.

"Don't worry, I'll be giving all the cats a shot of morphine just before we go," he said. "It's better than leaving them to starve. Or worse."

AROUND NOON, a four-seater plane appeared overhead and settled down on the landing strip. The pilot waited for me on board with the engine running. All morning I'd been helping

Dupont and Clara prepare for the general evacuation, and we hadn't had much of a chance to talk. They took a few minutes to come and see me off at the plane.

Dupont shook my hand and wished me well.

"I'm so sorry about this," he said. "I hope we'll run into each other again."

Clara gave me a peck on the cheek and looked at me with her huge eyes.

"Remember," she said. "You can't run away from love. It's the baggage we carry with us on all our travels."

Dupont laughed.

"Advice, right till the last minute," he said.

He helped me climb up onto the wing and I took my place in the little cabin behind the pilot, who shut the door. He began to rev the engine, making the plane shudder so much I feared it might fall to pieces. After just a few seconds, it leaped forward and raced along the strip for a hundred yards or so before soaring upwards abruptly. As it banked westwards towards the coast, I looked down. The hospital was already so far below that Dupont and Clara were only the tiniest dots.

I'd never been in a plane before, but after the terror subsided, I felt pure exhilaration at hurtling through the air. That sensation was quickly erased by the realization that I had just left behind the only people who cared about me on this huge continent, or anywhere else in the world, for that matter. I knew I'd never see them again and suddenly felt empty and lonelier than I had at any time since my parents died.

BARELY AN HOUR LATER, I was in Racca again. The pilot, a gaunt German national who'd barely spoken to me in the plane and whom I'd had difficulty hearing anyway because of the noise, hadn't much more to say when we landed. He directed me to an airport truck that took me to the Seamen's Union Hostel at the docks.

I stayed there for just two nights then found a berth as a deckhand on an outgoing freighter. Being hired was easier than I'd expected, thanks to my "previous experience" at sea, but even more because ships were recruiting crew quickly so that they could get clear of the region in case of general civil war.

"You were lucky," said the bosun of my new ship, the SS *Charybdis*, bound for South America. "We were about to sail short-handed, never mind maritime law."

That was how he greeted me after I'd climbed the rope ladder onto the ship's swaying deck. The ride out on a small boat through huge breakers with attendant sharks had seemed even more dangerous than when I'd first came ashore with Dupont.

"Yes, the Fates are on your side," said the bosun.

I was beginning to doubt that some great power was watching over every human move, including the last-minute appearance of a deckhand to satisfy official requirements. But Fates or no Fates, here I was on a sea-going vessel, the most junior member of the crew once more. I didn't at all mind when the bosun informed me that the ship wouldn't be sailing directly to South America but would be zigzagging along the way, taking on and depositing cargo at various remote spots in the Atlantic. The more zigzagging the better, as far as I was concerned: no one was desperately awaiting me and I wasn't desperate to arrive anywhere.

Much later that day, when the anchor of the *Charybdis* was securely nestled in its bed in the hawse pipe, I realized that ever since Dupont had awakened me that morning I'd barely given a thought to Miriam Galt, the cause of my broken heart.

PASSAGES

1

Early in this voyage I felt sick again, but it seemed to be only plain old seasickness and I got over it quickly. Even though my job kept me busy on deck most of the day painting, scraping rust, and swabbing salt from exposed surfaces, I spent a lot of my free time up there, too, enjoying the ocean's various moods. When strong winds and whitecaps meant a storm was coming, I was no longer overanxious—I now had more faith in ships and their ability to stay afloat.

Socially, too, things were better for me this voyage. The crew now regarded me as something more than a complete novice. After nightfall, I was often invited as a matter of course to join the other deckhands at poker in their quarters in the fo'c'sle.

Mainly, though, when I was off-duty I read constantly, for the SS *Charybdis* had its very own library under the rear deck. It consisted of two large cabins, whose well-filled bookcases were a feast to my eyes. Most of the books had suffered some degree of water damage but were still quite readable. A sticker on their inside covers indicated they'd been donated by the Mariners'

Guild for the purpose of providing seamen, over the course of a life at sea, with a basic education.

The top shelves contained a set of encyclopedias and dictionaries as well as a variety of general fiction and poetry. Some of these were "great books" I hadn't got round to at university, such as *War and Peace*, *Dead Souls*, *The Magic Mountain*, *The Anatomy of Melancholy*, *The Charterhouse of Parma*, *Religio Medici*, *Remembrance of Things Past*, *Samson Agonistes*, *Leviathan*, and *The Laws of Ecclesiastical Polity*.

The books in the middle shelves had no Mariners' Guild stickers and were the most water-damaged. Surprisingly, considering the crew of the ship consisted of masculine types of men, these books were mainly paperback novels of the popular romance genre. They had dramatic covers and such memorable titles as *Sweet Passion of the Prairies*, *Brides of Belladonna*, *The Gallant Gambler and the Lively Lass*, *A Man for the Kissing*, *The Star-Spangled Mistress*, *Her Temptress Tongue*, *Cherished Foe*, *Blue Moon Blonde Lady*, *Amazon Amy*, *Lovelorn My Love*, *Apache Woman*, *True Love and the Parson from Moose Jaw*, *Wife for Rent*, *The Neurosurgeon and the Nymph*, *Savage Embraces*, *Whisper Love in My Earnest Ear*, *Cupid's Tangled Heart*, *Island of Love's Flame*, *Lure That Lady*, and *Affaire Immemoriale*.

The bottom shelves contained a number of obscure books of fiction that looked as though they'd never been read. Early in the voyage I skimmed through the pages of some of them and must have stumbled on the worst—even their titles still haunt me: *Inspecting the Faults*, *The Paladine Hotel*, *The Wysterium*, *Last Blast of the Cornet*, and *A Dutch Life*. Each of them was as incoherent as dreams.

THE DAY I DISCOVERED the library, no one else seemed to be around, so I took my time looking over what was available. In the midst of my browsing, a woman's voice startled me: "Would you like to check anything out?"

The voice's source had been in the library's other cabin. She now came towards me and shook my hand. She was a short, elderly woman in a flowery dress, her hair short and grey, her face rather serious.

"I'm Mrs. Pradhan, the ship's librarian," she said. "So you've been having a good look round?"

THAT WAS MY FIRST of many meetings with the librarian of the *Charybdis*. She was a Londoner and the wife of the first mate, whom she'd met at the Mercantile Law Ministry in London when she was a research assistant there. He'd come to do some work on an impending inquiry and had asked for her help.

"Love at first sight," she told me.

After their marriage, she sailed with him on all his ships and voluntarily looked after their libraries, which were usually in a state of utter neglect. "My labours of love," she called her work.

IN MY SUBSEQUENT visits to the library, she grilled me about my life. She was a sympathetic listener and, of course, before long I'd told her my whole story. She was especially fascinated by what she called my "tragic love affair" with Miriam Galt and would ask me to repeat the details of it over and over.

"Talking about it will make you feel better," she'd say.

In my view, if just talking about a broken heart made the sufferer feel better, it obviously wasn't all that serious a blow in the first place. But I didn't tell Mrs. Pradhan that. To keep her happy, I did talk about those days in Duncairn as often as she wished.

"How sad," she'd say. "But how wonderful!"

By then I'd discovered that she was the one who'd acquired the collection of popular romances for the *Charybdis*, two years before. They were so noticeably water-damaged because they'd been on a ship that had run aground on a dangerous shoal off Plymouth. A major part of the cargo had been books headed for bookstores abroad. A salvage company had subsequently retrieved whatever it could and auctioned them off by the hundredweight.

"The boxes of love stories were the cheapest," said Mrs. Pradhan. "I thought they might be especially good for lonely men at sea and help preserve their idealism about love. Don't you agree?"

To be polite, I did agree. But as far as I could tell from listening to their tales about the various brothels they'd visited, my shipmates were anything but idealistic about love. Nor did I ever see any of them reading her romances, or much else for that matter—aside from the comic books and erotic magazines they'd brought aboard with them.

HER HUSBAND, First Mate Srinivas Pradhan, seemed about the same age as his wife. He was a small, dapper man from Calcutta, with silver hair slicked back. He was always impeccably dressed, unlike many of his fellow officers, who looked more at home in dungarees.

Because I'd become his wife's favourite client, I was invited on several occasions to either dinner or high tea with them in their cabin. Mrs. Pradhan herself would prepare the meals in the ship's galley, then bring them to the cabin where a formal table was set up with tablecloth, napkins, wine glasses, and silver cutlery.

The food was always extremely bland, out of regard for the first mate's stomach. He'd been diagnosed as having a stomach ulcer, which he attributed entirely to the stresses of his job. He often reminisced about the delightful spicy foods of his youth, but his stomach could no longer stand them. Now he was condemned to boiled rice, liver cooked in milk, and custard pudding. His wine glass was used only for water.

So I much preferred it when they asked me to high tea. Then the food was much more palatable, with jam sandwiches and apple tarts specially baked by Mrs. Pradhan.

At all these meals, she would wear her floral dress and the first mate would put on his best uniform. I'd change into a fresh shirt and make sure I shaved. In the stifling heat of the cabin, we'd talk about this and that in the most civilized way, as though we were in some vicarage in the southern counties of England and not sweating it out on a dirty freighter in the southern ocean.

AS I GOT TO KNOW the Pradhans better, I could see how impor-tant his ulcer was in both their lives.

"How does it feel, Srinivas, dear?" Mrs. Pradhan would ask her husband if he was noticeably quiet during dinner or high tea. He didn't need more encouragement than that to launch into a description of his ulcer's fluctuating moods in the course of a given day. We'd listen respectfully.

I foolishly mentioned that I sometimes had slight headaches that might be the aftermath of malaria, or whatever my original fever had been. Thereafter, when the first mate had finished talking about his ulcer, he'd inquire about my headaches. He may have thought he'd sound like less of a hypochondriac if I made a contribution. If so, I let him down, and my motives were quite self-centred: talking about those headaches sometimes brought them on, or made them worse.

All in all, the Pradhans seemed a happy enough couple. Though I wondered if it wasn't The Ulcer that held them together as much as love.

Love, true love. I often thought about that once-in-a-lifetime rarity I was sure I'd possessed, then lost. In the course of the voyage I actually did read dozens of those popular romances from Mrs. Pradhan's library—she recommended them as therapy for a broken heart. But the heroines in them were so unconvincing they only made me feel, even more deeply, the loss of the real thing—Miriam Galt.

2

After calling in at several small coastal islands to deposit and pick up cargo, the SS *Charybdis* headed out into the Atlantic, leaving the sultry air of Africa in her wake. Three days later, a high column of cloud began to appear on the distant horizon. Under the column, in time, we could make out a smudge, which became in due course the outline of a mountain. Finally, the *Charybdis* took us close enough to see the shores and forests of the island on which the mountain stood: Isla Perdida.

Of the islands we'd so far visited, this was the first one I could find an article about in one of the library's encyclopedias. Isla Perdida had an occasionally active volcano, four thousand feet high. The island had belonged over the centuries to Portugal, Spain, and France before becoming part of the British Empire. The main town had had a variety of non-English names but was now known as Stopover. It had served as a base for fishing fleets, a slaving station, a military outpost, and a penal colony.

The town's prison, in fact, had only lately been closed down. The present small population of the island reflected its history: African, Portuguese, Spanish, French, and British bloodlines were mingled, the descendants of prisoners had intermarried with the children of former wardens, and so on. Socially, life on Isla Perdida was apparently quite harmonious. Any havoc now was caused only by occasional eruptions of the volcano.

WE SAILED RIGHT UP to Stopover's dock, which lay at the narrow end of a deep fissure in the cliffs, safe from the Atlantic's storms, though this day was perfectly windless anyway. As the *Charybdis* nestled alongside the high seawall a team of local stevedores, burly men with close-cropped hair, tied the ship to huge bollards. Aside from these stevedores, none of the local population came out to greet the ship.

First Mate Pradhan was on an upper deck beside me, keeping an eye on the docking operation.

"We'll only be in port twenty-four hours," he said. "We're picking up some cargo dropped off here a few weeks ago for delivery to South America. The ship's engines will get some routine maintenance, too." He looked at me as though he'd just thought of something. "You should take the opportunity to see the island's medical officer about those headaches of yours."

I was reluctant, he persistent.

"Once we're tied up I wouldn't mind stretching my legs," he said. "You can come along with me and I'll show you where the Medical Office is. I visited it when we were here last year. Some of these out-of-the-way places have homegrown cures, so I thought I'd give it a try. Of course, I'd no luck—nothing seems to help this ulcer of mine." There was a touch of pride in the way he said that.

SO, SHORTLY AFTERWARDS, Pradhan and I walked into the town of Stopover itself, about a quarter mile from the dock. Along the way, we were assaulted by armies of mosquitoes and biting flies enjoying the windless conditions. We swatted at them in vain.

As for the town itself, it was an odd place. It was built in that narrow crack between the huge walls of black rock and seemed to consist of a single street of paintless and weather-beaten clapboard buildings, including a post office, a general store, and a bar. Several ancient-looking passenger cars and trucks were parked on the potholed road. As we walked along, we passed some of the townspeople. The men were all of that burly, short-haired type we'd seen tying up the ship. The women wore black headscarves and baggy dresses with flowery designs. Pradhan observed how, though we surely stood out as strangers, these islanders ignored us, just as they'd paid no attention to the ship's arrival.

"Now you know quite literally what 'insular' means," he said.

As we walked on, I noticed that the street didn't have any trees, only a few shrubs and little plots of grass, no bigger than graves, outside some of the clapboard houses.

"The volcanic rock's just below the surface, so trees can't take root," said Pradhan. "Most of the soil here is imported, and sometimes it's blown away by storms."

WE EVENTUALLY CAME to the only noteworthy building in town, a cube-shaped structure made of stone blocks and filling an entire corner at the upper west side of the street.

"Here we are," said Pradhan. "The building's all that's left of the old prison. See where the cell blocks were dismantled when it was closed down?" Heaps of rubble stretched over a wide area behind the building. No effort seemed to have been made to remove them.

The heavy wooden front door bore a brass plate:

> ## PRISON MEDICAL OFFICER
> ## DR. MACHLA CHAFAK

"Just give the door a rap," said Pradhan. "I'll get on with my walk and see you back at the ship."

After he left I knocked and a small elderly woman came to the door. She had eyes that were astute but small on either side of quite a large nose. I told her I'd like to see the medical officer.

"I *am* the medical officer," she said. "I'm Dr. Chafak."

Pradhan hadn't said anything to indicate the medical officer was female. I'd assumed from her appearance that this woman was the maid—she wore one of those baggy dresses like the other townswomen we'd seen. She didn't, however, wear a headscarf to cover her shoulder-length grey hair.

"Come in," she said.

I followed her into a large, well-illuminated room. A big window with bars on it looked out onto the ruins we'd seen at the back. The room had a desk, an examination table, various rubber tubes, a sink, and some medicine cabinets—the usual items in a doctor's consulting room. Usual, but for one thing: an elderly German shepherd lay on a rug in the corner. When I came in, it slowly got up, growling and baring its fangs.

"Pongo! Don't be silly!" Dr. Chafak said to the dog. "Am I not allowed visitors?" She spoke with an accent similar to that of some of the Eastern European sailors I'd met.

The dog reluctantly crouched back down on the rug and the doctor indicated a chair for me by the examination table.

She then put on a white labcoat from a hook on the wall, hung a stethoscope round her neck, and sat in the chair opposite. Now, looking much more the part, she asked me who I was and what was troubling me.

I explained that I was from Scotland, now a deckhand on the *Charybdis*, that I'd contracted some kind of fever either in or on the way to West Africa, and that although I was feeling much better now I still had occasional headaches.

She took my pulse and checked my back and chest with her stethoscope. She peered into my eyes with another device.

"You do show signs of having had malaria," she said. "In that case, your symptoms aren't unusual." She went to the biggest medicine cabinet, which had shelves of pills and liquids. Then she poured some yellow pills into a paper pillbox and gave them to me. "Take one of these each morning for the next week. That should help clear up the headaches. If they continue, see a doctor at your next port of call."

I took out my wallet to pay for the medicine.

"No charge," she said, and before I could thank her, she went on: "By the way, if you don't mind my saying so, you have a most interesting nose."

I didn't know how to respond to that. She'd been looking at my nose all through the examination. She'd even allowed her fingers to touch it gently for no apparent reason.

"The nose is an unjustly neglected area of medical research," she said. "I had the good fortune to study in Edinburgh under a famous physician—Dr. Cornelius MacVittie?" She was sure someone Scottish, like me, would know the name.

Of course, I'd never heard of him.

"He was renowned for his pioneering work in phrenology—that's the study of the shape and size of the cranium," she said.

"Dr. MacVittie believed that the human skull can reveal the psyche of its owner. A highly trained phrenologist, like a perceptive art critic, should be able to grasp precisely what the exterior characteristics convey about the inner person."

She paused a moment, smiling while I took that idea in.

"At the suggestion of Dr. MacVittie," she said, "I myself moved from the general study of anatomy into phrenology, and from there into a subspecialty: rhinology. That's the technical name for a specialization in the nose alone. Dr. MacVittie was convinced that through the use of various methods he'd developed, nose studies would inevitably come to replace psychology—which he regarded as a dangerously unscientific discipline."

As she talked, I couldn't help but notice again how conspicuous her own nose was. I wondered if it was possible for a rhinologist to do a self-analysis. But I was afraid I might laugh, so I didn't dare ask.

"Now, in the case of this nose of yours," she said, "I wonder if you'd allow me to schedule a few sessions to give it a careful examination?"

I told her that wouldn't be possible, for we sailed the next morning.

"That's a great pity," she said. "But if you like, perhaps I could make a few general observations right now—though you mustn't put too much stock in them. A nose is as individual as a fingerprint, and the nuances are everything. After a rigorous scientific analysis complete with follicle samples I might arrive at quite different conclusions over the course of a few meetings."

I thought this experience might be amusing, and I was in no rush to get back to the ship. So I told her I'd be most interested in her findings.

"Very well," she said. "Sit back and relax."

I did sit back, and Dr. Chafak began to run the tips of her first two fingers along the contours of my nose. Her nails were clean and rounded, her touch delicate. She spoke, almost to herself, as she worked. "Nostrils: medium wide, conducive to adequate inhalation. Bridge: a little on the large side in proportion to cheekbones and brow. Septum: notable deviation from rectilinearity. Skin: tending to desiccation."

At that point, she stood back for a moment, thinking. Then she took a pencil-thin flashlight from her labcoat pocket. She pushed my head gently back and shone the light up each nostril.

"Well, well," she said, in that same meditative way. "What a very pleasing interior architecture. Caverns: unusually capacious. Nostrils: narrow and absolutely symmetrical. Olfactory bulb: globose and delicate as could be wished. How paradoxical that the deviation of the septum has had no effect on the inner harmony." She put her flashlight back in her pocket, smiling admiringly at my nose. "All in all," she said, "a most instructive first inspection."

By now I really was curious about her findings.

"Now remember, I can't be definitive, but I'm willing to pass an informed opinion," she said. "*Physically*, you have nothing whatever to worry about concerning your nose. All the parts are in exceptionally good order and will continue to be of service throughout your life. If, as we believe, a healthy nose is an excellent predictor of longevity, you will certainly live to at least three score years and ten—accidents aside, of course."

I supposed that was good news. Dr. Chafak had more to say, however.

"But *psychologically*, what your nose tells me is another matter." She considered her words carefully. "The interior and the exterior are in surprising conflict with each other. You remember I noted that extreme aridity of the outer skin? Yet the inner surface is totally humid and lubricious. What this generally implies in an individual is extreme difficulty in reconciling conflicting elements of the psyche."

This sounded to me as vague as the horoscope section of a newspaper. But she was obviously serious, and what she said next caught my attention.

"Within the last year, you've apparently suffered a great emotional shock," she said in a gentle voice. "On the one hand, you've had to deal with the death of at least one of those you loved most. But your condition has been exacerbated by something else, almost certainly an affair of the heart."

On hearing this I was, to put it mildly, surprised. I'd told Dr. Chafak nothing whatever about the deaths of my parents, and certainly not about Miriam Galt.

"You see, the first thing I noticed," she went on, "was that the interior veins of the exumenta, which were already quite fragile, have slight ruptures in them. In my experience, it takes the double emotional trauma of a death and a tragic love affair to cause this kind of damage." She looked at me with great compassion. "I'd guess it's because of these things you've wandered so far from your native land."

She asked for no confirmation from me and I volunteered none.

"But there is very good news, too," she said. "Those inner vestibulants are already healing noticeably. In other words, you're gradually getting over your emotional hurt. Your mind may not be fully aware of that yet, but your nose is."

With those consoling words, the session was over. As Dr. Chafak was showing me to the door, Pongo the dog rose from his rug and hobbled along at her side.

"Pongo used to act as a guard dog when I had to treat violent inmates from the prison," she said. "Now he's just a pet." She fondled his ears.

Pongo then came to me, sniffed at the back of my hand, then licked it. I made some comment about the infallibility of a dog's nose.

"That's true," she said. "But who knows what a dog's thinking? When the prison was still in operation, he'd sometimes lick the hands of monsters."

I thanked her for seeing me and went outside. I walked fast all the way back to the *Charybdis* but not fast enough to outpace the stinging flies and mosquitoes.

FIRST MATE PRADHAN was at the top of the gangway, waiting for me.

"Well, what did you think of her?" he said. "I presume she insisted on analyzing your nose? Was it illuminating?"

I answered somewhat vaguely. Then he told me about his own experience with Dr. Chafak and about her analysis of his nose.

"She claimed my nose indicated that no medicine would do my ulcer any good if I didn't really want to be cured," he said. "Have you ever heard such nonsense?"

Of course, I nodded sympathetically.

AT TEN THE NEXT MORNING, the *Charybdis* sailed out of Isla Perdida. Aside from the stevedores who cast off our lines, the islanders paid no more attention to our departure than they had to our arrival. Having already resumed my major duty of swabbing the deck, my work took me alongside two big wooden crates that had been loaded at the island and were tied down on the foredeck. The canvas shroud on one of them flapped loosely, so I was able to see these words stencilled in large block letters:

SMITH'S
HYDRAULIC PUMPS & VENTILATOR SYSTEMS
CAMBERLOO
CANADA

Camberloo? Wasn't that the name of the university where Dupont had studied for his medical degree? How curious it was to see, stencilled on this wooden box on the deck of a rusty freighter in the middle of a southern ocean, the name of the Canadian town I'd first heard from Dupont's lips. What a small and strange world.

DURING THE FOLLOWING weeks, as the *Charybdis* made its slow and steady way towards La Guaira, the seaport of Caracas, I made my own way slowly and steadily towards a decision regarding my future: that when we reached port, I would retire from the life at sea. It had been enjoyable in some ways, but its rituals were too confining. By definition a sailor touches only the margins of the real world. I felt I was now ready for the hinterland.

Accordingly, I warned the bosun I'd be signing off at La Guaira. He was grateful for the courtesy. Crew members would often just quit without notice, giving him problems in finding replacements.

"It's a pity you're leaving," he said. "You've got the makings of a real sailor."

First Mate Pradhan and his wife were sorry to see me go, too, and I felt sad about that: they'd been very kind to me. Some of the first mate's sadness was no doubt on behalf of The Ulcer, which had been like a silent fourth guest at all our meals.

The night before we sailed into La Guaira, we shared a farewell dinner and talked about what I might do ashore.

"Your money won't last long, you know," said the first mate.

"So you should find some useful work quickly," said Mrs. Pradhan. "If you don't find something that keeps your mind occupied, you'll start moping. That's the problem with life at sea—it gives you too much time to think."

She was referring, of course, to my tragic love affair. I didn't dare tell her that now sometimes when I tried to remember Miriam's face, it almost completely evaded me.

"There's always a need for English-language tutors," said the first mate.

"Srinivas is right about that," said Mrs. Pradhan.

Why not? I thought. After all, I'd almost become a teacher once before, in another world, in what seemed another century. Maybe I'd give it a try.

3

And, indeed, after a few restless, lonely days in a cheap Caracas hotel room, I ventured out and managed to get myself hired on a three-year contract as an English tutor with InterMinas, a big mining conglomerate. My job was to travel to the sites of various mines and teach advanced English to Spanish-speaking mine managers and supervisors. They already knew fundamental English but needed to improve their skills to communicate better with their mainly gringo owners and the big investors who occasionally flew down from the north to inspect their fiefdoms.

Those hours of class preparation I'd done at Duncairn and never used now proved useful.

The mines themselves were often located in the most inhospitable areas of the southwest, where jungle ran into mountain. The scorching sun, drenching rains, and hostile insects together made life especially hard for the mine workers.

I became the most itinerant of teachers, travelling between assignments mainly on small planes, or diesel trucks, or occasionally on narrow-gauge railways that had been converted from use in sugar-cane fields to the task of transporting ore. But the most relaxing mode of travel for me was in dugout canoes. I'd just lie back and rest as I was paddled along muddy jungle rivers. Like my earlier journey on those roads in Africa, I imagined these primal forests sliding by on either side like bookcases in some endless library filled with lookalike books.

As for the types of mines: most were open-pit or strip mines because the minerals were near the surface and tunnelling wasn't required. Hundreds of miners would crawl around, day and night, picking at the red earth in the broiling heat like flies on a massive sore.

Some of the mines, however, were underground. The miners who worked in them were of that universal type I'd seen on their way to and from work in Duncairn. They were small, wiry men doing a dangerous job that made them a close-knit group. But to the owners, the men's safety seemed of little importance, so deaths and maimings were daily affairs.

No matter the type of mine, the administration offices and the supervisors' bungalow residences all had the same cinder-block walls and corrugated tin roofs. As a visiting tutor, I was usually allocated a room in one of these bungalows for the length of my visit.

In proximity to each mine, a shantytown of sorts would spring up, consisting mainly of long bamboo huts that were split into flimsy apartments for the married men and dormitories for those without wives. Hospitals and churches were really just adaptations of the same bamboo structures, as were the entertainment establishments: movie theatres, brothels, liquor stores, cockfighting rings, and mescaline dens.

I sampled some of the offerings now and then.

THAT FIRST CONTRACT passed slowly, and I soon began to wonder if I was the right kind of man for this work. I didn't mind the teaching, but I couldn't help being afraid I might die of some exotic illness, as so many did in this part of the world. If so, my body would probably be buried in a shallow grave in the jungle, where it would be disinterred and ripped apart by nightmare creatures. Soon the weeds would protrude from the gaps in my bare, gnawed ribcage.

The thought of such an end led me on jungle evenings, to the accompaniment of a billion chirruping insects, to write a journal for the first time in my life. In it, I recorded the true story of myself: my upbringing in the Tollgate, the violent deaths of my parents, my love for Miriam Galt and the breaking of my heart in Duncairn, my subsequent illness—or whatever it was—in Africa, my voyage of recovery on the *Charybdis*, then this present work as a tutor. If I were to die in obscurity, someone might stumble on the journal and know I once existed. The thought of that consoled me to such an extent that I might have resigned myself to my lot.

Then Gordon Smith appeared.

GORDON SMITH

1

I'd just spent several weeks at the La Mancha gold mine conducting conversation tutorials when he arrived, late one afternoon, in a company jeep used to bring passengers from the little airfield that had been slashed out of the jungle a few miles away. From the open-walled hut where I held my class, I saw the mine's general manager get out of the jeep, then this other man.

He looked about fifty, of middling height, with thin, grey hair swept back. There was something hawkish about his face, with bent nose, noticeable eyebrows, and eyes that took in everything as he walked past—including my little classroom and me, looking out at him. He had a neatness about him, not just because of his spotless tropical whites but in his entire bearing. In this part of the world where everything tended to be sweaty and sloppy and ready to revert at the first opportunity to chaos, he seemed utterly in control of himself.

One of the students in my class that day was the mine office clerk. He told me that the man passing by was the Canadian engineer, Gordon Smith. Smith had been visiting another mine in the region when InterMinas asked him to help with a problem that had arisen. He had a special knowledge of the conditions at La Mancha, for his firm had supplied its specially built pumps.

I remembered the big crate the *Charybdis* had picked up on Isla Perdida and the stencilled name on its side. Could this man be that Smith?

"That's right," said the student. "Señor Smith, of Smith's Pumps."

I'D ALREADY HEARD about the problem Smith was being consulted on. In fact it had been the talk of my students for a week now, and had to do with the location of the La Mancha mine. The mine workings were at the base of a low mountain, only a thousand feet high. The mountain seemed misplaced in a region of flat swamplands and thick jungle. It had even been designated a holy place by the traditional forest people. None of these original inhabitants were around anymore, though. They'd long ago been wiped out by tuberculosis, syphilis, and the usual cluster of imported diseases for which they'd no resistance, as well as by alcohol, which to them was just as deadly.

This mountain lay right on top of the La Mancha mine. Three crude tunnels had been burrowed a hundred feet deep into the earth beneath it. The first two tunnels were no longer in production—the vein of gold in them was exhausted. The third, most recent tunnel was still quite profitable. Then the problem arose.

An early sign that something wasn't right was the exodus of all the bats and cave iguanas that had taken up residence in the tunnel, as they always did at these jungle mines. The tunnel was a half-mile long when the animals disappeared. Then one day, shortly after the morning shift had begun blasting a new section, the miners themselves came rushing up out of the tunnel in a panic. They'd been attacked by "evil spirits," they said—the old forest people who'd once worshipped in this area must have laid a curse. The miners refused to go back down, despite threats of firings.

One of the foremen, a tough old Argentine named Juarez who'd been in the administration office at the time of the panic, volunteered to go down on his own. He wasn't at all superstitious and would show the men there was nothing to worry about. The miners stood watching at a distance as Juarez entered the mine. They didn't have to watch long. After a few minutes, they heard a scream and saw Juarez come stumbling back out of the tunnel entrance. His eyes were wild and he kept glancing back over his shoulder as though being pursued by something awful.

The general manager now had no option but to suspend all work. He got in touch with InterMinas headquarters and was told the Canadian engineer, Gordon Smith, would come to the mine and diagnose the problem.

THE NIGHT OF SMITH'S arrival, the general manager asked me to a special dinner with his visitor, who was staying in the guest room at the big bungalow. I was surprised at the invitation and delighted at the prospect of a good meal.

Around seven, I went over to the bungalow and met Gordon Smith formally. His eyes were shrewd and his handshake firm. As we sipped aperitifs and chatted before dinner, he said he'd spotted me in my classroom when he'd arrived and had asked the general manager who I was.

"I told him he should invite you over for dinner," he said. "I didn't want the entire evening to be nothing but business." From close up, his face was a mesh of tiny wrinkles—like one of those paintings that look solid from a distance. And his brilliant blue eyes had, perhaps, a certain weariness behind their gleam.

I thanked him for asking me to dinner and mentioned the curious coincidence of seeing his name on wooden crates a thousand miles away on an island in the middle of the Atlantic. I also told him I'd heard of the town of Camberloo, too, before seeing it on the crates, for I'd met a doctor who had trained at the university there. It was as though there must be some other law of gravity that brought certain people together, from halfway round the world, in a most unlikely way.

"I wouldn't go quite that far," he said with a little smile. "It's just that the world's not so immense as we sometimes think."

I mentioned Dupont's name in case he might know him. But he shook his head.

"I can't say I've heard of him," he said. "Though, who knows, I may have passed him often enough on the street."

He spoke in the calmest of voices and looked so neat I felt refreshed by his presence. In the jungle, I'd become accustomed to passionate outbursts and extravagant displays of emotion over even the most trivial of matters. Clearly, it would take a lot to ruffle Gordon Smith's composure.

We talked for a while about Scotland. He asked this and that about my life in Glasgow and told me that, like many early Canadians, his ancestors had been exiled from the Highlands several generations back. But although he'd travelled widely he'd never been to the land of his forebears.

I wasn't ready for his next question.

"Are Scots trustworthy?"

Some of them were bound to be, I said, meaning to be amusing.

He didn't smile but just watched me with those hawk eyes so that I began to feel less than comfortable. I was relieved when the general manager, who'd been in another room answering the telephone, came back in. He asked Smith if he'd any preliminary notions about this problem at La Mancha.

"Well, I've heard what some of the men have reported," said Smith. "I'll have to go down the mine myself and find out whether there's a scientific explanation for what happened."

The general manager looked surprised.

"Señor Smith, you're a scientist," he said. "Could there be an *un*scientific explanation?"

"I'm a scientist by training—that doesn't mean I'm a cynic," said Gordon Smith. "Anyway, after the discovery of quantum physics, scientists should perhaps be more open-minded." He looked at me. "I've seen so many weird things in my travels, I'm not superstitious about not being superstitious."

I had to think about that one—my father would have enjoyed the double negative.

THE DINNER OF pineapple chicken was excellent and the wine tasted good. The general manager had other business to attend to and excused himself right after the coconut cream dessert.

Gordon Smith and I stayed at the dinner table for a while longer, but he didn't drink much. I made up for that and, inspired by the wine, I needed no encouragement to talk. Before long I was telling him all about Duncairn and Miriam Galt and my broken heart. How I often dreamt about her, and when I woke to her absence, it was as if my heart had been broken again.

"These matters of the heart can be so complicated, especially when you're young," said Gordon Smith. "I hope in time you'll get over her."

We sat silent for a few moments, then again he said something unexpected.

"I've never been much of a dreamer myself," he said. "I used to think that was good. I was under the impression that when you dream, you see the world the way a madman sees it. So maybe it's better not to dream in case the dreams, or nightmares, or whatever they are, start to affect your waking life."

I'd never heard that before. I assured him that, speaking from personal experience, it was just nonsense.

"I'm sure you're right," he said. "In fact I read somewhere recently that dreams are a natural way of clearing out the mind's overflow. You know, like a kind of mental Smith's Pumps system. If you don't dream, the unpleasant things stuffed in there have no way of getting out."

I wondered what kinds of unpleasant things a man like him might have in his mind. But he didn't enlarge upon it and once more changed the subject.

"Do you enjoy tutoring?" he said.

I explained how I'd just drifted into the job, and, for that matter, lacked the skills to do anything else. But from what I'd seen, I didn't really like how the mining industry acted in some of these out-of-the-way places. They polluted the earth and the air, were located where they'd no right to be, and destroyed the native cultures while they were at it. Nor did I much like the fact that I was helping them conduct their unpleasant business in good English.

The hawk eyes were locked onto mine.

"Maybe you should try another line of work," Gordon Smith said.

I suggested that wouldn't make any real difference to me. After what I'd been through—I meant, of course, my broken heart—I doubted I'd ever find contentment in any job, anyway.

As I said this, my voice was fuzzy from the wine and I knew I sounded melodramatic.

He nodded his head in sympathy, but his eyes were still taking my measure.

2

We moved to a screened verandah and sipped brandy. Above, the moon was breathtaking in the midst of a billion stars. The buzz of insects and the piping of tree frogs were all at once silenced by the scream of some animal in pain. But in a few seconds, everything returned to normal.

Gordon Smith remarked that these tropical regions involved perils not just for animals, but for human beings too. He himself, for example, had been smitten by a variety of illnesses in the era before modern drugs and vaccines were available.

"Yes, I caught my share," he said. "Malaria, several times. Yellow fever, too—no one in that era knew it also came from mosquitoes. Believe me, it wasn't a pleasant experience. And no matter how careful you were in some parts of the world, you couldn't really avoid all the sand flies, black flies, fleas, ticks, and lice. Because of them I caught things I'd never heard of—a lot of Greek-sounding medical terms like onchocerciasis and leishmaniasis.

"Then of course there was cholera—if you had to drink unpurified water, you inevitably got it. And even if you didn't drink the water and only used it for washing yourself, the bug went through the skin and gave you schistosomiasis. Unless you completely stopped washing yourself, as some people did, which led to even worse problems, aside from just the smell. Like most travellers, I contracted hepatitis—it was as normal as sunburn and there were so many possible causes you'd have had to stay home to be safe." He sighed and sipped his brandy. "Just running off the names, it sounds as though I'm boasting, but believe me they took quite a toll. Thank goodness I at least managed to avoid bubonic plague—as you know, it's not so good. Or hemorrhagic fever, where your whole body starts to bleed—if I'd run into that, I wouldn't be talking to you today."

After listening to this catalogue, I knew I should be grateful for only having had to deal with malaria, or whatever it was, in my own brief travels. I told Gordon Smith I'd be much more careful in future.

"Very wise," he said. "Things are a lot safer now if you're careful with the water and keep up with your vaccinations. In the old days, it was much riskier. I used to be strong as an ox, but I've paid the price."

HE NOW BEGAN talking about his home and the home of Smith's Pumps—Camberloo, in Southern Ontario, more or less in the middle of Canada. He lived there with his only child, a daughter, his wife having died many years ago.

"It's a town with no remarkable landmarks, or works of architecture, or any of that sort of thing," he said.

I'd already heard about Camberloo from Dupont: he too had thought it quite a bland place.

Gordon Smith considered that.

"Yes, I suppose Camberloo looks about as bland as a place can be," he said. "Bland *on the surface*, that is." He gestured out beyond the verandah. "Here, in the tropics, everything's exotic and hits you over the head like a hammer, demanding to be noticed. In Camberloo, things are more subtle. The town has its quotient of drama, too, but you have to be astute and patient to spot it." The night insects were so noisy that his voice barely rose above them. "These tropical countries have an immediate appeal to some area of the mind that's adolescent and unformed. Whereas a place like Camberloo—it's for adult, mature tastes. I have to admit, I'm still not sure which I prefer."

After another drink he said he needed to get some sleep, for he had a busy day ahead. I took the hint. Before I went out the door, he invited me to join him for breakfast at seven in the morning. I thanked him and staggered across the compound to my own sleeping quarters.

THE SCREECHING of parrots and a host of noisy morning birds woke me not long after sun-up. I could have slept much longer despite the noise, but I remembered my breakfast appoint-ment, got up, showered, and went over to the big bungalow. The general manager had already eaten and gone to his office. Gordon Smith had waited for me. We didn't talk much as we munched orange slices and banana along with corn bread. I drank four or five cups of coffee.

"Feeling a bit better now?" he said.

I assured him I did.

"I'm just about to head for the mine and see if I can pin down whatever has been causing the problem," he said. "I'll have to use a machine for measuring air quality. I'd like to check in case there's some kind of gas down there."

The hawk eyes were on me and I could guess what was coming.

"I was wondering," he said. "If you're feeling up to it, would you mind helping me carry some things down into the mine? I

can't really trust any of the locals in their present state of mind—
even if I could persuade one of them to come with me, which I
very much doubt. Besides, I wouldn't mind having someone else
along to act as a witness, or a second pair of eyes."

I hesitated. I didn't feel at all brave.

"Maybe you're a bit under the weather?" said Gordon Smith,
watching me. "I'd quite understand if you don't want to."

I told him I just needed one more coffee. To my satisfaction,
my hand was quite steady as I poured.

3

We wore coveralls and miners' hats, Gordon Smith and I, as
we went into the La Mancha mine. He had a small backpack
that ticked loudly and a shoulder bag for rock samples, and was
carrying a trowel. I brought a pickaxe and a long-handled shovel.

I was hoping there might be a few spectators at the mine
entrance to witness my bravery. But since the incident, the
workers had thought it best to stay well away from the mine,
and this day was no different.

As we entered the gloom of the tunnel the sultry morning
sun was cut off. By the time we'd advanced about thirty paces, a
sharp bend almost eliminated any remnants of natural light, so
the occasional electric bulbs strung overhead now became our
main illumination. The silence was broken only by the crunch
of our boots on the gravelly floor and the metallic ticking from
Gordon Smith's backpack.

Soon we could no longer walk side by side, for the tunnel
began to narrow, with many sharp rocks protruding. Gordon
was in the lead and had become more cautious, pausing every

few moments and peering ahead. I walked a couple of paces behind.

This single-file advance went on for about a hundred yards into the mountain. The tunnel widened again and we could see the rock face where the work had stopped. A dozen wheelbarrows, some of them full of gravel and ore, had been left by the fleeing miners. In the light of the bulbs, veins of gold gleamed in the half-excavated wall. Power drills and discarded shovels lay around.

Gordon Smith stopped beside one of the wheelbarrows. He bent over it and began to trowel up some of the smaller pieces of ore into his shoulder bag. All at once, he stiffened and then straightened up, head cocked, as though to listen to something.

The little hairs on my neck tingled.

He was about ten feet away and had begun to make a peculiar, growling sort of noise. He turned very slowly towards me.

The face that looked at me was no longer Gordon Smith's but rather seemed like parts of a number of faces superimposed on one another, with noses, mouths, and ears all misplaced and distorted. A huge pair of eyes dominated in the midst of that awful face, bulging and cold like a predator's.

I knew this transformation was illogical and impossible, but my heart was pounding nonetheless. I tried to say something when the thing that had replaced Gordon Smith started to shuffle towards me with its claws reaching out.

That was enough for me. I threw my shovel and pickaxe at it then turned and ran as fast as I could. The thing scuttled along behind me, its breath rasping horribly. When I reached the narrower part of the tunnel, I had to slow up because of the protruding rocks. I was terrified it might catch up to me, but it too was having trouble avoiding the rocks. At last, glimmerings of daylight appeared ahead. I raced round the final corner of the tunnel and out into the open air.

The thing was right on my heels. I could run no more, so I turned with my fists raised, ready to defend myself to the death.

The monster slouched over in front of me, gasping, was Gordon Smith. He was the only living creature around, aside from myself, and he was trying to smile.

BACK AT THE big bungalow, I drank some coffee and gradually got my nerve back. The general manager, like me, was wondering what exactly had happened. Gordon looked at me.

"I was taking a sample of some of the ore and I turned to ask you for the shovel," he said. "To put it mildly, you didn't look at all like yourself. In fact your face was so ugly, it frightened the wits out of me. You threw your tools at me as though you wanted to kill me, then you turned and ran. So I just grabbed my sample bag and ran out after you. See, this is where you hit me with your shovel."

He slowly unbuttoned his shirt and we could see, on the left side of his chest, a red and purple welt. He flexed his left shoulder gently and winced. "This is real enough, anyway," he said.

I was shocked that I'd done this to him. I told him he'd seemed to me to be transformed into something awful and I'd only been defending myself.

Gordon addressed himself now to the general manager.

"Clearly we both experienced some kind of hallucination," he said. He took out the ticking instrument that had been in his backpack. The arrow on one of the dials pointed at a red zone. "You see, it's registering a high quantity of some kind of gas other than methane or carbon monoxide or any of the usual things you find in mines. My guess is it's from some vegetable component in the rock. The miners may have released it into the air when they were boring deeper inside the mountain. If so, it'll be in the rock samples I brought out.

"If I'm right, there's no miracle involved. Though whether you'll be able to convince your miners of that is another problem."

"*Claro,*" the general manager said.

Throughout, Gordon Smith had seemed more amused than anything else about what had happened. I really had thought he'd somehow been turned into a monster.

"For a moment, I thought the same about you, too," he said. "But I knew that couldn't be. One of the advantages of being a scientist is that we're loath to consider the *impossible* as the cause of anything."

As for me, I should have been reassured by his rational explanation of the event, sitting there in the orderly calm of the bungalow, with a cup of coffee in my hand and the sound of birds through the screens. But I wasn't quite at ease. The entire incident reminded me of too many weird things I'd come across—in the Tollgate, in Duncairn, and in Africa—that never seemed quite resolved by common sense.

LATER THAT DAY when the rocks were analyzed in the mine laboratory, Gordon found traces in them, in various concentrations, of a hallucinogen.

"It has the same makeup as various peyote mushrooms," he told me and the manager. "Perhaps they were petrified in some ancient upheaval of the earth in this region. The original inhabitants may have stumbled on this place, had their visions, and decided the mountain was holy."

Now he got down to business. He recommended that the

manager advise the owners to invest in a ventilator system. Smith's Pumps would, of course, be happy to custom-build one for them. In the meantime, the wearing of oxygen masks by the miners would be adequate protection.

Even as he talked about business matters, I could still catch glimpses in his face of that monstrous image I'd seen in the cave. And from his sideways glances, I knew he could still see aspects of it in me.

We even joked about it.

But I wondered if perhaps we'd each seen a truth about the other, the kind of truth no one would want to believe about himself. And, having seen it, would two people ever be able to look at each other in the same old, relatively innocent way?

At any rate, the next morning, he took a jeep to the little airfield. From there he'd fly to the capital, and then on, back to Canada. The last thing he said to me was that he hoped we'd meet again.

GORDON SMITH'S scientific analysis made no difference to the fate of the mine. In the weeks that followed his departure, the unscientific view of the incident spread and intensified. It was believed that any miner who went down into the La Mancha mine, and any gold extracted from it, would be accursed. The owners went so far as to hire a local shaman to come and perform some ceremonies to placate or exorcise the spirits. But that did nothing to reassure the miners. So eventually it was decided that the entrances to all three tunnels should be dynamited over and the workers deployed to other mines.

Almost overnight, the shantytown that had grown up around La Mancha was depopulated. The townspeople were now convinced that after the shaman's intervention some of the mountain spirits might flee the mine and, instead, take up residence in the town.

One way or another, "ghost town" soon became an apt description of that collection of shacks.

MY TUTORING TOOK ME to other mines. But those few moments of terror down the La Mancha tunnel had a lasting, if not permanent, effect on me. Certainly, from that point in my life I felt I became less naive about people, less reliant on first impressions.

Which, surely, was a good thing.

4

InterMinas had sent me to tutor a group of administrators at the Segura strip mine, which was located in a low-lying region of thick jungle. I'd been warned that the climate there was very humid and especially hard on gringos. After a few weeks, just when I was congratulating myself on my strong constitution, I suddenly came down with a high fever and upset stomach. Within a day or two, I'd developed severe pains in all my muscles and a severe rash.

InterMinas arranged for me to be transported by jeep to a regional hospital. It had been established by the company exclusively for its workers.

"HOSPITAL" WAS A grandiose name for what was a large bamboo hut in a jungle clearing. It had a tin roof, fly screens instead of glass windows, and mosquito nets over each of the twenty beds. In spite of the window screens, the place was abuzz with flying insects that didn't seem to grasp the difference between indoors and outdoors.

The only sort of cooling in this hospital consisted of three ceiling fans. These depended on an electrical supply that seemed to fizzle out regularly during the stickiest part of each day.

Three nurses took turns looking after the patients day and night, and a physician did a morning round. He diagnosed my problem as a case of dengue fever, a quite painful form of malaria inflicted by a species of daytime mosquitoes. He assured me that although the illness was painful—it was known as "break-bone fever"—it wasn't likely to recur.

I was relieved to learn I had a mere case of dengue, which I'd heard about before. I'd been worried it might be the dreaded Guinea Worms. These worms got into the intestines from drinking untreated water. They were as thin as wire and grew to several feet long, popping their heads out through the belly of the sufferer from time to time. At other mines, I'd seen afflicted miners wind the worms out of themselves on twigs.

Only five other patients were in the hospital, all noticeably bandaged from such work injuries as fractured skulls, legs, and arms. You'd never have suspected any of these patients were in pain. Like all the miners I'd met, no matter how awful their condition, suffering in silence was the only acceptable behaviour. I did my best to muffle my own groans.

IN ABOUT A WEEK, I was starting to feel much better. One afternoon I'd had a good lunch of small meat-filled burritos, with mangoes and other fruit for dessert. I must have nodded off.

I dreamt one of those strange dreams in which I was aware I was dreaming. I was standing at the entrance of a tenement in a crowd of people, their faces as detailed and memorable as those of any strangers you see in any real street in the waking world. A man came through the entrance and looked out over the crowd.

It was Gordon Smith. He eventually saw me, raised his right arm, and pointed towards me. His eyes were bulging and cold, the way they'd been that day in the La Mancha mine. I knew that was impossible, that there was a scientific explanation, and that this must therefore be a dream.

Nevertheless, to be on the safe side I tried to run away. I couldn't move my limbs so I attempted to say something, and the sound of my own voice awakened me.

There, by my bed, looking down at me in a friendly and concerned way, stood Gordon Smith himself. I blinked to be sure I wasn't dreaming still.

"I'm sorry I startled you," said Gordon Smith. "May I sit down?" He pulled a cane chair towards the bed and sat. "I happened to be down in this region checking the pumping system over at the Segura mine and one of the managers mentioned that the young Scottish tutor had been brought here sick. I realized it was you he was talking about, so I borrowed a driver and a jeep and came over to pay a visit. Unfortunately, I only have fifteen minutes then I have to get to the airport—I'm flying out tonight. How're you feeling?"

I didn't mention just seeing him in my dream and told him instead about the dengue.

"I know it well," he said. "It's not the most pleasant thing."

A nurse appeared with two cups of coffee for us. I almost thought I was dreaming again, that was so unusual. Clearly we were being given special treatment.

As we sipped, Gordon Smith asked about my work and we talked about the various mines where I'd been tutoring since I last saw him, nearly six months before. We chatted for a while about some of the managers he knew. He kept checking his watch and eventually gave me one of his keenest hawk stares.

"I don't have much time so I'll get to the point," he said. "When you're fit to travel why don't you come to Canada and stay a while at my place in Camberloo? The change will help you recuperate properly."

I was so surprised I didn't know what to say.

"Look," he said. "This isn't a spur-of-the-moment idea. I've been thinking about it since we met at La Mancha—and my motives aren't entirely benevolent. The fact is, I'm getting a bit too old myself for all this travelling, and I badly need a reliable assistant. I've had my eye out for someone suitable for quite a while, and I have a notion you might be just the man for the job. You'd still see lots of the world if that's what you want—and you'd have a good income and a home base to come back to."

He could see how stunned I was.

"If you do come and visit Camberloo, you can find out for yourself what's involved at the business end of Smith's Pumps," he said. "I'm quite aware that you're not a scientist or an engineer, and that you're not really familiar with pumps or air-exchange systems. But your job wouldn't be building the machinery. That's already taken care of. All you'd need to learn is how to persuade potential clients to consider our products. And I can teach you how to do that." He checked his watch again. "I know it's a lot to take in, but give it some thought. Whatever you decide in the end, it'll be a few months' holiday for you."

What could I do but accept his generous offer? The idea of a holiday, with no strings attached, was very appealing—and I'd certainly think over what he'd said about working with him at Smith's Pumps.

He seemed pleased enough at that, for he shook my hand warmly. Then he reached into an inside pocket of his jacket and handed me an envelope bulging with banknotes. "This'll cover your expenses."

I protested that I could pay my own way.

"Not at all," he said. "This is a business matter. As soon as I get home, my travel agent will arrange an open first-class ticket in your name on any ship of your choice from Panama to Quebec City. A sea voyage'll give you another few weeks to relax in the fresh air—and this time you won't be a deckhand. From Quebec, you can catch a train to Camberloo. I'll look forward to seeing you there in the not-too-distant future."

We shook hands again and he rushed off to his jeep. No sooner had he gone than the hospital doctor, in the best of spirits, came to see me. Apparently Señor Smith had slipped him a few thousand pesos in return for taking especially good care of me till I was ready to leave.

He did take good care of me. Two weeks later, I was fit to travel.

ALICIA

1

During the three-week voyage from Panama to Quebec City on a recently built cargo ship, the SS *Gardeyloo*, I avoided my fellow passengers as much as possible. It was easily done, for there were only a dozen or so and they didn't seem all that interested in socializing with a walking skeleton. I read and ate and drank in the privacy of my cabin, which was as big as the combined living quarters of the *Charybdis's* entire group of deckhands.

Some remnants of my bout of dengue fever persisted in the form of occasional dizziness and a fear of the mosquitoes that made half the voyage with us. But I'd started to put on a little weight again, despite how emaciated I might have looked to others. I was feeling alert by the time the ship was sailing up the Gulf of St. Lawrence. That sensation of slowly entering the gullet of a great beast, which must have affected centuries of immigrants, moved me too.

In the end, the *Gardeyloo* moored at the docks in Quebec City. Passengers and cargo alike were deposited at the harbourfront on a hot and windy July day. From there, I went to the railway station and caught the train for the ten-hour journey westwards.

THE LAST HUNDRED miles of the approach to Camberloo were through a landscape with no lakes and no mountain ranges, in fact scarcely a hill of note. The near-empty train rolled past enclosed fields, some with stone farmhouses that might have been imported from the pastoral Lowlands of Scotland, and neat little towns with glimpses of quiet streets and church steeples. There were occasional patches of forest, some of the trees quite ancient-looking—relics, perhaps, of the original great forests that had once covered the land.

At last, the train slowly crossed an iron bridge over a placid-looking stream—the Grand River, according to a flaking sign on the bridge—and came into the outskirts of Camberloo, which seemed to be a larger version of the other towns we'd passed. A mile or so of further reluctant slowing down and the train squealed to a halt at Camberloo station.

The time was three o'clock.

I WAS THE ONLY passenger to climb down onto the sunny, deserted platform. The overwhelming heat surprised me—I'd expected the summer weather here to be nothing to me, after being so long in the tropics. Perhaps I'd become too used to the air-conditioned climate of the train, so this dry, stifling heat made me feel a little dizzy. I'd trouble sucking in oxygen and my knitted sweater bought especially for Canada's arctic chills prickled my flesh.

Behind me the train slowly began to move away from the station. In the background of all its roaring and hissing and thumping, a mad voice was howling. But there wasn't another person around. When the train had passed, I realized the howling was actually the noise of another, higher-pitched machine. It came from just across the tracks where an old factory with hundreds of sooty windowpanes vomited yellow smoke into the blue sky.

As I stood in the awful heat, I couldn't help wondering why I'd ever agreed to come to such an unprepossessing place. Yet here I was and it was too late for second thoughts.

Nor was there any point in just standing there broiling in the sun, for no one would be coming to meet me. Gordon Smith had telegraphed the *Gardeyloo* the day before it arrived at Quebec City to say a room was reserved for me at a place called the Walner Hotel. Whenever I arrived, I was to make my own way there and he'd be in touch with me. So I picked up my canvas holdall and went into the station waiting room.

Immediately I felt much better. This waiting room wasn't air-conditioned, but after the heat and glare of the platform it was quite refreshing. There was no one around except for a ticket clerk who looked up from his wicket when I came in. He was a middle-aged man with lank, sparse hair, carefully draped over his skull in a way that drew attention to his near-baldness.

I asked him how to get to the Walner Hotel.

"It's about a ten-minute walk," he said, looking me over doubtfully. "It's a fairly expensive place, you know."

With my unsuitable wool sweater and canvas bag I must have seemed an unlikely guest for the hotel in question. I told him that a room had been reserved for me there.

His eyebrows rose.

"Ah," he said. "Well, it's just along King Street. I can call you a taxi if you like."

I felt a walk might be good for me after sitting so long in the train. So I asked him for directions to the hotel, went outside again, and with my bag in hand—it had nothing in it but a change of clothes, some paperbacks, and the jungle-stained notebook that was to be my epitaph before Gordon Smith came on the scene—I began to walk.

To get to King Street, I followed a side street the clerk had told me to take. It was lined with trees and big houses built in what I took to be the Gothic style, many of them with fake turrets and cupolas. They were so alike they might all have been designed by the same architect. But the old oaks and maples, which in some places formed a leafy archway over the street, grew according to their own rather individual plans. These trees, like many of those I'd seen from the train, must have already been huge long before Camberloo came into existence.

Eventually I got to King Street, which was treeless. The architecture here was of a different type, too—though, again, there was a sameness about it. Red-brick buildings of a commercial sort dominated. Some were big and square, some were small and square, but otherwise they were mainly distinguished from one another by such overhead signs as *Grimm's Tailor*, *The Hardware Company*, and *The Pig's Eye Pub*.

The buildings all seemed to be of much the same age—as though on a given day eighty years ago, perhaps, King Street in its entirety had been plopped down here. If any of the buildings were more recent, it was hard to tell, they'd been made to fit in so unobtrusively.

No sooner was I on King Street than I began encountering flies. These Camberloo flies were big and unpredictable, so it was hard to avoid bumping into them. After these collisions, they'd just buzz a little louder and continue on their way. In that sense, they were unlike those persistent little jungle flies I'd learned to hate—flies that howled and never missed an opportunity to bite or sting.

On this first walk along King Street I didn't see a great number of pedestrians. Most of those I did pass were ordinary-looking and forgettable and avoided eye contact.

Except for one couple. The man's face shone red in the sun and he clutched a walking cane with which he jabbed at the sidewalk viciously. She, a little woman with a black headscarf and thick glasses, staggered along some feet behind him. As they came closer I saw, quite clearly, that they were connected by a studded leather leash roped round both their waists. I couldn't tell if he was pulling her along by it, or she was trying to hold him in check.

Naturally, I gave them lots of room to pass.

The only children I saw on that walk weren't pedestrians. They were two boys of maybe ten years of age playing in an alleyway between buildings, kicking a ball made of some scraps of black cloth bound loosely together. As I passed by, one of the boys kicked the ball towards me in what looked like a friendly gesture. I made to kick it back then saw it was actually a dead crow, trussed up with string. I shrank from it, causing the boys to laugh in a most unpleasant way.

I NOW ARRIVED at the junction of King Street and Princess where, just as the railway clerk had promised, stood the Walner Hotel. The structure was certainly the tallest and most imposing on the entire street, jutting out prominently into the junction like the prow of a ship built of red brick that had somehow become beached in this landlocked place.

I pushed open the brass-bound swing doors and stepped

into the hotel lobby. Away from the brilliant sun, all colours became muted. The lobby was long with a floor of green tiles. Couches and reading tables with the usual scattering of newspapers and magazines took up much of the space. I could see a large mural on the wall alongside the reception desk. It looked like a nineteenth-century country scene: men in black hats and trousers with suspenders seemed to be at work bringing in the hay, or doing other agricultural tasks, with horses and wooden wagons in the background.

How charming, I thought: probably a depiction of pioneer days, part of Camberloo's history.

But as I walked towards the desk, a startling feature of the painting caught my eye. In a remote corner of the field where the work was going on stood the figure of a naked man with upraised arms. His entire body was impaled on a stake that exited from his mouth. I could hardly believe that such a horrific scene would be displayed in a hotel lobby.

Of course, when I looked at the painting more closely, I saw that what I'd taken for an impaled man was only an upended red wheelbarrow leaning against a post, its handles reaching in the air.

THE RECEPTION DESK itself was a long, polished mahogany counter backed by a framed mirror and the usual pigeonholes for keys and mail. No one was there, so after a moment I palmed the "Ring for Service" bell.

Immediately, from a room to one side of the mailboxes, a small man in uniform with swept-back grey hair emerged. He was quite handsome, except that where his nose should have been he wore a black leather cone tied behind his head with a lace. That made quite an impression on me, but I tried not to stare at the cone and concentrated on his eyes as I told him who I was.

"We've been expecting you," he said. He had a pleasant smile and a lilting, nasal voice. Everything about him was pleasant except for that sinister cone. "Mr. Smith has reserved a room for you on the second floor. He's left a message."

He took a folded paper from one of the boxes and gave it to me. It was a brief note from Gordon, welcoming me and saying that a car would pick me up at six.

The little man now handed me my room key.

"The elevator's in the hallway by the door, just past the mural," he said. He smiled. "What do you think of our mural? It usually makes a big impression on visitors."

I glanced towards it and made some flattering comment, happy not to have to avoid looking at his cone. I picked up my bag and began walking towards the hallway.

"The elevator's around the corner to your right," he called cheerily after me.

When I automatically looked back to thank him, I saw the man with his cone and then my own image, distantly reflected in the mirror behind him. I quickly found the elevator and pressed the solid brass number two.

MY ROOM IN THE Walner Hotel turned out to be cool and luxurious, with a big bed and heavy, expensive furniture. The bathroom had a dozen towels as well as soaps and shampoos. I lay down on top of the bed, enjoying the silence after the constant noise of travelling, and soon dozed off.

2

The he bedside phone woke me: the voice of the little man with the nose cone informed me that the time was six o'clock and a car had arrived for me. I quickly pulled myself together and went down to the front door where a black limo with darkened windows waited. A chauffeur in a cap with a shiny visor showed me into the back seat. We drove west for a few miles into an area that gave glimpses of old trees and the manicured grass of a golf course. The houses were of a modern design and looked even bigger than those in the town. At one of these mansions the limo pulled into a long driveway and stopped beside a white-pillared portico.

I was halfway up the set of marble steps when the double doors were opened by Gordon Smith himself. He wore a dark formal suit rather than the tropical whites I associated with him. His hawk eyes that had seemed quite at home in the jungles of the south didn't quite fit this civilized setting.

"Harry!" he said. "Good to see you." His handshake was firm and cool.

He led me into a large white-painted hallway with a high skylight and open doors through which I could see spacious rooms. On the right was a wide stairway to the upper floor. Several discreet-looking paintings that might have been landscapes done in some abstract, geometrical style adorned the walls.

"This way," said Gordon Smith.

We went through one of the doors into a room with full-length windows looking out onto a neat lawn with trees and shrubs of the unobtrusive sort. The main furnishings of the room consisted of leather armchairs and white rugs. The paintings on the walls were watercolours of palm-clad tropical islands. Both the vegetation and the ocean were muted and tamed.

From a cabinet Gordon poured us both a glass of wine and we sat opposite each other on the leather armchairs. He inquired about my health and I assured him that I felt fine and was almost completely recovered from my sickness. I thanked him for his kindness in arranging the voyage for me.

"I'm glad you enjoyed it," he said. "I've always found travel by sea to be a great way of relaxing."

I understood what he meant. Being a passenger was very different from voyaging as a crew member, swabbing the decks, polishing brasses, doing anything that needed done, in no matter what weather.

"And the train from Quebec City?" Gordon said. "Was it comfortable?"

I told him how much I'd enjoyed the cleanliness and the spacious compartments. It had been worlds away from those little jungle trains crowded with people carrying babies or chickens or even pigs for the market, with the claustrophobic jungle on either side of the tracks and the glassless windows that allowed in insects as well as engine smoke.

Gordon Smith knew those experiences well, and smiled his agreement.

"And now, what about Camberloo?" he said. "What's your first impression?"

I was honest in my answer. I mentioned the two people on the street who seemed to be leashed together and the boys playing with the dead bird. Then that I'd misperceived the wheelbarrow in the hotel mural, which had made me wonder if perhaps the lingering effects of my fever had distorted my grasp of things. I couldn't even be sure now if the little man with the nose cone actually existed.

"Oh, he exists all right," Gordon said. "The rumour is he lost his nose because of syphilis. But your general confusion is quite natural. You've been through a lot and it'll take time for you to be completely at ease. That's what you're here for."

OFTEN THROUGHOUT this conversation he'd been glancing towards a doorway to his right. Now his eyes lit up as we heard the tapping of high heels on polished wood, followed by the entrance of a young woman in a blue silk dress.

Gordon Smith stood up and so did I.

"I'd like you to meet my daughter, Alicia," he said.

The young woman held out her hand and shook mine lightly.

"How nice to meet you," she said in a soft voice. Her eyes were dark brown, not blue like her father's. But they were just as unflinching, looking me over quite frankly, the way you'd appraise a photograph.

For my own part, I was certainly appraising her, though I was trying not to make that too obvious. She was of middling height, with an oval face. She was carefully made up, with black mascara framing those brown eyes. Her hair was dark brown, too, and striking in the way it hung over the left side of her face, like a veil. The more I looked at her, the harder it was to spot her father in her aside from that quality of her eyes. She was one of those children whose physical resemblance to a parent isn't all that obvious even when you see the two of them together.

I was about to make some such remark to Gordon when I saw he'd been watching me closely, as though anxious about my impression of his daughter.

I suddenly understood.

From perhaps the time of our very first meeting at the La Mancha mine, Gordon Smith had been assessing me not just as a potential employee, but as a possible husband for his only daughter.

I BEGAN, THEREFORE, to look quite differently at this Alicia Smith, who, after pouring herself a glass of wine at the cabinet, came and sat down on the couch opposite and made polite conversation.

I guessed she'd heard all about me. I, on the other hand, didn't know much about her. Had she lived in Camberloo all her life, for example?

"Yes. I love it here," she said.

"In fact, she's always lived in this very house," said Gordon Smith. "I had it built before she was born. It was meant to be my gift to her mother but she died without ever seeing it."

They both smiled sadly at this private allusion.

"However," said Gordon, "Alicia doesn't mean she's been confined solely to Camberloo. Right, Alicia?"

Thus prompted, she began to tell me more about herself, in the course of which I realized she'd had an altogether different kind of life from mine. She'd attended a private girls' school in Toronto and spent a year at the Sorbonne studying fine art. And, of course, every year she'd go "roughing it" at their cottage in the north country, sailing on the Great Lakes, skiing in Vermont, or basking in the sun at their apartment in Key Biscayne.

Not that her entire life was play. She was a member of the board of the Camberloo Art Gallery where she spent several mornings a week as a volunteer. Gordon, it turned out, was a major supporter of the gallery. The muted paintings on the walls around us were part of the collection he was allowed to borrow.

I asked if she'd ever travelled with her father on any of his business trips.

She shook her head, and because of the head-shaking, I realized she kept that veil of hair over the left side of her face to partly cover some sort of discoloration on her cheek.

"I much prefer to stay here and look after the house," she said.

"And I always look forward to coming home to her," said Gordon Smith.

They looked at each other with great fondness.

Of course, I couldn't help noticing that her account of her life had made no mention of a husband or boyfriend.

DINNER WAS SERVED in the dining room by an Asian maid who was also, I gathered, their cook and cleaning woman. They complimented her upon the main course—a dish that was one of Gordon's favourites from his travels in the East. It consisted of tofu, eggs, shrimp, and rice done in various exotic spices.

I tried to look as though I enjoyed it.

The entire dinner took more than an hour, with short course after short course. The Smiths only pecked at them, as though this was more of a daily ritual than a means of sustenance.

I'd been feeling rather nervous, but the wine loosened my tongue and I did a lot of the talking, mainly about my life as a sailor and my experiences in Africa and South America. I wanted to be amusing, and they seemed amused. Even after the remnants of the meal were cleared away, we stayed at the table a while, drinking coffee and chatting.

Then Gordon Smith glanced over at Alicia, they nodded to each other, and she stood up. We stood too.

"I'll leave you two now to talk business," said Alicia. She kissed Gordon briefly on the cheek. She shook my hand again, perhaps a little more warmly than at our introduction.

"I've enjoyed meeting you," she said. "I do hope you'll visit us again."

She seemed about the same age as me, so her enormous self-possession impressed me all the more. I mumbled something to the effect that I'd no idea how long I'd be in Camberloo but I hoped I'd be invited to dinner again.

"I'm sure you will be," she said. Then she left the dining room.

3

Gordon Smith now said, "Time for brandy and cigars."

He led me into an adjoining room lined with bookshelves and let me have a look around. He called the room "the library" and indeed it was full of books, mostly matched sets of classical works as far as I could see—Plato and Shakespeare and Dickens and Tolstoy and so on—that looked as though they'd never been opened but were for decorative purposes. Near the fireplace, a smaller bookcase beside two comfortable armchairs with reading lights was clearly dedicated to books that were actually read. I glanced at a few of the titles: *A History of Technology Throughout the Ages, The Hydraulic Deep Earth Pump, Clear Thinking in a Complex World*, and *Business: Strategic Approaches*. I didn't notice any fiction. A number of what appeared to be catalogues from galleries and large-sized art books were lying flat on the bottom shelves.

When the maid came in carrying a tray with a bottle and glasses and a box of cigars, we sat down in the armchairs.

She placed the tray on a little table near Gordon and silently retreated. He poured two sizable brandies then picked out two cigars. He snipped the tops off and handed me one.

"Cuban," he said.

He lit them, we puffed, then we sipped the brandies. It was a most enjoyable sensation.

"Harry, it really is a pleasure to have you here," he said.

We clinked glasses, puffed and sipped some more, then Gordon put down his glass.

"You remember when I came to see you in the hospital?" he said. "As I told you then, it wasn't simply an act of kindness. I'd been looking for someone I could have complete trust in to represent the firm overseas. We're doing very well, but I ought to be spending the bulk of my time here in Camberloo dealing with our expansion plans, not gallivanting around the world. In addition my doctor says my heart isn't as good as it used to be and it's time I cut out the rigours of long-distance travel." The hawk eyes narrowed on me. "When I met you, I came to the conclusion that you were a fine young man, wasting your talents in those mining camps. I really think you could do a great job for us."

I'd been thinking about this moment for weeks now and answered him carefully, letting him know I was very flattered by his interest in me. But, equally, I didn't want him to put his faith in the wrong man. How could someone as ignorant as I was— even of basic science—be of any use as the representative of a highly technical, specialized firm like Smith's Pumps?

"You probably don't realize how refreshing it is to hear that," he said. "It's a quality we don't often find in business. Some people would claim they were experts on pumps and ventilators because they'd lived for a few months in a town that had a coal mine—what was it called? Duncairn?"

We both laughed.

"Look, as I told you before, it's not another engineer we need," he said. "It's someone who's smart and adaptable and doesn't mind travelling. Our clients have their own engineers and they're the ones who decide whether our design and performance specifications will do the trick for them. But they'd much rather deal with someone they can trust. If they buy one of our machines, they want to be sure they can rely on us if problems arise during the warranty period and that we'll be fair and helpful thereafter. Clients appreciate that kind of commitment."

I was still worried about my lack of technical expertise and reminded him that he'd only been at the La Mancha mine that day because he could handle the technical equipment for testing the air. His ease with that weird device was something that had impressed me deeply at the time.

He shook his head.

"Honestly, in twenty years in the business, I've never had to do anything like that," he said. "I went down to perform the test, not because I was an engineer, but because their own engineers were too superstitious to go down and do it themselves. One of them actually had to show me how to switch the testing machine on and off. A child could have done that."

He saw I was still hesitant, so again he tried to allay my fears.

"If you agreed to give the job a try, I wouldn't just send you off on your own," he said. "No, naturally I'd go along with you on your first few trips to show you the ropes and let you see for yourself what's involved. I'd go with you till you were totally confident."

I still couldn't make up my mind, so he tried another tack.

"Back then, when we first met," he said, "I remember you gave me a little sermon on the failings of the mining industry, with its pollution of nature and destruction of cultures. If you took this job, you'd have the opportunity to do something about those things—at the very least by providing machines that do the minimum damage."

WHILE I WAS THINKING about that, he got up out of the armchair and went to the window, puffing at his cigar, looking out onto the lawn. I looked out too—it was getting dark now. Bats, or maybe small birds, flickered in and out of existence in the light cast by the window.

After a while, he turned to face me and I sensed he was about to play what he hoped would be his strongest card.

"Alicia's a great girl," he said. "Her mother died just after giving birth to her and her brother. He was stillborn and that made Alicia's birth very difficult. I've never told anyone about this, but did you notice the blemish on her cheek? It was damaged getting her out of the womb and it's never quite cleared up. She's very conscious of it and adjusts her hair to cover the mark."

I was a little embarrassed at how he was confiding in me. I pretended, of course, that I hadn't noticed any blemish. He had more to say, however.

"I never remarried but tried to be both father and mother to Alicia," he said. "I'm very proud of how she's turned out. As you can guess, over the years, a number of men have wanted to marry her." He paused a moment. "We didn't approve of any of them."

I couldn't help but notice the "we."

He now sat down opposite me and, as he talked, his eyes glinted like one of those jungle hawks when it's about to strike its target. Indeed, that was how he seemed to me: outwardly a scrawny creature, but with startling energy when focused on his prey. What nimbleness and willpower it would take for me to counter him. If, that is, I'd even wanted to counter him. He hadn't said outright that he wanted me to be the husband of his beloved daughter, but I'd no doubt about it.

What a temptation his implied offer was to one whose dreams were still haunted by the slums and oppressiveness of the Tollgate. The job might not be ideal, but if I accepted, I could travel the world, I'd live in comparative luxury for the rest of my life—and I'd have Alicia. Not long ago the idea of such treachery, such a betrayal of the memory of my love for Miriam on such mercenary considerations, would have been quite unthinkable. But, after all, wasn't it Miriam who'd broken my heart? Was I to mourn the loss of her forever? Alicia certainly was beautiful— might I not, in time, fall in love with her?

"Well," said Gordon Smith. "What do you think of my proposition?"

I came right out with it: yes, I'd really like to give it a try.

His eyes widened momentarily in pleasure, or triumph. He stretched out his thin hand.

"Great!" he said. "I'm delighted. I really am."

I knew he meant it.

4

For two months following that conversation, Gordon Smith oversaw much of my life. He arranged a work visa for me as well as a furnished apartment. It was on the top floor of a building he owned, overlooking Camberloo Park with its fine old trees and elaborate flower beds.

Most weekdays, wearing one of my newly bought business suits, I'd walk the half mile from my apartment to Gordon's office in the city square. He or Lew Jonson, his business partner and right-hand man, would coach me in the characteristics of the various types and sizes of the company's pumps and ventilators.

Some days, we'd go to the factory a few miles west of Camberloo where the machines were assembled from the parts made at various steel foundries. The factory was quite small, with only a dozen skilled employees headed by Jonson. He was a plump, balding engineer and co-designer, with Gordon, of the pumps. As he showed me the various machines, he'd pat them affectionately as though they were dogs. His temperament was of the placid sort and clearly he'd have been unable to take Gordon's place as a salesman.

My head was soon bursting with unfamiliar terminology: centrifugal and positive displacement, radial, mixed, or axial flow, single and multiple rotors, circumferential pistons, diaphragms and progressive cavities, pneumatic and centrifugal exhaust fans. Gordon Smith assured me that a display of my expertise in the *language* of our products was the passport to acceptance by future clients. To my surprise, it didn't take too long for me to understand what the words meant and where the parts they named were located in the machines.

MOST EVENINGS after work, I'd eat in a little steakhouse in Camberloo Square then walk the mile or so back to my apartment and settle down with a book. But once or twice a week, Gordon Smith would bring me home with him for dinner.

Alicia always looked pleased to see me. I soon realized she wasn't much of a talker—it was as if she'd said most of what she had to say on that day we first met. But I was flattered by the fact that she seemed to enjoy hearing me talk and would listen attentively, nodding her head in such a way that her curtain of hair gave only occasional glimpses of the blemish on her left cheek.

Not that we were alone together very much. Mainly, all three of us would eat dinner, then Gordon and I would adjourn to the library for brandies and cigars and he'd instruct me in the business. When he dealt with the profit-and-loss side of Smith's Pumps, those eyes looked as though they could shatter glass. But when he talked about the art of selling, the human side of him would dominate and his eyes would soften.

Sometimes, these talks would go on so late that he'd insist I stay overnight in the guest room at the top of the stairs. Indeed, the overnight stays became frequent enough that I even left a change of clothes there. I'd often fall asleep in the guest room thinking of Alicia, who was just a few doors away.

In the mornings, her father and I would have breakfast and be on our way to the office before she was up and about.

ONE NIGHT when we were sitting in the limo on our way to his house for dinner, Gordon told me he'd be leaving for Toronto immediately after we ate.

"I have to catch the overnight train to Montreal," he said. "I'm having problems with a major supplier there so I'd better go and see what's going on. I probably won't be back till tomorrow night, at the earliest. Jonson will keep you busy at the factory. He wants to show you some of the latest components."

The dinner was pleasant. Gordon was, naturally, somewhat preoccupied. I talked quite a bit and Alicia was, as usual, the perfect listener. When we'd finished eating, we accompanied Gordon out to the limo. He ducked into the back seat and, before closing the door, spoke directly to me.

"Harry, why don't you stay overnight and keep Alicia

company?" he said. "It'll give you both a chance to talk without me in the way." He said goodbye to us, shut the door, and the limo took off down the street.

SO, FOR THE FIRST TIME, only Alicia and I went into the library. We sipped brandy and I puffed away at one of the Cuban cigars. Gordon's parting words had been ambiguous enough to make me feel nervous and uncertain, so the conversation was rather stilted and general. After a while, the maid put her head in for a second to tell us she'd finished tidying up and was on her way home.

Now that we were completely alone in the house I felt even more nervous. To my relief Alicia put on some classical piano music that was being considered for background at the art gallery. We sat listening and smiling approvingly. Around ten, when the music ended, Alicia finished the one small glass of brandy she'd been sipping all along and put it down.

"Well, it's time for bed. Goodnight," she said, looking into my eyes calmly. She left the library and I heard her climb the stairs.

Now that she was gone, I felt quite depressed. I poured some more brandy and glanced without much interest through the illustrations in *The Hydraulic Deep Earth Pump*. At about ten-thirty, I thought I'd better go to bed myself if I was to get up in the morning. I switched off the library light and climbed the stairs to the guest room.

ALICIA'S DOOR at the end of the little hallway was ajar, showing the muted light of her bed lamp. I was halfway inside my own door when I decided to take a chance and call out goodnight to her.

"Why don't you come in for a while?" she called back.

My heart began pounding. I caught a glimpse of myself in the hall mirror: an anxious and nervous-looking stranger. So I took a deep breath, went along to her room, and pushed the door open.

She was lying on top of the bed in her nightdress. As I came in she closed the book she'd been reading and put it on the nightstand. She was still wearing her makeup, her eyes mascaraed, her lips red. Her hair had been brushed back, so I could see the flawed left side of her face—a kind of bruising on the skin.

"You took a long time coming up," she said. She held out her hand.

I could hardly breathe as I went to her. I murmured her name.

"Don't talk," she said in the softest of voices.

WE DID TALK LATER, long after midnight, lying in each other's arms. The bed lamp was still on and I was admiring her.

"I was beginning to think you didn't like me," she said.

I protested that she couldn't have been more wrong, that I'd been in a state of tension all night, that I'd kept thinking about telling her how much I wanted her, that I'd kept quiet only because I was afraid if I tried to take advantage of the situation she'd be deeply offended.

She snuggled against me.

"Men know so little," she said. "Most women are quite flattered to be asked—after all, the worst that can happen is that they'll say no. I mean if a man doesn't ask, how is he ever to find out?" Her brown eyes, dark in the low light of lamp, were on me. "I'll bet there are women in all those places you've travelled wishing you'd asked them," she said, laughing softly. "Aside from just the fun of it, if a man and a woman don't spend some time in bed together, how are they to know whether they're compatible?"

This down-to-earth approach to something I'd always tended to think of in a semi-mystical way astonished me.

She hugged me tightly for a while then let me go.

"You've got to be up for work in a few hours," she said. "You'd better go to your room if either of us is going to get any sleep."

Of course, she was right. It was a hard thing to do, but I went back to my own bed and lay there for a while wondering what it would be like to be married to such a woman. I had just decided it might be a very good thing when I did indeed manage to fall asleep.

<h1 style="text-align:center">5</h1>

Next afternoon I was at the factory with Jonson, studying the specifications of a variety of spare parts, when Gordon Smith phoned and asked for me. He'd arrived back from Montreal earlier than he'd expected and gone straight home. He'd had a successful trip and wanted to discuss something.

"Would you be able to come over again for dinner?"

I said I would.

"By the way, I've chatted with Alicia," he said. "She tells me you both had a good talk last night." He sounded amused, but I couldn't be sure. I made some inconsequential reply about how we'd stayed up too late.

"Anyway, we'll both look forward to seeing you at dinner tonight," he said.

I ARRIVED AT THE HOUSE by taxi around seven. The conversation over dinner was quite normal. I tried to behave towards Alicia in a way that wouldn't give any hint of what had happened the night before, difficult though it was with Gordon watching. His eyes seemed more than ever impossible to deceive.

Yet he was clearly in the best of moods, talking about Montreal in general and the various fine hotels and restaurants he usually frequented on his trips there. He didn't say much about the reasons for this latest journey—he rarely discussed business at table. I gathered there had been a problem with the production of valve linings in a Montreal factory, but it was now satisfactorily resolved.

Later, he and I went into the library, drank brandies, and puffed on Cuban cigars. After a while he talked about the reason he'd wanted me to come for dinner.

"You've been with the firm now for about three months," he said. "I know that's not very long and I don't want to press you unduly. But you've seen for yourself how much I have to do at the office, keeping on top of the running of day-to-day business affairs. Then there are trips like the one to Montreal that are symptomatic of the kind of thing that's been happening more and more as we've expanded. The truth is, from now on I'm going to have to spend the bulk of my time dealing strictly with the business end, especially making sure we get the highest-quality parts. In other words, I need to be here in Canada. Jonson and I believe it's high time someone else took over the travelling part of the job."

I knew what was coming.

"We both agree you're the man for it," he said. "You've worked hard and Jonson's been very impressed by how quickly you've come to have a sound grasp of the ins and outs of the machinery. So, what do you think? Could you see yourself dealing with our customers abroad? As I promised you before, I'd keep you company at first to make sure things go smoothly. If you say no, we're back to square one."

I could hear the anxiety in his voice, so I immediately put him at his ease: if he thought I could do it, I'd like to give it a try.

I'd never seen him look so happy.

"I couldn't be more pleased," he said. He shook my hand warmly. "Alicia will be thrilled, too. You should go up and tell her."

AS OPPOSED TO the night before, this time I ran up the stairs straight to Alicia's room. I knocked on her half-open door.

"Come in," she called.

She was sitting on the edge of the bed, looking at me expectantly. I told her Gordon had asked me to take over the foreign travel, and that I'd agreed to do it. She came to me and we hugged each other.

"What wonderful news," she breathed. "How wonderful, wonderful."

I held her out at arm's length and looked resolutely into her eyes. I told her that this day could only be bettered if she'd consent to become my wife. Though I'd rehearsed my little speech, hearing my own mouth utter the words shocked me a little.

She was not at all shocked.

"Of course I will," she said.

Her body leaned into mine, her dark eyes gleaming. My heart was beating at the thought of last night and all the other nights to come.

Did she think Gordon would approve?

"He most certainly will," she said. "He talked and talked about you when he came back from South America that first time he met you. I heard your life story, even the part about your tragic love affair. We thought it was so romantic. I was dying to meet you, and when I did I liked you right away. Then, after last night …" She said no more, but snuggled against me.

I was a little surprised to hear that Gordon had told her about my love for Miriam—I'd thought it best not to mention that to her. This father and daughter were such a strange pair, I wondered if they kept any secrets from each other. Fortunately, in this case, it was clear that Alicia not only didn't hold my confession of undying love to another woman against me, she actually regarded it as a point in my favour.

After a few more moments of tenderness, she stood back, rearranged her hair, and looked into my eyes.

"Are you absolutely certain this is what you want?" she said.

I assured her I was.

"Then let's go downstairs and tell him."

I did notice neither of us had once said that we loved the other. If I had any misgivings about that omission, I put them aside. Somehow, in a very short period of time, I'd come to the conclusion that perhaps all those notions I'd once had about undying love were probably no more than the delusions of an immature mind. I was, at last, on my way to becoming a realist.

We went downstairs hand in hand.

Nobody realizes that some people expend tremendous energy merely to be normal.

Albert Camus

PART THREE

THE CURATOR AGAIN

Several more weeks had passed since I'd received the curator's letter. Then, to my surprise, the man himself phoned me at work one afternoon. By now I had a mental picture of him as the typical bearded, half-starved-looking scholar—except for his fairly loud voice.

"I wonder if you could be a little more specific about where and how you came upon *The Obsidian Cloud*," he said. "I'm curious to find out if there's any direct link between this man Macbane and Mexico. Though the book may only have been brought there by an early traveller who discarded it somewhere along the way. I certainly doubt a modern-day tourist would lug something that big halfway around the world. Anyway, perhaps nothing will come of looking into a Mexican connection, but you never know—it might be a useful line of inquiry for us."

I'd been hoping this phone call was to announce some dramatic development in his research on *The Obsidian Cloud*. But he'd already warned me in his last call that these things took time, so I tried not to sound disappointed.

"Didn't you mention finding it in an old bookstore of some sort?" he said. "Tell me a little more about that."

So I told him about the actual finding of the book. How, on my third day in La Verdad, as I was walking along the Avenida del Sol, the skies darkened, the rain began lashing down, and I took shelter under the awning of an impermanent-looking store with a half-English name:

Bookstore de Mexico

Normally, I'd never have bothered going into such a place. In my quest for oddities over the years, I prided myself on having a nose for bookstores with the potential for hidden treasures.

The Bookstore de Mexico definitely wasn't one of them.

But on this day, to pass a few minutes till the downpour passed, I went inside this unprepossessing place—and came across *The Obsidian Cloud*.

"Well, I must say this bookstore doesn't sound like a very promising lead," said the curator. "I was hoping it might be one of those old-established businesses—they often keep records of their acquisitions. Anyway, if this Bookstore de Mexico still exists, we'll certainly check it out. Now what about the city itself—La Verdad? What kind of place is it—and what were you doing there, anyway?"

I explained that I'd been in La Verdad only because its turn had come as venue for the AMCA—the Annual Mining Convention of the Americas—which I always made a point of attending. This particular gathering had been as unremarkable as these events tended to be. I'd connected there with several of the mining industry people I'd come to know over the years. I'd also dozed through lectures by various professors of engineering on advances in mining technology.

In fact, I myself gave a short presentation to a group of potential customers on how Smith's Pumps had incorporated the very latest developments into our new models. My small audience had listened politely enough, but their questions showed where their main interest lay—in our prices.

As for the city of La Verdad itself? It was a rather undistinguished Mexican state capital that hadn't much to offer the stranger. Most of it was of a modern, shoddy construction, and its unemployment and crime rates were higher than the national average. I stayed in one of the two newish hotels that had joined forces to accommodate conventions like the AMCA. Non-conventioneers would have had to make do with smaller, old-fashioned hotels that lacked air conditioning, or with rundown boarding houses that had once been mansions.

These mansions were mainly located in the pre-twentieth-century area of the city, the Old Town of La Verdad (the *Ciudad Vieja*). It was advertised as a tourist attraction, but I certainly didn't find it all that attractive. For the most part, it was just a warren of huddled streets whose residents didn't go out of their way to help tourists. Equally unfriendly were the sudden, obscene odours that would sneak up through ancient drain covers into the nostrils of unwary visitors. Some of the Old Town mansions were certainly quite imposing, but uninviting. I noticed that a number of them were guarded by high, vine-entangled walls and iron gates. The carved heads of jaguars glared down on passersby from the gate pillars.

In the midst of the Old Town, appropriately, was the El Centro Plaza. It was surrounded by the customary arched *portales* to protect walkers from the sun, and under their shade some little cafés had been established. I went there once or twice looking for a place to enjoy a mid-morning coffee. But the crumbling architecture of the plaza as well as the statues adorned with chicken wire (to keep birds from perching and leaving souvenirs) made the idea of lingering for any length of time in one of these cafés unenticing. The fact that many of the statues were of ghastly-looking sixteenth-century conquistadores holding out the severed heads of Mayan guerillas didn't do much to improve the flavour of the coffee, from my perspective.

The pride of the Old Town was its cathedral. It had been built by the Spaniards in the 1580s to let the vanquished Maya know that a European god was now in charge. In fact, a tourist brochure said that the cathedral stood on the very ruins of a temple erected by the Maya, centuries before, to celebrate a massacre of the Aztec. Some materials from the temple had even been used to build the cathedral. After reading that, I thought I could make out the faces of pagan deities, peering helplessly from inside some of the big stones.

The old temple had also supplied the cathedral's massive wooden door, a door that was, according to a plaque beside it, considered miraculous. Apparently the wood was of a rare species, so dense that the conquistadores' efforts to incinerate it actually made it tougher.

THOSE WERE THE kinds of impressions of La Verdad I rambled on about to the curator.

He asked an occasional question for clarification—I could hear him scribbling notes. Finally, he thanked me for the information.

"You never know," he said. "Perhaps there's some connection between La Verdad and Duncairn. At any rate, I'll contact the city authorities. There may be records in some vault that would be of interest."

That was fairly well the gist of our conversation, though he did mention my donation once again.

"On behalf of the Board of Trustees, I want to thank you very much. We work on a tight budget, as you can imagine," he said. "If you do happen to be in Glasgow one of these days in the course of your travels, you'd be very welcome to drop by. You could see the kind of thing that goes on at the Rare Book Room and I could give you a verbal report on the current status of our research into *The Obsidian Cloud*."

I assured him that such a trip to Scotland at this time was unthinkable—we were right in the thick of the busy season at Smith's Pumps. That, of course, wasn't quite the truth. How could I tell him that, above everything, two memories had always made me shudder at the idea of a return to Scotland: one concerned a bombing, the other a broken heart.

MARRIAGE

1

So IT WAS THAT at the age of twenty-five, I married Alicia Smith. Gordon's dislike of "public displays" was more than reason enough for us to hold the marriage ceremony in the Camberloo Registry Office, with only Gordon himself and Jonson present as guests and witnesses.

The wedding reception was equally small—just the four of us. Alicia had reserved one of the little enclosed dining areas upstairs at the Hanging Gardens Tavern in the village of St. Herbert, just north of Camberloo. She and I had sometimes gone there for lunch and enjoyed the antique atmosphere. The interior was wood-panelled, with bare roof beams and heavy oak furniture.

But it was the exterior that delighted Alicia most. The three-storey-high front wall was clothed in ivy. During the summer months, from little alcoves amongst the vines, hundreds of flowering plants and flowers protruded. When they were in full bloom, the wall looked like a perpendicular garden, or a marvellous painting. Presumably that was how the name The Hanging Gardens came about.

Though a piece of local folklore gave an alternative explanation. According to it, one of the nineteenth-century builders of the tavern hanged himself from a roof beam because of a failed love affair.

I liked that version, but Alicia, being Alicia, never gave any credence to it. I think she really doubted that human beings could be soft-hearted enough to kill themselves for love.

Our honeymoon consisted of a week at a remote, luxurious inn amongst the Muskoka lakes, a couple of hundred miles to the north of Camberloo. It was late September, so in that region the leaves of the deciduous trees were already changing colour.

On our return to Camberloo, I was permanently installed in the Smith household. Gordon gave up the main bedroom, which was actually a two-room suite with its own huge bathroom, to Alicia and me. He took over what had been her bedroom.

Otherwise, my presence seemed not to disturb in any major way the customary rhythms of the Smiths' existence. Not that they had to go much out of their way to absorb me into their routine, for I tried to make myself, as much as possible, a seamless fit. On weekday mornings while Alicia slept on, I'd join Gordon in the kitchen for breakfast. We'd have toast and coffee, and skim through the newspapers without much talk. The limo would pick us up at eight-thirty.

My typical workday, as before the marriage, was spent at the office, where Gordon instructed me further in the art of sales. Occasionally I'd go to the factory. There, Lew Jonson would patiently explain the more subtle aspects of pumps and ventilators (p's and v's, as I learned to call them).

After work, our routines were quite fixed. At six-thirty, Gordon, Alicia, and I (and, occasionally, Jonson) would assemble in the dining room and await the serving of dinner. For the first time in my life, I learned to experience food as a sensual delight in itself and not, as in the Tollgate, simply the way of staving off hunger. I came to marvel at mouth-watering smells and flavours so refined I often didn't know whether I was eating fish, lamb, poultry, or beef.

When the meal was over, we'd all head to the library for coffee and brandy and the men would smoke cigars. We'd talk about this and that, or we'd read quietly. We were all comfortable with each other. At ten o'clock, Gordon would say his goodnights and adjourn to his room (if Jonson had come for dinner, he'd already have left). Shortly thereafter, Alicia and I would go upstairs. She'd take her nightly bath—her second of the day, for she always liked to have a bath in the early afternoon, too—while I'd read in bed, waiting for her.

She'd eventually come to me all soft and perfumed with rosewater. By midnight we'd be asleep in each other's arms. Often, when we woke in the mornings, I'd tell her about particularly interesting dreams I'd had. She'd lie there, half asleep, listening. As for her own dreams, she said she rarely remembered them but that, when she did, they were too unpleasant to talk about.

I didn't press her.

DURING THE DAY, when Gordon and I were gone, Alicia was busy in her own way. She didn't cook or do housework, but she did advise the maid, whose duties these were, on possible menus for dinner and on special cleaning tasks. Then there was the gardener to be dealt with, and so on.

Several mornings a week, as a member of the acquisitions committee at the art gallery, she'd visit local artists' studios in search of potential exhibits. Being the daughter of a successful citizen of Camberloo, she also sat on the boards of St. Polycarp's

Hospital and of the Camberloo Symphony. These obligations involved fund-raising activities which kept her occupied.

Her membership in the symphony board surprised me a little. I'd never heard her or Gordon humming or whistling a tune, the way my parents used to. Apart from the night Alicia had put on a record when Gordon left for Montreal, music was rarely heard around the house. They'd both listen to the news on the radio, but if music came on, one or the other of them would switch it off as though tidying something up.

IN FACT, they often may have put me in the category of an untidiness. They made a fuss—though in a good-humoured way—over replacing my books in exactly their proper spots on the shelves, adjusting the cushions on chairs I'd been sitting on, or lining up my discarded shoes neatly on the doormat beside their own.

Eventually, I got the hang of it. But from time to time I'd leave something out of place, just to give them a chance to put it back where it ought to be.

On occasion, one of Alicia's board meetings might be held at our house during daytime when Gordon and I were at the office. The board members were invariably gone by the time we came home. When I'd ask about them, Alicia would wrinkle her nose to let me know I wasn't missing much. But I'd no doubt she was the perfect hostess.

Only rarely did she or Gordon have anyone else over to the house on a purely social basis—except for Jonson. In fact, aside from him, they seemed to desire no close friends outside of each other, and now me.

In that sense, things hadn't changed for me since my life in the Tollgate: I was part of another very un-extended family.

2

Gordon, as promised, came with me on my earliest sales efforts during that first year. These journeys meant we were both gone from Camberloo, sometimes for as long as a month. Alicia didn't complain. She'd been well trained in the demands of running a business.

As for the journeys themselves: we always went first class if it was available, whether by ship, or plane, or train, and we stayed in good hotels. Of course there were exceptions. At times we could only travel on roads so primitive we needed Land Rovers to tackle them. Once in a while there weren't even roads of any sort and we had to resort to riverboats or even smaller craft such as canoes, which were particularly hard on Gordon.

"If I have to spend another hour in one of these things I'll never be able to stand up again," he used to complain.

Nor was it always possible to find decent hotels. In bush towns or on remote islands, the hotels were often so primitive they even lacked electricity. The toilet might consist of a little cubicle on stilts over a river or where tidal water would scour away the evidence. Sometimes, the only shower was an overhead tank of water located outdoors, amongst palm trees and flowering shrubs. We'd have to tiptoe cautiously around to avoid scorpions or spiders. Such hotels weren't much better than the vermin-ridden huts I'd sometimes stayed in when I was a tutor.

At the actual business meetings we attended on these trips, Gordon was always just as sharp and efficient as when I'd first seen him at the La Mancha mine. But at night, back in our quarters, those remarkable eyes were sometimes almost lifeless, his face pale and drawn. I fully understood then how wearing these trips had become for him and why he'd been so keen on passing them on to me.

And, for the first time, I really began to confront the ethical problems that went along with the job.

THAT FEBRUARY we were in La Coruna, a provincial capital in the northwestern region of the Andes. Gordon had given a successful presentation at one of the big strip-mine companies and they'd bought two of our pumps and a ventilator.

Out of the blue, another opportunity arose. We were at the hotel preparing to head back to Canada when Gordon received a lengthy phone call from the manager of an old-established gold mine near the town of Santa Cruz, eighty miles away, asking for his help.

Apparently, for at least a hundred years, waste water from this gold mine had emptied into the Rio del Sol, a river that ran past Santa Cruz. Out of deference to the town, the waste had always been directed round it by means of a pipe that opened into the river a mile or so farther downstream.

In the course of a hundred years the townspeople had benefited economically from the mine and never had any cause to complain about the waste.

But just three days before, a tricky situation had arisen. The pump controlling the waste pipe had become sluggish, as it often did over the years if too much debris gathered in the metal grille over its intake valve. Stopping the pump to clear this debris safely and then restarting it could take as long as a full day.

So, the usual procedure was just to keep the pump running while workers removed the grille. In that way, they could clean it and put it back on without any major suspension of work.

Two workers had been delegated to perform this very operation. With the pump still running, they'd managed to unscrew the rusty bolts that held the grille on. But as they were trying to lift it out they slipped and were sucked into the uncovered intake valve. The huge impeller blade then became a very efficient meat grinder.

This kind of horror had happened, apparently, on several occasions over the decades during grille-cleaning time, and not much fuss was made about it. What caused the present crisis was that the oversized spanners and crowbars the men had been using were also sucked in. As a consequence, the impeller, its gears, its massive cast-iron valve, and its housing were shattered, as was the connection to the escape pipe. The lagoon immediately began backing up and spilled directly into the Rio del Sol just above the town. The fact that the river flowing past the town had turned bright orange, the fact that the fish all floated belly up—these might have provoked only a mild reaction.

But the smell! It was a public relations nightmare for the gold mine. The stink of rotten eggs given off by the chemical-filled water permeated Santa Cruz day and night, causing babies to cry and appalling their parents and the citizens in general. Especially upset were the mayor and the bishop, whose town hall and palace, respectively, stood on the riverbank.

Civic outrage resulted. For the first time in its long, profitable history the gold mine was ordered closed.

"AND WHAT EXACTLY would you like me to do?" I heard Gordon ask the manager on the other end of the phone.

Gordon was well known amongst the mining fraternity. The manager of the Santa Cruz mine wondered if he could come and make a speedy assessment of the condition of the broken pump.

"If you send transportation, I'll come down tomorrow morning," Gordon said. "I'll bring my colleague with me."

IN THE MORNING, a company car picked us up at our hotel and took us to the mine, a two-hour drive away. It was a typical sprawl of buildings with corrugated roofing amidst high mounds of broken rocks. The river ran nearby. We were met by the manager, a small, hollow-chested man who reminded me a little of my father: a cigarette dangled from his lips and he had a chronic cough.

The broken pump, he informed us in quite good English, was located in "the lagoon." That was the romantic-sounding word used by the mining industry for the septic ponds that resulted from cleaning the gold with a mix of chemicals. The cleaning process lasted for two weeks out of each month. The contaminated water was then forced, by means of a huge hundred-year-old cast-iron pump, into a two-mile-long pipe. The pipe, in turn, disgorged its contents into the Rio del Sol safely below the town. The only human beings affected by it were natives whose villages were on the banks of the river far below when the waste pipe was in use. These villagers would see the Rio del Sol turn an orange colour, for the waste water contained clay from the galleries of the mine, mixed with cyanide and a number of other chemicals used to clean the gold.

For two weeks after such a discharge all the fish in the river would die. Then the water would clear, the fish would return, and everything would seem normal. Or relatively normal, though there were unsupported reports of villagers who had died from what appeared to be cyanide poisoning.

The mine manager told us the owners wanted things returned to that quite acceptable situation.

"They say the pump must be repaired or replaced *pronto* so that we can begin operation again," he said.

He now took us to see the problem for ourselves.

The lagoon was several hundred yards away along a pathway from his office. In the sticky heat, in the silence broken only by the squawking of birds in the surrounding jungle, I sweated. Gordon looked as cool as ever and impervious to our escort of mosquitoes.

As we got nearer to the lagoon the stink became eye-watering. The path was lined with bushes of red and yellow frangipani in full blossom, but whatever fragrance they might have given off was undetectable in the manmade stench.

We were soon on the bank of the lagoon itself. It was the size of a football field, with walls about ten feet high. Most of the water it once held had already seeped back into the river. The ancient pump stood half immersed in sludge, like some primeval water creature. From the bank, the engineer pointed out the jagged cracks in the shell of the engine and the areas where the impeller's blade and housing had shattered. The manager translated for him, then asked Gordon hopefully:

"You can repair it, *señor?*"

Gordon shook his head.

"I'm afraid its days are over," he said. "The miracle is that it's survived so many years."

WE WENT BACK to the office and began discussing the specifications for a new pump with the manager and his engineer. Gordon did all the talking. We'd brought along the briefcase of brochures and diagrams. He showed the engineer our most powerful model, made of alloys incomparably tougher and more flexible than the cast iron of the old pump. He said he was confident that our engineer, Jonson, could very quickly adapt it to their needs.

Questions were asked about price and installation date—less than a month, in Gordon's view. The manager said he'd consult the owners and then get back to us with a decision that evening at our hotel in the city.

ON THE RIDE BACK to La Coruna, Gordon was in a very good mood. The road was newly paved and the company car was air-conditioned.

But I wasn't so happy. I'd seen during my experience as a tutor just how mercenary the mining industry often was. The only thing the owners seemed to care about was keeping their mines operating and maximizing profits. In the case of the Santa Cruz mine, giving it a new, better pump would only ensure that it would carry on just as before, and might make the men work even harder. As for the pollution of the river and the poisoning of the natives downstream, they would be carried out even more efficiently.

I told Gordon what was on my mind.

"I agree, to a certain extent," he said. "But if we don't sell them a new pump, one of our rivals will. That's how business works." He could see this didn't cheer me up. "Look, Harry. Our pump *will* make things better for the miners, if the owners go for it. It'll be much more reliable and won't need cleaning the dangerous way the old one did."

I didn't say anything, so he knew I still wasn't as excited as he thought I ought to have been.

"Surely you can see it's not our job to tell our customers what we think is right or wrong about their practices," he said. "If we did that, believe me, we'd soon be bankrupt. I'm not saying we don't have our own moral responsibilities and that we don't have to adhere to them as well as we can. For example, we use the very best materials and we make our machinery as safe and reliable as possible. Isn't that a benefit to the miners who depend on them?

"Another thing is, we never cheat our customers. We sell our products at a fair profit and we stand by the quality of our workmanship. Those are our ethical responsibilities and we live up to them. The business world's just as complicated as the rest of the world—that's something you'll find out. There are no simple solutions, so we can't expect everyone to do what we think is the right thing when perhaps it isn't."

I wasn't convinced by that defence. Perhaps because the manager had reminded me of him, I wished my father were here to make one of his astute comments. But of course, he was long gone now and I couldn't think of anything astute to say.

LATER THAT NIGHT, the manager phoned Gordon at the hotel to tell him to go ahead with the new pump. Afterwards we went down to the bar to celebrate the sale—the pump in question was our finest, most expensive model. This sale had been an unexpected bonus.

Back in my hotel room, I phoned Alicia to tell her I missed her.

"Me too," she said. "I can't wait to see you again. Gordon called me a couple of hours ago to say the trip's been very successful."

He hadn't mentioned to me that he'd already spoken to her. I wasn't as surprised as I used to be that they'd communicated with each other without involving me. Nor did I tell her about my own mixed feelings about the sale. She was too much like Gordon to appreciate my squeamishness. Perhaps they were both right and I was taking too personally what was really only a business deal.

Her voice over the phone was seductive. "You and I will find a special way to celebrate when you're home."

THAT NIGHT I LAY in the hotel bed for a while, unable to sleep, thinking over what had happened. Eventually, I convinced myself that the Smiths' common-sense way of looking at the world was probably a very reasonable one and that the scraps of idealism I'd retained were nothing but a sign I hadn't really grown up.

Then I slept an uneasy sleep.

3

On our return to wintry Camberloo, Alicia did try to make my homecoming more than usually enjoyable. Gordon and I had arrived from the airport late in the day. We'd eaten a light meal and Alicia had toasted our success with a glass of wine. Soon Gordon, exhausted by the journey, bade us goodnight and headed off to bed.

Shortly afterwards, Alicia and I went upstairs. She prepared the tub in the bathroom, surrounding it with candles which she lit while the tub filled. We lay together in the warm water for a while. Then we dried each other off and made good use of a jug of aromatic oil before entering into the most pleasurable of exertions.

BUT WHAT MADE this occasion particularly memorable was something Alicia revealed to me later, as we lay in each other's arms.

"Do you remember the first time we made love?" she said.

How could I ever forget that night Gordon went off to Montreal, leaving us the house to ourselves?

"I told him all about it when he came back," she said.

Surely she didn't mean *all* about it?

"Yes, all about it," she said, nuzzling into my shoulder. "I'd always made it clear to him that I couldn't marry someone I wasn't comfortable with in bed. That's why he told you to stay with me that night. He wanted me to have a chance to try you out. When he came home and asked me about it, I assured him it was a great success."

She saw how surprised I was at hearing this. Not that I hadn't suspected he'd connived with her to get us alone together—maybe even as far as the bed. But that she'd then given him an evaluation of our love-making! That struck me as very unromantic. I thought of asking her if she'd "tried out" those previous suitors Gordon had mentioned. I knew she'd tell me the truth if that was what I really wanted, for she was by nature a truth-teller. But I didn't want to know.

"Did I say the wrong thing?" she said, laughing at my reaction. "I'd have kept it to myself if I'd realized that's what you preferred."

She was looking at me now, her brown eyes warm and affectionate. I think she was fond of me, as much as anything because I was so guileless—just as I was fond of her, as much as anything because she was so honest. Perhaps that was a good enough basis for a marriage.

BUT LOVE? True love? On that matter, I felt I had some basis for comparison. If I loved Alicia at all, it was a lesser kind of love than the all-consuming kind I'd experienced with Miriam. Just

remembering that love made me both sad and happy: sad that it
didn't work out, but happy that the possibility of it existed and
that I'd once known it. Or, at least, so I believed, and I'd held
on to that belief in the way others might hold on to a belief in
a great power that makes sense of their world for better or for
worse.

So, I tried to make a case on my own behalf. A man—myself,
for instance—might behave in a practical and self-serving way
such as marrying for advancement, or working at some lucrative
but unethical job on the pretext that if he didn't do it, someone
else surely would. Yet that man—myself, again—might still, in
his deepest being, cling to principles fundamentally at odds with
his actual behaviour. Indeed, this was perhaps how most men
lived. Despite their failure to live up to a higher ideal, their belief
in its existence allowed them to be relatively happy.

The logic of my case seemed somehow defective. Still, as
before, I'd almost convinced myself of it.

On this note of relative happiness, lying beside the honest
Alicia, I fell into a sound sleep.

At some point in my dreams, I was young again, running
along a grey street in the Tollgate—or perhaps it was Duncairn—
being pursued by a stranger with a scar on his cheek. Terrified
and out of breath, I could run no longer and crouched with my
hands up to shield myself. Then, in that odd way dreams work,
I was all at once aware that I was looking into a mirror and that
the stranger was no stranger—he was only the grown-up version
of myself.

When I awoke the next morning, that dream was stuck in
my mind. It seemed a concrete image of my ongoing anxiety
over who I was and what I'd become. But, of course, it was only
a dream and not to be taken too seriously.

4

That spring was important for me. Gordon and I made a week-long trip to a large uranium mine in Northern Ontario. There, I took the leading role in presenting an offer to sell two new pumps as well as spare parts for older equipment. I'd also warned Gordon that I was going to propose the mine buy a ventilator. In most of these older mines, the workers depended on the feeble drafts of air that penetrated the tunnels—natural ventilation, it was called. Miners almost invariably suffered from lung problems caused by breathing in dust particles and gases, had to take a lot of time off work, and generally died young.

So, in my presentation I suggested to the mine's negotiators that an efficient ventilation system would actually be a good (I didn't use the word "ethical") investment in the long run, and they agreed. Gordon was delighted and surprised. He'd been noticeably worn out during much of our trip and was more than happy to leave the sales up to me.

WE'D BEEN BACK in Camberloo only a week when he called me into his office at work one morning with a smile on his face.

"Well done, Harry!" he said. "Look what's just arrived by courier." He was holding the signed contracts for the deal at the uranium mine. "As far as I'm concerned, your apprenticeship is officially over. You are hereby promoted to Head of Sales for Smith's Pumps and Ventilators. Congratulations!" He shook my hand vigorously and added, "This is altogether quite a significant day for us."

I naturally assumed he was still talking about my promotion.

But when we got home from work that night, Alicia met us at the door.

"We're going to have a baby!" she said to me, her dark eyes warmer than I'd ever seen them. "The doctor told me this morning. Isn't it wonderful? Father was thrilled to bits when he heard."

"Indeed, I was," said Gordon, smiling.

She'd told him before she told me. She'd phoned him after she left the doctor's—hence his comment to me about the great significance of the day. It was his idea that she should surprise me with the news when we came home, then we'd all go out and celebrate the pregnancy as well as my promotion. But it was clear which was more important to them.

I tried to sound enthusiastic, for Alicia's sake, though I felt quite let down.

We went to a restaurant for dinner and Gordon ordered an expensive bottle of wine for the occasion. He and Alicia speculated excitedly about the baby throughout. I chimed in from time to time and they smiled fondly at me. Not much was said about my promotion.

THE BABY WAS BORN in Camberloo General Hospital at six-thirty on a bitterly cold January morning. Gordon was determined he'd be present at the birth, so I went with him although I knew I'd feel squeamish.

It turned out to be very hard to watch—an agonizing, protracted struggle. Alicia must have been suffering badly but didn't complain. The baby was in the wrong position for delivery, so a lot of forceps work was needed. Eventually a boy emerged, but by then Alicia was in such a state she really didn't care. Before he was swathed in cloths, a brief glimpse of the baby's face showed he had a large bruise on his right cheek. An attending nurse assured Gordon and me that the bruise, caused by the forceps, was superficial and would soon disappear.

For the next twenty-four hours, Alicia lay in the recovery room, heavily sedated. Gordon and I took turns at her bedside, but we both happened to be present when she eventually awoke. Right away, she asked to see the baby. When the nurse laid him down beside her on the bed, Alicia had to be reassured that the mark on his cheek was only temporary. Then she concentrated on him and a look came into her eyes I'd never seen before. She began cooing words to the baby, her speech a little slurred: "Shweet 'ittle Franshish. Shweet 'ittle Franshish." She kept repeating this over and over.

Gordon explained the meaning to me.

"We'd agreed that if it was a boy we'd call him Francis, in memory of my father," he said. "I hope you don't mind? Everyone called him Frank."

I really didn't mind, but I wished they'd asked me. Though the name was really quite fitting. There was indeed a frankness in the blue eyes of the little boy with the bruised cheek who lay there on the bed, staring up now at his wounded mother, now at his grandfather, and now at me, his father, as though appraising us. I couldn't help wondering what he might have thought of a father who'd had no say in his son's naming.

ALICIA EVENTUALLY came home to heal. A series of nannies helped look after little Francis, or Frank, which we all preferred. Much as she loved him, Alicia tired easily and often had to go to bed early.

When we got home from work at night, Gordon and I tried to abide by some of the old rituals. We still went to the library to sip a whisky and read. At that time he was reading an illustrated *History of Scotland* and would ask me questions, now and then, about some of the old customs. Around nine, the nanny would leave for home after making sure Frank was asleep in the nursery, which was the room adjoining our bedroom. At ten, Gordon would go to bed and I'd look in to check on Frank before slipping into bed beside Alicia, careful not to disturb her sleep. If Frank woke during the night, I'd see to his needs.

Such was our new routine for many weeks as we waited for Alicia to regain her strength.

5

One night during that period, when Gordon and I had made our ritual retreat to the library after dinner, he sipped his brandy, cleared his throat, and embarked on what I soon realized was to be a fatherly talk. The subject: a mature relationship between husband and wife.

"I often think about what you told me when we first met— about your great love affair in Scotland," he said. "Your idealism was one of the things I liked about you at the time.

"As you've no doubt gathered by now, idealism isn't in my own makeup. I've always been a much more pragmatic type. Take my marriage to Alicia's mother, for example. I was very fond of her and deeply saddened when she died so young. But neither of us had married strictly for love. No, it was for much more practical reasons. I worked for her father, who owned a small engineering firm that manufactured machine parts. He and I had an understanding that if I married his daughter I'd become his partner. Which is exactly what happened. Then when he retired, I changed the firm's direction to more specialized work: it became Smith's Pumps and Ventilators.

"So, in the business sense, the marriage was clearly a great success. And, of course, it produced Alicia. What more could a man ask for? What would have been the purpose in my getting married again?"

The preliminaries of Gordon's speech were over. His eyes seemed to become even more brilliant as he was about to come to the point.

"From what I've read, up till recent times men of ambition wouldn't have thought of marrying just for love. I mean, if there wasn't some material advantage to be got from it, they wouldn't have considered it. Marriage was strictly about property, or inheritance, or business.

"You see what I mean? The idea of love as a basis for marriage was apparently one of those notions invented to keep ordinary folks happy. It allowed them to believe their marriages were just as important as anyone else's—especially those they had to work for.

"Now if that sounds cynical, I don't mean it to be. As far as I'm concerned, even in a marriage based on practical, business considerations it's better if a man does love his wife.

"But what I'm trying to get at is this: let's say, for any reason, a man's wife can't give him what he needs physically. Yes, physically—you know what I mean? Well, in that case, surely there's no harm in him finding his satisfactions elsewhere. Discreetly, of course. It doesn't mean he's not a loving husband and she's not a loving wife. It's just that men can't be expected to do without certain things. And anyway, most men enjoy … a bit of variety, shall we say? So from our point of view, it's not all that bad."

The tone of these last remarks of his really surprised me, as if a cloistered monk had said something of the sort. For Gordon had always seemed to me monklike in the service of Smith's Pumps.

"Any wife worth her salt understands these things," he went on. "As long as there's discretion, she knows that a marriage is based on much more substantial elements—mutual business and family interests.

"Now in your case, Harry, when you lived in Scotland, putting love on a pedestal was quite understandable. You were young and poor then—you'd nothing at stake. But now you're a partner in a thriving business. You and Alicia have produced a son—an heir. These are the things marriage is all about. The rest isn't really important."

Gordon sat back and sipped his brandy. He seemed quite pleased with all he'd said on the matter of marriage. He took it for granted there would be no questions.

About that, he was right. I might have asked why he'd even raised the matter—I suspected that he and Alicia had planned it together—but I kept quiet. In fact we never spoke of it again.

6

By mid-summer, Alicia had almost totally recovered from the birth. Frank was now six months old.

I'd just come back from a five-week sales trip to some diamond and bauxite mines in northern Australia. The travelling itself had been exhausting, and so I was happy when Gordon told me to take a week away from work and "get reacquainted," as he put it, with Alicia and Frank. Accordingly, I stayed home and he went to the office alone each day.

On one of those mornings, Alicia and I were playing with Frank in the backyard when the phone rang. The time was ten-thirty. I ran to the kitchen and picked up.

It was Jonson on the line, calling from St. Polycarp's Hospital. Apparently, shortly after arriving at work an hour before, Gordon had slumped over at his desk. Jonson had immediately called for an ambulance. He rode in the back beside Gordon till they got him to the hospital. This was the first chance Jonson had had to phone.

Alicia and I left Frank with the nanny and drove immediately to the hospital.

THE DAY WAS ONE of those incomparable summer days in Camberloo. The sky was a flawless blue, the trees were in full leaf, and the townspeople wore bright summer clothes. The red-brick hospital itself looked at its best, with ranks of blue and yellow flowers all in blossom along the gardens at the Emergency entrance.

Jonson greeted us at the door.

"They've managed to contact his doctor," he said to Alicia. "He was out on a house call but should be here any minute." He then led us to a little private ward on the main floor and we all went in.

Gordon was lying on the bed, his head propped on a pillow. When he saw Alicia come in, his eyes brightened and he smiled weakly. He moved his hand towards her and she held it.

"How are you feeling?" she said.

"Now that you're here, I'm fine," he said to her in a quiet voice. He tried to say something else, but his eyes narrowed and he looked puzzled. Then the puzzlement evaporated from his face and the light went out of his eyes. And he was dead.

HIS HEART HAD BEEN bad for a long time. So his doctor, a plump man in a polka-dot bow tie who arrived at the hospital just minutes after Gordon died, revealed to us. He was surprised Alicia didn't know that in recent years her father had consulted a number of specialists. All of them had told him he shouldn't be working. He'd been on a strict regimen of pills.

That night, Alicia found several bottles of these pills hidden under layers of underwear and socks at the back of a drawer in his dresser.

TWO DAYS AFTER his death, Alicia and Jonson and I sat together miserably in the chapel of the Final Gateway Crematorium. The plain wooden coffin lay on the catafalque. I had my arm round Alicia, who was weeping quietly. Gordon, in line with his dislike of public displays, had requested that his body be cremated, that only we three be present, and that there be no funeral service of any sort. It was cold in the crematorium because of the air conditioning. Outside, the day had been humid, the sky heavy with the threat of a storm.

The undertaker appeared and whispered that we might wish to take our last look at the deceased. So we went up to the coffin. The top had been lifted and we could see what had once been Gordon lying there, his eyes closed, his face like a shrivelled apple. The undertaker's efforts to redden his lips and cheeks had failed to make him look alive.

Alicia sobbed at the sight of him. Jonson and I gripped her arms to support her.

As we were standing there, the chapel door swung open and footsteps approached the catafalque. It was Gordon's doctor, in the polka-dot bow tie he'd been wearing the last time we saw him. He was now carrying an alligator-skin doctor's bag.

Naturally, we wondered what he was doing here.

He was a little embarrassed that the undertaker hadn't

informed us. The fact was that Gordon, more than a year ago, had told him about his wish to be cremated. He'd commissioned him to come to the crematorium in the moments before incineration and make sure he was quite dead.

"It's just a formality," the doctor told us. "That is, if you've no objection."

We had no objection.

Our final goodbyes to Gordon having been said, the undertaker ordered the coffin to be wheeled out of the chapel into the committal room, its last stop before the oven. The doctor, with his bag, accompanied the coffin. He'd been in the committal room for only a few minutes when he returned.

"Everything was fine," he said to us.

Soon after that, a blue light began to flicker on and off in the chapel. That was the sign the final act was about to take place out of our sight. We could hear the ignition roar of the gas jets, followed not long after by the squeal of a conveyor belt's rollers as the coffin slid into the oven.

The undertaker appeared again and advised us to go home. The process of incineration and preparation of the ashes would take several hours. We could pick them up that evening if we so wished.

Before we left the chapel, I went over to Gordon's doctor and thanked him for complying with Gordon's final request, whatever it was.

"All he wanted me to do was a simple little surgical procedure on his body," he said. "His carotid arteries were to be severed, right there in the coffin. I did the procedure, with the undertaker as witness. We can both attest that Gordon's blood was totally coagulated."

He saw I was surprised to hear this.

"I can only suppose he wanted to be on the safe side," said the doctor.

THE NEXT MORNING, we planted a young rose bush amongst his ashes in the backyard. That was my idea. In my tutor days, the natives who'd lived near one of the mines claimed that the very best orchids grew from rotting corpses. I thought if there was any truth to that, it might somehow apply to the ashes of the dead, too. So, with Alicia's consent, I mixed Gordon's ashes with some bags of potting soil and planted the rose bush in the midst of them.

7

Gordon's death shocked me. I'd become very attached to him—he'd been a second father to me and seemed to care about me in that unconditional way my own parents had, though he was very different from them. Why he'd taken to me so much and chosen me as a suitable husband for Alicia, I never quite understood.

I'm not sure he himself knew. In spite of his theories, he may have let himself be guided by a feeling or an intuition— something a practical man like himself would normally have ignored. Perhaps he had an instinct that someone unlike himself might be the very man for Alicia.

Another enigma was that weird final request of his about the severing of his arteries. On the one hand, it might have been a matter of simple logic—the wish of a competent and efficient man to remain in control of his body right up to the moment of its disintegration. On the other hand, perhaps it revealed an aspect of his mind he generally kept to himself, one that was imbued with the ancient terror of being wrongly pronounced dead.

His incineration made me think yet again about the terrible deaths of my own parents in that inferno in the Tollgate. I'd never permitted myself to consider the possibility that they'd been quite aware of what was happening as the flames of their burning tenement engulfed them. The idea was still too much to bear.

ALICIA WAS DEVASTATED by her father's death. For weeks she could barely hold back her tears. I think if it hadn't been for little Frank, she'd have had a complete breakdown.

I tried to comfort her, but I knew the closeness of her bond with Gordon. They weren't just father and daughter, they were each other's confidants about everything. Or, not quite everything. He'd withheld his heart problem from her, no doubt so that she wouldn't worry unduly.

I suggested it was only natural for a parent to try to protect his daughter in this way. But she seemed to regard it as a kind of betrayal by him, no matter how much they loved each other. It would take a while yet for her to forgive him entirely for that. Naturally, I didn't mention the business of the severed arteries.

I MADE A FRESH discovery about her, too, a few weeks after the cremation. In the middle of the night she began fidgeting with the blankets and making whimpering sounds that woke me. In the glow of the night light, I could see she was actually still asleep. I shook her shoulder gently and she awoke, her eyes wide with fear.

I told her she'd been making noises.

"Did I disturb the baby?" she said, looking towards the door of the adjoining room where Frank slept.

I assured her he was sleeping peacefully and asked her if she'd been dreaming. I held her hand—it was very cold. I said talking about the dream might help.

"All right," she said. Slowly she began translating whatever she'd dreamt into language.

"I was in freezing cold water," she said. "It must have been winter and I'd somehow fallen out of some kind of boat into an ocean or a lake. It was nighttime and I couldn't see any shore. But there were lights in the distance so I tried to swim towards them. Then my arms wouldn't move, as though they were paralyzed. I shouted for help and I couldn't get any words out, I could only make noises. Then you woke me up."

I hugged her and reassured her. Her bad dream was surely related to Gordon's death and her shock over the loss. She'd soon be having good dreams again.

"No, you're wrong about that," she said. "All my life that's the only kind of dream I've ever had. I try not to think about them."

I didn't ask any more. I just kept holding her and soothing her and after a while she went back to asleep. But this revelation about her harrowing dream life disturbed me and kept me awake. Surely in some major way, this woman beside me, the mother of my son, was really a stranger.

AFTER BREAKFAST the next day when we were out in the yard playing with Frank, Alicia suddenly turned to me.

"Talking about that dream last night didn't help at all," she said. "In fact, putting it into words only made it seem worse." She was looking right at me. "Not only that, I can see in your eyes that it's got you worried, too."

I denied that this was so, but it was unnerving to realize just how transparent I was to her.

DEATH OR NO DEATH, business had to be resumed. I was soon taking Gordon's place behind his desk at the office, guided by two middle-aged secretaries who'd worked for him for many years and now had to get used to me. Jonson made sure the factory was back in full swing. Whatever sales trips I had to go on, I tried to make as brief as possible and was always anxious to get back to Camberloo.

But my homecomings had changed. Those sensual bedtime rituals we used to indulge in on my return didn't occur. Eventually, when I alluded to them, Alicia (who was still as enticing to me as ever) made it clear, without being unpleasant, that they were over.

I was aware of how much the birth of Frank, physically, and the death of Gordon, emotionally, had wounded her. I assumed I was being too hasty and apologized for my thoughtlessness.

"Oh, no," she said. "It has nothing to do with you. I just can't. I don't have any desire anymore." And before I could say anything, she added: "Why don't you find someone else to satisfy you in that area? Don't men enjoy … a bit of variety?"

"A bit of variety"—the very phrase Gordon had used in his little talk to me not long before his death. Right away I was certain of what I'd suspected then: that they'd discussed this matter of my "needs" just as they'd discussed so much else. No doubt that was the very reason for Gordon's heart-to-heart talk with me about what he considered the realities of marriage.

"I wouldn't mind," Alicia was saying. "Honestly, I wouldn't."

Honesty was, indeed, her trademark. At times, depending on the mood I was in, I'd wonder if this honesty of hers wasn't so much a virtue as a lack of sufficient imagination to make up pleasing lies. For Gordon, a quality like honesty was probably a more-than-adequate alternative to true love. Whether he was right or not was something I'd have to find out.

FRANK

1

In my role as Gordon's successor at Smith's Pumps, I spent a good part of the next number of years travelling. My itineraries brimmed with exotic-sounding names. In the East, I visited Kamchatka, Ulan Bator, Quingyang, Tanaga, Tuvalu, Banjarmasi, Port Moresby, the Tuamotus, Bangalore, Jabalpur, and Oamaru. I crossed and recrossed Africa, from Timbuktu and Addis Ababa to Nova Lisboa and back. The continent of South America, from Cochabamba, San Fernando de Atabapo, and Paysanchi to Rio Gallego in Patagonia, was part of my territory. In fact, the world was my territory.

The very sounds of these names at first had the effect on me of poetry, the way they did when I was a schoolboy, poring over an atlas and wishing I was anywhere but in the Tollgate.

But the more I travelled, the more disillusioned I became. These places with the lyrical-sounding names were now home to such unromantic realities as the modern hard-drug enterprise and its accompanying violence. The only kinds of ancient

traditions the new thugs still honoured consisted in such barbari-
ties as cutting off the hands of an enemy.

That made me feel less guilty about my own "legitimate"
business.

DURING MY FREQUENT absences, Alicia had to act as both mother
and father to Frank. They both looked forward to my return,
especially Frank, to whom I was the bearer of gifts. At first, when
he was very young, I'd bring animals of one sort or another, so
that the spare bedroom became like a private zoo. A parrot from
Australia would shriek "Good day, mate" to him alone whenever
he brought it food. A pair of fierce-looking salamanders and a
basilisk from Africa were also big successes—he was fascinated
by how their apparent immobility was transformed into violent
bursts of energy as they pounced on the insects that made up
their dinner. The gift he loved most, however, was a three-foot-
tall Oaxaca cactus inhabited by a colony of pygmy rats. Frank
fed the rats several times a day with birdseed and spent hours
trying to make friends with them. But he was so gigantic they
never seemed able to conceive of him as a fellow creature.

BY THE AGE OF NINE, he became less interested in exotic animals,
so I looked for other gifts that might stimulate his imagination.
In a bazaar along the Malabar coast of India, I saw a trader selling
some half-inch-tall, painted marble figurines from the sixteenth
century. They were quite expensive and I'd no idea why anyone
would have made these objects so small. But on a whim, because
I knew how much Frank had enjoyed the pygmy rats, I bought
the figurines for him.

When I got them home and he saw them, he immediately

loved them, more than all his regular toys. With the help of a magnifying glass, he was able to transform these tiny fragments of stone into fully individualized men and women from another era.

"Look," he said. "It's like magic."

And indeed, through the glass, the diminutive people seemed to leap into life in their colourful Eastern gowns and turbans, some of them wielding curved scimitars, their eyes looking directly into the observer's. It was as though they'd been shrunk five hundred years ago and had been waiting for some shaman like Frank to restore them to their real size.

On the basis of his reaction to those figurines, I kept an eye open. When I was in Paris at a mining convention, I bought what looked like a box of matches, except that the matches were little ivory sticks made by the Inuit. The tips of the sticks were actually carvings of a variety of bears, foxes, sharks, whales, char, halibut, and cod, all done with marvellous precision. When Frank saw them he was captivated, and spent innumerable hours admiring the little creatures through his magnifying glass.

THE BIGGEST SUCCESS was a model railway. I found it in a classic toy store in Zurich, where I was overnighting on my way back from the Far East. The clockwork engine and the passenger cars were from the turn of the century and were meticulously engineered. The station buildings, the bridges and the scenery, the faces of the train crew and the passengers were detailed and convincing.

Frank, who had just turned ten, was ecstatic. For weeks he played exclusively with that train set, hour after hour. He gave names to the little people who inhabited its world, made up backgrounds for them, and talked to them. He introduced them to his figurines and to the creatures on the ivory sticks.

Alicia often had difficulty persuading him to leave them so that he could eat his meals or go to bed.

FRANK WAS ALWAYS curious about how and where I'd acquired these gifts. For him, this seemed to be a vital part of the pleasure in having them. Mainly I told the straightforward truth, but I'd sometimes embroider the facts just to make the story a little more dramatic. On retelling it, I'd worry about forgetting some of the invented details.

It was those ivory sticks that led to a revelation.

One day, Frank was examining them at the table in the library while I was poring over the manual for one of our latest pumps. Out of the blue, he asked me once again for the story of how I'd got hold of the sticks. Almost without thinking, for my mind was so taken up with the technical jargon of the manual, I slipped up and told him the truth: that I'd seen the sticks in the window of a jewellery store near my hotel in Paris and bought them for him.

"But what about that old gypsy on crutches, begging at a street corner near Notre Dame, who told you about them?" Frank said. "You gave him a twenty-franc note and he was so grateful he took you to a secret shop that had the ivory sticks. It was up a dark side street at the top of a long set of stairs and you'd never have found it if he hadn't hobbled alongside you to show you where it was."

Having been caught out, I thought it best to confess that I'd invented the old man, and his crutches, and the secret store. That I sometimes made up stories around the gifts, to add to the fun. In other words, the stories weren't the absolute truth.

Frank looked at me without blinking.

"I know that." The abrupt way he said it sounded like a reprimand.

I was very surprised, and I promised to continue as before. But I knew I no longer needed to be anxious about forgetting some detail. He, of course, no longer had to pretend he didn't know truth from fiction.

MINIATURE BOOKS were soon to become Frank's great passion.

I'd been passing through Athens on one of my trips and had gone for a stroll in the Monastiraki area, near the Acropolis, looking for something for his upcoming twelfth birthday. A bookstore I went into specialized in rare books, including miniatures, some of which weren't much bigger than postage stamps. I examined a number of them on a lectern that had a magnifier to assist the reader. All were beautifully printed, often with coloured illustrations that seemed as exact as in any book of regular size.

One tiny leather-bound book in particular caught my attention: *The Book of Seasons*, printed in Brussels in 1450. It was a three-hundred-page prayer book of some sort, with beautifully ornate capital letters at the beginning of each prayer. It wasn't the Latin prayers or the ornate lettering that won me but the fifty pages that contained meticulously lifelike illustrations of medieval people and their activities. The book was expensive, but I'd a feeling Frank would like it, so I got it for him.

My instinct was good. From the moment he looked at it through a magnifying glass, he was enthralled. The very notion of an entire book in miniature, with all the attributes of a full-sized volume, astonished him just as much as it had me. Those illustrations, most of all, fascinated him.

One evening in the library he'd been studying them for a long time.

"Come and see this," he said, sounding quite excited.

I went to the desk and he handed me the magnifying glass.

Through it the tiny painting he'd been examining immediately became as large and clear as anything you might find in a gallery. The subject matter was religious: a saintly figure complete with halo was riding on horseback alongside a river that ran through a mountain pass, perhaps in the Alps. The mountains, the swirling currents of the river, the horse's gear and its bulging muscles, the details of the rider's medieval clothing, his somewhat pious but determined face as he looked upriver—all were rendered realistically and convincingly.

"Look more closely over there," said Frank, drawing my attention to a particular area of the painting.

So I did look carefully. Holding the magnifying glass at a different angle, I could make out different species of birds in a variety of different types of trees. Farther up the riverbank were cottages with smocked peasants working in gardens. In one of the cottages, I could even see a figure looking out of a casement window down towards the distant rider, as though in expectation of his coming.

"But look at the boat," Frank said.

I hadn't seen any boat. But once again, adjusting the magnifying glass, I discovered that what had seemed like a tiny mark far up the river was actually a rowboat with three men in it, their features and clothing quite distinct. Two were concentrated on the work of rowing, straining against the current.

"Look at the other man," Frank said. "See what he has in his hand?"

I fiddled with the magnifying glass a little more. This third man did indeed seem to have something in his fingers which he was staring at. I manoeuvred the glass again and the object in his hand wavered into focus for a moment. There was no doubt. The object in the man's hand was a book.

"Do you think it's *this* book he's reading?" Frank said.

I was quite startled that Frank should have even thought of such a thing, for it was a dizzying idea to me. For the first time I think I understood something of the spell these miniatures might cast with their suggestion of microscopic worlds within worlds, and we ourselves as giants looking down on them, observing. Or even that our own world might be nothing more than a tiny speck in an infinite universe being observed by infinitely larger giants.

Of course, I certainly didn't mention that last thought to Frank. I worried that such ideas might drive the fragile mind of a young boy to madness. Yet, young as he was, I never knew quite what to make of him. He often seemed to me to be made of tougher stuff than his father.

2

For the next six years, as Frank was proceeding through high school, I regularly brought home miniature books for him. Some of them were reputed to be classics of the genre: *Portraits of the Town of Madrid*, 1741, *Le Petit Poucet*, 1800, *Customs of the Hindu Kush*, 1834, and *The English Bijou Calendar Poetically Illustrated*, 1841. They were all famous for their brilliant illustrations.

I also found a miniature bookcase built with little shelves that would accommodate Frank's collection. He fell in love with the bookcase, too.

TO MARK HIS eighteenth birthday as well as his acceptance into university, I searched for a special miniature book for him. While I was on business at a mine near Erzurum, in Eastern Turkey, I borrowed a car and drove to the ancient village of Gez, where I'd heard there was a fine bookstore. I found it halfway along the village's axle-threatening, cobblestoned main street.

The store was full of leather-bound books of all shapes and sizes and ages, as well as glass cases displaying dozens of beautiful old quill pens and inkwells. But even after looking around for almost an hour, I could see no miniature books.

I then spoke to the owner, a sophisticated Istanbul Turk who spoke English. He told me that, as a matter of fact, he did have a miniature—only one. It wasn't on display because it was too expensive to leave out. He took me to his office, opened a squat safe, and lifted out a cardboard box. He took the lid off the box and gave me a little book to examine.

It was about two inches tall and one and a half inches wide, with a leather cover and a silver latch that seemed smooth with use. The owner said it was a fourteenth-century Turkish edition of the erotic classic, the *Kama Sutra*. I undid the latch and skimmed through it. The book contained sixty-four tiny, full-colour illustrations of the famous intimate positions—at least, I presumed that's what they were; they were too small to see.

The owner offered to find me a magnifying glass to convince me of their lifelikeness, but I told him that wouldn't be necessary. I'd already decided this might be the perfect eighteenth-birthday gift for Frank and was soon engaged in the customary haggling over price. In the end, I paid more than I wanted but left the store with the book in my pocket.

WHEN I ARRIVED back in Camberloo from Turkey, Frank wasn't home. He was apartment hunting in Toronto, where he'd be attending university. I was glad of his absence, for I wasn't so sure any longer about giving him the little book. I'd had a good look at the illustrations now through the magnifying glass, and I wondered if it was a proper kind of gift from a father to a son, even though the book was a classic.

I told Alicia about my doubts and she said she'd have to have a look at it. She began examining the illustrations through the glass and was soon laughing out loud, something she rarely did.

"Good gracious! Would you look at that!" she said over and over. In the end, she'd no doubt. "Of course you must give it to him. What a great gift for anyone his age. What fun!"

So when Frank came back from Toronto, I did give it to him and he seemed delighted with it. But we never talked about its subject matter—I wouldn't have known what to say. Nor did he point out to me any interesting features of the illustrations, as he usually did. But I did see him and Alicia looking through them together and laughing.

That September, he went off to Toronto for his first semester. He left the other miniatures at home, but he took his *Kama Sutra* with him.

Alicia really missed him and I did, too, but not as much as she did—though, of course, I didn't tell her that. The fact was, since he'd grown up, he'd become more and more a mystery to me. Unlike my relationship with my own father, which had been based on an unquestioning warmth and love, there was a certain distance between me and Frank. I feared he could see right into me and found some characteristic he couldn't tolerate. I was so aware of that, it was impossible for me to be spontaneously loving towards him, as a father would like to be with his son. Even in our conversations, I was never quite sure what he wanted from me. Perhaps he needed me to be something I wasn't capable of being. Accordingly, he withheld himself from me in return.

AS FOR THE *KAMA SUTRA*, Alicia's response to the book was typical of her attitude to all things sexual. She regarded them in the same common-sense way she'd always done. I knew she felt bad about our own lack of activity in that area since the birth of Frank.

Every so often, she'd ask sympathetically if I was "doing all right," and I'd reassure her.

In spite of her natural bent for truth in most things, she didn't mind deceiving others when it came to the public image of our marriage. Whenever, for example, we had dinner guests— an infrequent occurrence—we'd behave like the ideal couple. Indeed, we both took a certain pleasure in giving convincing performances, as perhaps many other couples do.

Mainly these dinner guests were men—mine representatives who were in Camberloo for a day or two to inspect machinery at the factory—and I could see they envied me. If they happened to have their wives with them, Alicia would put on an even better show.

THE MATTER OF Lew Jonson was similar, in a way. His wife had died years before I'd arrived in Camberloo. They'd been child-less and Lew had come to regard Alicia almost as a daughter. When I was away from home on business, he'd worry she might be lonely and would phone her. Often this would end up in her inviting him to dinner.

Alicia told me about the curious rituals that took place at these dinners with Jonson. He was an opera lover and, since she was on the symphony board, he naturally thought it would be a treat for both of them to listen to some of his records after dinner. He'd no idea how much she dreaded that. Like her father, she really wasn't all that fond of music.

I once asked her why she didn't just tell him straight out and be done with it.

She shook her head vigorously.

"A dislike for music's not something I care to admit to," she said. That was as near as she ever came to acknowledging it might be a defect.

So, when Jonson brought his records along, she'd make an effort to maintain a polite interest in them. But the ecstasies of the divas and tenors that so delighted him were pure agony to her. Jonson's image of father–daughter musical soirées was as much a charade as the perfect marriage she and I presented to the world.

I'D FREQUENTLY CATCH myself thinking how wonderful it might have been if I'd married Miriam Galt. But those moments of wishful imagining were a kind of sadism, one part of my mind tormenting another. I'd immediately try to make myself think about something else, and if that effort of will didn't work I'd head out into the garden and mow the lawn or hack at the weeds. As a last resort, I'd even go up to the library and force myself to concentrate on some very technical article in the latest *International Journal of Pumps*.

On such occasions, I convinced myself that my self-discipline was necessary to avoiding madness. But I couldn't stave off the doubts—that perhaps the real madness was my ongoing attempt to forget such an important episode from my past.

Anyway, I had no defence against my dreams. In one of the most persistent of them, I'd be tramping the purple hills of Duncairn on my way to Miriam's house, my heart pounding in anticipation.

To awake from that dream, pounding heart and all, to my present reality was a refined form of torture.

OLUBA

1

In early March of Frank's first year at university, I had to leave the snows of Camberloo behind and head for the southern hemisphere on business. Gordon had had to go there often, and had told me about the rigours of getting to Fiji in the old days—it involved, amongst other things, an arduous sea voyage of several weeks and the likelihood of spells of very rough weather. But for me now it was just a case of catching a trans-Pacific flight and emerging a few hours later into warm air scented with frangipani and who knows what other perfumes.

The major business of this particular trip was done in Suva, the capital of the main island, Viti Levu. I attended numerous meetings and sold six new pumps and a variety of parts to Consolidated Minerals, the biggest mining organization on the island. We'd been trying for years without success to interest them in our pumps, so all in all it was a very satisfying piece of work.

But I didn't head home right away.

Some weeks before I left Camberloo, Jonson had received a letter from the manager of a phosphate company on Bird Island, one of the islands of the Oluban chain in the vicinity of Fiji. The gist of the letter was that Gordon, twenty-five years ago, had sold the company two pumps used in the phosphate-extraction process. The pumps were now wearing out. Records of the sale had been found by the present manager at Bird Island and he'd decided to get in touch with Smith's Pumps and inquire about possible replacements or repairs.

Jonson had shown me the letter and we'd decided I should make a side trip from Fiji. The Bird Island manager and his engineer agreed to come and meet me on the main island, Oluba.

So, after the Fijian business was settled, I set out on an inter-island schooner headed southwards for the Oluban Archipelago, a scattering of volcanic islands and coral atolls spread across three hundred miles of ocean. On the map, the chain of islands looked like some half-immersed monster, with the main island—Oluba itself—being the monster's head. I remembered how Gordon had mentioned the island to me several times, and remarked on how kind the people had been to him.

During the long day and overnight sail on the inter-island schooner, I once more suffered from the curse of seasickness. At dawn, I couldn't stand the nausea anymore and stumbled out of my cabin onto the deck to gulp in the fresh air. I noticed that what had been a smudge on the horizon the night before had turned itself into an island.

I managed, without vomiting, to ask a sailor who was coiling a line near me on deck if we were near our destination.

"Yes," he said. "That's Oluba, the main island, off the bow. The women there have tattoos and strong legs."

That was a curious remark. But I was feeling too sorry for myself to ask what he meant.

OLUBA WASN'T QUITE as near as it had seemed at dawn. In fact, my watch showed four-thirty in the afternoon as the schooner hurtled through the narrow opening in the reef into the smooth waters of the lagoon. At the same time, magically, I lost my desire to vomit and even took enough interest in my surroundings to notice a few dozen sailing ships at anchor as well as some freighters. A luxurious-looking motor yacht was moored at the same dock where our schooner tied up. Several islanders began helping our crew with the discharging of various crates and other cargo.

Dusk was already falling as I set out, bag in hand, for my hotel. I was a happy man to be on dry land again.

From what I could see, Oluba was a typical native village along a beach. It consisted of one main street and a sizable dock that protruded into the lagoon. There were the usual structures—a church, several stores with colourful signs above them, and a post office—all of them built with bamboo and other local woods. The houses had grass roofs and walls flimsy enough to let the fresh air blow through. Toilet facilities for the most part consisted of dilapidated outhouses perched over the tidal waters.

At the end of the street, I came to a hotel with an especially large sign—*The Mango Tree Hotel*. According to Gordon's records, this was where he'd always stayed when he was here. The sandy compound contained a number of bamboo huts, dominated by a main building with a woven grass roof. I made my way inside it.

Behind the check-in desk sat a woman in a blue smock with long sleeves. In the light of the overhead lamps—the hotel obviously had its own generator—the skin of her face and neck looked so damaged I thought at first she'd been in some awful accident. Then I realized the blemishes were, in fact, ornate tattoos of grasses and flowers and vines.

That brought to mind the comment of the sailor on deck, earlier that morning, about the women here. I'd never seen anyone, in all my travels, tattooed to this extent. The camouflage effect made it hard to tell her age accurately, though I guessed she was in her twenties. She had a friendly demeanour but spoke no English, not even pidgin, so we communicated in sign language. Finally she gave me a little card with the number of the hut that had been allocated to me. Written on it in several languages was the information that dinner would be served at seven. I wrote my name and business in the register and headed for my hut.

It turned out to be at the rear of the main building and had a lagoon view. The bamboo walls were painted white and the floor was covered by a rattan carpet. There was a large bed, a desk and chair, and a wardrobe. I was most pleased by the fact that the hut also had a shower and an indoor toilet.

The bedside lamp highlighted an odd feature of the room. Running above the whole length of the bed was a rounded, hardwood beam supported by posts. A flimsy mosquito net hung from that beam, which seemed to me somewhat excessive for the purpose.

After a shower to wash the salt of the voyage off my body, I put on fresh clothes and went back to the main building. To get to the dining room I had to pass through a well-stocked bar, where I ordered a scotch from the bartender, a slow-moving, bald man of about sixty. He wasn't an islander, though he did wear the traditional waist cloth. A plain white shirt bulged over his sizable belly.

As I sat at the bar with my drink, he talked to me about himself and the hotel. His name was Joe; he was an American with a slow drawl that no doubt suited the pace of life in Oluba. He'd been a soldier down here during the Second World War and had liked the place so much he came back permanently when the fighting was over.

"The hotel belongs to Anata," he said. "She's in the kitchen cooking tonight's dinner."

He was also very interested to hear about my connection to Smith's Pumps.

"I know Smith's Pumps," he said. "Gordon Smith used to come down here. We haven't seen him now in maybe twenty years."

I told him that Gordon had actually been dead for eighteen years.

"Gordon's dead?" He seemed shocked. "Well, I'm sorry to hear that."

He turned and called out into the dining room in the local language. A grey-haired island woman emerged from inside and joined us.

This was Anata, the owner of the Mango Tree Hotel, and she certainly made an interesting first impression. She had long grey hair, and her face and bare shoulders and arms were completely covered in tattoos of what appeared to be vines, lianas, and tropical plants. These tattooed plants seemed to be wilting with age, like Anata herself. She wore a kind of sarong that was slit from ankle to thigh, so I could see that her legs were also tattooed with vegetation. Those legs looked remarkably muscular for a woman past the prime of life.

Joe spoke quietly to her in the local language. Gordon's name was mentioned several times.

She looked shocked at what he'd said. She turned to me and began to talk quickly in her own language. What with the tattoos all over her face, it was almost as if she was talking from behind a potted plant. Of course, I couldn't understand what she was saying, though again I heard Gordon's name.

When she'd finished, Joe gave me the very briefest of translations.

"She's very upset to hear about Gordon," he said. "He was very generous to her."

He would have said more but just then a half-dozen or so other diners appeared—apparently, sailors from one of the freighters anchored off shore. Joe had to turn his attention to bartender duties for the new guests and Anata had to get back to her cooking.

THE DINNER CONSISTED of fresh fish from the lagoon, washed down with palm wine. The latter was surprisingly pleasant tasting, and I had a little bit too much. The sailors at the other tables were drinking it, and getting quite rowdy, so I went back to my room. I was tired after my sleepless night on the voyage, so I thought I'd read for a while then get to bed early.

Before I could even open my book, though, the lamp had attracted mosquitoes and the little biting insects they called *nonos* in Fiji. So I undressed and got into bed under the mosquito net with the book, *Unveiling the Islands*. I'd found it in a bookstore in Suva and was attracted to it because the cover mentioned that it dealt with Oluba and was written by one of the first Western travellers there, an anthropologist named Ireneus Fludd.

In the first chapter, Fludd talks about the pervasive use of tattoos, especially amongst the Oluban women. He attributes the practice to a vegetation and fertility cult that was widespread in the region. He also makes particular mention of the women's legs:

Muscular legs are regarded as most desirable attributes amongst the Oluban women. As I walked along the
beach on my first days on the island, I observed the male
islanders mending their fishing nets and the woven sails
of their outrigger canoes. But much more fascinating was
to see the women of all ages doing vigorous knee bends
and other leg exercises. Upon my inquiry, one of the Oluban chiefs explained that the exercise was for the rite of
paratac, a word unfamiliar to me at that time.

Fludd was soon to discover both the meaning of that word
and the purpose of those leg-strengthening routines.

He'd been invited by the Oluban chief to attend a banquet.
When the festivities were over, the chief, following an Oluban
custom to help make strangers feel at home, presented him with
one of his daughters as a temporary gift.

The chief's daughter took him to a nearby dwelling place.
Inside, about five feet above the floor, a thick wooden beam had
been erected in the manner of a horizontal training bar used in
gymnastics.

Fludd faithfully records what happened there:

She divested herself of her sarong and, with an acrobatic move, she hooked her legs over that heavy beam
and hung there upside down, her black hair dangling to
the floor. She held out her arms to me, then slowly lifted
me up by the waist, her own great legs taking the combined weight of us both, and turned me upside down till
we were face to face. In this position, she inserted me into
her and clung to me.

"*Paratac*," she said.

She began gently to swing back and forth, back and forth, causing me to move, by the law of gravity, up and down, up and down.

Soon she was gasping and howling words in her own language. I felt I ought to participate so I began shouting appropriate words in English. My vocal participation seemed to rouse her even more, which, I feel I must confess, aroused me still more.

After a brief frenzy, we dangled silently. Then she slowly turned me upright again, lowered me to the ground, and unhooked herself. I understood that *paratac* was finished.

I looked from the book up to that beam over my bed. Surely it must have been put there originally for the purposes of *paratac*. The whole exercise, as described by Fludd, sounded anything but enticing.

I went back to my reading. The next chapters in Fludd's book consisted of rather technical analyses of the complex system of totems espoused by the Olubans. That acrobatic sex act of *paratac*, for example, was itself totemic: it mimicked the behaviour of fruit bats, which Fludd said he himself thereafter observed propagating upside down in the heights of coconut palms.

These technical chapters were, no doubt, the kinds of things an anthropologist might savour. But for me, lying there sweating under the mosquito net, exhausted from my journey, drowsy both from the palm wine and the effort of trying to keep my eyes open, they were too much. I gave up the effort, switched off the lamp, and fell asleep.

2

The next morning, I showered and dressed for the business that had brought me here: my meeting with representatives of Bird Island Phosphates. The island was actually a hundred miles south of Oluba itself, but to spare me another sea voyage, the manager and the chief engineer had come to Oluba's harbour. We were to conduct our business on the company vessel before they caught the noon tide back to Bird Island.

I strolled down to the harbour and realized that the company boat was none other than that expensive-looking motor yacht I'd noticed tied up at dock. The manager of Bird Island Phosphates and his engineer welcomed me aboard. Both were Englishmen of about my own age and appeared to be good friends. Our meeting was held under the deck awning.

That morning it was low tide and the lagoon was shallow, with weeds and corals protruding. The air was full of the strong smell of rotting vegetation as well as whatever other dead things lay exposed to the sun. In the distance we could see the surf breaking on the reef against a backdrop of the endless dark blue of the ocean.

The engineer had brought photographs of the two pumps Gordon had sold the phosphate company so long ago. They were an early model and the cylinder blocks and valve plates were very worn, which meant the pistons were no longer able to function with much efficiency.

From the engineer's comments it was clear that he was hoping the old pumps couldn't be repaired. He devoted much of his time on Bird Island trying to keep them running but felt it was now becoming a losing battle. He'd seen our recent catalogue and was keen on buying new pumps. Either way, a decision had to be made quickly. The pumps were vital because much of the phosphate was beneath sea level and the diggings were prone to flooding.

The manager obviously sympathized with his friend, but his job was to consider finances. He wondered if by replacing the worn parts he would save money and also have pumps that again ran efficiently.

I could see they'd had this debate often before. Indeed, I'd often heard it in similar situations.

"Sure, we could buy new parts," said the engineer. "But they'd just reveal other weaknesses in the pumps. Then we'd have to buy even more new parts. It's a vicious circle." He looked to me for support. "We might end up replacing so many parts that it would be like buying new pumps at ten times the expense, isn't that so?"

I couldn't have made a better sales pitch myself. Diplomatically, however, I told the manager he was right that it might be possible to repair the pumps. But that his engineer was right, too, about the problems that might result from putting new parts in old machines.

Now I played the card I'd discussed with Jonson before leaving Camberloo. Because of Bird Island Phosphates' loyalty to Smith's, I'd offer a substantial discount on two new pumps as well as free delivery and a ten-year warranty.

After hearing the details, the manager was won over. His friend, the engineer, was delighted. A deal was signed.

"Let's drink to it," the manager said.

SITTING THERE SWEATING under the deck awning, we drank several glasses of scotch and we talked. I learned that their brand of phosphate was in demand throughout the world for agricultural fertilizer. The workers who extracted it were brought in

from other islands. These two Englishmen, like all their predecessors, were hired on three-year contracts. They made it clear
they'd stay for that exact time and not a day more.

"No one could live on Bird Island for longer than three
years without going mad," said the engineer. "It isn't a fit place
for human beings. It shouldn't even be called an island. It's just
thousands of years of bird droppings heaped up on a coral reef.
The flies are so bad that when you approach from the sea, you'd
swear they were clouds of smoke from a volcano."

We laughed at his description. I remembered such pillars of
flies over the battlefield near Dupont's hospital in Africa.

"Thankfully, by the time the new pumps are installed, our
stint will be just about finished," the manager said. They'd go
back to England for six months' rest and recuperation, then they'd
be assigned to some other remote place. It certainly couldn't be
any worse than Bird Island.

I could see in their faces signs of the ravages of malaria and
isolation. So I was curious to know, in view of what they'd told
me, why any man would willingly spend part of his life in a place
like Bird Island.

The engineer looked at me for a moment, sizing me up.

"There's a Bird Island in everyone's life," he said.

We all laughed at that, probably because of the scotch.

3

After dinner that night, my last night in the Mango Tree Hotel,
I went to the verandah of the main hut and settled down in a
deep rattan couch that looked out over the lagoon. I'd brought
along my glass and the remains of a jug of the palm wine.

It was one of those idyllic South Sea Island moments, only slightly spoiled by the angry whine of mosquitoes that couldn't make up their minds between the verandah lantern and my neck. On the beach below, palm trees creaked and sighed in the warm night wind. The lagoon was dotted with outriggers from which Oluban fishermen dangled lanterns to mesmerize the fish. In the skies far above, an oversized moon hung amidst endless clusters of stars.

AFTER ONLY FIVE minutes or so, I heard a squeaking of floorboards and a rustling of clothing. I looked round.

At the entranceway to the verandah was the woman who'd signed me in at the reception desk upon my arrival. She stood there, watching me through the foliage of tattooed vegetation covering her face. She was wearing a red sarong and carrying a little woven purse. Her hair was long and black, with a white orchid over her left ear.

Since she spoke no English, I gestured to a rattan chair beside the couch and waved an invitation to her to come and sit. But instead of sitting on the chair, she came and sat down beside me on the couch with her woven purse in her lap. Her skin glistened with some sort of perfumed oil. What with that and the plant tattoos, she was like a scented garden.

I pointed at myself.

"Harry," I said.

She pointed at herself.

"Maratawi."

The word sounded to me like a song.

"Would you like some wine, Maratawi?" I said, holding up my glass.

She nodded.

In my drunken state, I easily imagined that the old custom in Fludd's *Unveiling the Islands* was still in effect and that this beautiful woman had been sent to me, a stranger, to make me feel at home.

And indeed, one thing led to another—or, one glass of wine led to another. And soon enough Maratami was in my hut, my clothes strewn over the floor and her red sarong beside them. On the bed, we massaged each other with a little phial of oil she'd taken from that woven purse. Her thighs didn't look at all muscular, but I couldn't help being aware of the heavy wooden beam that supported the mosquito net above us. I prepared myself mentally for the delicious ordeal ahead.

There was no need.

What we proceeded to do was done in bed in the good old-fashioned way, a bit noisy but most satisfying. Afterwards, we both fell asleep. About two in the morning I awoke and saw that she was gone. I didn't stay awake long. Owing to the combined effects of the palm liquor and my exertions, I fell back into a deep sleep.

THE NEXT MORNING I awoke with a splitting headache and a great deal of remorse over my activities of the night before. On my way to the dining room for breakfast I had to pass the reception area and was relieved to see that Maratawi wasn't there. Joe, the bartender, brought me breadfruit rolls and coffee right away.

"You look tired," he said. "No wonder. You and Maratawi had quite a time last night. Our room's at the other end of the hotel and we could hear you. We thought we'd never get to sleep."

Clearly, a hotel made of grass wasn't the best place to keep secrets. I didn't answer him but he stayed by the table, wanting to talk.

"Maratawi won't be in today," he said. "She's home with her husband and her two children."

That unwanted information made me feel much worse. But more was to come.

"You've heard of *paratac?*" he said.

I nodded, not knowing quite what to expect.

"Gordon and Anata used to do it together," Joe said. "That was in the days when the women still did it. The last few times he was here, he said he was too old to do it anymore and felt bad about that. After *paratac*, I guess it was hard for him to go back to the usual thing."

I was speechless. Gordon used to indulge in athletic sex with that tattooed Oluban woman! Again, it wasn't quite the image of the business-monk I'd usually associated with him.

Joe, the bartender, wasn't finished with his revelations.

"Maratawi's their daughter," he said. "That was one of the reasons he kept on coming down here—to see how she was getting on."

Now I was really shocked. If what he said was true, I, who was legally married to one of Gordon's daughters, had just slept with another whose existence he'd never mentioned.

"You can thank Anata for sending Maratawi to you last night to keep you company," Joe said. "It's no big deal down here so long as you both had fun."

At that moment, the tattooed Anata came shuffling in like a plant with legs.

It was hard enough for me to comprehend how a mother could have done such a thing to her daughter. What would she think if she knew I was married to another of Gordon's daughters—or would she even mind?

"When Gordon found out Anata was pregnant with Maratawi," he gave her the money to buy this hotel and make it what it is," Joe was saying. "He wanted them to be comfortable for the rest of their lives. With Gordon's blessing, Anata took me for a husband and we really cleaned this place up. Businessmen and sea captains usually stay here when they're in town. We hope you'll do the same any time you're here. Maratawi will always be happy to come and keep you company."

AROUND FIVE THAT afternoon, I was on the deck of the inter-island schooner looking back at Oluba. Anata and Joe waved to me from the dock and I waved to them. We navigated the opening in the reef successfully and entered the open ocean, heading for Fiji. The wind was fair and the blue sky was pocked with tiny clouds.

The figures on the beach were now becoming quite small. I borrowed a pair of binoculars from the first mate and focused them. Anata and Joe were waving, and they'd been joined by a third figure—Maratawi. I waved back, though I doubted they could see me any longer. But they stayed there waving, tinier and tinier, and I, out of courtesy, waved back till at six o'clock darkness fell like an axe.

ON THAT RETURN voyage to Fiji, when I didn't feel too seasick, I went over again and again the significance of my Oluban experience.

I'd had my night of pleasure with Maratawi in an updated version of an ancient Oluban custom. But the more I thought about it, the more I flinched at the idea of having been to bed with another of Gordon's daughters. Technically, it may not

277

have been incest. But if I'd known before the act took place, no amount of palm liquor would have enticed me into it. I did know now, even if no one else ever would, so I'd have to live with it.

I also pondered the stunning discovery I'd made about Gordon Smith's exploits on Oluba. Once again I realized that though I'd been close to him, I'd barely known him. Which should, of course, have been no surprise. When we take such care to disguise our true feelings from others, why would we expect them to be an open book to us?

These things filled my mind for that entire journey. By the time the schooner sailed into the harbour at Nani the next day, I'd made up my mind on one thing at least: Oluba would never see me again.

<h1 style="text-align:center">4</h1>

A bitterly cold northeaster, precursor of a late March blizzard, was scouring the streets of Camberloo on the morning of my return. But Alicia's greeting was unusually warm. With me away and Frank at university in Toronto, she'd felt lonely. She'd adopted a cat to keep her company, which surprised me. Both she and Gordon had never seemed fond of pets—cats especially, perhaps for their unpredictability.

I went to bed at noon and slept for several hours to make up for the disruption caused by the change in time zones. When I woke I felt much better. At six o'clock, Alicia and I had dinner together then went into the library for coffee and brandy. I sat in the armchair near the blazing fire. Alicia sat opposite on the sofa.

On her knee was her cat, Miss Sophie, a little ivory Siamese who already seemed very much at home.

As ever, I couldn't help admiring Alicia, sitting there. How beautiful and mysterious she looked, with her dark eyes and her long hair partly covering her face. She was in an unusually talkative mood and asked more questions about my trip than she normally did. I told her that after Fiji I'd spent a couple of days on an island called Oluba.

"Oluba?" she said, suddenly very interested. "I didn't know you were going there."

I explained it had been a last-minute addition to my plans.

"Please tell me more about Oluba," she said. "Gordon used to love it there."

I went on at length about the coral reefs, white beaches, and palm trees, then about my interesting meeting with the two men from Bird Island and the horrors of their situation.

"Is the Mango Tree Hotel still there?" she said.

Her familiarity with that name surprised me. I admitted that was where I'd stayed.

"Gordon used to talk a lot about it," she said. "That was where he always stayed, too. The owner back then was a woman called Anata. I don't suppose you met her?"

I was cautious now, for Gordon's sake as well as my own. Yes, as a matter of fact, Anata still owned the hotel. She was an elderly woman.

"Gordon said she was one of the most beautiful women he'd ever met," said Alicia. "He gave her the money to buy the hotel—apparently it had a lot of potential."

I didn't like the way this was going.

"In a way, it was repayment for services rendered," she said.

I put on a puzzled face.

"Oh, yes," Alicia said. "She was quite an athlete in bed—at least in those days. *Paratac*, or something like that, I think he called it."

To hear her use that word and to realize Gordon had actually told her about his bedroom activities in Oluba shouldn't have surprised me, but once more it did. What an unorthodox father–daughter relationship they'd had.

More was to come.

"Anata didn't mention they'd had a little daughter together?" she said.

A daughter? I put on a surprised look and explained I'd barely seen Anata, and anyway she spoke no English.

"Maratawi was the name they gave the little girl," said Alicia. "Isn't that a delightful name? I was six when she was born. 'You have a little half-sister at the other end of the world,' Gordon used to say. She must be quite grown up by now." She was looking right into me. "You're sure you didn't meet someone called Maratawi?"

Of course, I denied it.

She was in so many ways a complete mystery to me, I often felt quite out of my depth with her. How would she react if I told her everything, including my drunken fling with her half-sister? Would she be upset? Or would she be amused? Of course, I just kept quiet.

"If you ever go back to Oluba," she said, "make a point of looking up Maratawi. After all, she is your sister-in-law."

I assured her I would do as she said, though I did wonder why she herself had never shown any great interest in meeting her half-sister. She was looking at me quite skeptically, still not satisfied with my account of the trip.

"You should know by now you can tell me the truth," she said. "If there's one thing I can't stand, it's not being told the truth."

I changed the subject and asked her if she'd ever told Frank about her half-sister in Oluba. After all, Maratawi was his aunt or half-aunt.

Alicia fell for the diversion.

"No, I haven't yet," she said. "Please don't mention it to him. I'm saving it as a big surprise for him someday soon."

IN THE END, I promised her I'd look up Maratawi next time I was in Oluba. I felt no need to tell her I'd already resolved never to go back there again.

THE EMPORIUM

1

Frank graduated with a degree in fine arts that had allowed him to make a special study of old furniture as well as rare books. He was by now a young-looking twenty-two and had the dark brown hair and eyes of his mother. In fact, physically he was like her in many ways. A stranger might have thought it ironic that the genes of a woman who tended to avoid society could be so domineering when it came to stamping their image on our son. The only noteworthy thing he took from me was his nose, which had a slight leftwards hook to it.

So I was always puzzled when Alicia would say, as she often did, "Frank's more like you than you think." I presumed she must mean in temperament, or personality, and was surprised she should think so.

After graduating he came back to live in Camberloo, but not with us. He wanted his own place, a natural thing for a young man to do. Alicia was, of course, disappointed at that but arranged an apartment for him in the building beside the park where I myself had lived on first coming to Camberloo. When

I helped Frank move in his things I felt quite nostalgic, thinking back to that period in my own life.

AS TO WHAT FRANK might make of himself, Alicia and I had assumed that in the course of time he'd take his place in the family business, though he'd never shown much interest in pumps. But it turned out he had his own ideas about his future.

He joined us for dinner one night not long after he'd moved into his apartment and presented us with a plan he'd clearly been thinking about for some time. It was this: he wanted to open a store that specialized in rare objects, particularly furniture and books. He'd done his homework and felt that such a store would be unique to Camberloo and the area around it.

"Those gifts you used to bring me when I was growing up—you know how much I always loved them," he said to me. "When I got to university, I began to think: wouldn't it be great to own a place that stocked things like that? It was at the back of my mind all through my degree."

That surprised me. I wasn't quite sure what I felt at being told I was the root cause of this unexpected announcement. Alicia—not surprisingly, for she always indulged him—didn't seem to mind too much that he'd no desire to join me at Smith's Pumps. And I suppose I didn't really mind much either, though for different reasons—I'd often worried that we might not work well together, and that when he fully understood those ethical compromises I'd made, he'd think even less of me.

We began discussing in a general way how he might put his plan into action by finding a suitable store for lease and stocking it with suitable items—naturally, we expected to play a major role in financial matters. We all agreed that a downtown location would be best, and encouraged him to make further explorations.

AFTER FRANK LEFT that night, Alicia and I talked about his scheme. We were both realistic about its lack of realism: the kind of store he had in mind probably wouldn't do much business. But we wanted him to be happy, above all.

That was when our talk took a quite unexpected turn.

"If anything ever happens to me, will you promise to look after him and make sure he doesn't mess up his life?" said Alicia.

I scoffed at the notion of anything ever happening to her— she'd outlive me by decades. But she was in a serious mood, so I promised her I'd always be there to advise him. Not that I really believed sons are inclined to take their fathers' advice in these matters—especially a son with whom the father had never really been at ease.

My promise seemed to alleviate whatever fears she had.

"Thank you for that." She smiled. "And don't worry. I fully expect to outlive you, too."

IN THE FALL, Frank leased a moderately sized old store—it had formerly sold shoes—on the corner of King and Delta near the City Hall. Much of the building looked as though it was unchanged since the 1920s, with crumbling brick walls and creaky plank flooring. Frank was especially charmed that it still had an ancient pneumatic-tube system: from the front counter, orders and cash would whiz overhead through a brass tube to the business office at the rear.

He himself was on the road quite a bit at this time, acquiring items for his store, but he also directed its renovations. Though that was hardly the right word. Frank's notion of renovation was actually more like a restoration of the building to its primal state, revealing the interior brick behind the plaster and uncovering the pipes of its antique heating system. If there had been some way to restore even the unique odours the store must have had in its heyday, he'd have been very pleased.

2

In November, Smith's Emporium opened for business without much fanfare. The use of the family name pleased Alicia a great deal. The night before the opening, while Alicia was attending one of her board meetings, Frank called and asked me if I'd like to come and have a preview of his collection.

"I'd like to hear your opinion of it," he said.

I must admit I was delighted at the invitation. Perhaps this was a sign of a positive development in our relationship. So I met him at the store for a guided tour.

EVEN THOUGH THE Emporium wasn't all that big, he'd split it into two distinctive areas, or "galleries" as he named them. The Furniture Gallery began just inside the front door and was guarded by four tenth-century Chinese temple lions. To fill this area, Frank had purchased almost the entire stock of a New York antiquities firm that had gone bankrupt. Included was an array of items from various centuries—armoires, walnut buffets, uncomfortable stool chairs, and heavy oak tables, as well as the four lions. All the acquisitions on display had little cards beside them to indicate their origins.

Some of the pieces were quite remarkable. Taking pride of place was an early Renaissance clothes trunk with inlaid panels that showed daily life in a ducal palace. Not far behind was a seventeenth-century French *vaisselier* containing porcelain serving plates, many of them broken and carefully glued together, depicting pastoral scenes.

A special section of the Furniture Gallery contained Frank's own personal favourites. Protruding from the wall above them was an armless female nude figurehead from a Spanish galleon found off the coast of Florida. A worn-looking black walnut credence table from Peru had been used by the servants of conquistador Hernán Cortés to check his food for poison—several of them had, as a result, died in agony. An elaborate Florentine commode was from the bedroom of Maddalena de' Medici, who'd been married to a son of the most depraved of pontiffs, the murderous Pope Innocent VIII. Near the commode were some folding military chairs from the American Civil War. A stain on the faded yellowish cushion of one of them had been identified as the blood of a Confederate officer at the Battle of Chickamauga.

THE FURNITURE GALLERY overflowed into the Book Gallery, which took up the rest of the store. It was mainly a repository of old leather-bound books in Latin. Their subjects weren't all that enticing—treatises on horticulture, collections of prayers and pious meditations—but it was an extreme pleasure for a book lover just to caress them, skim through their ancient pages, and even inhale their ancient dust.

Some of the books in the "erotica" section were certainly eye-catching for other reasons. These were privately printed and hard to obtain. Amongst them were such titles as *The Fair Concubine, Venus the Flagellant, The Discreet Copulator,* and *The Dildoad—An Epic.* The authors of these books had wisely chosen to remain anonymous, for the most part.

FOR ME, the most fascinating part of the Book Gallery was a glass case near the back, with a sign over it: *Four of the Great Lost Books of the West*. The four books on display in the case had printed cards beside them with information on the books themselves as well as on the reputable European dealerships from which Frank had acquired them.

The books were aligned in chronological order.

The first was a tattered-looking volume entitled *Inventio Infortunata*. This was an anonymous, fourteenth-century eyewitness account of the seemingly impossible: a visit to the Arctic. The book had been mentioned by various scholars in subsequent centuries, but no other copy of it had ever been found.

The second book was a stained, cloth-bound work, *Les Journées de Florbelle*. Apparently this was volume nine of an erotic epic handwritten by the Marquis de Sade while in the lunatic asylum where he spent much of his life. Scholars had formerly believed that the entire work was destroyed by de Sade's son after its author died in the asylum.

The third of the books was really just a smoke- and fire-damaged writing tablet with the title, *My Secret Love*, scrawled on the cover. This was a pen-and-ink account, by Robert Louis Stevenson, of his affair with a Samoan woman. His wife, Fanny Osbourne, had found it in his bedside drawer after his death and thrown it into the fire. It was later retrieved by a servant.

The fourth wasn't a published book either, but a hefty manuscript in a peculiar, leathery-looking binder. Typed on it were the title and the author's name:

The Poor Man and the Lady
by
Thomas Hardy

This was a draft of Hardy's first novel, the only one not published. He'd held on to the manuscript nevertheless, and used parts of it in other of his works. Upon Hardy's death, according to his biographers, his heart was surgically removed from his chest to be buried in his wife's grave. The excised heart was left momentarily in a biscuit tin on his kitchen table. When no one was looking, Hardy's favourite cat crept in through an open window, knocked the lid off the tin, and devoured part of his master's heart. The leathery-looking binder holding this manuscript was actually made from the skin of that cat.

THAT FIRST TIME I looked into the glass case containing *Four of the Great Lost Books of the West* and read the accompanying notes, I asked Frank if these literary works really were authentic.

"Well, in their day, they were considered genuine by some experts and were included in authoritative bibliographies," Frank said. "But now scholars using the latest scientific research tools have discredited them. There's no doubt about it. They're all definitely forgeries."

I wondered in that case why he'd acquired them. I couldn't believe anyone would want to read or collect such frauds.

"The truth is they seem so genuine you'd like to think they were the real thing," Frank said. "Collectors are willing to pay a lot for fakes of this high calibre. Even when you already know they're fakes, you can't help admiring what perfectionists the forgers were and the sweat that must have gone into the work. First of all they had to master the exact mannerisms and styles of the authors—even their handwriting. Then the paper, the bindings, and the inks had to be so authentic looking that even experts would be taken in. I really believe the authors they were copying would have been flattered."

I was skeptical about this downplaying of the difference between the fake and the genuine.

"You're entitled to your point of view," said Frank. "But I'd argue that some fake books, just like some fake paintings, are actually *better* than the artists they imitate. In fact, they're too good—and that's how they give themselves away."

He offered to let me read the four books whenever I had time, and see for myself. The very idea made me uneasy.

RIGHT AT THE BACK of the Book Gallery, in a corner by his office, Frank kept his miniatures in an illuminated bookcase with glass doors. All of those I'd given him through the years were there, along with others he'd since bought. His latest acquisition was a nineteenth-century *Complete Works of Shakespeare* handwritten on the backs of seven hundred Victorian Penny Black stamps.

This masterpiece of crazed devotion was apparently produced in a penal colony in Australia by an Englishman—an actor who was serving twenty-five years for a botched bank robbery. The robbery was undertaken in London to help finance a travelling performance of *The Tempest* with himself playing Prospero. He was sentenced to deportation to Van Diemen's Land for twenty-five years. He worked on his miniature *Shakespeare* for exactly that length of time, finished it, and promptly died.

"He copied it all out with strands of his own hair," Frank told me. "You need a triple-strength magnifying glass to read it."

HE WAS ESPECIALLY proud of the desk in his small office. One entire wall and most of the floor space were taken up by it. It was a labyrinthine Georgian bureau, five feet tall and four feet wide, checkered with drawers and cubbyholes and sliding panels. The bureau was made to be assembled in any location the buyer wanted. It could be taken to pieces and reassembled if it ever needed to be moved.

"We discovered that it's a few days' work to put it together, but it's well worth the trouble," said Frank. "I bought it from an Irish dealer who thought it was possibly the very desk where Swift wrote *Gulliver's Travels*." He opened one of the drawers and handed me what looked like a pair of eyeglasses. "The dealer found these in it. Try them on."

I did try them on: the right eye magnified objects and the left minimized them. Frank was either a giant or a tiny puppet depending on which eye I closed. I started to feel quite nauseated and quickly took the things off.

"Glasses like these really were used in the Middle Ages by students of ancient philosophy," Frank said. "They were fascinated by the idea of proportion in nature and in the universe in general. So that dealer who sold me the desk could have been right about Swift having owned it. You remember in *Gulliver's Travels* the little people from Lilliput and the giants from Brobdingnag? Swift may have worn this very pair of glasses as part of his research."

He saw I was impressed and smiled.

"On the other hand, Irish antiquity dealers are notorious for their far-fetched sales pitches, so he probably put the glasses in the drawer himself," he said. "Anyway, Swift or no Swift, I love the idea and I've no intention of ever selling this desk."

Another of his acquisitions was on display above the desk—a weird-looking wall clock. The preserved skeleton of a hare was stretched out in full flight, with an old-fashioned clock mechanism set into its ribcage. The clock's ponderous *tick-tock, tick-tock* was quite at odds with the suggestion of the hare's breakneck speed.

Frank could see how the clock delighted me.

"I hate to disappoint you, but it's not for sale either," he said.

I was beginning to get the feeling that he wouldn't care if no one bought anything from Smith's Emporium—it was more his private museum than a commercial enterprise.

From that night onwards, something changed in the way Frank and I got along. He couldn't hide his satisfaction that I'd been so clearly impressed by his collection. That very fact, in turn, was gratifying to me, too, for till then I hadn't been sure my reactions would have been of much importance to him.

Alicia had occasionally worried that this collecting obsession of his was a substitute for "real living," and in the past I'd tended to agree with her. But after that night of the guided tour, I tried to persuade her that, even though his collecting might not seem practical and useful in the sense of a normal business such as Smith's Pumps, perhaps it was a much more fulfilling and sane occupation for a human being—especially one we loved. Much as she did indeed love Frank, I could see she wasn't quite sure what I meant by my defence of his choice of work, for she was still Gordon's daughter.

3

Frank certainly did love his work, and would often stay at the store long after six o'clock, its official closing time. Occasionally, if I happened to be driving past and saw his office light still on, I'd ask the chauffeur to drop me off and go on home. Then I'd rap on the store window to get Frank's attention. He seemed to enjoy my visits, and that pleased me immensely. Besides which, I liked to have a look at his latest acquisitions—his reasons for having chosen them might perhaps give me some deeper insight into Frank himself.

He even displayed a sense of humour to me now, something he'd rarely done before.

One particular night when I knocked on the store window, he came and opened the front door just as a man passed by with two dogs on leashes, out for their evening walk. One of the dogs was big and slow moving, with a melancholy hound's face. The other was a tiny bright-eyed terrier, snarling and snapping at the big dog's legs.

"Just like a married couple, eh?" Frank said.

Laughing together, the way a father and son should, we went inside the store. There he showed me an ancient Egyptian cube he'd just bought. It was made of marble, about six inches tall, with hieroglyphs sculpted out on all four sides. Egyptologists had apparently been unable to decipher their meaning.

I speculated that, in time, someone would surely figure it out.

"I hope not," said Frank. "There's something very appealing about the idea of a mystery that never explains itself—just like our own minds." He looked at me as though that might apply to us, and the fact that we didn't really understand each other might not be such a bad thing.

HE HAD A GIRLFRIEND at that time who was a reporter for *The Camberloo Record*. By pulling some strings she arranged for an article on the store to appear in the newspaper's weekend edition, together with a photo of Frank sitting at his big Georgian desk. The headline read: *The Emperor in His Emporium*.

For a few weeks, as a result of that publicity, quite a number of townspeople dropped by just to see what all the fuss was about. Naturally, the bulk of them found the pieces on display either too expensive or too odd for their tastes, or both.

It was hard to imagine, for instance, that many customers could envisage on their living-room tables one of Frank's very latest acquisitions—a yellowing glass laboratory bottle found in the south of Tierra del Fuego. It contained the pickled genitals of a Russian explorer who'd participated in one of those doomed expeditions to Antarctica at the end of the nineteenth century. The card beside the bottle explained that the contents were all that was left of his body. Apparently the survivors of the expedition had cannibalized the rest of him.

At any rate, after the early interest roused by the newspaper article, the flow of visitors to the store began to dwindle. Frank clearly didn't mind. As I'd already come to suspect, for the most part the Emporium was really his private collection, masquerading as a place of business.

4

Almost a year of relative tranquility followed the opening of the Emporium. I was in my office on a Friday afternoon in the fall discussing some business matter with Jonson, who was about to leave for home. He was putting on his raincoat and looking out the window over Camberloo Square at the big trees, already changing colour.

I couldn't help remarking on how beautiful they were.

"That depends on your perspective," said Jonson. "From a scientific standpoint, this changing of colour is a kind of strangulation. The mottling of the leaves is the effect of the deprivation of sunlight. To say it's beautiful is like saying a man who's being suffocated turns a beautiful colour."

I didn't make any comment. I was just thankful I was no scientist. Jonson had barely shut the door behind him when the phone rang.

It was Frank, and his voice was anxious.

"I dropped by the house for a cup of coffee with Mother," he said. "She's here, but something's wrong. Please, come quickly."

A VERY WORRIED-LOOKING Frank opened the front door for me when I arrived.

"She's in the bathroom and she won't answer," he said. "I can't get the door open and I didn't know what to do."

We were both aware that Alicia's midday bath was one of her indispensable rituals. But it was after three o'clock now. She should have finished long ago.

We went upstairs to the main bathroom. The cat, Miss Sophie, was prowling outside the door. I knocked and called Alicia's name. Just as Frank had, I tried the handle but it was locked on the inside. So I put my shoulder to the door, it burst open, and I went in.

Miss Sophie ran past me, jumped onto the ledge around the tub, and saw what I saw.

ALICIA WAS LYING on her back in the almost-full bathtub. The marble ledge held a half-dozen candles, two of them guttering, near burnt out, giving off an incense fragrance. The water was very clear, and she looked quite beautiful and peaceful, her breasts and her arms slightly afloat. Her eyes were open, looking up at me, her lips slightly apart, showing her teeth. You might have thought she was alive and well but for the fact that those eyes were under an inch or two of water. I bent over and touched her shoulder. It was cold and the water was cold.

Frank was still outside in the hallway.

"What's wrong?" he called to me.

I told him his mother had drowned.

"Oh, no," he said.

I thought it just as well that he shouldn't see her dead and naked. So I told him to go downstairs and call the police. Meantime, I sat on the toilet seat. Miss Sophie, disappointed at Alicia's lack of responsiveness, jumped on my knee to be petted.

There was something comforting about the whole scene: the candles still burning, the cat purring, Alicia half floating in her tub, quite relaxed looking, as if meditating. You might even have thought she had a little trace of a smile on her face, except that the water was cold, which I knew she wouldn't have liked one bit.

THE POLICE QUICKLY ruled out foul play: the bathroom door and the window could only be locked from the inside. When the coroner arrived not long after and let the water out of the tub to examine her, he found a bad bruise on the back of her head. That enabled him to rule out suicide. In his view, she'd most likely slipped getting into the tub and been knocked unconscious when her head hit the marble or the faucet. Nor were her lungs full of water, so the combination of the blow to the head and the rapid blocking of the nasal passage probably caused her death.

"I'm sorry for your loss," he said to Frank and me when he eventually came downstairs. He was an elderly man with a sad, lined face and had the air of someone who'd seen many awful things but retained his humanity. "It's always distressing for the loved ones when the death's so unexpected," he said. "For what it's worth, I can tell you the way she went was just about as pleasant as any of us could ever hope for."

I thanked him. Then he and his assistants left with the body.

Frank sat on the living-room couch sobbing quietly. He was in the kind of shock I'd once experienced myself. This, his first real experience of death, was the death of the person who'd adored him.

FOR MYSELF, I was deeply affected by Alicia's death, indeed much more than I'd ever have guessed. All these years, I'd convinced myself that whatever my relationship with her had been, it wasn't a union of soul mates, the kind that ends with broken hearts— the kind I'd had with Miriam.

But now I was beginning to grasp that, while Miriam had become a ghost, receding more and more into the corners of my memory, Alicia had been my unfailing best friend and ally. She'd loved me totally in her own way. Without realizing it, little by little, I'd come to love her too.

I thought of what the coroner had said—that it wasn't a bad way for her to go. The image of her sliding unconscious into the warm water, her last breaths scented with spices from her candles, was somehow consoling. If I'd died like that, she'd probably have felt much the same way.

THREE DAYS LATER, we cremated Alicia. An unexpected guest, Gordon's doctor—twenty years older now, but still wearing a polka-dot bow tie—showed up for the occasion. I was taken aback to learn from him that both Alicia *and* Gordon had requested their carotids be slashed before being wheeled into the incinerator.

That reminded me of how, one night not long after Gordon's death, I'd picked up the illustrated *History of Scotland* he often read. The corner of a page was turned down at a section on premature burial, which was relatively common right up to the nineteenth century. To avoid this unpleasant possibility, some of the dying would ask that after being pronounced dead, their carotid arteries be cut. They didn't want to wake up and find themselves underground in a coffin—or even worse, in the hell of a crematorium furnace.

I'd torn that page out of the book and destroyed it, thinking it might distress Alicia if she came across it. But all these years, she'd kept their pact secret, knowing it would distress me.

LATER THAT DAY, in a light rain, Frank, Jonson, and I buried her ashes under the very rose bush where Gordon's ashes had been intermingled with the earth decades before. The bush had always looked healthy enough but had produced no roses, despite Alicia's loving care for it.

Afterwards in the house, over drinks, Jonson asked me about the derivation of our little burial service. I told him about the South American tribes who believed that the best orchids grew on top of corpses, beauty springing out of tragedy.

"Ah" was all he said. He wasn't the sentimental type.

But I liked the idea of the ritual, even if only as a symbol. Surely there was no harm in wishing that out of the dust of Gordon and Alicia, two people who'd done so much for me—loved me—something beautiful might arise.

5

A year had passed since Alicia's death. I hadn't realized how much I'd miss her, and tried to immerse myself in work to keep my mind occupied. Notice arrived that the Annual Mining Convention of the Americas was scheduled to take place in La Verdad. I'd attended most AMCA conventions over the years and, this time, had actually been invited to give a presentation on our latest pumps. I had no intention of going, however. Frank and I had become much closer in the aftermath of his mother's death and I didn't like the idea of leaving him on his own. But when he heard about the AMCA meeting, he insisted that I go—a week in Mexico would be good for me.

So I went to La Verdad reluctantly. Indeed, I would have adjudged the entire trip to be a waste of time. Till that few minutes sheltering from a storm in a shabby bookstore where I discovered a book—*The Obsidian Cloud*.

When I brought it home, I lent it to Frank to find out what he thought.

He was excited—it was just the kind of oddity he loved. I'd mentioned to him my own Duncairn connection, but only in the most general way. That was one of the reasons why I'd spent a considerable amount of my spare time at the university library, doing whatever research I could on the book's origins and its author. Without the slightest success.

Frank wasn't surprised.

"Look," he said. "I know from experience, this isn't the kind of thing an amateur can do. You need to give the book to an expert, then you might get results."

I thought he meant himself, for his collection of oddities included rare books. He'd already hinted he wouldn't mind putting *The Obsidian Cloud* in his collection at the Emporium— not for sale, of course, but just to show it off.

In fact, of course, he had in mind the curator of rare books at the National Cultural Centre in Glasgow.

"I haven't met him," he said. "But I've read articles by him in various journals. He really knows his stuff."

So I did what he suggested, and the curator eventually became enthusiastic about the task. While his research was underway, another important figure from my past reappeared.

DUPONT RETURNS

1

It was a Friday, and I was in my office later than usual preparing for an important meeting on Monday morning with the representatives of a consortium of mining companies. The phone rang and I picked up, expecting it to be Jonson. He'd gone over to the factory earlier to check on machinery parts and said he'd call if there were any shortages.

"Harry, is that you?"

The voice wasn't Jonson's.

"This is Charles Dupont."

My mind was full of the upcoming Monday meeting, so the name didn't quite register at first.

"You know—Dr. Dupont. We were together in Africa, more than twenty years ago?"

Dupont! I was surprised and delighted. I told him I'd often thought about him over the years and wondered what had become of him. He was one of those who'd been kind to me when I badly needed a friend.

"Well, it's nice to hear I haven't been forgotten," said Dupont. "I've often wondered what became of you."

I gave him a brief account of my life since we'd last met, and he did the same. After leaving Africa he'd gone on to various postings in other foreign parts. Most recently, in fact for the last three years, he'd been director of surgery in an institute of some sort in Upper New York State, near the Canadian border.

"Which is how I came to hear about you," he said.

Apparently, a technician from Canada had been brought in to repair a defective magneto in one of the generators that ran the institute's labs. He'd finished the job just that very day, and before heading back over the border had reported to Dupont. This technician happened to mention that he'd learned some elements of his trade at Smith's Pumps in Camberloo, and my name came up. Dupont asked a few questions and realized it must be the same Harry Steen he'd known so long ago in Africa.

"You can imagine what a surprise that was," Dupont said. "But it was also such a coincidence, for I'd just been thinking about you. It happens that this very weekend I've a visitor coming who spent some time in that little mining town in Scotland you were always talking about. Duncairn, wasn't it?"

I was even more surprised to hear that name yet again, so soon after the discovery in La Verdad, and that Dupont had even remembered it from so many years ago.

"Well, you talked about it often enough back in those days—that and your broken heart," he said. "Anyway, as soon as that technician left my office I found the Smith's Pumps phone number, and I'm so glad I caught you. Here's what I want to ask: I know I'm not giving you much notice, but is there any chance you could come down here this weekend? The two of us could catch up and you can meet my friend and hear all about Duncairn, too."

How could I refuse such a tempting invitation? Of course I'd drive down and see him on Saturday. But I'd have to leave again early on Sunday to get back to Camberloo for an important early-morning meeting on Monday. Was there a hotel near his institute where I could stay on Saturday night?

"Don't even think about a hotel," said Dupont. "I have my own living quarters at the institute and I'll put you up in the guest room overnight. Now let me tell you the best way to get here. We're a bit off the beaten track."

2

I set out early on Saturday morning, but with the roads so busy with weekend traffic, the drive took longer than I'd hoped. Eventually, after seven weary hours, I turned off the interstate at the junction Dupont had indicated. For the next hour I found myself driving through forests of spruce and maple on roads that got narrower and narrower until there was hardly room for two cars to pass. At times I startled families of browsing deer and even one tall, scraggy wolf. It was standing in the middle of the road, driven mad perhaps by the mosquitoes that were thick in the shady bush at this time of year.

Around three in the afternoon, the road dead-ended at what looked like an army barracks: a cluster of long huts with semicircular, corrugated roofs in an area the size of several football fields. It was surrounded by a high mesh fence topped with razor wire. The gables of the huts were a faded khaki colour. The windows and doors looked in need of some paint. The tin roofs were rusted. All in all, the place wasn't very impressive, though it blended well with the surrounding forest.

I parked alongside several official-looking vehicles in a small lot and got out of the car into the hot sun. The buzz of insects was the only sound. I began to wonder if perhaps I'd made an error and taken a wrong turning.

But no, attached to a big iron gate in the fence was a sign:

```
FEDERAL INSTITUTE 77
NO TRESPASSING
```

That was the name and number Dupont had told me to remember in case I got lost. I couldn't see any bell, so I tried twisting the handle of the gate. Immediately, the door of the nearest hut opened. A young man in a soldier's uniform accompanied by an elderly man in a white labcoat came down a cinder pathway towards me. The soldier unlocked the gate and motioned me in. The other man, who wore narrow sunglasses, held out his hand to me.

"Harry," he said. "How good to see you again."

It was Dr. Dupont.

I'd never have known him, he looked so much older and thinner. His hair was short and grey and he was clean-shaven—the twin beards I always associated with him in my memory were gone. With his white labcoat and striped tie, he looked the epitome of a government scientist. Then he took off his sunglasses and I recognized those green eyes with their amused gleam.

THE SOLDIER GOT my bag out of the car and we walked over to the hut they'd come from. Going into it was like entering a huge barrel that had been cut down the middle and was lying on its side. The hut contained several well-worn tables and a hatch opening into a kitchen. Apparently this was both meeting place and dining room for the institute, but it wasn't busy, since this was a weekend.

Dupont and I sat at a table and were soon drinking strong coffee and talking, quite at ease, as though decades hadn't passed. I told him in more detail now about my experiences after our parting in Africa. How I'd sailed across the Atlantic, tutored in South America, met Gordon Smith of Smith's Pumps, eventually married his daughter Alicia, and together we had a son. Sadly, Alicia had died last year.

Dupont listened quietly, nodding at appropriate moments.

Then I asked him about his own last days in Africa. I remembered only too well my final glimpse of him and Clara from the window of the plane.

"I remember that, too," he said. "We envied you flying away from it all, but we had to wrap up things at the hospital. Then, the day before the rebels were to arrive, we managed to find places on a truck headed for the coast. We were afraid they'd come after us and I was determined we wouldn't be captured. I didn't tell Clara, but I brought along two cyanide pills for us to take, just in case. You saw the kinds of things they did to anyone they caught.

"The roads were worse than usual, and it was such a slow journey that the truck had to stop overnight and park amongst some trees for camouflage. Clara and I slept in the truck bed. Just before dawn, a snake of some kind dropped from a branch overhead and bit her. The venom spread all through her body in minutes. I'd never seen anything like it. After an hour, she was half paralyzed and could hardly breathe. I just watched her swell up and die in agony.

"I had those cyanide pills, and could have given her one to put her out of her misery. If she'd been a stranger I wouldn't have thought twice about it. But because I loved her, I kept waiting and hoping."

I could see the pain in Dupont's eyes.

"It was selfishness on my part to let her die that way," he said. "I've never been able to forgive myself for that."

To comfort him I suggested that what he'd done was quite understandable, but he obviously didn't agree.

AFTER A WHILE, he began telling me about the work he'd gone on to do in various other parts of the world, some of them also dangerous. Eventually, age took its toll and he was no longer able to put up with the rigours of such a life. He looked for something a little safer, but still challenging, and was offered this position as director of Institute 77. It called on his anthropological as much as his surgical expertise.

"When I say the job here's safer, I mean in a relative way. It has its risks, too—but mainly for my patients," he said.

He looked at his watch: we'd been talking for more than an hour.

"Time to go." He stood up. "I'll show you where your room is, then we'll head for Waterville. It's a town about an hour's drive from here. That friend I told you about—the one who knows Duncairn—will be joining us there for dinner."

SEVERAL OF THE HUTS served as shared living quarters for the staff of the institute. Dupont, being director of surgery, had an entire hut to himself. It had a fairly large living room with a carpeted floor and comfortable couches and chairs.

When we first went in, a white cat with enormous green eyes jumped from a couch where it had been sleeping and ran towards Dupont with little excited squeals. It leapt onto his shoulder, purring noisily and rubbing itself against his face. He stroked its coat in return. His affection for animals was one of the things I'd liked about him.

Now this white cat, from its lofty perch on his shoulder, was examining me with a superior air.

"She's called Prissy," Dupont said. "She makes sure mice don't get to be too much of a pest, at least inside this hut. The whole institute's full of them, especially when winter comes."

With the cat still on his shoulder, he showed me where the bedrooms were at the back of the living area. The guest bedroom where I would stay for the night was plainly furnished with an iron bedstead and a deal table with a lamp. A private bathroom was attached.

I took the opportunity to wash my face and put on a fresh shirt. By the time I'd rejoined Dupont in the living room, he'd exchanged his labcoat for a regular suit jacket. Prissy had settled down again on the couch.

"I need to look in on my patient before we head for Waterville," he said. "It'll only take a few minutes. Would you like to come with me? You might find it interesting."

3

We passed several huts, some of them with pathways full of weeds.

"These huts haven't been used since the last days of the war, when this place was an active military base," Dupont said.

The next building was a modern-looking brick structure with an air-conditioning system rumbling by its side wall. I assumed we were headed in there.

"No," said Dupont. "That's our operating theatre. It's very up to date, but it's not what I want you to see."

Our destination turned out to be another of those army huts, one that looked proportionately much larger than any of the others we'd passed and was in better condition on the outside. The paint on the gables was fresh and the corrugated roof seemed to have been de-rusted recently. Glistening black iron bars protected all the windows.

"This is the recovery room," said Dupont. "There's always a guard on duty."

He knocked on the door and we heard the sound of bolts sliding. A thick-set soldier with an ammunition belt and a hand gun in a holster opened the door.

"Come on in, Doctor," he said.

"I have a guest, too," said Dupont.

The soldier gave me a quick look-over.

"No problem," he said. He let us in and bolted the door behind us.

A corridor ran all along the left side of the hut, narrowed a little because of the rounded roof. The soldier led us down past a number of doors on the right. The last had a peephole in it. He stopped there and used a key to turn the lock, but didn't open the door. He stepped to one side and stood with his arms folded.

Dupont looked through the peephole in the door, knocked softly, and listened. No sound came from inside. He turned the door handle and motioned to me to follow him into the room. The soldier shut the door behind us.

Dupont and I were alone in a spacious room whose walls were painted a light blue. A faint odour, perhaps of ammonia, permeated the air. The only sound came from some flies loudly buzzing at the barred window in one corner, above a sink and toilet. An unmade bed, a chair, and a desk were the sole furniture. The floor was littered with newspapers.

All at once, I realized we weren't alone in the room. A thin woman was sitting at the bottom of the bed. Even though her blue dress was much the same colour as the walls, I wondered how I could possibly have missed seeing her. She seemed to be fortyish, with close-cropped grey brown hair and grey eyes. Her face was heart-shaped and her skin quite pale. On the left side of her forehead, a livid scar about three inches long ran from her hairline to her eyebrow.

The woman was certainly aware of our presence. She smiled a wan, grey smile at Dupont and he smiled back.

"Good evening, Griffin," he said. "Just a quick visit. I hope you're feeling well."

"Oh, yes," she said. "I was just resting. I'm so tired these days."

I had to strain my ears, she had such a soft voice and what might have been a slight foreign accent.

Dupont gestured towards me.

"This is my old friend, Harry," he said.

I was going to reach my hand out to shake hers, but Dupont put his hand on my arm to stop me.

Griffin was looking me over, up and down, head to toe. Her grey eyes had brightened and she was even, I thought, sniffing the air a little in my direction.

"I just wanted to check and see if you needed anything to help you sleep tonight," Dupont said.

"No," she said. "Not at night."

"Good," Dupont said. "That's all I wanted to know. I'll be back to see you in the morning for our usual session."

We left without another word. I glanced back as we went out the door and saw that she was still watching me. The soldier locked the door behind us.

EVEN THOUGH IT WAS only a short walk to the parking lot, in those few minutes darkness seemed to have grown like a mushroom. Dupont chose an institute van and we got in and headed towards Waterville. By the time he'd driven a mile, the first stars were making their appearance.

"We'll be there in about an hour," he said as we sped along the tree-lined road.

I'd been thinking about only one thing: why hadn't I seen that woman, Griffin, when we went into the room? Was there a secret compartment, or somewhere she might have been hiding? Dupont laughed at my question.

"I understand just how you feel—it can be disconcerting," he said. "But let me assure you, Griffin was there in plain view when we went into her room, though you didn't see her at first. Why not? Well, as has been observed over and over again by scientists and philosophers, our eyes aren't all that reliable in many things. Those stars you see up there?" He pointed at the night sky through the windshield. "Our eyes tell us they're there, but we know from astronomers that many of them don't even exist anymore.

"Or, take the movie screen. Our minds grasp a single image, but a film actually consists of thousands of them strung together and we can't see the joins, they move so fast. Then again, even the slowest movement isn't visible to us either—for instance, the minute-by-minute growth of a tree.

"Or, closer to home, what about you and me, Harry? You must have noticed I'm quite elderly now, just as I noticed how you'd aged, too—though not quite as badly! But if we'd been in contact daily over the years, we'd barely have noticed the ravages of time on us.

"Anyway, you know the kind of thing I'm getting at. For example, you recognize someone at a party and go over and speak to them, only to discover your eyes were mistaken. Or you see your cat asleep in the corner and it turns out to be a pair of socks rolled together. And so on.

"Now, in the case of Griffin, it's not quite the same thing, but similar. You know that sensation everyone sometimes experiences: you're looking for something—say, your car keys—and you just can't find them. When you're about ready to give up in frustration, suddenly you spot them more or less where they ought to be and you can't believe you could possibly have missed them.

"Well, Griffin's had something of that characteristic since she was very young—of being almost undetectable at times, even though she's right in front of you. A lot of animals have that gift, like the chameleon in the way it changes colour to blend in with the terrain. And there are birds that are so adept at fitting into their backgrounds, even trained birdwatchers have difficulty spotting them."

I suddenly remembered that time on the truck in Africa when he'd pointed out the nightjars. I reminded Dupont of how surprised I'd been that those great black birds were almost invisible even though they were sitting on tree stumps in broad daylight.

"I remember them, too," he said. "But in Griffin's case, unlike the nightjars, she wasn't born with her gift—she had to develop it. Her family situation was probably at the root of it. Her mother died young and she was left to be brought up by a deeply religious father who should never have been a father in the first place.

"He was a man congenitally unable to imagine the devastating effects of his words on a small child. Whenever Griffin did something he disapproved of, he'd tell her she'd die in agony as a result of her sins, or that her flesh would be devoured by fire in perpetual darkness.

"For a certain type of child these were terrible things to hear, especially coming from the voice of authority.

"Griffin's aptitude for disguise, if that's the word, seems to have developed as a response. She tried to make herself as inconspicuous as possible, first of all to her father, and afterwards to the world at large. By the time she was in high school, she'd become so adept she could be amongst other students and they'd barely notice her.

"Sometimes her near-invisibility didn't really protect her—in fact it often brought her even more grief. After she left school, for example, she managed to get a job in a typing pool. Her co-workers used to gossip about how unsociable and weird she was, not realizing she was right there in the room, listening to them. In the end, situations like that became too much for her. She had a breakdown and was hospitalized.

"That was when she came to our attention," Dupont said. "We're always on the lookout for people who might be suitable for our research."

BY NOW WE WERE approaching the main highway and a full moon made everything almost as clear as in daylight. This seemed the perfect moment to ask Dupont outright what exactly the purpose of Institute 77 was and what his function was within it. So I did.

He didn't begin answering till we were on the main highway.

"Look, Harry, what's going on at the institute is all very hush-hush. We sign nondisclosure agreements when we agree to work there. But you're not a scientist and we're old friends, so I trust you to keep to yourself what I tell you. Okay?" he said.

I was gratified by his faith in me.

"It's not a simple matter to explain, but I'll do the best I can," he said. "The institute is the base for a collaboration between the government and experts in the fields of medicine and anthro-pology. I'm in charge of the surgical side of an experimental procedure that deals with those areas of the brain that distin-guish human beings from the other primates. Our patients—we prefer to call them volunteers—are individuals who've suffered from severe kinds of recurrent psychological problems that have ruined their lives. We ask them if they're willing to act as subjects for a certain type of brain research we do. They all have to be clear-headed enough to understand what our program is about, and to participate of their own free will. Griffin's a good example." He glanced at me. "Following me so far?"

More or less.

Dupont now launched into a little lecture on the makeup of the primate brain and the various components of its two hemispheres. I tried to follow him as best I could, but the bevy of technical terms—ventromedial cortex, hippocampus, cerebellum, frontal, parietal, and temporal lobes, amygdala—soon overwhelmed me.

Eventually, Dupont put the matter more simply. Research

had demonstrated that the brains of *all* primates contained the elements he'd mentioned. But in the *homo sapiens* brain alone, some subtle variant in the linking mechanism between the parts had led to the emergence of reason and morality, which in turn produced what we might call conscience.

This was the focus of the institute's investigations. By careful, progressive pruning of the connective tissues in volunteers' brains, experimenters hoped they might eventually understand precisely how the link functioned.

At first, non-surgical methods were used. The volunteers were plied with various drugs aimed specifically at modifying the linking tissues. But the drugs were too diffuse and numbed the surrounding areas of the brain, too. When their effects wore off, the patients had no recollection of whatever altered perceptions of the world the drugs might have induced.

A more precise, if irreversible, route was indicated—surgery. A research program was launched to find a procedure for targeting little parts of the brain for destruction while leaving its other functions intact. Dupont's predecessors had tried the approved methods of the day—inserting electrodes or ice picks through the eye sockets into the designated target areas of the brain and gently stirring them around. Predictably, such a chopping method was still too random. Some of the volunteers died and others lost their sight, or sense of taste, or motor function, or control of the bowels.

Dupont shook his head. All in all, the results had been very disappointing for the experimenters.

I was appalled to hear him say this. Surely the disappointment of the experimenters was trivial compared to the horrors inflicted on the volunteers. But I kept my opinion to myself.

THE BIG BREAKTHROUGH occurred at the very time Dupont became head of the surgical team at Institute 77. The team began using the latest diamond-bladed skull saw to make an opening in the forehead, through which the most up-to-date loboto-mizing instruments could be inserted robotically. These could be directed to slice out minuscule segments of the brain—just a cell or two, here and there. The method was found to be almost one hundred percent effective. Successful operations had now been performed on several volunteers.

"Preliminary analyses of the outcomes are still being done," Dupont said. "These things take time, but everything looks very promising."

I wondered exactly what "outcomes" he was looking for. He chose his words carefully.

"First of all, you have to understand this, Harry," he said. "The purpose behind our work at Institute 77 diverges quite radically from traditional neurosurgery. The normal aim of brain procedures is to turn badly impaired patients back into mentally sound human beings, if possible."

He hesitated again, making me even more curious. I really wanted to understand this research that Dupont was so involved in.

"In fact, our goal is the exact opposite of the traditional one," he said. "Our volunteers are indeed significantly impaired when we accept them into the program. But what we try to do here is to transform them into mentally sound *pre-human beings*." He paused to let that sink in. "We believe that if we succeed in eliminating from their brains the dominance of such traits as morality and reason—the very traits that signal mental health in human beings—they stand a good chance of becoming perfectly normal representatives of the primate class before conscience developed in it—in other words, the way our species used to be. Take the case of Griffin, for example. When she came to us she suffered from a debilitating guilt complex. After the procedure, she was 'cured,' in the traditional sense, for she no longer had a conscience to make her feel guilty—she was essentially what we'd call a sociopath. But there was much more to it than that."

He saw how startled I was and became more passionate.

"Imagine what it must be like, Harry," he said. "A modern human being, at last able to experience the world through the eyes of a not-yet-human primate! That's the gift we've given Griffin and the other volunteers. Just think of the gifts they'll be able to give us in return, for they still have language and will be able to articulate their primeval perceptions and sensations. What extraordinary contributions individuals like Griffin will be able to make to our understanding of exactly how our ancestors thought and behaved. Anthropology, above all, will be revolutionized.

"Already, even in the early stages of the experiment, we've made some strange discoveries. For example, we're able to use only female volunteers for our procedure. It isn't that we've had any scarcity of male volunteers. On the contrary—we've had hundreds of them. But X-rays of the male brain indicate that those parts of the brain we need to excise are already of negligible size. It's a rather puzzling finding, but valuable, too. I'm sure it'll become an important research topic in the future."

While I was thinking about the implications of that, Dupont went on to talk about other fascinating and challenging findings. The fact that Griffin used words at all seemed to contradict the long-established view that language and conscience were interdependent. Though I must have noticed she now spoke with a strange accent—as did each of the other volunteers so far who'd undergone the procedure. They'd all been native speakers of English, but no longer seemed to use it quite as spontaneously. They spoke with deliberation, as if trying to remember the vocabulary of a foreign language.

This trait was so noteworthy that Dupont's team planned, in the near future, to perform the procedure on a volunteer whose native language was French. A linguistic specialist from the Sorbonne would be on hand to study the after-effects, particularly whether the volunteer's French accent would now sound like a foreigner's.

Griffin also seemed quite unaware she'd had part of her brain removed. The team had tried showing her the scar on her forehead in a mirror. But as with the other candidates, she didn't identify with the mirror image any more than a dog or a cat would. Even when she was shown her consent form and other documentation she'd signed before the operation, she still didn't accept that any procedure had actually been done.

This inability of recruits to grasp that they'd had the brain surgery was actually quite fortunate. Dupont's team, as yet, knew no way of reversing the procedure if certain things went wrong—as they were bound to do in an area so new. While it was now relatively simple to take the designated bit of brain out, it was quite impossible to stuff it back in and reconnect it to the tissue in exactly the right place and start the conscience up again. But even after the procedure, the team was curious to find out if, perhaps, another part of the brain might eventually take over the functions of conscience, morality, and related matters. Only time would tell.

Another peculiar result of the procedure was that the volunteers no longer responded to their actual names. Griffin's real name was Winifred Burke, but now she wouldn't answer to that.

She insisted on being called "Griffin" because that was the name of the hero in H.G. Wells's *The Invisible Man*, which she'd read in high school. Experience with the other volunteers, however, suggested that she wouldn't stick long with that first choice. They tended to change their names as frequently as once a month. The team thought this fickleness might mean that the volunteers had lost any overwhelming sense of themselves as unique individuals.

The phenomena of the odd smell and the torn newspapers in Griffin's room were also common to all those who'd undergone the procedure. If the janitorial staff tidied up their rooms or sprayed deodorant around, the volunteers became very unhappy, like animals whose dens or natural smells are tampered with.

Griffin herself had become violent with a janitor who tried to clean her room, to the extent that the guard had to rush in and restrain her—and remember, Dupont pointed out, she's a sociopath, so who knows what she might be capable of? In the end, the cleaning effort had to be abandoned and more newspapers were made available to her. She immediately began tearing them up and spreading them around. As for the smell, she preferred fresh water for grooming but absolutely refused to use soap.

One last noteworthy characteristic of the volunteers was their preference for staying awake at night. The research team at first thought this might be insomnia brought on by the surgery. Now it was believed that the operation somehow released a primitive hunting instinct and turned the volunteers into night creatures. Like the others, Griffin would prowl restlessly around her room in the darkness, but sleep on and off during the day, just like a cat.

4

The institute's van was negotiating a series of small hills and curves. Dupont had to pay attention and was silent for a moment. Then he went on with his description of the Griffin case.

"When she leaves us, she'll be sent to one of our facilities in the South," he said. "There, in addition to daily interrogations by a number of distinguished anthropologists, she'll be put through a rigorous program to correct her little post-surgical eccentricities. Naturally, someone who tears up newspaper to make a den and won't use soap will have trouble fitting into society again, which is our hope. Indeed, with her gift of virtual invisibility, she'll be an ideal observer of how our society appears to a pre-human primate—in a way, she'll be an anthropologist in reverse. Her reports should be groundbreaking in the field.

"Isn't it curious that, if she can be taught just to act like a normal human being, no one will be able to tell the difference between her and the rest of the world? We can only judge other people by what they say and what they do. We've absolutely no certainty about what's going on in their heads—even the people who are closest to us don't know that. Fortunately, in the case of Griffin, we're well aware she's a manufactured sociopath, so we'll be keeping a close eye on her for the first few years at least, just in case something goes badly wrong."

DUPONT COULD TELL that I was taken aback by all these revelations. He began to defend himself before I could ask any questions.

"Now, Harry, you're probably surprised that this is the kind of work I do," he said. "For some people, it doesn't quite fit with the ethics of the medical profession. For that very reason, our team from academia and industry had to be chosen very carefully—hence the secrecy agreement in advance, for we knew some of them might be reluctant to be involved in research of this nature and might even try to have it stopped.

"Let me assure you, we always adhere strictly to protocol regarding the volunteers who are about to undergo the procedure. I make doubly and even triply sure they do so willingly and with full knowledge of the consequences. It's an odd thing, but without exception they don't mind at all the prospect of having part of their brains excised. Some of them, like Griffin, have suffered so much in their lives they're actually keen on having the procedure done on them for their own sakes—and for the advancement of science.

"In that I believe they're right," Dupont said, in conclusion. "Our procedure isn't just revolutionary in terms of surgical and anthropological research. In my opinion, philosophy and psychology will also be its major beneficiaries. Because of what we're doing at Institute 77, for the first time in recorded history researchers will be on a scientific path to finding out what actually leads to the development of the human mind."

OUR VAN HAD BEEN labouring up what seemed like an endless hill as Dupont offered this defence of his work. His claim—that he was advancing knowledge by deliberately dehumanizing others—was the traditional argument used to support questionable scientific experiments. Ironically, the more he tried to make it sound rational and logical, the more immoral it seemed. Claiming human superiority over other life forms, while using one of our great intellectual achievements—advanced science—in such a perverted way, was patently absurd. Surely that was evident to him.

But I kept silent. I couldn't help wondering: was it possible that after witnessing so much cruelty and inhumanity in the course of his work in some of the most unstable and brutal areas of the world, he'd become infected by them—had himself become a monster? When I first knew him he'd never pretended to be a great humanitarian, even though he'd imperilled his life practising his profession in those dangerous places. His efforts back then just happened to have a more benevolent purpose. But he'd made no bones about his love of adventure and the exotic.

Indeed, in my eyes at that time, the very fact that he didn't pass himself off as some kind of saint made him all the more human and likable. Also, he'd been a friend to me—a good, reliable one at that.

Even now, after telling me about this dubious scientific experiment, he still seemed essentially no different from the Dupont of old. And anyway, who was I to judge anyone else? What did I have to brag about on the matter of ethics? I'd married for reasons that had little or nothing to do with love. I'd profited for more than twenty years from industries that wreaked havoc on the earth and damaged the lives of countless innocent people. Whereas at least Dupont's victims had "volunteered" to be damaged.

SO I WAS ON THE brink of reassuring him, for I sensed he was trying too hard to persuade me—and maybe himself—that his work was ethical. I was about to tell him that I and probably most other human beings were guilty in some way or other of some awful self-betrayal.

But just then our van surmounted that final hill and the lights of a substantial town were spread out below.

"Waterville, dead ahead!" said Dupont in a quite cheerful voice. "I hope my friend's there by now."

5

Our destination turned out to be Ye Olde Mill, a nineteenth-century ruin turned into an upscale hotel, restaurant, and bar on the edge of Waterville. A plaque on the fieldstone wall of the lobby informed us that a hundred years ago the place had been a "manufactory."

"That's the fancy word for 'factory,' which is yet another fancy word for 'sweatshop,'" said Dupont as we went inside. He seemed to be in good form, maybe relieved at having made his confession to me or maybe because he didn't think of it that way at all.

The maître d' led us to our table. There a striking woman with long blond hair rose to greet us. She was dressed in some kind of silken gown that fell to her ankles and had a loose, open weave that was pleasing to the eye.

Dupont kissed her lightly on the lips then introduced her.

"This is Marsha Woods," he said to me with a little wink. All along, he'd let me assume we were to meet a male friend and not a breathtaking woman.

"This is the Harry Steen I mentioned—the man from Duncairn," he said to her.

I shook her extended fingers and we all sat down.

"I just arrived a few minutes ago," she said. "I left my suitcase at the front desk. I haven't even had time to order a drink."

Now that my eyes were becoming accustomed to the dim restaurant lighting, I realized she was older than I'd first thought—in fact she must have been much my own age. Her makeup didn't quite mask the tiny wrinkles around her eyes.

"Marsha flies to Washington at noon tomorrow," Dupont said to me. "She'll be staying with us overnight at the institute and we'll have breakfast together. One of my staff will drive her back to the airport in time for her plane."

DUPONT ORDERED A bottle of wine and we sipped and talked till dinner was served. Marsha, I discovered, worked for the United Nations. She and Dupont had met only a few months ago. He'd amused her with stories about his various postings around the world and the strange customs he'd encountered.

"One thing led to another," she said, glancing at Dupont affectionately.

"Including the bedroom," Dupont added. They both laughed at that.

The more wine I drank, the more I liked the look of her. She was really quite the opposite of Dupont's long-dead lover, Clara, who'd been aged prematurely by the African sun and made no attempt to disguise it. Marsha was in fact middle-aged but, by artifice, tried to appear younger. She didn't smile much and I wondered if even that was an attempt to discourage the wrinkles.

WE WERE ALL HUNGRY, so while we ate the main course, talking was minimal. But as we relaxed awaiting dessert we began to talk more. Remembering that Dupont had spent some time in the Pacific, I told them about my trip to Oluba and seeing the tattooed women there. I mentioned that in recent years the fertility cults associated with full-body tattooing had disappeared, but it was still a form of female ornamentation.

"How interesting," said Marsha.

I liked how she looked cool and curious at the same time.

"Well now, Harry," said Dupont. "You say the women's tattooing was full body, eh? How did you find out?"

We all laughed.

"Still, the fact that tattoos don't have a ritualistic significance in Oluba any more might be taken as a sign of progress," said Dupont. "Some of the other island chains used to cling hard to old customs, and that interfered with any efforts to bring them into the modern world." He began to reminisce about his years on Manua, which was a long way south of Oluba. He remembered especially his attempt to set up a clinic there and coming up against traditional beliefs—a story he'd told me back when we first met. The Manuans had a complex belief system centred on reincarnation. They wouldn't take his medicine for they didn't want to be cured of any illnesses they suffered in this life. If they did, they were convinced they'd be smitten even more painfully in their next incarnation.

"So how did you get them to use your medicine?" said Marsha.

"I didn't," said Dupont. "I tried every way to persuade them, with no success. It was actually quite humbling, as a man with a scientific background, to be completely baffled by a view of the world that hadn't changed since the Stone Age. Part of the problem was that we didn't share any common ground for arguing the point.

"For example, their head shaman couldn't even grasp what I was getting at when I tried to explain the basic concept of two and two adding up to four. He showed me how wrong I was. He took two pieces of string and tied two knots in each of them. Then he said to me: Look, you can't join them without another knot! See? He tied the two strings together and pointed out that now there were five knots. After that, he treated me like one of their pre-adolescent children."

We were amused at such perversity.

"Couldn't you have claimed that your knowledge came from the gods, just as a shaman's did?" Marsha said.

Dupont shook his head.

"The power of rational thinking is the one thing a scientist must believe in. It's more important than life itself," he said, not in a pompous way but as though he really meant it—and didn't work at an institute where he cut out parts of people's brains in the name of scientific research.

From the way Marsha looked at him it was obvious she was impressed. Oddly enough, in spite of what I knew about his work, I envied him his conviction, at least to an extent. Long ago, it seemed to me, I'd lost sight of any principle worth more than life.

AFTER DESSERT, we left the restaurant and went to the barroom with its great stone walls and fireplace. We found a quiet table where we could sit and enjoy our brandies. I told them about my recent trip to La Verdad, my finding of *The Obsidian Cloud*, and its description of a fantastic occurrence over the skies of Duncairn back in the nineteenth century.

"Duncairn!" said Dupont. "Well, well. I've already told Marsha you lived there years ago."

She'd been listening to my account with great interest.

"Yes, he did tell me you'd been there," she said to me. "I'm afraid the days of fantastic happenings are gone now, from Duncairn and everywhere else in the Scottish Uplands. I know that only too well, for my department's concern is with depopulation in various parts of the world. We try to determine its causes and possible remedies for it, if remedies are called for.

"About five years ago, I was assigned to study the situation in the Uplands because of the steady exodus of its people. I drove from one end of the region to the other interviewing as many of the remaining inhabitants I could find, as well as occasional visitors such as hunters and anglers.

"As for Duncairn specifically ... well, the town isn't really there anymore. At least, not as you'd remember it. That entire area doesn't have many permanent inhabitants now, except for the occasional shepherd."

MARSHA NOW LAUNCHED into a devastating history of the decline of the region during the decades since I'd left it. The main cause was that the coal mines, which had employed most of the male population, were shut down—either because they'd run out of coal or because changing economic and political times made it an unpopular form of energy. Towns like Cumner, Rossmark, Lannick, Taymire, and Gatbridge—which had all existed in some form since at least the Middle Ages—were now abandoned.

"It's almost as though the land was cursed," said Marsha.

Hearing her use the word "cursed" reminded me of how Miriam, long ago, had described some of those strange happenings in various Upland towns: Stroven, with its sinkhole into which the entire town was gradually sliding, and Muirton, with its regiment of one-legged men. Then there was Carrick—strangest of all—its population smitten with the mysterious and deadly talking plague. They had indeed sounded like towns that were cursed.

"I'm afraid I've never heard of those cases," Marsha said. "But when I visited Duncairn, the mine had been shut down for ten years. That was really the end for the town. Today there are only a few inhabitants, and the buildings are falling into decay. Though there's still an old hotel, mainly for passing tourists and hunters."

THIS NEWS OF Duncairn's fate was a blow to me. Like most people who've left their native land and not returned for many years, I'd preserved it in my mind just as it had been when I lived there. That image of Duncairn defied all such common-sense notions

as the passing of time. The same applied especially to Miriam
Galt—for me, she must be as young and beautiful as ever. If the
more practical side of my mind ever intruded to point out that
this simply couldn't be so, I'd push it away.

And so to hear this objective, eyewitness account of the
depopulation of the Uplands and the decline of Duncairn upset
me deeply. It was as though some vital component of myself as a
human being was likewise erased. The idea that there was once a
young man who'd lived for a few short months in Duncairn, full
of hope, was all-important to me. The common-sense view—
that in the course of our lives we're many people, some less
pleasing to us than others, that the young man who'd spent time
in Duncairn was only one character in the long story that makes
up a person—was at times very hard for me to accept.

DUPONT GUESSED something of what was going on in my mind.

"I didn't tell you that when Harry was a young man in
Duncairn, he loved a girl there who broke his heart," he said to
Marsha. "That was why he left and never went back. Isn't that
so, Harry?"

That was all the encouragement I needed. Influenced by the
wine, I told Marsha all about my love for Miriam Galt, and how
it had come to a devastating end. Thinking of it brought everything back, and telling it was so like reliving it that I was moved
by my own words.

By the time I'd finished, Marsha was looking at me with new
interest.

"How very sad," she said. "But why don't you go back and
pay a visit before there's no one at all left there? For all you know
she's one of those people still living in Duncairn. Wouldn't it be
wonderful to see her again? Wouldn't it be very romantic? The

Upland roads are all in good condition for driving. And I imagine the hotel's still there—the Bracken Inn, I think it was called."

Her eyes were warmer when she looked at me now, or perhaps the brandy made them seem that way to me.

"So she really broke your heart? How marvellous to have been so much in love," she said. "Even once."

It sounded to me as though Marsha believed in true love. It also sounded as though she'd never experienced it.

AROUND ELEVEN, it was time for us to head back to the institute. Dupont took Marsha's claim check to the front desk to pick up her suitcase. Then we got into the van and set out along the now deserted roads. Visibility was excellent under a bright moon. For some reason the term "hunter's moon" came into my mind, but Dupont assured me it was much too early in the year for that.

We were all in the big front seat of the van, with Marsha in the middle. She talked a little more about other places where she'd worked but I found it hard to concentrate, being so conscious of her presence beside me and the smell of her perfume. When the van would round a bend, she'd lean against me and once even put her hand on my thigh for support, leaving it there for a while after the road had straightened out again.

I didn't know what to think.

6

We pulled into the institute at about midnight. When we got to Dupont's hut, he insisted we sit at the table and have another glass of wine as a nightcap. His white cat, Prissy, usually so friendly, stood by the window and meowed noisily.

"She wants out," said Dupont. He went to the window and opened it, murmuring fondly to the cat. Marsha, at the same time, kept looking at me in a meaningful way, slowly blinking her eyes.

"She'll come back during the night, so I'll leave the window ajar for her," Dupont said, returning to the table. "She just likes to prowl around for a while, frightening the doves out of their sleep."

After the glass of wine, I stood up and made my excuses, for it had been a long day. We arranged to meet for breakfast in the dining hut at seven the next morning. Then I'd have to start back on the long drive to Camberloo. Before I went to my room, Dupont shook my hand warmly, saying what a pleasure it was to see me again. I kissed Marsha on the cheek, avoiding her eyes.

In the guest bedroom, I undressed, set my watch alarm, switched off the light, and stretched out on the bed. The only sound was from the direction of the window—the occasional rustling of doves' wings, scared out of their nests by Prissy, perhaps.

I couldn't help thinking about how Marsha had acted. Even if I'd interpreted the signs correctly, how would she be able to get out of Dupont's bed during the night and come to my room without disturbing him? Any movement made these old floorboards creak and even squeal in the night stillness of the northern woods.

I MUST HAVE FALLEN fast asleep, for I didn't hear her come into the room. I just felt her slide under the covers and press her naked body against me.

"Ssshhh!" she whispered.

I didn't need the warning, for Dupont's room was only a few

yards off. But that final glass of wine must have knocked him out and she'd managed to slip away.

The blinds were drawn so there was no hint of light in my room. But in the utter darkness, our exertions were a kind of Braille that required no training. We made virtually no noise but for involuntary gasps and sighs, the bedsprings groaning an accompaniment. In the end, we both lay back with an incomparable sense of contentment and completion.

Shortly afterwards she left, opening and closing the door soundlessly. Those suspect floorboards gave off no alarm as she made her way back to Dupont's room. Even as I was straining to listen, I fell asleep again.

7

The alarm woke me around seven. I was quite hung over, so it took me a few moments even to remember what had happened during the night. When I did, I felt awful. What a shameful thing to have done to an old friend. I could only hope Dupont had slept too deeply to notice. As for Marsha, she would surely understand that our little fling was only the result of too much wine, certainly on my part.

After showering and dressing, I steeled myself and went out into the main area of the hut. Dupont's door was still closed and I couldn't hear any sounds coming from inside. Either they were still asleep or they'd already gone over to the dining hut for breakfast.

I stepped into the glare of the morning sun and walked towards the dining hut, breathing the fresh air deeply into my lungs. Then I noticed something going on in the grassy alleyway between two of the other huts. Three men were bent over, as though examining the ground. Two of them wore uniforms, the other the same suit and tie as the night before.

It was Dupont.

He signalled me to join them. He seemed quite agitated.

"Look," he said.

There, in the short grass, was something horrific—a mess of white fur with blood and intestines scattered around.

"It's poor old Prissy," said Dupont. "They found her here this morning."

"Most likely she was attacked by one of those big weasels they call 'fishers' around here," said the soldier next to me. "They come in from the woods—fences can't keep them out. They prey on small animals, and that includes cats."

"It was my own fault for letting her out at nights," said Dupont. "I was warned about the fishers, but she was always so insistent."

THE SOLDIERS SHOVELLED the remains of Prissy into a garbage bag and, though we'd no appetite, Dupont and I went to the dining hut for coffee and bagels. I was relieved to see that Marsha wasn't there. With any luck, I'd be on the road back to Camberloo by the time she got out of bed.

"What a way to start a day," said Dupont as we ate half-heartedly. "I was already exhausted. I barely got a wink of sleep last night."

At those words, I tensed up. If he hadn't slept well, he must surely be aware that for part of the night Marsha wasn't in bed with him but in the room next door with me.

But in fact, he wasn't aware of it. When he told me the reason for his sleepless night, I felt even sicker.

AFTER DINNER the night before, when we'd been leaving Ye Olde Mill, Dupont had picked up Marsha's suitcase at the front desk. Or so he thought. Actually it was the wrong suitcase, full of men's clothing. It wasn't till they were getting ready for bed at the institute that they noticed. Marsha was very upset for she'd left her passport and other confidential documents in her suitcase.

Dupont immediately phoned the Mill and discovered that one of their guests had taken the wrong suitcase and brought it back. So at least the mix-up was now resolved.

Marsha persuaded Dupont that they absolutely must go back to Waterville right away or she'd never sleep. Since she hadn't had nearly as much wine as Dupont, she'd do the driving. They got to the Mill well after two in the morning and the suitcases were exchanged, to everyone's relief. Marsha and Dupont were in no mood for the return drive to the institute and took a room at the Mill for the night. The concierge would arrange for the Mill's limo to take her to the airport for her noon flight.

"SO I WAS ON the road by myself at the crack of dawn this morning," said Dupont. "I wanted to make sure I was in time for breakfast with you before you left. I have a general staff meeting scheduled right afterwards, too. I hope I can stay awake.

"I got here about half an hour ago and the guard told me they'd found what was left of little Prissy. I'm glad Marsha didn't come back with me and see that. By the way, she's sorry she didn't get a chance to say goodbye to you. She really enjoyed meeting you and hopes we'll all get together again sometime soon."

As he told me all this, the sun was shining through the hut window directly on him, giving his face a golden sheen that was rather eerie and unsettling. My bagel had turned into sawdust.

Not Marsha? Marsha wasn't the woman who'd been with me in bed in the pitch darkness? Then who was it?

"Well, I know you need to get on the road," said Dupont, and we both stood up and shook hands.

"It was great to see you again," he said. "It's hard to believe so much time has passed since we met. I always feel I can really talk to you. Next time, we'll make sure we're not in such a rush."

We promised each other we'd keep in touch. He went off to his meeting and I returned to the hut to pack my bag.

MINUTES LATER I was just about ready to go to my car when Dupont, quite out of breath, rushed into the hut.

"I'm glad I caught you," he said. He was looking at me with great curiosity. "I just found out it was Griffin who killed Prissy. I thought you ought to know that." Apparently, on his way to his meeting, Griffin's guard had called him over. He'd just seen bloodstains on the door handle of her room. Dupont went with him and saw the blood for himself.

The guard opened her door for him.

Griffin was sitting quietly on her bed. She wasn't quite as hard to spot as usual because of the blood smeared all over her dress. She admitted it was the blood of a cat she'd killed.

"It seems," Dupont told me, "she slipped out last night when the guard left the door ajar to pick up her dinner tray. He didn't notice she was gone because he's so used to not noticing her."

He was watching me now in that inquisitive way, but I tried to look as unperturbed as possible.

"Let's not beat around the bush," said Dupont. "She told me she was with you, Harry. And that from the moment she saw you, she felt very attracted to you. When we came back from Waterville she was already in the guest room, waiting for you.

She was watching you while you undressed. Of course, you wouldn't have seen her even when your light was on."

But I had *heard* something—that sound I'd taken to be doves' wings disturbed by Prissy outside the window. It must have been Griffin, watching me, excited at what was about to happen.

"She asked me if you'd be there again tonight," said Dupont. "She wants you again. You might say you're her idea of love at first sight."

My stomach was upset. I could hardly believe what I was hearing.

"Believe me, Harry, I'm telling you the truth," said Dupont. "It was after leaving you, on her way back to her room, that she killed Prissy. She just picked her up and ripped her to pieces. I asked her why, and she said why not? Of course, when she said that, I knew the procedure must have turned her into a predator as well as a sociopath. Maybe the sliver of her brain we removed had something in it that would have blocked the violent impulse. If so, that's another valuable finding for us—there may be some way of reversing the problem by more snipping in that area of her brain."

I was shocked but Dupont was looking at me with admiration, or perhaps envy.

"Well, well, Harry," he said. "You do realize she might just as easily have killed you, too? She was the most dangerous lover you've ever had."

I didn't know what to say. I could see he thought I'd been well aware it was Griffin who was in bed with me. I couldn't protest that I'd actually believed it was *his* lover, Marsha.

Dupont now tried to coax further information out of me. What kind of sexual activities did Griffin prefer? Was her role in them of the dominant sort? Were there any notably bestial aspects to her methods?

I refused to answer.

"I know it's embarrassing to be asked about such intimate things," Dupont said. "But this is just the kind of insight that's invaluable to our research. In the past, we've always had to deal in speculation and not hard facts in these matters." He then made a quite surprising admission. "That's why, at one point, I even considered having the procedure done on my own brain. If a trained scientist like me could communicate how the world appears to a pre-human primate, what a contribution to knowledge it would be." Dupont shook his head. "But what if the surgery destroyed the very part of the brain that values such knowledge? Until we find that out, we can't risk operating on an expert."

I was shocked to hear he'd even thought about such a crazy thing.

"You know, Harry, you might be a good candidate, too," he said. "I mean, especially after your antics with Griffin last night. Like a lot of Canadians, you're actually a very strange person disguised as someone very ordinary!" His eyes lit up and he laughed. "Don't look so worried. I'm only kidding."

With that, we shook hands again and he hurried off to his meeting.

I headed to the parking area, bag in hand. The guard unlocked the gate for me and I went to my car. The parking area was covered in leaves, as if from a big wind during the night. But when I stepped onto those leaves they took flight and I realized they were, in fact, copper-winged butterflies, dozing in the morning sun. A moment later, I turned the key in the ignition and the entire remaining surface of the parking lot seemed to ascend. The mass of butterflies, like a flying carpet, swooped away magically into the air, blocked out the sun for a moment, then disappeared over the treetops to the south.

DURING THE EARLY stages of my long drive back to Camberloo that day, I was tormented by Dupont's assumption that I was the kind of man who'd knowingly go to bed with someone like Griffin.

Of course I might have told him straight out that I'd thought it was Marsha who was in bed with me. But rather than admit to that conscienceless act against my host and old friend, I'd preferred to let him go on believing that I knew it was Griffin, herself a being without a conscience. Morally speaking, I suppose I got what I deserved.

Suddenly, a foolish thought hit me. I pulled off the road, parked, and adjusted the rear-view mirror so that it focused on my forehead. I examined my brow up to the hairline from every angle, this way and that, probing it gently with my fingertips.

Nothing. No pain, no sign of any post-operative scar. Nor did I feel any different from when I'd arrived at the institute, except for being a little hung over. Of course, Dupont had said not feeling any different was the common reaction to the procedure.

Still, there was no scar.

MY MOMENT OF extreme paranoia over, I started up the car and drove on northwards. But I didn't begin to feel more completely at ease with myself till several hours later, when I crossed the border into Canada once more.

The mind loves the unknown … since the meaning of the mind itself is unknown.

René Magritte

PART FOUR

THE CURATOR AGAIN

Several months had passed since my journey to Institute 77. At first, no matter how hard I tried, I couldn't get out of my mind that midnight visitation to my room of the half-human, Griffin. Everything else—the reunion with Dupont, the revelation of his involvement in a horrific surgical-anthropological experiment, the description by Marsha of the decline of the Uplands—took a distant second place to the memory of what had occurred in the guest room of Dupont's quarters. At the meeting with the mining consortium the next morning in Camberloo, I was still in a fog. I pretended I'd caught a bit of a cold and allowed Jonson to take the lead role.

Time gradually worked its magic on me, however. Soon enough the incident with Griffin began to take its place alongside that other weird erotic experience with Maratawi in Oluba. I no longer thought about either of them too much—and when I did, it was almost as though they were somewhat disturbing episodes in another man's life rather than my own.

ANOTHER CALL FROM Curator Soulis came for me one morning when I was at my office desk studying some fairly dull engineering documents. He wanted to give me another brief report on how the research on *The Obsidian Cloud* was progressing. First, however, he again referred to how delighted his board was at my financial contribution—so much so, in fact, that they'd approved his request to commandeer an excellent researcher to assist him in his work on the book. Together with her, he'd quickly completed his work on the format and they'd managed to track down the company that printed the book.

In addition, they were vigorously hunting down some biographical leads on Macbane himself, as well as consulting various experts about the actual phenomenon described in the book. He knew these were the kinds of things that would be of interest to me and, probably, to book readers in general, so he thought he'd call and let me know.

I was, of course, all ears.

"We've already talked to some meteorological specialists—we had very little expectation of anything useful coming from them. We were wrong. They've made some rather interesting speculations," said the curator. "We've also had extensive communications with academic historians about precedents for the black cloud. We still have a lot to do before we'll be able to say anything definitive on that. All in all, it's been quite a refreshing adventure for us—very different from our usual sort of research. As for who this man Macbane actually was, so far we haven't had any luck finding anything tangible. But we do have some leads, and we haven't by any means given up on that part of the quest. At any rate, I wanted you to know that I'll be sending you all the details when we do arrive at our preliminary conclusions."

Naturally, I looked forward to reading them.

"Well, always remember what I told you last time," said the curator. "If you ever happen to be in Glasgow in the course of your travels, you'd be very welcome to drop by and see us. I know you're a busy man, but I'd be delighted to meet you in person and bring you right up to date on our latest discoveries about the book."

On that note, the call ended.

THAT SAME AFTERNOON, I left work early and went to see Frank at the Emporium. In his office at the back, I filled him in on the curator's phone call. He was as thrilled as I was to hear about these latest developments.

"Why don't you take him up on his invitation?" he said. "It would be great to go and talk to him directly about the book." He suddenly had an idea. "Not only that, if you had time, you could even make a side visit to Duncairn and see what's left of it." He knew that all the Upland towns were now in a sorry condition.

I suppose this encouragement from Frank should have been all I needed to hear. Indeed, in my own mind, it wasn't so much the meeting with the curator that tempted me as the prospect of a return to Duncairn. As Marsha Woods had said, wouldn't it be wonderful if the woman who'd played such a major part in my emotional and mental life all these years—Miriam Galt—still lived there and I could see her again?

Yet no sooner had Frank urged me to pay a visit to Duncairn than the whole idea began to seem distasteful—a betrayal, a disloyalty both to him and to the memory of Alicia. So I made the excuse that it wouldn't be possible: I had pressing business matters to deal with here in Canada.

"Oh, come on," Frank said. "Jonson could look after things for a while. After all, what an opportunity to talk to an expert about *The Obsidian Cloud*. It really would be exciting."

So, I convinced myself I ought to go, just to please Frank as much as anything else. After all, our shared interest in the mystery of Macbane and his book was, for me, an implicit acknowledgment of our newly discovered bond as father and son.

When I got back to my own office, I phoned the National Cultural Centre. Soulis had left for the day, but I was able to arrange an appointment with him for the following Monday morning. I made my travel plans accordingly.

SOMETIMES, NOW, I wonder what might have happened if I'd decided not to go on that journey. But, of course, that's not something worth dwelling on. Presumably, if there really is such a thing as destiny, none of the obvious actions a person could take would change it. For all we know, the very flimsiest material—a word misheard, a false assumption, an excusable miscalculation—might actually be the most potent link in the chain.

SOULIS

1

From the window of the plane the first signs of land—the western islands—appeared. Between gaps in the clouds I could see them outlined in snow against the dark ocean. There were even glimpses of isolated villages and tiny houses. That anything as fragile as life, never mind love, could survive down there was hard to believe.

By the time we landed at the airport just south of Glasgow an hour later, it was after four o'clock on a Sunday afternoon and already dusk. Snow was falling here, too.

I hired a car and was very careful at first, for I wasn't accustomed to driving on the left side of the road. It made me feel rather disoriented, as if some reversal of the natural order had occurred. I eventually got used to the sensation of being in a looking-glass world. But I still had to go slowly, for the snow turned to sleet, then a heavy rain.

BY THE TIME I got to the edges of the city, night had fallen and the street lights were on. I'd taken the long way round so that

I could approach from the east side. That way I passed directly through the Tollgate, which I hadn't seen since the time of the explosion, all those years ago. I'd braced myself to confront bitter memories but instead was stunned at what had taken place in the intervening years. While the contours of the main streets were much the same, the entire area where I'd been brought up was transformed. The tenements had all been demolished, and newish apartment blocks with little rows of well-lit stores and fast-food restaurants had sprung up to replace them. As though no nightmare had ever occurred.

Quite bewildered, I just kept driving towards the city centre, keeping an eye out for a hotel. Soon I found myself near the docks, with the river alongside glinting in its old, menacing way. From what I could see through the lashing rain, the ships tied up at the wharfs looked as rusty as ever. But otherwise, this whole part of the city was also unrecognizable. The dangerous slums that used to crowd both banks had disappeared to make room for clusters of high rises and flashy office blocks. A few of the more historic buildings seemed to have been spared and spruced up—including one with an illuminated sign: *The Strath Hotel*. It looked inviting, so I parked on the street as near as I could and hurried back to it out of the cold wind and the rain.

Since the lobby was warm and a room was available, I checked in. I was famished, and so after depositing my bag in the room, I made my way down to the hotel's low-ceilinged pub-cum-restaurant. It was thick with the smells of fried food, beer, and cigarette smoke. A dozen or more customers were sitting at the various booths. Some of the men wore uniforms— perhaps from the ships I'd noticed—and were accompanied by female companions in noticeable makeup.

A small table by a window looking out onto the wet street

was vacant, so I sat there and ate a filling meal of fish and chips with a pint of strong dark beer. As I looked out the window, I couldn't help marvelling at how much the city had changed. Yet the changes saddened me, too, for some reason. In the case of the Tollgate, it was hard to accept the fact that the bombed-out ruins from that far-off day of horror were now gone. Without them as a marker, the very existence of my parents was made to seem doubly transient and forgettable. I had to console myself with the knowledge that they still lived on vividly in my mind— the only memorial they both would have valued.

I then turned my thoughts to my meeting the next morning with the curator, as well as my return journey to Duncairn. The prospect of these things should have been exciting, but I hadn't slept on the plane and was starting to feel very tired. By the time I'd got halfway through a second glass of that excellent beer, I couldn't stop yawning. So I paid for my meal, plodded up to my room, and went to bed, even though it wasn't long after nine o'clock. The rain drumming against the window mixed with faint sounds from the restaurant beneath lulled my senses.

DUPONT SHOWED ME into a cell where the volunteer, a pale man, lay quite still on his cot observed by keepers in labcoats. When this man held a fossil up to his forehead and closed his eyes, he'd be transported back millions of years. One of the keepers gave him an old rock and he began to describe strange plants and trees. Then he became aware of a huge animal approaching and he shrank back in the cot, screaming, the veins in his brow pulsing. The keeper prised the rock out of his sweating hand, for fear he'd die of shock. The man's eyes suddenly opened and he stared up at me just as the iron door of the cell behind me slammed shut.

THOSE ACCUSING EYES and that slamming door startled me out of my dream. It took me a few moments to remember I was in the Strath Hotel. Perhaps the door next to mine in the corridor had really banged shut. Certainly, through the wall I could hear the laughter of a man and woman. The bedside clock indicated it was three in the morning.

I tried to put the foolish dream out of my mind and concentrated on getting back to sleep, for the day ahead would be a busy one. Sleep, however, refused to oblige. I started thinking about the Tollgate and reliving that other day, so many years ago, when my parents had been blown to pieces.

Only when I began to hear early-morning traffic in the streets outside the hotel did my grief-stricken and exhausted brain at last close down and I slept.

2

The rain had stopped overnight and there were even brief glimpses of a winter sun as I walked to the National Cultural Centre, about a mile from the hotel.

I arrived at the centre five minutes before my eleven o'clock appointment. It was a newish, boxy structure, but for one noteworthy feature: its east wing was actually a round clock tower, the remnant of a much older stone building.

Inside, I asked for the rare books curator and was directed to that old tower. There, I had to climb a flight of stairs that led directly to a large, circular room with walls of smooth stone and a polished wood floor. Several round windows had been cut in the stone, giving the effect of a ship's portholes. Lamps dangled from the high plank ceiling. Dozens of grey metal filing cabinets fanned out from the middle of the room like an oversized set of dominoes. Beside them was an array of solid-looking tables and wooden chairs. But I couldn't see any collection of rare books.

A SHORT, BALDING man whom I hadn't noticed, for he'd been behind one of the rows of filing cabinets, came towards me with hand outstretched.

"Mr. Steen?" He had that familiar loud voice. "A pleasure to meet you. I'm Neale Soulis, the curator. We've talked on the phone."

He wasn't at all the elegant scholarly type I'd envisaged. He was fiftyish with a bulbous nose and wire-rimmed glasses. His blue suit was wrinkled, the knot of his tie askew: he was clearly a man uninterested in fashion.

We shook hands.

He had just begun to say more when a most alarming thing happened: the solid stone walls and the floor began to tremble so much I was afraid the tower was about to collapse. Then an ear-splitting noise came from above us: the bell of the clock was slowly chiming the hour of eleven. Soulis waited till the chiming ceased before he spoke again. At least, his lips were moving, but I'd such an after-echo in my ears I could barely make out what he was saying. He waited a moment more then spoke again, or shouted:

"Can you hear me now? I'm afraid you arrived just a bit too early. I should have warned you against that. Can you believe that clock used to go off every quarter of an hour before I got them to adjust it? Now at least it only chimes on the hour." The reverberations had ceased but he was still talking very loudly. "This tower used to be part of the official residence of the Lord Provost of the City till it was bombed in the last war. The bell was cast in Hungary back in 1850. Did you know the Hungarians used to be the great bell makers of Europe?"

I backed away from him just a little. Perhaps the constant ringing of the bell over time had damaged his ears, for he had the loud voice of someone hard of hearing.

I looked around. If this was the Rare Book Room, where was the collection? All I could see were filing cabinets and study tables.

"Ah, we don't keep the actual books here—they're in Special Collections at the university, a few miles away," he said. "If you're around tomorrow, I'll take you there and you can have a look at our collection. It's extremely interesting."

I told him that wouldn't be possible, since later that day I intended to drive through the hills to Duncairn—strictly for nostalgic reasons. I might stay in the Uplands for a day or two, then I'd have to return to Canada and get back to work.

"I understand perfectly why you'd like to visit Duncairn again," he said. "Well, perhaps on your next visit you'll have more time. You see, this location is just a research facility. No other department was keen on using it because of the noise, so I volunteered for the sake of getting the extra space for our files. As you can tell, it's not ideal, but it serves as a useful office for me, too. Visitors who come to see me are usually scheduled for a few minutes *after* the hour. I warn them to leave a few minutes before the next hour strikes. One advantage is, it helps keep meetings to the point."

I couldn't tell whether that was meant to be amusing.

"So, don't worry. I'll make sure I get you out at five to noon," he said. His voice was becoming more bearable now.

HE LED ME OVER to a cluttered desk half hidden amongst the filing cabinets.

"This is what passes for my private office," he said apologetically. He sat behind the desk and I sat in front. I could see, lying beside a sheaf of papers, my copy of *The Obsidian Cloud*. He caressed it with his fingers from time to time throughout our entire interview.

"I'm very glad you were able to come and see me," he said. "As I communicated to you, I consider this book a fascinating find. Isn't it incredible that you actually lived in Duncairn when you were a young man—and then to discover this book in the middle of Mexico? And, as you said, but for the name 'Duncairn' on it, you probably wouldn't have taken any interest in it. Believe me, the really exciting discoveries in our business are often made in just that fortuitous way—as though some god of books was at work." His smile displayed rows of uneven and yellowish teeth. "There's probably nothing to the entire Mexican connection, but we'll check it out thoroughly. Perhaps some identifiable traveller brought it to Mexico, or some book collector acquired it long ago. In the trade, we call that part a book's 'provenance.'"

He then looked down at the pile of papers on his desk and began to sort through them, putting them in order.

"Now, let me tell you what I've been up to," he said. "My assistant and I have already managed to do quite a bit of the preliminary research on when and how *The Obsidian Cloud* came to be published, who its author might be, and so on. Here's what we've found out so far.

"As I said in my letter, even the physical dimensions of the book are quite uncommon."

3

The irregular size of *The Obsidian Cloud* was what had caught the attention of Soulis when he first saw my copy. He'd taken a ruler to it—it was fifteen inches long by eleven inches wide. This was an unusual format known as an "imperial quarto," which had gone out of style by the end of the nineteenth century. That was partly because these quartos were so large they didn't fit into regular bookcases. But they were also unwieldy, as though they'd been designed more for lying on a sloped reading table or a lectern than being held.

And even in their heyday, imperial quartos tended to appear in limited editions, for they were very expensive to produce. The printing presses had to be adjusted to suit them, and that resulted in extra labour costs.

Some collectors of rare books called them "Scottish quartos," because, for the most part, only printers based in Scotland would agree to produce them. With the Scots' reputation for thriftiness, they believed they could make an acceptable profit out of these quartos by using up the remnants of quires of paper that would otherwise be discarded.

SOULIS HAD MANAGED to find some facts on The Old Ayr Press—the printer of *The Obsidian Cloud*—in a comprehensive history of Scottish printing. The firm, which was very small, had operated in the Ayrshire town of Kilcorran for a hundred and fifty years but had gone out of business during the Great War. The building where it was once situated had been demolished and the land was now part of a public housing development. The firm's records had probably been consigned to the rubbish dump, too, so the exact publication date of *The Obsidian Cloud* might always remain a mystery. The title page gave the year of printing only as 18-something. The last two numbers had been so obscured by mould that the date could have been any time in the 1800s.

SO MUCH FOR THE PRINTER. But what Soulis would have preferred by far was information on who published the book. The publisher, in consultation with the author, would get a book ready for print and make sure the finished book was distributed and read. So knowing the publisher always opened a fruitful channel of inquiry for later researchers.

Sadly, in the case of *The Obsidian Cloud*, no publisher was listed in the front matter of the book. Possibly the Rev. K. Macbane had preferred to have the book printed privately—a lot of clergymen authors used to do that so they couldn't be accused of seeking either fame or commercial success. In that case, The Old Ayr Press, having receiving payment from Macbane for the printing of *The Obsidian Cloud*, would simply have sent the entire print run to him to dispose of as he wished. It would be up to Macbane to send copies to his friends, or to magazines and newspapers. If he was ambitious enough, he might try to place them with various booksellers around Ayrshire, or even Scotland at large.

But no record of any such efforts had so far been found. Soulis had been methodically searching all the usual places: nineteenth-century book catalogues, literary journals, national and local newspapers, even registries of Scottish clergy. As yet, he hadn't come across any mention of a Rev. K. Macbane, or of *The Obsidian Cloud*.

All of this made Soulis a little suspicious. Surely a book and an author dealing with such a sensational incident were bound to have attracted at least some attention, somewhere?

"In our business, it's unusual to come across a rare book that presents so many interesting challenges," he said. "I'm determined to get to the bottom of this one."

I wondered: was it perhaps it a fake? Might someone have put it together to look like an old book, when it actually wasn't?

Soulis assured me that he'd considered that possibility right from the start. He did that, as a matter of course, with any rare book.

"We're not as easily hoodwinked as some people think," he said. "One of the first things we do nowadays is to conduct a lab analysis. In the case of *The Obsidian Cloud*, the paper, the ink, the glues, and the bindings are completely genuine. So if any fakery's involved, it's certainly not in the materials the book's made of."

But what about this fantastic cloud at the core of the book? Surely, in the natural world, such a thing couldn't really have happened? I put those questions to him outright.

"For myself, I don't have the slightest doubt," said Soulis.

He saw the look of surprise on my face.

"By that I mean I, personally, don't have the slightest doubt the cloud's nothing but a figment of Macbane's imagination," he said. "But, just to make sure, I had to see if there was any possible historical basis for it."

He knew I wanted to hear much more on this, so he dug around for another paper amongst the pile on his desk and told me what he'd found out.

A PROFESSOR IN THE university's history department, who took a special interest in the effects of weather-related events on history, had assured Soulis that some cases of exceptional weather did indeed make themselves so noteworthy as to be well documented. The great drought of the year 530, for example, was the direct cause of the massive outbreak of bubonic plague that devastated the Roman Empire. Then there was the unexpected hurricane that struck the Spanish Armada in 1588 and thus changed the entire course of European history. Another famous instance was the period known as the Little Ice Age, which brought about the Salem Witch Trials of 1692—the women who were hanged were found guilty of causing the unseasonable cold.

But most other "weather matters" were, from the standpoint of historians, recurrent and predictable. It was a quite normal Russian winter, for example, that was in large part responsible for wiping out Napoleon's armies in 1812. Those Cape Horn tempests we hear so much about? They had, for centuries, sunk flotillas of ships and hindered exploration and trade. No ship's captain with a modicum of competency could complain he was taken by surprise if he ran into one.

As for what might be called non-scientific accounts of history, there were any number of symbolic, or mythic, or allegorical appearances of weather events—Noah's Flood, or the Parting of the Red Sea, to cite well-known instances. Indeed, religious literature was prone to searching for omens in sea and sky, or for any other obliging antics by the elements.

In short, the professor of history concluded, *The Obsidian Cloud* surely belonged to this latter, non-scientific category, for he had found no record in any reliable historical source of such an event ever having happened in the skies over Duncairn, or Scotland, or anywhere else on this earth.

I PRESUMED THAT settled the weather matter: Macbane's cloud was an invention, as we'd already suspected. But I could see from Soulis's expression that there was more to come.

"The professor's conclusion would have satisfied me

completely, but I was in for a bit of a surprise," he said. "You see, I'd also written a letter to the Royal Meteorological Society in London to request an opinion on the cloud. I eventually got a lengthy response from the society's nubionomist—that's what they call their expert in cloud formations." On his desk, Soulis found several pages stapled together. "Here it is. I'll just summarize it for you."

ACCORDING TO THE nubionomist, Macbane's cloud certainly ought *not* to be dismissed out of hand as a piece of fiction. "A black cloud that acts as a mirror to the earth beneath may seem astonishing," he wrote, "but like a magnitude ten earthquake, or a tsunami the height of the Eiffel Tower, it's certainly in the realm of theoretically possible natural phenomena."

In his mind, it was quite feasible that silica dust from some distant volcanic eruption, carried by high atmospheric winds, might indeed bring about what could be called an "obsidian cloud." The high concentration of shiny particles in it might well be similar to the mirror effect produced by those tinted windows in some modern buildings. And if a cloud of that makeup were later to dissolve into rain, that rain itself would in all probability have black properties.

Even the rather grisly notion of eyeballs bursting during the height of the occurrence would be consistent. "In extreme weather situations, sudden catastrophic increases in atmospheric pressure are common," the nubionomist explained. "In hurricane conditions, for instance, doors and even walls have to be protected to prevent implosion—the external atmospheric pressure is greater than the internal. Also, ear barotrauma, which laypersons know as ear-popping, is frequent during hurricanes. It is just possible that in an extreme case, something as fragile as the human eye might indeed be vulnerable, in the same manner as air can be sucked out of a glass container."

The nubionomist did, however, finish this astonishing letter on a cautionary note. Yes, an event like an "obsidian cloud" was possible—*in theory*. But, to his knowledge, in the entire history of nubionomic scholarship no such phenomenon had ever been recorded. "Surely," he wrote, "especially in more recent times and in a small, populous country such as Scotland, any happening of this sort would have been observed and reported in appropriate publications by any number of qualified persons. That it should have been recorded in only one little book of dubious origins and that it should cite *no credible scientific witnesses* give cause for a warrantable skepticism."

The nubionomist promised to keep Soulis informed if any future developments were to moderate his findings.

"THE CLOUD SPECIALIST probably didn't know just how right he was about the credibility of the witnesses named in *The Obsidian Cloud*," said Soulis. "I'd already checked them out, and they weren't what you'd call credible, by any means." He looked at his watch. "I can tell you about them briefly if you like."

I urged him to go ahead.

He glanced at another paper on his desk.

"Do you remember that Dr. Thracy de Ware who was supposed to have seen the cloud?"

I did remember the name.

"In the book he's referred to as a 'well-known naturalist and astronomer,'" said Soulis. "And it's quite true that de Ware was well known in the early nineteenth century—but as an *astrologer*, not an *astronomer*. He used to go round the rural parts of Scotland predicting the future on the basis of the movement of the stars and planets. Nor was he a stranger to the justice system. I found his name in a number of court documents in connection with fraud—some of his clients lost fortunes on the basis of his predictions. In other words, he'd hardly be what scientists would call a credible witness."

Soulis looked at his paper again.

"The book specifically mentioned the name of only one other witness—Meg Millar," he said. "She was a poet and folklorist in Ayrshire around the same time as de Ware. According to one of the histories of Upland literature, she was called 'The Moorland Minstrel.' She compiled a collection of local legends and myths, which is very interesting. She also wrote hundreds of sonnets about the flowers of the region." He rolled his eyes. "Only a few of them have survived, and maybe that's just as well."

I told Soulis I'd recognized Meg Millar's name, too, when I first saw it in *The Obsidian Cloud*. I'd once read a story of hers about a disappointed man looking for a pot of gold. I didn't tell Soulis that it was Miriam who'd given me the story, in Duncairn, and that the night I'd read it I was so full of love for her I'd no idea of the crushing disappointment she had in store for me. I'd sometimes wondered, looking back, if giving me the story was to prepare me for the blow.

"Yes, I'm familiar with that story, too," said Soulis. "It's one of her best known. In cultural studies they call it a 'Dream' story: versions of it are found in societies all round the world. They're always about a hero who dreams of buried treasure then looks for it in the place the dream indicates. Sometimes he finds it, sometimes he doesn't." He added, "Naturally, in the Scottish versions, he doesn't!"

We both smiled at that.

"As for Meg Millar's life, not much is known about her, not

even whether she was actually born in Ayrshire, or the dates of her birth and death," said Soulis. "But the very fact that a collector of fantasies is used by Macbane as one of the authoritative witnesses to the cloud would again suggest it's pure fiction."

4

He checked his watch again. He'd been talking a little faster and louder the last few minutes.

"Well, it's five to noon," he said. "I think I've caught you up on everything of interest I've come across so far. If you want to get out of here before those chimes begin again, you'll need to be on your way." His fingers stroked *The Obsidian Cloud* once more. "Would you mind if I keep the book until my inquiries are finished? I could work with a photocopy, but it's not quite the same thing as having a real book in hand."

I assured him that he could keep the original as long as he wished, and he thanked me profusely. I could see he'd become very attached to it.

On our way to the stairs, he kept talking.

"Let me assure you once again, we'll keep working hard to solve all the problems," he said. "As you can probably tell, from my perspective *The Obsidian Cloud* has been an exceptional find. It may not be a work of the very highest literary quality, but it's in a tradition of Scottish fantasy literature going all the way back to the Middle Ages. In fact it's really quite a bizarre example of the genre and may have vague links to the even earlier European tradition of the *speculum*—have you come across that? It's the Latin word for 'mirror.' Some of the ancient metaphysical scholars thought that every single thing in this world was a symbol of everything else—that in a way, they mirror each other. A clergyman such as Macbane might well have been familiar with that tradition. Anyway, my assistant and I are determined to find out everything we can about just who the Reverend K. Macbane is. Though there's always the chance we've already come to a dead end."

WE SHOOK HANDS at the top of the stairs and he promised he'd write if any other discoveries were made.

"I hope you enjoy your journey to the Uplands," he said. "Wouldn't it be interesting if you ran into someone who still remembered you?"

That was precisely what I was hoping, but I didn't say so. In fact I'd no time to say anything, for he spoke first:

"You'd better hurry—the clock's about to strike noon!"

I ran down the stairs as fast as I could and got through the front door just as the building began its pre-chime tremor. The noise of workday traffic in the street only partly muffled the first enormous clang from the clock tower as I rushed along the sidewalk away from it.

BUT I DIDN'T GO BACK in the direction of the Strath Hotel. On my way to the centre I'd realized that the area wasn't all that far from the house where I'd lived with Deirdre, the cat lady, and Jacob, the violinist. I'd never forgotten the kindness of that odd pair to me in my time of need and wondered if they might still live there. When I arrived at where their house should have been, however, I saw that the entire part of the street had also been levelled long ago. A number of ultra-modern university residences now took up the space.

Again I felt sad, as well as slightly paranoid—as though some malevolent force had set out to erase all of these important traces of my former life. But of course, that was nonsense. Time and Progress were at work—there was nothing personal in it. They'd not the slightest interest in the nostalgic longings of Harry Steen from the Tollgate. I turned away and walked back towards the Strath.

I ATE SOME LUNCH then went to my room and scribbled a few pages of notes on what the curator had told me while it was fresh in my mind. I'd promised Frank I'd give him as complete an account as I could when I got home. Afterwards, still quite tired after my restless night, I lay down and tried to nap for an hour. But it was useless. Two main contenders—fascination over the new information the curator had given me and uncertainty about the upcoming journey to Duncairn—fought an all-out battle for my attention. Mere sleep didn't stand a chance.

In the end, I got up, packed my bag, paid my bill, and set out for the Uplands. By the time I'd got to the outskirts of Glasgow, a mix of city smog and snow had slowed traffic enough for me to realize that the journey might take a good deal longer than I'd planned. The drive south was like a funeral procession all the way to the coastal town of Ayr, where I stopped for a sandwich and a cup of coffee. It was pitch-dark now, and I contemplated finding a hotel for the night. But the snow had begun to slacken off enough that I decided to keep going. I set out along the winding eastern road into the hills.

THE UPLANDS

1

Even though the snow was light, I had to drive cautiously, so it was all of two hours before I came through a pass in the hills—and suddenly I was in Duncairn. The road from the coast now became, for the next half mile, the main street through the town. It was lined at intervals by lampposts of the gallows type, with feeble bulbs hanging from many of them.

I'd been prepared for a town that was more or less rubble, after what Marsha Woods had told me. But from what I could see the roofs and walls of the buildings were fairly intact, though many of the windows were broken and there was no sign of people. Certainly, there were no footprints on the snow of the sidewalks or tire marks on the road. So Duncairn was still here, though it seemed to be a ghost town.

I reached the town square, noting the deserted buildings that had once been Kirk's Pharmacy, the police station, and Mackenzie's Café. The war memorial in the little park seemed to have survived, the three bronze soldiers with bayonets still at the ready, straining with blind eyes towards an invisible enemy. The Bracken Inn, on the corner of the square, was the only building that was lit up. I parked on the street in front, got my bag from the trunk, and hurried through its door.

During my long-ago stay at Duncairn I'd never been inside, but from the look of the lobby, it probably hadn't changed much since then. The floral carpet was wilted and worn, a set of yellowing stag horns jutted out over the front desk, and the photographs of long-ago revellers on the walls were mostly in black and white. Scratchy piped music and the smell of fried meat filled the air.

I rang the desk bell and waited. A thin, middle-aged woman came along a dark passageway to greet me.

"Yes, there are indeed rooms available," she said in answer to my inquiry. She had a southern English voice. I filled in the various pieces of information she needed. She gave me a room key and said the dining room would be open till eight.

My room on the second floor was ordinary enough, with the usual hotel furnishings. I stood for a while at the window—it looked over the square—then sat on the bed, overwhelmed with sadness. No doubt it was a normal reaction, coming back to a place you haven't been in for many years—a deeper awareness of your own mortality, and that the world will persist without your presence.

Again, I wondered if that was why I'd never returned to Scotland. Often, over the years, whenever I'd tried to envisage myself as I was when I last saw Duncairn, it was like remembering a character from a book I'd read a long time ago.

It was almost eight o'clock and I thought of going downstairs for dinner, but suddenly I felt drained of all energy. It wasn't so much the physical miles I'd travelled in the last two days, but the much vaster journey backwards in my mind that seemed to have exhausted me. I undressed, got into the cool bed, and within minutes was fast asleep.

I WAS UP THE NEXT morning around seven-thirty, hungry. I went downstairs to the dining room with its old-fashioned checkered-cloth-covered tables. The bacon and eggs were good and I ate with relish.

Afterwards, as I passed through the lobby, the Englishwoman was back at the desk doing some paperwork. She asked me how I'd slept and we chatted for a while. She seemed to welcome the opportunity to talk to a stranger.

She was, in fact, the owner of the inn: she'd inherited it fifteen years before from her uncle. Around that same time, the town's decline had begun when the coal seam in the mine started to peter out, making the extraction process lengthy and unprofitable. The English owners of the mine (one of them was the uncle who'd left her the inn) decided to shut the operation down.

From that moment, according to the Englishwoman, the townspeople began to leave. Within a few years Duncairn became more or less deserted, the inn being used mainly as a base for visiting fishermen and grouse shooters. Occasionally, though, her guests were old townspeople who'd come back to visit the cemetery, or just to look over what was left of the place where they'd been born and brought up.

"They're very sentimental about Duncairn, and I appreciate their business," said the Englishwoman. "But I'm not sentimental. If there's any charm in the ruins of things that were once useful, I haven't noticed. I'd sell the inn at the drop of a hat if anyone would buy it."

I confessed to her that I myself had once lived in the town a very short time: I'd been hired to teach here, but the job didn't work out. I wondered about the school.

"Ah, the school," she said. "Well it's gone now too. It closed around the same time as the mine, and the school building's been demolished. The principal carried on living in Duncairn for years afterwards, though. He'd often drop in for a glass of beer." She frowned, remembering. "Sam Mackay was his name, a very nice man. He's dead now. His wife died five or six years ago, too."

I didn't show how shocked I was to hear this.

"Yes," she said. "I saw her quite a few times, but I didn't really know her. She was buried beside him in the graveyard. Most of the townspeople had already moved out of Duncairn by then, so not many attended either of their funerals. You can still see their big house up in the moors. No one lives there anymore, so I'm sure it must be quite rundown by now."

BACK IN MY ROOM, I sat for a while trying to absorb what I'd heard. Over recent years, I'd considered the possibility that Miriam might be dead. But I hadn't considered it often or seriously. Rarely had a day passed, in fact, when I hadn't thought about her and hoped she might be thinking fondly of me. Now the shock of hearing about her death made me feel empty to the core. I suppose in many ways she'd always been central to my entire sense of who I was.

Now I would never know for certain why she'd rejected me. But she had gone ahead and married Sam, just as he'd told me she would.

Ah, well. Knowing she was dead, there wasn't much reason for me to prolong my stay in Duncairn. I made up my mind to leave the very next morning. For today, I'd walk the hills one last time and visit the house up in the moors.

And, of course, her grave.

2

I was glad of my winter coat when I set out across the moors into an eye-watering wind that morning. The natural landscape was unchanged from thirty years ago, as—no doubt—it wasn't much changed since the last great geological upheaval of planet Earth. Mine were the only human footprints in the snow, but in sheltered areas I could see the delicate tracks of hares and rabbits and birds as well as various other moor creatures. Their patterns were so elaborate they might have spelled out some message, if only I had the wisdom to interpret it.

After I'd walked for a while, one of those black moorbirds darted past me, bringing to mind how Miriam and I had met, how she'd climbed the rock to warn me against their rather gruesome taste for human eyeballs.

And the rock! Yes, there it was, away to the west, a dark outline against the snow. It looked smaller now and the hills behind it less impressive. But at least they still existed, whereas Miriam was dead and her face was now only a ghostly image in my mind. Surely that, too, was one of the saddest things: how time and distance become a frosted window through which we can barely make out the features of those we love.

IN THIS MELANCHOLY state of mind, after a half hour of walking I reached the house.

At first glance, it too looked smaller, though perhaps it was just that the windbreak of evergreens had grown bigger. The oak tree on the front lawn was taller, but skeletal, with only a few leaves clinging to the branches, pretending winter hadn't come yet.

The house, close up, looked neglected. A coat of moss made the name *Duncairn Manor* on the lintel only half legible. The paint on the door was peeling away. The thin layer of snow on the roof didn't conceal the fact that some of the tiles were broken or missing. One of the chimney pots was cracked and another had fallen over. The downstairs windows were unbroken but had been shrouded with white cloths, so nothing inside was visible.

I knocked on the door just in case, then I tried turning the knob. The door squealed open and I stepped inside.

THE SMELL WAS the first thing I noticed—the damp smell of mould and abandonment. It might have been my imagination, but there seemed to be a hint of sweetness in it, too, as though a residue of the old man's opium had lingered all this time.

Enough light came through the white cloths over the windows for me to see that the floor was dusty and swaths of faded wallpaper were in the process of detaching themselves. In the living room, chairs and couches and other furniture had been draped in dark blue cloths and looked like oddly shaped monsters asleep. Even the pictures on the walls were hung with these cloths.

The door of the library was ajar. Remembering that night long ago when I'd first seen Miriam's father on the sofa before the blazing fire, I went over cautiously and looked in.

The room was deserted. The furniture was covered with cloths, the books were all gone from the shelves, and the grate was cold. From the window, there was a buzzing sound. I drew back the cloth just a little. Lying on its back on the sill was a huge bluebottle that must have somehow got into the house during the last days of summer and managed to survive. As I watched it trying to right itself, the wind suddenly whipped up outside. The tips of the evergreens bent over a little and the house groaned.

That was enough of this sad place for me. I began to make my way out.

All at once I remembered something and went into the living room again. Above the mantelpiece was a covered picture. I carefully lifted the cloth away.

Yes! It was the photograph of Miriam, intact after all these years. I stood there at the dead fireplace for the longest time, absorbing the image of that face I'd almost forgotten. She was indeed as beautiful as I'd always dreamt. My eyes filled with tears of pleasure mixed with grief.

At that very moment, I heard a measured creaking on the floorboards above my head. On that morning long ago when Miriam had gone upstairs to get me a book, I'd heard that same noise from her movements up there. Now, I was overwhelmed with the feeling that, quite impossibly, it was happening all over again: she was up there waiting for me.

I went to the bottom of the stairs, but I didn't go up. The dust looked as though it hadn't been disturbed for many years. I called out her name. I called it again and again.

Of course, no one answered.

I walked back into the living room, took the picture down from the wall, and tucked it under my arm. I stepped outside into the cold wind that no longer seemed so cold. Then I pulled the door shut behind me and left that haunted place without looking back.

3

For several hours after leaving the manor I walked the moors around Duncairn, putting off and putting off the moment. In the end, by a great act of will, I made my way to the eastern outskirts of the town—and the graveyard. It was a flat plot of land, surrounded by a low, weathered stone wall. The entranceway was through rusty gates wide enough for a hearse to pass, with gargoyle figures leering down from each gate pillar. My footprints were the only ones on the layer of snow along the central path, which was flanked by the most ancient headstones, many of them tilted and crumbling, the inscriptions on them too worn to make out.

Amongst the plainer headstones and slabs that marked the more modern burials, I soon found the grave marker I was seeking. It was a small, granite headstone with three names:

JOHN GALT
SAMUEL MACKAY
MIRIAM MACKAY

There were no dates or inscriptions.

Feeling quite miserable, I stayed only a few minutes. Then, as I was leaving, I noticed a slight protrusion in the snow on the surface of the grave. I stooped and brushed at it with my fingertips. To my surprise, a tiny bunch of red carnations was lying there, still in its paper wrapper. Some of the petals were unwithered.

WHEN I GOT BACK to the Bracken Inn, I removed the photograph of Miriam from its frame and put it carefully into my suitcase.

After dinner that night, I went to the front desk to tell the Englishwoman when I'd be checking out next morning. I also mentioned to her that I'd visited Sam Mackay's grave and seen some flowers on it that appeared quite fresh.

"Oh yes, that would be their daughter who put them there," she said. "She comes a few times a year to visit the grave. She sometimes stays the night here in the inn. She was here two weeks ago, in fact—that would account for the freshness of the flowers."

Their daughter? I was surprised to hear that.

"Oh yes. Sarah. Sarah Mackay. She's a very nice girl," she said. "She's an administrator of some sort at Eildon House." This was, apparently, a government institution located in an isolated area of the Border country southeast of Duncairn. Sarah was clearly devoted to the care of her parents' grave, as Eildon House was at least a three-hour drive away on the treacherous roads at this time of year.

"I could give you her phone number," said the Englishwoman before I could ask.

She rummaged in her card index and found me the number.

"Eildon House is a strange place for such a nice girl to work," she said, looking around as if to make sure no one was listening and lowering her voice: "It's for people who've gone wrong in the head."

BACK UP IN MY ROOM I dialed the number and got Sarah Mackay's secretary.

"Miss Mackay's gone for the day," she said quite brusquely.

I explained that I was a visitor from Canada who used to know her parents. I was hoping to meet her and talk to her about them.

The receptionist became much more pleasant.

"I'm sure she'd love to talk to you, but I'm not allowed to give anyone her home number," she said. "I'm afraid you'll have to try phoning her here in the morning and see if you can meet her. Unless ... let me have a look." Papers rustled. "Oh yes, according to her schedule she *is* free between ten and noon tomorrow. I'm not supposed to do this, but I could always book you in for that, if you want?"

I did want.

"Good. I'll make a note you asked to see her about a personal matter." She made me spell out my name for her.

"All right, Mr. Steen," she said. "I'll leave her a message that she can expect you around ten tomorrow."

SARAH

1

The next morning, it was barely daylight when I checked out of the Bracken Inn. I had to drive very carefully: not only was the road slippery from a thin layer of fresh snow, but a winter fog made vision difficult.

As I passed the graveyard on the edge of town, thicker wisps of fog seemed to sway from the tops of the tombstones, especially those at the back where Miriam lay, as if she and all the dead of Duncairn were waving goodbye to me. A solitary raven was perched on the horn of one of the gargoyles at the graveyard entrance. Both raven and gargoyle were glaring at me with mad eyes.

The driving was slow for about ten miles, then the fog cleared sufficiently for me to go at a more or less normal speed for the next couple of hours. Near ten o'clock I at last saw the sign, *Eildon House E.R.C.*, and began to make my way along a tree-lined road leading past acres of lawn and a half-frozen pond of green slime. Through the gaps in the trees, I caught glimpses of a huge mansion with arches, buttressed walls, pillars, and innumerable windows of the Gothic and Palladian sort: this must be the house itself.

I found a parking lot and from there walked to the front door. A set of stone steps bevelled with use led up to a portico supported by thick columns. The portico floor was of worn flagstone and the door itself was massive. When I twisted the ornate knob of the doorbell I could hear only the faintest of clangs from the inside.

After a moment, a man in a dark blue uniform with a guard's insignia over the breast pocket opened the door. He checked for my name on a clipboard he was holding then let me into a high, gloomy lobby. He shut the door behind us and directed me to a corridor leading to the west side of the building: there, I'd find a waiting area.

My footsteps echoed as I walked along the wood floor. The smell of fresh polish was so strong it would disguise, if need be, anything less pleasant.

Around a corner, I arrived at the waiting area. The atmosphere was like that of another era, with dark wainscoting and murky oil paintings of unsmiling men with Victorian pork-chop whiskers looking down from on high. Several wooden upright chairs surrounded a low table. A small, barred window of bottle glass was embedded in the three-feet-thick wall, and through it I could see some huge flies gathered on the outside sill. I was relieved to find they were only distorted sparrows, which flew away when they saw my equally distorted figure through the glass.

From the elaborately moulded ceiling, a cord dangled with a single, unshaded electric bulb. The light it cast was so feeble it would have been difficult to read by—though, in fact, no reading material was lying around, not even out-of-date magazines. I sat on one of the wooden chairs—it wasn't made for sitting in long.

In fact, the entire waiting room didn't encourage waiting.

ALL WAS SILENT for a minute or two—then I heard the echo of brisk footsteps and a young woman came round the corner. She too wore an official uniform, but it was of a greenish colour with the word *Director* on her badge. She came right to me.

"Mr. Steen?" she said in a pleasant, friendly voice. "I'm Sarah Mackay ... Miriam's daughter." She shook my hand.

I could hardly speak. Close up, she was so like Miriam in the photograph I'd removed yesterday from the house in Duncairn, I felt transported back in time. The blue eyes had the same honest quality as her mother's when they'd first scrutinized me over the edge of that rock on the moorlands all those years ago.

"I was delighted to hear you were coming," said Sarah Mackay. "I almost feel I know you, my mother spoke your name so often. She always wondered how life had worked out for you. I know she'd have loved to see you again."

To hear that I hadn't been forgotten by Miriam touched me deeply. I couldn't think of anything to say.

"Let's go to my office," said Sarah Mackay, glancing round the waiting area with its grim furnishings. "At least it's a little more comfortable than this."

2

I followed Sarah Mackay along a maze of corridors, deep into Eildon House.

As we walked, she explained that the place had originally been the residence of Andrew Eildon, one of those nineteenth-century industrial barons. He'd spent much of his fortune on this house, acting as his own architect. Newspapers in his day had called it "Eildon's Folly." By the early years of the twentieth century, none of his descendants could afford the upkeep.

"Ultimately, the government took it over and converted it to its present use," she said.

I guessed its "present use" must be as a place of confinement of some sort. The intersections of many of the corridors had checkpoints manned by uniformed guards with pistols in their belts. They nodded respectfully to Sarah Mackay as we passed.

I was curious about the letters E.R.C. I'd seen on the *Eildon House* highway sign.

"It means 'Enforced Residential Community,'" she said. "For most people in this country, that's a polite designation for 'prison.' Though only about half of our inmates have actually done anything criminal. Anyway, we think of them all as patients, not prisoners."

By now we'd turned so many corners and walked along so many lookalike corridors that I was rather lost. I remarked that the place was like a rabbit warren.

"Quite so," she said. "This labyrinthine design seems to put the inmates more at ease. They don't feel regimented or spied on. That's quite different from the more orthodox prisons. If you've ever seen any photographs of them, you'll have noticed they look like a big wheel, with its spokes containing rows of cells and its central hub for observing the inmates at all times."

I thought back, too, to Dupont's reconstituted military camp, with its razor-wire-topped fence making it look like a prison camp. I told Sarah Mackay about my visit there. I wondered whether, no matter what the design of these places of confinement, the workers in them came to feel as though they were prisoners, too.

"There's a good deal of truth to that," she said. "Here in Eildon House, in the case of guards and other service workers, their salaries have to be high enough to keep them from looking for work elsewhere." She frowned. "But as for those of us who're professionals, we don't mind spending the better part of our lives in places like these. It's our calling—our vocation, you might say—and we'd do it for no money at all. Indeed, we're sometimes accused of being attracted to those with afflictions of the mind by a kind of sympathetic hypochondria. Some of our critics even say that our sensitivity to the sufferings of others is a mental illness in itself."

She must have seen that I was genuinely interested, so she talked more as we walked.

"I should have mentioned that Eildon House specializes in artists and academics who've somehow gone wrong," she said. "By that I mean many of them have undergone the kinds of psychological traumas associated with people in their professions.

"Of all the artistic types referred to us, writers are in the majority by far. It's no exaggeration to say we'd need ten Eildon Houses to accommodate all the writers with severe problems.

"Our academic inmates are often quite brilliant, as you'd expect. Yet they have a tendency to commit the most disproportionately awful criminal acts—for example, they might stab a department head to death over their teaching assignments, or shoot a dean who's denied them even a tiny research grant. One of them is particularly infamous in this country for other reasons. His name's Professor Artimore—you've probably heard of him?"

Naturally, I hadn't.

"Well, he's a very interesting case" was all she said.

3

By now, Sarah Mackay and I were walking along a corridor lined with century-old black-and-white photographs. The subjects wore the uniforms of Eildon House employees and were assembled in groups, like football teams. Their faces were unsmiling and wary, as is often the case with people who've never seen a camera before.

We arrived at a door with the sign *Director* on it and she led me inside.

The office was spacious, with a number of filing cabinets and a wide desk in front of a big window. Thick iron bars on the outside marred an otherwise beautiful view of the hills. The office walls were a plain, greyish colour with no ornamentation aside from several more of those old black-and-white group photographs I'd seen in the corridor.

Facing the desk were a shiny black leather couch and armchair. Beside them was a kneeling stool, the kind of thing you'd find in a church. She noticed me looking at it.

"Eildon House used to have its own chapel," she said. "After the government took the place over, they put many things in storage, including the chapel furniture. That *prie-dieu* had actually been used by Andrew Eildon exclusively. When I saw it, I thought it might be useful in my office and had it brought up. Sure enough, some of the inmates now prefer to kneel when they come to see me." She smiled. "You're welcome to use it, if you wish."

I assumed she was joking and smiled back. She seated herself in the armchair and I sat on the couch. Despite its expensive appearance, it was unyielding.

WE'D BARELY SETTLED when a young, pretty woman wearing a white housekeeping uniform came in. She was carrying a tray with a pot of coffee and two cups on it.

"Thank you, Georgina," said Sarah Mackay.

The woman laid the tray on the desk and left.

"Georgina's one of our inmates," said Sarah in a matter-of-fact way. She saw my surprise. "Yes, half of our inmates are female. Madness is one of those areas where women have always had equal rights."

I wondered why this Georgina wasn't under lock and key.

"It's a long story," said Sarah. "She likes to help out and her medication makes her quite sociable, so most of the time there's no need for her to be locked up. She's here because she wanted to be a writer. Would you like to hear about her?"

GEORGINA, after graduating from university at the age of twenty-two, had decided to write a novel and bought a typewriter for the purpose. For a year following that, she stayed home every day, and for almost every hour of the day did virtually nothing but write—*tap, tapping* out her first novel, hour after hour, seldom leaving her room. She was so dedicated she rarely took time to eat, so that after a few months her body began to wither away and the tips of her fingers blistered, eventually bleeding onto the typewriter keys as well as down over her clothing.

Inevitably, Georgina's family could no longer deal with her and a series of institutions for the mentally infirm became her home. If they took away her typewriter, she'd fall into a catatonic state. If they gave it back to her, she'd immediately revert to her suicidal typing. There seemed to be no middle ground. Drugs and extended counselling were ineffective.

"IN THE END, she was committed to Eildon House," said Sarah Mackay. "When she first came here, her file contained some of the many hundreds of pages of the novel she'd been writing. I read them carefully. It wasn't really a surprise to discover that her main character was a woman who sat in her room all day, writing a novel. In the course of writing, this woman came to understand that all the other inhabitants of the world outside her room were conspiring against her. What was worse, they weren't actually people at all but huge rodents disguised as human beings. She could hear them hissing and scratching at her door trying to get in. She herself was the last real human being on this earth, and she knew that as long as she kept up her desperate typing the rodents couldn't get at her. Hence, her compulsion—and, by extension, Georgina's."

After hearing this I felt curious: what was wrong with Georgina to make her believe such frightening nonsense?

"You've put your finger on a dangerous aspect of the writing profession—the inability of writers to separate reality from fiction," said Sarah. "In an invented story, it's quite all right for a heroine to believe that all the human beings in the world have turned into rodents. In fact, it contains interesting possibilities. And Georgina must have been sane enough at first, for she wrote about her heroine in the third person. But as she herself began to lose her grip on reality, she began to write in the first person— she'd come to identify completely with her character.

"As I mentioned, we've tried all the latest psychotropic drugs on her and at times they seem to help. She can wander about Eildon House doing little jobs—such as delivering coffee and so on, as you've just seen. If I let her have her typewriter back, she's fine at first and writes about her character in the third person. But after a while she gradually reverts to the first-person narrator—a sure sign she's returned to the manic state. So we have to take the typewriter away from her. That deprivation makes her catatonic again and we give her more of the drug till her behaviour's quite balanced once more. It's been a vicious circle so far, but we haven't given up on her. If we can't get her to stop reverting to the first person, we may try another mix of drugs that'll make her give up writing altogether and become a normal human being on a permanent basis. But that'll only be as a last resort."

4

The story of Georgina being out of the way, Sarah Mackay now began interrogating me closely about my own life history. She applied herself to the task in the way, no doubt, she would question a new inmate. Only detailed and considered responses satisfied her. I had to tell her at some length where I'd gone after I fled from Duncairn, how I'd ended up in Canada, about my marriage, and about my work. She listened with great concentration, drawing me out with shrewd questions about Alicia and Frank. She seemed especially interested in the complexities and recent development of my father–son relationship with him.

Finally, she turned to the purpose of this present trip to Scotland. I was required to tell her all about my meeting with the curator, my finding of *The Obsidian Cloud* in Mexico, and the mystery of its author, Macbane.

Sarah listened to all of this with rapt attention.

"How fascinating," she said. "His story sounds just like some of those old Upland legends Mother used to tell me."

WE THEN CAME to the matter of how I'd discovered she worked at Eildon House. I explained that I'd driven to Duncairn after meeting the curator, partly just to see what the place looked like now. I'd also hoped I might even come across her mother, still living there. I'd found out she was dead, visited her grave, and seen the fresh flowers. Through that I'd learned about her own existence from the owner of the Bracken Inn and decided to track her down.

She sat back, apparently satisfied with my account of myself.

"I'm so glad you did track me down," she said. "Miriam would have been thrilled to know what had become of you." She sometimes called her mother by her first name, as though they'd been more like friends or sisters than parent and daughter.

I understood—my own parents liked me to use their first names, though for other reasons.

"She might have been surprised at the kind of work you do," Sarah said. "She seemed to think you had more of an idealistic streak."

That hurt a little, but I said nothing.

"Did you know she herself was an only child?" she said.

I'd always assumed that was the case. As in other matters, I'd known so little about her.

"Yes, her mother—my grandmother—was a fragile woman with a weak heart who died at home just a few days after Miriam was born, and Grandfather never married again," said Sarah. "When I was a child, Mother took me on a trip to see her birthplace. The people who owned the house didn't mind us coming in to have a look round." She recollected the scene for me. "It was on the east coast, north of Edinburgh—one of the big houses you find on the cliffs with a bow window in the parlour looking out over the sea. There was a huge rock a mile or two off shore, completely covered in bird droppings. When we were there, it was glimmering in the sun like the dome of a cathedral. But apparently the day Grandmother was dying the sky was overcast and the rock grew less and less visible till you couldn't see it anymore. That was always the sign of a storm approaching the coast.

"After Grandmother died, Grandfather sold the house and rented a rowhouse in Edinburgh. He wasn't really cut out to be a parent, so he hired nannies to look after Miriam. When she was ten, she was enrolled in a girls' boarding school in Edinburgh. He wasn't around much during her childhood, for he was a partner in an export–import business and had to make a lot of voyages back and forth to the Far East. That was where he developed a liking for opium. You knew about that?"

Indeed, I did. How could I forget Miriam's distaste as she tended the opium pipe for that wreck of a man?

"Eventually," Sarah went on, "he sold his share of the firm, too, and moved everything to the house in Duncairn, lock, stock, and barrel—yes, there really *was* a barrel with a lifetime's supply of opium in it. Who knows why he chose Duncairn? We used to wonder if it was because the sight of the ocean stirred up bad memories for him and Duncairn was about as landlocked as it was possible to be in the Uplands.

"When Miriam was sixteen she left school and went to stay with him. Even though he wasn't very old, he already needed looking after. The townspeople of Duncairn barely knew him, but they did get to know Mother and they liked her. After she married Sam Mackay, they lived together in the manor with Grandfather. Sam had the kind of temperament that was able to put up with him.

"In the course of time, I was born. I didn't have much to do with Grandfather. He always seemed only vaguely a member of the human species, inhabiting his corner of the manor, with his strange smells and habits. I was only seven when he died of complications resulting from the opium. After his death I missed him—I suppose it had become normal to have such a weird creature at home.

"A much worse loss occurred when I was fourteen, and Sam died. He looked so big and strong but his heart was never good and it let him down too soon. His death seemed to take most of the zest out of Miriam.

"After I graduated from university, I worked in various institutions like this. Perhaps I was drawn to them because of having grown up with the enigma of Grandfather always close by. When I became director here at Eildon House I tried to coax Mother to come and live nearer to me. But she just couldn't imagine not being in Duncairn.

"One morning five years ago, she was found by some fishermen at the foot of Tam's Brig, a place up in the moors. What she was doing up there, I don't know. She may have fallen off the bridge or she may have jumped. Either way, I suppose it was a good thing: by then she was ready to die. I just wish she'd found a less horrible way to do it."

I was shocked to hear the way Miriam had died. The owner of the Bracken Inn, tactfully perhaps, hadn't mentioned it. I'd never forgotten that day long ago when Miriam and I had gone up into the hills and looked down from the ruined bridge into the turbulent waters and rocks beneath. I tried not to think of her crumpled body at the bottom of the gorge.

But Sarah's narrative was unrelenting.

"The worst thing was that when they found her on the rocks,

the birds had pecked out her eyes," she said. "She used to warn me never to fall asleep in the moors because of them."

To hear about Miriam's death and the mutilation by the birds was very hard to bear. The very first time we'd met, she'd warned me about them, too.

"She was buried in the cemetery alongside my grandfather and Sam," Sarah said. "When she died, I lost my best friend. I loved her and Sam very much and they loved me. It took me a long time to be able even to think about them without crying. I still go to Duncairn from time to time to lay some flowers on Miriam's grave—and talk to her."

5

After a while, perhaps because of the confessional aura of the room, I began to justify myself to Sarah. I made it clear to her that I'd never have willingly deserted her mother, for my time with her had been the happiest in my whole life. The day Sam Mackay told me they were going to be married, I'd rushed straight up to the manor to ask Miriam how that could be possible, to beg her to change her mind. She knew I was there, she even looked out the window at me, but she wouldn't open the door.

Yes, I was the innocent party—the party sinned against—no matter what Sarah might have heard to the contrary.

"But I didn't hear anything to the contrary," Sarah said. "Mother told me precisely what happened that last day when you came to her door, much the same way as you describe it. That moment preyed on her mind and was one of the major causes of her unhappiness all her life afterwards." She spoke slowly and emphatically. "Refusing to see you was the hardest thing she ever did. But you must believe this: she did it for your own sake. She *knew* you loved her—in fact, that you loved her too much to give her up. So she took matters into her own hands. She decided to make the sacrifice herself."

I didn't understand.

"She'd come to the conclusion that it would be an awful thing for you if she were to inflict herself and her family baggage on you," Sarah said. "She was aware of how uneasy you were about Grandfather and his addiction. But she couldn't just up and leave him to fend for himself. And if you'd come to live with her in the manor, would you really have been able to put up with the sight of him every day, year after year? She felt she'd be ruining your life, and she couldn't accept that. So she just cut you off." Sarah looked right into my eyes. "She knew you'd be badly hurt, but she was sure you'd be able to recover as time passed."

Hearing this, I felt a little uncomfortable, but I knew Miriam's assessment of me had been right. When I wasn't deluding myself about my eternal love for her, I'd actually spent long periods of my life getting along quite well without her.

"She was very wise about love," said Sarah. "She used to tell me that first love is often a kind of self-love, a delight in the idea of being in love. In your case, she was afraid that to preserve that idea you'd have insisted on staying with her no matter how harmful it might be to you in the long run."

Again, I understood how well Miriam had seen through me. I'd been so smitten with the notion of myself as the great lover I'd barely given a thought to the reality of what might have happened if we'd stayed together. Would it have taken very long for me to start resenting her—even hating her—for being stuck with her and that old man in their gloomy manor? But instead of facing the truth about myself, I'd spent my life blaming her for making true love impossible for me thereafter. My "broken heart" had become an excuse for my self-serving behaviour over the years.

"Sam knew all about your relationship with her because she'd told him everything, even before you did," said Sarah. "But he still loved her and wanted to marry her. She tried to be as good a wife to him as she could. But unfortunately, you were the only one she really loved. She never got over you."

The only one she really loved. What a grim irony, to hear that. All these years I'd convinced myself that I'd loved her and that she hadn't loved me. Now I had to face the truth: my broken heart had never been more than a piece of self-indulgent nonsense— whereas she'd truly loved me.

"Yes, for the remainder of her life you were like a ghost that kept haunting her," said Sarah. "She knew you'd always believe she'd treated you badly, and that made her feel tremendously guilty." She paused and shook her head slowly. "If there's one thing I've learned in my profession, it's how good we are at guilt. My mother just piled it on herself for having done something in your best interest." She sighed. "What a price we have to pay for being human."

WE SAT SILENTLY for a while. Then, I suppose to get away from this sad topic, Sarah told me that she herself was engaged.

"We're planning to get married in the next year or so," she said. "He's a lawyer in Edinburgh. We'll try and find a house in some little town between there and here so that we can both continue with our work."

Children? I wondered.

"We're not planning on having any," she said. "Mother would

probably have thought that was a good thing. She was sometimes afraid that our family was cursed. Even if her fear wasn't rational, it was quite understandable."

OUR TIME WAS RUNNING OUT. Sarah made me promise, next time I was in Scotland, to come and visit her again for a more extended period. She'd love to show me more of the kinds of patients she had to deal with at Eildon House—she knew I'd find them fascinating.

This keenness, like a child wanting to show off her toys, reminded me of Dupont and how proud he'd been when he introduced me to his prize volunteer, Griffin. At the thought of what that had led to, I shuddered.

THE PHONE ON HER DESK RANG. She talked into it for a few moments then replaced it with a sigh.

"Oh dear," she said. "The people from the ministry have arrived for our meeting. I'm afraid it's something I can't get out of."

I assured her I understood. Anyway, it was probably about time for me to start heading for the airport—my flight was due to leave at four, with a much earlier check-in. She said there was no need to drive back the same route I'd taken. She pulled a map out of her desk and showed me a quieter, alternative road to the coast. At that, we both stood up.

"I'll walk with you to the front door," she said. "If you'd like, I've time to let you have a look at Professor Artimore. We'll be passing near his cell on our way out. You remember I mentioned him—the most notorious by far of those criminal academics? People have actually offered to pay just to see him in the flesh. His research caused an uproar when it became public at the trial.

He's one of the strangest types we've ever had to deal with at Eildon House."

Of course I was happy to go with her.

SHE TOOK ME ALONG a side corridor that led to a room with a door that differed from any of the other doors we'd passed. It was reinforced with metal struts and had a small, barred rectangle for viewing the occupant.

Sarah Mackay glanced through it then waved me over.

"Take a look," she said.

I peered into a small, sparsely furnished room with a caged bulb in the middle of the ceiling. Under it an elderly man sat strapped by the arms and legs to an upright wooden chair bolted to the floor. His grey hair was straggly and long. His face was grey, too, except for some angular bluish marks right in the middle of his forehead—they looked like letters of the alphabet, but from where I stood I couldn't quite make them out. His cheeks were lined with anxiety or pain. His eyes were half closed with a faraway expression, as if concentrating on some problem.

After I'd had a good look, Sarah and I continued on our way. She was obviously keen on hearing my impression.

"Well?" she said. "He looks relatively ordinary, don't you think?"

I actually thought he seemed more than a little stressed.

She smiled at that.

"You're quite right, of course," she said. "And he certainly has good reason to be. Let me tell you about his case.

"Artimore was a renowned professor of linguistics at Edinburgh University. His main interest was in finding out how language first began to develop amongst human beings. I'm told that's still one of the great mysteries for scholars.

"In the course of his historical research, the professor came across a rather sadistic, unethical linguistic experiment that had been tried without success as far back as the Egyptian pharaohs. Indeed, over the centuries it had been repeated over and over again—there was even a Scottish connection: in the late fifteenth century, King James IV of Scotland, who fancied himself quite a student of linguistics, had tried the same experiment, in vain.

"Linguistic scholars, including Artimore himself, had always denounced the entire effort as barbaric. But at the back of his mind, he believed his colleagues would feel quite differently if the experiment were to lead to a breakthrough in linguistic studies. So he made up his mind to try it."

I'd no idea yet what exactly this Professor Artimore had done, but his rationale did sound similar to Dupont's—that the end will justify the means. I readied myself to be appalled.

"The professor got in touch with some kind of underground market in human flesh," said Sarah Mackay. "Through it, he acquired two newborn infant girls."

I didn't really need to hear any more than that. But human curiosity, like a dog's nose, can't control itself. I waited for more.

"He was a bachelor and lived alone in a Georgian villa in the New Town, one of the most exclusive parts of Edinburgh," said Sarah. "He'd already had a room specially prepared in the basement, so he put the two infants down there with a serving girl to look after all their needs. The serving girl was a deaf-mute—that was vital for the experiment. She would be the only human being the children came into contact with, so they'd never hear language being used.

"From the day of their arrival in his house, and for the next five years, Artimore spent hours each day behind a one-way glass, observing the infants develop. Every grunt or gesture or attempt to communicate with either the maid, or with each other, he made meticulous notes on.

"But disaster struck.

"One afternoon, he had to attend the university for a meeting. During his absence from home, a massive thunderstorm engulfed Edinburgh. A bolt of lightning struck his villa and set it aflame. Because of fallen trees and flooding all over the city, it took the fire brigade a long time to arrive. They managed to pull the deaf-mute servant out of the basement alive. They understood enough from her frantic noises and pointing to hack their way down again into the basement. There they found both children already dead from smoke inhalation. The rest of the house was in ruins and the professor's study and all his notebooks were incinerated."

PROFESSOR ARTIMORE, Sarah told me, had subsequently been charged with numerous crimes, including human trafficking, kidnapping, unlawful confinement, and manslaughter. The deaf-mute girl testified against him by sign language and in writing.

The professor would say nothing, but through his counsel, pleaded guilty to all charges.

At the sentencing, this same counsel argued, in mitigation of his client, that his was by no means the first attempt at such an experiment. He cited the well-known historical precedents— even that king of Scotland. He also maintained that similar experiments were still being conducted by a variety of linguists in less enlightened parts of the world, where the concept of human rights for children wasn't taken seriously.

He went further. Even in our own hemisphere today, members of various professions were permitted to subject children daily to horrific behaviour-modifying procedures. These were often drug-induced and unproven, yet the practitioners garnered not the slightest disapproval from the authorities. His client, Professor Artimore, may have been misguided, but he was essentially a humane man. He'd taken every measure to ensure the children were well treated—aside from confining them in a basement and depriving them of language. In reality, it was a violent act of nature that killed them, not the professor's research.

The judge wasn't impressed. Artimore was sentenced to life in a maximum security prison. He was later transferred to Eildon House as a more suitable place of correction for a scholar-criminal to serve out his time.

At first, several of his former colleagues used to visit him. Before the fire, he'd apparently hinted to them that he'd made the most astonishing, groundbreaking observations on the origins of language. These colleagues now told him he still had a scholar's obligation to publish his research and make his discoveries known for the benefit of linguistic science. Yes, his behaviour had been atrocious in the eyes of humanity, but what was done was done— publishing his findings would be a clear way to make amends.

The professor maintained his silence in the presence of these former colleagues, and soon all visits ceased.

"He's been here now for ten years," said Sarah Mackay. "He hasn't said a word to anyone since he arrived."

I'd been curious all along about those marks that looked like letters of the alphabet on the professor's forehead. It was as though someone had rubber-stamped them there.

"You're almost right," she said. "When he was in the penitentiary they caught him in the middle of the night carving them into his forehead with a piece of broken glass. They're the capital letters THGIR. It's been speculated that he'd been trying to write 'THE GIRLS'—you know, as in an inscription on a gravestone. But he didn't have a mirror, so it could have been 'RIGHT.'

Anyway, whatever it was he didn't get it finished."

Hearing about Artimore's research had recalled Dupont's work and his attempt to give an ethical justification for what outsiders might consider his criminal behaviour. That in turn reminded me of Sarah's comment that my own line of work would have disappointed Miriam, in view of the "idealistic streak" she'd seen in me. So I smiled and tried to make some facetious remark on the irony of "right" the wrong way round.

Sarah Mackay didn't smile.

"'Right' and 'wrong' are words we rarely have much use for at Eildon House," she said. "That's one of the reasons it's not easy for certain types of people to work here."

AFTER THAT we just walked together, silent for once, along the corridors of Eildon House and were soon standing on the front steps. The sky was overcast, suiting my mood at parting with Sarah Mackay. She looked directly into my eyes.

"You can have no idea just how curious I was to see you after having heard about you so often from Miriam," she said. "This visit really has been lovely. And it's been a special treat for me to know how interested you are in what I do here. You really are a kindred spirit."

I assured her that it had been a great pleasure for me to meet her and learn about her work. I was especially grateful for everything she'd told me about Miriam. Knowing the truth was a comfort to me, at last.

She seemed about to say something else, then decided against it.

So I thanked her again for seeing me and told her that she was a remarkable young woman. Miriam and Sam must have been the proudest of parents.

Her blue eyes became resolute. I could see she'd made up her mind to say whatever it was that was on her mind. In fact, I had one of those disorienting feelings of anticipating what's about to happen, as if it's happened before. Those questions she'd asked earlier about Frank, and about my relationship with him, flashed through my mind and I knew almost with certainty what she was about to say.

"Yes, they were proud of me," said Sarah Mackay. "But Sam wasn't my father. You are."

THE DRIVE WEST was quite straightforward, though the weather again turned into a mix of rain and sleet. I had to keep my mind on the winding road, especially when passing trucks sent up a blinding spray. But I couldn't stop myself from thinking about that final revelation.

Sarah Mackay, my daughter! Apparently she'd been aware of that ever since she was a child. Miriam and Sam had believed she ought to know, and so they told her the truth. Miriam's rejection of me hadn't been based only on her belief that I wouldn't be able to deal with her father. She'd also found out she was pregnant. Those two things together were, in her mind, too much to ask a young man—a boy, really—to put up with.

Over the years it had occasionally crossed my mind that Miriam's final act towards me might have had something to do with what she felt were her obligations towards that old man. Never that she was pregnant. What an irony. As often as not it's the man responsible for the pregnancy who runs from his responsibilities. In our case, Miriam knew I *wouldn't* run—that if I'd known she was pregnant, I'd have insisted all the more on staying. So she'd told me nothing and driven me away. Though she was in love with me, she probably didn't trust me to stay with

391

her through thick and thin. She didn't have the same kind of love for Sam, but she trusted him.

She'd made the hard choice and the right one.

That was exactly what I told Sarah after hearing this startling news on the front steps of Eildon House. I begged her to forgive me. She hugged me and told me there was nothing to forgive. We both had tears in our eyes as I got into my car and drove away.

AT THE AIRPORT, a heavy afternoon sea fog delayed all flights, so it wasn't till well after four that we boarded the plane and took off. I had a window seat and glanced out from time to time, but my mind was still full of Sarah's final revelations. By now, my feelings about what she'd told me had become more complicated. One minute I'd again start feeling sorry for myself: Miriam, by forsaking me, had killed my capacity for ever truly loving someone else. But the next minute self-loathing would take the place of self-pity: Miriam had realized, all too clearly, a basic truth about me—that I was really only capable of loving myself. And so it went, back and forth, endless variants and combinations of self-justification and self-condemnation.

The plane had circled back over the Uplands before heading out towards the ocean. There was just enough light to make out beneath us the low hills streaked with snow and the patterns of ancient fields enclosed by walls of heaped-up rocks. In one of these fields, the earth seemed to have been combed into rows that were exactly symmetrical but with occasional protrusions. A lone man with a long-handled hoe jabbed at one of the protrusions, then picked it up and hurled it onto a pile nearby. It appeared to be a human leg, blackened and mouldering. The pile held countless other such decayed body parts.

The man's eyes turned upwards towards the plane, searching for mine.

CONVENIENTLY, the clatter of the drinks trolley jolted me out of this vivid dream and I got myself a pre-dinner scotch. While I sipped I wondered, as I often did, whether there was any sense to be made of my dreams. Perhaps in this case it might have been spawned by the sensation of flying above the world at an immense height—something no animals except birds had ever been able to do. Surely this novel experience must have altered the way humans now perceived their world. In the dream, the geometrical structure of those fields far below had seemed to me like humanity's flimsy attempts to scratch a semblance of order out of nature's chaotic state. The fields themselves were only fertile because the soil was fed by the rotting flesh, just under the surface, of generation after generation of men whose brief lives were snuffed out in yet another piece of human ingenuity— those old mine tunnels that failed to hold up the weight of the earth. To walk in those fields was, therefore, to walk on the remains of the dead.

As for the man in the dream who used the long-handled hoe, I was having trouble making sense out of him. I didn't like the look of him or the way he'd looked up at me. So maybe he was Death, warning me that even though I was flying high above with a glass of scotch in my hand, my own turn would come.

Altogether, this interpretation of the dream, though a bit on the melancholy side, was quite pleasing to me. Indeed the brief nap, the dream, the scotch, or all three seemed to have got rid of the angst I'd been feeling over Miriam's choice. Instead I was now full of elation at the thought of two much more significant revelations: that she'd only done what she did because she loved me, and that her daughter—the astonishing Sarah—was my daughter, too.

Add to these two things the memory of that illuminating visit to Curator Soulis in his strange bell tower, and I'd more than adequate cause for celebration. So when the drinks trolley came by again, I ordered another scotch in their honour.

6

I got back to Camberloo in the early morning, slept till late afternoon, then phoned Frank. Naturally, he wanted to know all about my trip right away. I had to check in at the office for an hour or two, but I promised I'd give him a full account over dinner later that night.

So, around seven, we got together at the Library, a recently opened restaurant in what had originally been one of those big old Camberloo mansions. Only a few diners were there that night. Frank and I sat at a table in the bow window of the former library of the mansion. The room was still lined with impressive mahogany bookcases, but the books themselves had been replaced by a wallpaper of false book covers. As for the meal: the tiny main course tasted all right but was so artistic-looking you felt like a vandal sticking a knife and fork into an oil painting.

Frank was full of questions about my visit to the curator and his research on *The Obsidian Cloud*. He made me go into detail on every aspect of it, even the characteristics of Scottish quartos— one of them might make a valuable addition to his collection at the Emporium.

So far so good. But now, after I'd brought him fully up to date on the curator's findings, Frank asked me if I'd managed to visit Duncairn.

I braced myself. It was time to come straight out with the truth, more or less: Frank already knew about my short spell in Duncairn as a young man, but I hadn't told him that when I was there I'd fallen in love with a girl named Miriam Galt. She'd eventually rejected me, and in despair I'd fled the country. But I'd always been curious to know how things had worked out for her. So I'd taken this opportunity to revisit the town, on the off chance she might actually be there.

Frank looked surprised at hearing all of this for the first time, but he didn't seem upset, nor did he consider my visit to Duncairn in any way a betrayal of his mother, as I'd feared. He encouraged me to tell him more about the visit.

So I described for him the present decayed state of Duncairn, and how I made the sad discovery that Miriam, my old love, was dead. Then I found out, almost by accident, the reason she'd driven me away all those years ago—she'd been pregnant with our child, a daughter as it turned out. I'd managed to track this daughter of mine down, and met her at a place called Eildon Hall where she worked. Her name was Sarah Mackay.

I was just about to explain that I'd actually known Sam Mackay, Sarah's proxy father. But Frank, my audience, had progressed from surprise, to incredulity, to delight.

"Do you mean I have a sister—a half-sister? That's great news!"

I could see he really meant it, and I was very relieved. Gordon must have felt this way about Alicia's reaction when he revealed she had a half-sister on a remote island in the Pacific.

"Tell me all about Sarah," Frank said.

So I tried to remember every detail about my visit to her and the impression she'd made on me. He was captivated by all he heard, and we both marvelled for a while about this new member of our family.

"I'd really love to meet her," he said. "Do you think she'd mind?"

Quite the contrary, I assured him. She'd asked all about him, too, and I knew she'd love to meet him. I'd invite her—along with that fiancé she'd mentioned—to come and pay us a visit so that Frank could get to know her.

The prospect seemed to please him immensely.

IN FACT, I was beginning to think that this making of confessions might be a good thing for me. Wasn't it time Frank was told, for example, that his grandfather, Gordon, had also fathered a child in a far-off, exotic land? In other words, that his own mother had a half-sister in Oluba who was, therefore, his half-aunt? And that I myself had had more to do with this exotic, tattoo-covered half-sister than I'd been willing to admit to Alicia?

But then I wondered if maybe it wasn't his mother's unexpected death that had prevented her from telling Frank about Maratawi. No, maybe even Alicia, with all her fondness for truth, had come to believe that some family secrets were better left untold.

If so, I agreed with her.

I thought back to my midnight fling with Griffin, for example, which still made me shudder. What if I were to confess my part in that little episode to Frank? Wouldn't that be a good one to get off my chest? I could share it with him, beg for his sympathy on the basis that I didn't know I was making love to a monster.

But the very idea that a father should try to offload his personal nightmares onto his son seemed unnatural. Indeed, by the time Frank and I had finished our meal at the Library, I'd come to a decision: the confessional path was strewn with a few too many thistles for someone like me.

THE OBSIDIAN CLOUD

1

The next month was a busy one at Smith's Pumps and I was preoccupied with office matters. I was at my desk early on a Monday morning, assessing upcoming requisitions, when I saw amongst the pile of mail that had just arrived a thick envelope from Curator Soulis.

The address was written in pen and was barely legible. I was amused at the thought of Soulis in his tower, his desk vibrating from the chimes of that great clock above him as he tried to write. Fortunately, the letter inside the envelope was typed and was accompanied by several other pages, which seemed to have been photocopied. I began reading.

Dear Mr. Steen:

Let me begin by saying again what a pleasure it was to meet you, and by reiterating how grateful I am to you for having entrusted The Obsidian Cloud to us here at the

398

National Cultural Centre. This letter is to bring you up to date on the results of our research since we met.

I have some rather exciting news, so I thought I'd communicate the details to you without delay.

As I intimated when you were in Glasgow, the major focus of our research would be to identify the author, Macbane. That task has been much more time-consuming than in many cases we encounter. My new assistant, Jean Murdo, and I had spent many hours poring over old book catalogues, journals, and newspapers but could find no reference to Macbane or to The Obsidian Cloud. We'd even looked up the Rev. K. Macbane in numerous registries of Scottish clergy from throughout the country. As I reported to you on your visit, we had no luck whatever.

Since then, Jean and I checked all available Registers of Birth. You may not be aware that till the middle of the nineteenth century in Scotland, many births went unrecorded. This is a major problem for the researcher. Nonetheless, we were hopeful we might find our author's name somewhere in one of the many registers, especially Old Parish Registers, which, though they're by no means comprehensive, are our best resource.

But even these registers present additional, chronic problems for the researcher: the handwriting can often be illegible and the spelling of names tends to be quite haphazard, depending on the whim of the Registrar — spelling in those days was not at all standardized.

Knowing this, we included in our search such variant spellings as Macbeane, Macbayne, Macbyne, MacVaine, and so on. To our chagrin, after we took the diverse spellings into account, we ultimately came across hundreds of possible candidates.

Using all sources at our disposal (census results, military lists, etc.), we were able to eliminate quite a number of them — some had died either at birth or quite young from disease, or as soldiers in various wars, or had emigrated to Australia or Canada where they'd disappeared from the records. As far as most of the others were concerned — farmers, shepherds, carpenters, doctors, etc. — we followed up on them to the extent we were able, but could find no information whatever to indicate they might be authors on the side. Though, of course, any one of them might have been our man.

We were beginning to think we'd exhausted all avenues. Then, by the purest chance, we found what we'd been searching for all along.

Jean Murdo deserves all the credit. She, like myself, had been quite captivated by The Obsidian Cloud and had often talked to her husband about it and about our hunt for the elusive Macbane. Now Jean's husband happens to be a barrister in a big law firm here in Glasgow, and when he came home from work just a week ago, he had surprising news for her.

Shortly before finishing for the day, he'd been searching for legal precedents regarding some matter his firm was involved in. He'd been obliged to consult the multi-volumed reports of Scottish court cases over the centuries. These books are usually written in such dry legalese that no one else can stomach them, except lawyers.

Jean's husband had been skimming through Volume VI of the mid-nineteenth-century Scottish Law Reporter, *which consists of brief outlines of the facts in many of the legally interesting cases of the day, with a few notes on the judgments and their significance.*

The title of one particular case quite unrelated to his own research just happened to catch his eye.

He glanced over the case and immediately realized its potential significance for Jean. So he photocopied the pages in question and brought them home to her. I've recopied the salient pages for you here. I suggest you refer to them now before reading the rest of this letter.

This sounded so exciting, I immediately did as he said. The photocopied pages were a little smeared and blurry, being copies of copies of a much-handled and ancient tome. But their contents were vivid and startling.

2

THE CROWN V ISABEL MACBANE AND ROBERT LEANIE

At the session of the Edinburgh Assizes held in the summer of 1866, Isabel Macbane (née Leanie) and Robert Leanie, her brother, were arraigned for the domestic murder of Macbane's husband, Revon Kenelm Macbane.

The Attorney General, who prosecuted the case himself, was satisfied from the evidence laid before him that he should prefer differing charges for the respective roles the accused played in the murder. Robert Leanie was therefore charged with the act of delivering the mortal wounds with a carving knife. Isabel Macbane, who was at the scene, was charged with "art and part," known in English law as "aiding and abetting."

Upon their arraignment, the prisoners refused to plead.

The trial proceeded before a jury, with Justice Alexander Weir as presiding judge. He entered a plea of not guilty on behalf of the prisoners, as is customary when accused persons refrain from cooperating.

Various witnesses were called to give evidence. It was established that the victim of the crime, Revon Kenelm Macbane, who had been educated in the parish school, was a clerk in the office of the Kilcorran coal mine. Isabel Macbane, to whom he was married for five years, was a farmer's daughter.

On the evening of June 12, the aforesaid Isabel Macbane entered her domicile in the company of her brother, Robert Leanie, a farm hand. They approached her husband, Revon Kenelm Macbane, who was writing in his papers at the parlour table, whereupon Leanie did intend to stab him to his death, in an act of murder with the assistance of Isabel Macbane. Which murder they duly did perform. The corpse having been mutilated further, the two accused did set about to burn all books and papers in the domicile. Thereafter they fled to England where they were arrested as they attempted to board the Dover packet for Calais.

Thus, the case against Robert Leanie and Isabel Macbane having been presented, Justice Weir attempted to question the accused. They did remain silent, jointly refusing a response.

Justice Weir then directed the jury, lacking any reason to do otherwise, to return a verdict of guilty: Robert Leanie of murder, Isabel Macbane of art and part, as being his accomplice and inciter in the act. The verdict having been so returned, Justice Weir subsequently donned the black cap and pronounced sentence of death by hanging. The prisoners were to be held for one week then to be executed upon a gallows erected in the town centre of Kilcorran, near the domicile where the crime occurred.

...

At the 1866 Michaelmas Assembly of Justices held in Edinburgh at the Chief Justice's chambers, consideration was being given by the Assembly to the better preventing of the horrid crime of husband-murder.

The Chief Justice alluded to the prevalent and traditional method used by Scottish wives in husband-murder, viz. the administering by said wives of covert doses of strychnine, causing the victims' certain deaths, slow and painful. The Chief Justice recalled that in previous eras, judges were given latitude in imposing penalties suited to crimes in order for the deterrence of similar offences by others.

In the instance of husband-murder, dissection after hanging or public gibbeting were the most common sentences imposed upon such wives. The Chief Justice averred that the sight of ravens feeding upon a gibbeted corpse in the Grassmarket was not easily forgotten by the populace. He regretted the diminishment of Scottish law through the subsequent abolition of such penalties by the Parliament in London in the Act of 1834.

Justice Alexander Weir now spoke. He adverted to the recent trial of Isabel Macbane and Robert Leanie over which he had presided. He revealed that in the women's cell of the Calton Hill prison on the day before her removal to the place of execution, Isabel Macbane discovered to him, in the presence of his secretary, the reasons and manner of her actions towards her husband, the cruelly murdered Revon Kenelm Macbane. For accuracy, Justice Weir read from his secretary's transcription as follows:

JUSTICE WEIR: Why did you request this interview?

ISABEL MACBANE: Because my death is near, I wish the full truth to be known.

JUSTICE WEIR: Proceed.

ISABEL MACBANE: My marriage to Rev Macbane was arranged through my father by means of a dowry. But Macbane was not a good husband to me. Within a year of our marriage, when he came home from work, he spent his time at his writing table. All the energy left in him was drained into his pen. Though he shared the same bed with me, he was infertile in it and I was thereby doomed never to bear offspring. But he was fertile enough with the other woman.

JUSTICE WEIR: To whom do you refer?

ISABEL MACBANE: The woman was she who tends the Kilcorran subscription library where he went many times. She could read his own writings. I did not learn to read for as a child I must tend the pigs on the farm of my father, so Rev Macbane had contempt for me.

JUSTICE WEIR: Was there adultery between your husband and this woman?

ISABEL MACBANE: Yes. My brother Robert Leanie at my request spied on them and witnessed the adultery through the window of her own dwelling. That woman was already much swollen in the belly as my brother did see with his own eyes. When Rev Macbane came home from her, we seized his arms at his back and fastened them with a rope. He admitted the adultery and I told him he would die for it as he only married me for the dowry for the printing of his books and that he planted his seeds elsewhere. He said he might have loved me if I was able to read. I promised him that I would burn every last one of his obsidian clouds and all his papers. He begged me to spare them for they were innocent of any offence.

JUSTICE WEIR: What are these obsidian clouds to which you refer?

ISABEL MACBANE: They were his books of which he had printed fifty copies by the use of my dowry.

JUSTICE WEIR: Describe the murder and the mutilation of the body.

ISABEL MACBANE: I brought the carving knife from the kitchen and gave the knife to my brother who stabbed Rev Macbane through the ribs five times, once for each year of our marriage. He was still alive and begged to be spared. From his desk I took his jar of ink and his pen with the steel nib. My brother held him by the jaw and I poured the ink down his throat and with the pen I cut open his throat like a Spring hog. Then the ink mixed with his blood spilled out of the cut and down his belly. I watched him till the light went out in his eyes. Then we gathered all his obsidian clouds and the other papers from his desk and threw them into the fireplace till they were burnt, so that nothing of them remained but ashes.

JUSTICE WEIR: Have you remorse for your crime?

ISABEL MACBANE: Only that my brother is now to be hanged because of me. He would not have killed Rev Macbane, for he acted only at my bidding.

The transcription having been read, Justice Alexander Weir declared to the Chief Justice and all those at the Annual Assembly of Justices that after the interview with Isabel Macbane, he thought much about the aptness of her sentence. He believed it was certainly commendable in her that she should have murdered Revon Macbane, her husband, outright by means of force, rather than by the act of poisoning him through stealth. But in Justice Weir's opinion, illiterate though the woman was, she understood well that exterminating the memory of Revon Macbane by the burning of his books and papers was the same as to kill him twice, and so a double crime. Upon this consideration, Justice Weir argued that in such cases the double penalty of gibbeting, in addition to mere hanging, ought to be restored as in the time before the Act of 1834.

The Chief Justice concurred with these remarks and proposed a motion: "That the new leniency in sentencing in capital cases is most regrettable and should be reconsidered for taking insufficient account of the deterrence effect generations of our predecessors on the Scottish Bench deemed necessary."

Motion seconded, by Justice Alexander Weir. Motion approved, *nem. con.*, by the Assembly of Justices.

3

I had to go over the photocopied pages more than once. I could hardly believe what I'd just read. The language in them was a little old-fashioned and sometimes hard to follow because of the legal terms, but the meaning was clear enough. I was in a state of shock as I returned to Soulis's letter.

I know you'll be as delighted as I am at the discovery of this documentary evidence, brief though it may be. Moments such as these are what a researcher lives for.

It had never for a moment entered our heads that "Rev" was an abbreviation of the given name, Revon, and not of "Reverend." We'd quite naturally assumed the writer was a clergyman. We've since discovered that Revon is in fact an old name (Middle Scots for "raven"), and is still used in some families in the Uplands, though infrequently nowadays.

Macbane himself may have actually hoped this confusion with the religious designation would help convince some publisher to take a chance on the manuscript. If so, the ploy was quite understandable. Hard though it may be for us to believe, at that time, even the most insipid books by a clergyman were guaranteed a wide readership.

But if such a ruse was intended by Macbane, it clearly didn't help him get a publisher. We now know from no less reliable a source than the Scottish Law Reporter that he had to pay out of his own pocket — or, more accurately, out of his wife's dowry — for the private printing of fifty copies of The Obsidian Cloud in large quarto format by The Old Ayr Press. The firm probably gave him a bargain price; as

I suggested to you when we met, they'd have been only too happy to use up the remnants of some old reams of paper. Macbane would have brought the fifty copies home for storage.

Obviously not every single copy was consumed in the fire set by his wife: you, for instance, found one in Mexico — more on that in a moment! — of all places. So perhaps Macbane had already managed to place a few with booksellers, or given some away as gifts. Perhaps he'd even persuaded the local subscription library to take one — after all, he seemed to have had more than the usual lender's privileges there.

Indeed that rather cynical suspicion led us down another track: looking for the identity of the woman at the library with whom Macbane had the adulterous relationship. We knew there were bound to be documents somewhere about Kilcorran's subscription library. Even if we could find nothing about the woman, it would be fascinating if we could at least discover what kinds of books Macbane read.

These subscription libraries, by the way, were very common all over Britain. Patrons had to pay a small fee (a "subscription") for the privilege of borrowing books. A history of the county of Ayrshire recorded that the Kilcorran branch was in operation for more than a hundred years and only closed in the 1890s when a free public library took its place. The original library had been housed in one of the wings of the old Kilcorran town hall, which was demolished at the turn of the century.

But we were sure the subscription library's records must be preserved somewhere in the town's archives, so we kept digging. We haven't so far found the membership and borrowing records, but we did stumble across a list of the librarians who served there.

Now here's the exciting part: from 1864 till 1866 the librarian in charge of the Kilcorran subscription library was a woman by the name of Ramona Vasquez — a citizen of Mexico — from the city of La Verdad! We discovered subsequently in the city's archives that her husband, Alonso Vasquez, was an official representative of the Mexican government's Ministry of Mining. He was based at Kilcorran for two years, studying mining operations in the Uplands before returning to Mexico. It seems that he brought his wife with him for his two-year appointment in the Uplands. She must have been proficient enough in English to be able to look after the Kilcorran subscription library.

We speculate (remember, this is only speculation) that Señora Vasquez may have met Macbane at the library, encouraged him in more ways than one, and possibly received a copy of The Obsidian Cloud, which she may have taken back to Mexico with her — conceivably this very copy which is now yours. We can't be certain exactly when the Vasquez family went back to La Verdad: we haven't been able to find any other reference to them in the Kilcorran archives. But if Macbane was indeed the father of Ramona Vasquez's child, we have yet one more possibly fruitful research avenue to explore. Vasquez is such a popular name in Mexico, future scholars will certainly be kept busy.

On the other hand, thanks to the Scottish Law Reporter, we do now have definitive, albeit limited, information on

The Obsidian Cloud *and on the life of Macbane himself: he was educated at a local parish school, he was married, he was murdered, and* The Obsidian Cloud, *published between 1864 and 1866, seems to have been his only work in print. This latter fact would account in part for the lack of success of our earlier inquiries. The most tragic aspect of the matter, from a researcher's standpoint, is that since all of Macbane's other papers were incinerated at the time of his death, his entire reputation may have to rest on this one book.*

Regarding Macbane's wife, Isabel, we were also hopeful of finding more about her on the basis of the trial record, but so far we've had no luck. Unlike Macbane, she seems to have been kept too busy on her father's farm to attend the parish school for a basic education. Illiteracy was the fate of most farm children of the day, especially girls. Sadly, it turned out to be one of the important factors in the murder of her husband.

Now that we know Macbane himself went to the parish school, we're trying to find some documentation on the one located at Kilcorran. These schools existed in every town in Scotland before government-supported education was introduced, so no doubt a file on the Kilcorran school is tucked away in a dusty corner of the vaults of the Ministry of Education. From it we might learn something more about Macbane's background and parentage, for example.

In sum, I'm very confident that there's much yet to be uncovered. In my profession we tend to be optimistic. These recent findings show precisely why a curator must never give up.

Now, on a final, related note, I venture once more to beg you to consider donating your copy of The Obsidian Cloud to our permanent collection. I regret that we don't have sufficient funds for any kind of remuneration, especially since you've already been most generous. But we would certainly issue a tax receipt to you for an appropriate amount, if it would be of any use to you in Canada.

My plan for the book would be to have it installed in one of our special book display boxes in the exhibit area of the centre. These boxes are generally used to show off the works of the great luminaries of Scottish literature: first editions of Hume, Scott, and Stevenson are in one of the boxes right now. But we pride ourselves on showcasing less well-known literary curiosities we feel are deserving of special attention. The Obsidian Cloud would certainly fill that bill.

I myself will be writing a detailed account of our discoveries regarding Macbane in the feature article of the spring issue of Archivists Quarterly. Naturally, you will be fully credited there for your involvement. I am certain the book will become a subject of great interest to scholars of the period. In the not too distant future, I fully expect to see new editions of it in print.

Again, thank you on behalf of the National Cultural Centre for having put The Obsidian Cloud into our hands in the first place. I do look forward to hearing your intentions regarding its ultimate disposal and hope you will consider this institution a worthy recipient.

Yours, etc.
Soulis.

4

I was as appalled at Soulis's findings as he was elated.

From his point of view as a curator, it was a job well done. He and his assistant had managed to unearth some key answers to what had at first looked like an insoluble mystery. Most importantly they'd established that a man called Revon Macbane really had once existed, and that this man was indeed the author of *The Obsidian Cloud*.

In his letter, Soulis barely mentioned Macbane's brutal death. For him the murderers' truly unforgivable action seemed to be the incinerating of Macbane's other papers, which would have been invaluable for scholars.

BUT I WAS NO CURATOR. My link to Macbane and his book was an intimate matter—I'd come to think of him as *my* author, *my* discovery. For me, the revelation of how he'd died was as shocking as if I'd just heard that a close friend had been sadistically tortured and murdered.

Indeed, reading the letter only strengthened the feeling that my relationship with Macbane was a special one. I'd always thought it curious enough that Mexico, of all places, was where I'd stumbled on the weird old book that evoked a moment in my own past in Scotland. Now, to find out that Macbane himself had had an actual, physical link—if only in the form of this Señora Vasquez—with Mexico!

Nor could I ever forget the most important way in which Macbane's life intersected with my own—that, but for him, I'd probably never have known of Sarah's existence. I owed him a profound debt of gratitude. Which made it all the harder to bear the thought that his brutal murder meant he'd never hold what might be his own child in his arms.

In my frame of mind, Soulis's letter really was appalling. If I'd even remotely guessed what his research would uncover, I wouldn't have considered putting the book into his hands. It was almost as though, by making that research possible, I myself had murdered Macbane.

SO THAT WAS my first reaction—regret that I'd ever sent *The Obsidian Cloud* to Soulis in the first place. By letting the book out of my safekeeping, I'd betrayed Macbane. Because of my curiosity, he'd been dragged into a callous world of "facts" where his weird book and his mutilated body would qualify equally as grist for the scholarly mill.

BUT IN TIME, when I calmed down, I realized that my instinctive response to Soulis's letter was just a selfish whim. Book lovers naturally do feel a kind of possessiveness and protectiveness in how they relate to certain authors and books, as though they were pets.

No, I'd done the right thing sending the book to Soulis. If by some miracle Macbane could have foreseen that over a century later a copy of *The Obsidian Cloud* would be found a world away from the Uplands in the Bookstore de Mexico, he certainly wouldn't have wanted the finder to keep it all to himself. His dying words clearly show that. He'd have hoped his book would become known to others, not kept hidden in a vault like some rare painting for a private collector's unique viewing pleasure.

He'd have applauded my decision to bring it to the attention of a man like Soulis, and maybe through him to a wider audience than he'd found in his life.

Anyway, one thing would always be mine alone: the experience of discovering *The Obsidian Cloud*. When I opened that old quarto for the first time and saw there on the title page the word "Duncairn," I could almost have believed the book had been waiting for me, had somehow chosen me—a man with his own private mystery in Duncairn—to bring its mysteries to light.

Of course, I'm aware that the very idea of a book having such powers is just romantic nonsense. Yet even to this day, thinking about that moment causes the little hairs on the back of my neck to rise, just as they once did in the oddly named Bookstore de Mexico in the sweltering heat of La Verdad.

EPILOGUE

Everything might have ended, as endings go, on that relatively pleasing note.

I say "relatively," for though my curiosity about the mystery of *The Obsidian Cloud* had been satisfied, along with it came the awful news of how Macbane had died. Likewise, though I now understood Miriam's reason for having rejected me, I'd always regret having missed so many years of my new-found daughter's life.

Ah well. I consoled myself with the thought that, outside of romantic fiction, completely happy endings are scarce, no matter how much one might wish for them.

I'd no idea something disturbing was still in store for me.

A YEAR PASSED before Sarah and her fiancé were finally able to come over to Canada to meet Frank. They had such busy work schedules that they could arrange to be away for only five days in July. They stayed at the Walner for the duration of their visit. Frank and I were able to show them the sights of Camberloo and the surrounding countryside at its summer best, and take them to several of our favourite restaurants. And we talked, talked, talked.

I'd dearly hoped Sarah and Frank would hit it off, though I'd been a little uneasy. After all, who knows how people will get along? Even our own minds can be quite a mystery to us, so I certainly couldn't take it for granted that two siblings who'd never met—never even known about each other's existence—would instantly find in the other some quality they were drawn to. On the other hand, surely it wasn't quite as improbable as, for instance, the appearance of a huge black mirror hovering over the Uplands sky.

As it turned out, my worries were needless. They did get along tremendously well together right from the start. I think they were both determined to like each other. She seemed to find everything about him quite charming, especially after a visit to the Emporium, which she obviously thought revealed a lot about him. Probably because of her profession, she wasn't at all shy about asking him the kinds of questions I'd never have dreamt of asking. For example, what did he think was the driving force behind his mania for collecting? Was he some kind of weird historical adventurer who needed, for some reason, to make physical contact with the past through these outlandish artifacts? And so on.

Frank answered that he just enjoyed building around himself a private world that interested him. Wasn't that what everyone did in their own way? Mightn't it be spoiled by overanalyzing the motivations behind it?

They both laughed. I could see that Frank already had complete faith in her. Like me, he enjoyed her earnestness, her aura of being in command of herself, though not in any forbidding way. Quite unconsciously, she took on the big sisterly role and he loved her for it, as though it was something he'd always needed.

Not only was I happy at that, but there was a spinoff for me, too. Sarah was obviously very fond of me because she'd found her real father. And that rubbed off noticeably on Frank. It was one of those incremental things. Seeing me through the eyes of someone he liked, who liked me, seemed to make him like me all the more, too.

As for Sarah's fiancé, he made a good impression on us. He

was a tall, quiet man, a lawyer from Edinburgh, with a dry sense of humour. At one point, for instance, I was updating Sarah on the curator's latest discoveries about *The Obsidian Cloud*. Her fiancé was especially interested in the legal aspects of the trial of Macbane's wife. When I got to the part about the Chief Justice's regret over the abolition of gibbeting, he nodded his head.

"Even today in Edinburgh, a public gibbeting would be guaranteed to draw a big crowd," he said.

We all laughed at that. If Sarah had needed our approval of him, she could see she had it.

OVER THE WEEKEND, Dupont's name came up several times in our conversations.

Sarah remembered I'd mentioned him at Eildon House and asked more about his work. I was evasive—I wouldn't like to say too much about it, for it was top secret. Of course, I would have invited him to meet her, but there was no way of contacting him. I'd tried the phone directory but was told that, if such an institute existed, its number must be unlisted.

From the way she looked at me, I'm not sure she was convinced by that excuse. But she left it at that, saying only that she was sorry Dupont didn't live nearer Camberloo—she'd have loved to talk to him. I amused myself thinking of the two of them engrossed in their own private debate on which would be the better way of modifying a damaged psyche—talk therapy, or an ice pick through the forehead? Sarah would assume that my old friend's passionate advocacy of the surgical route must only be for the sake of argument.

The truth was, I was glad I hadn't made any attempt to invite Dupont. With her astuteness, she might have got him talking about Griffin, and even about my own involvement with her, too.

JUST LAST NIGHT, this all-too-brief visit by Sarah and her fiancé came to an end. Frank drove us all to the airport. Before they left us at the security check, Sarah invited us to come to Edinburgh for their wedding, in the fall. We said we'd be delighted. In the meantime, we'd all miss one another.

From the airport, Frank dropped me off home around midnight. He then headed for his own apartment beside the park.

The disturbing thing I mentioned was about to happen.

I SAT ON THE DECK for a half hour with a glass of scotch to help me relax, enjoying the warm summer night and the sky full of stars. When I eventually got to bed, I left the bedside lamp on, for I thought I might glance through the latest issue of *Pumps International* for a while. It was on the nightstand, lying on top of Soulis's letter, which I'd gone over so many times since the day it arrived I almost had the pages by heart.

I soon gave up trying to read my *Pumps International*—I just couldn't concentrate on it. My mind was still full of Sarah's visit and the fact that she'd got along so well with Frank. I also wondered if I'd tried hard enough to locate Dupont. And that got me to thinking, once more, about the Griffin episode and the frightening words he'd used when he realized she'd shared my bed that night at Institute 77. "She was the most dangerous lover you've ever had," he'd said. I'd congratulated myself on surviving whatever menace he believed her capable of.

But now, lying there in bed thinking about those words, I suddenly began to worry. For some reason, I felt paranoid.

Acting on instinct, I then did something quite bizarre. I got out of bed, went down to the garage, and found my old long-handled chopping axe, quite rusty from lack of use. Glad that no one could see my foolishness, I took it with me to the bedroom and put it beside the nightstand. I climbed back into bed and switched off the light. In the dark room, as I lay there listening, the slow blades of the ceiling fan above me were like the legs of a huge spider circling its web.

SURE ENOUGH, after no more than ten minutes, I thought I heard a peculiar noise coming from the area of the walk-in closet—a rustling, snickering sound. My heart began hammering so fast I could hardly breathe. I'd absolutely no doubt that was the sound I'd heard in the guest room at Institute 77 on the night Griffin paid me a visit.

I tried to calm myself, then reached out cautiously and switched on the little bedside lamp. A quick glance around the room revealed no sign of any intruder. Of course, that was small comfort in the case of someone so hard to detect as Griffin.

So, I lifted the chopping axe from beside the nightstand with my right hand and slithered out of bed. I heard that sound again—it seemed to be coming from behind the half-open door of the closet. I took a deep breath and, reassured by the heft of the axe, began to tiptoe across the floor. My left hand I kept stretched out in front of me, sifting the seemingly empty space with my fingers in case of an unseeable predator.

In this way I arrived outside the closet, the half-open door revealing only its dark and fearsome interior. I took several more deep breaths. Then with my axe held high, I crouched in the attacking position, snatched the door fully ajar, and switched on the closet light.

Nothing. But the garments were swaying ominously, back and forth, back and forth, back and forth.

I had no intention of retreating. I steeled myself once more, stepped inside the closet, and began moving cautiously along the array of shirts, jackets, and pants. My free left hand probed amongst them, feeling for her almost-human flesh.

Nothing.

I was about to breathe again, to relax. When all at once that sound—a rustling, a snickering—was right behind me.

The hair on the back of my head bristled. There was no room for me to squirm away or turn and lash out with my axe. I hunched over like a rabbit paralyzed with fear, waiting for the predator to strike me down.

Nothing happened.

I waited and I waited. But still no blow came, no predator struck me down. Instead, very soon, what did begin to strike me was the absurdity of what I was doing—a grown man with a rusty chopping axe in his hand looking for a monster in his clothes closet! Of course I couldn't see Griffin there—because she wasn't in this closet, she wasn't anywhere in Camberloo, she wasn't even in Canada! The sound I'd taken as her mocking laughter must have been the innocent rustling of sports coats and office shirts and striped ties on their hangers, caused by the draft from the ceiling fan on this warm summer night. The clothes had swayed that ominous way only because I'd jerked the closet door open with such force.

In fact, the one genuine thing had been my terror. The rest was just the result of tiredness and an overstimulated imagination. The entire scene had come from that workshop in the mind that begins its operations when the rational part shuts down for the night.

BACK IN MY BED once more, I thought about the significance of what had just happened. It hadn't been a dream: I'd been wide awake when I tiptoed across the bedroom with a chopping axe at the ready. I really *had* been standing there in the clothes closet feeling like an idiot. That surely meant that for the very first time, the world of nightmare had intruded into my waking life. Long ago, Gordon Smith had told me he was glad he wasn't a chronic dreamer because of this very possibility—and I'd laughed at the idea. But now I'd experienced it, and I didn't like it. In fact, I was so worried by it that I lay there for the longest time, trying to keep myself awake. In the end, I did fall asleep and—of course—I did dream.

Dupont, complete with twin-pointed beard and bells, was showing me Griffin through iron bars. She was quite visible, sitting on her bed, her skin much greyer than before—a deathly grey. In her thin, grey arms, she was cradling a tiny baby and was leaning forward as though to kiss it. Then, not unexpectedly, the crunching sound began: she was devouring its tiny fingers. She held it out towards me, as if to share the hideous feast. Her eyes were silver slits and her face was grey. Her open mouth was a bloody cavern.

"What a tasty meal," Dupont was saying, his little bells all a-jingle.

NOW, THE MORNING AFTER, I'm sitting here in the kitchen drinking my coffee beneath the photograph of Miriam I retrieved from Duncairn Manor. But neither its presence, nor the faint songs of birds through the window, the distant swish of cars and trucks—these reassuring, mundane sounds—have done much to put me at ease after a night such as I've just passed. Even though Griffin didn't actually visit me, the aura of menace in the bedroom was so real it still makes me shudder. The dream that followed was equally powerful, and its horrific images are still prominent in my mind.

When I think about the two disquieting experiences in broad daylight, in a calm and objective way—as an engineer might consider them—it isn't hard to figure out a rational explanation. Their genesis is really quite logical. During Sarah's visit, Dupont's name and his work at Institute 77 came up several times. Naturally, those conversations led me to think about Griffin. She, in turn, eventually became the centrepiece of my recent terror in the closet as well as in the subsequent dream.

Even that image of her feasting on the baby has a simple explanation. It's just a skewed version of the incident in my real-life African journey with Dupont—when my fellow travellers ate the little tree monkeys on skewers. That grisly scene had been imprinted on my memory.

The point I'm making is that when I'm being calm and objective, I have no trouble whatsoever finding reasons for the state of mind that made me so susceptible last night. Indeed, I could add to them the fact that I've been under some stress—needlessly, as it turns out—over how Frank and Sarah would get along when they met. I could even include the traumatic news about the awful death of Macbane, a man with whom I have a unique connection, a man I'd come to consider, almost, as my closest friend. I suppose I really haven't got over that yet.

The accumulation of all these things must have made me vulnerable.

SO MUCH FOR when I'm being calm and objective.

But when that state of mind passes, the catalogue of rational explanations appears to me desperate and empty. They're nothing but self-deception, a way for me to avoid acknowledging the thing I'm really terrified of, so much so that I'm almost afraid to put it into words, in case the words become prophetic.

That dreadful truth is as follows.

I was indeed euphoric over the finding of my daughter, Sarah, and being able to witness her joyous coming together with Frank. But my happiness was moderated by a frightening notion that began lurking in a dark corner of my mind. It emerged from hiding, full-blown, last night.

What I'd been trying not to think about was this: the possibility that Griffin, too, might have had a child by me, as a result of our night together at Institute 77.

If that were the case, her primitive maternal urge to share her child might well drive her to come looking for me, its father. Then I'd have to acknowledge to the world—especially to my own children—my paternity of her baby. After that, would Frank want anything to do with this other half-sibling, with its half-human mother, or with me? And as for Sarah—when she found out what I'd done, would she be left with anything but contempt for the newly-discovered father she'd almost come to love?

On the other hand, there is yet another, simpler reason for my fear. That Griffin has no baby, but is searching for me because she craves me as her lover, one more time. And that afterwards, she will tear me to pieces.

AT THIS POINT, the sensible part of my mind again tries to assert itself.

"Harry Steen," it says. "All of this is just speculation based on nothing more than an overripe imagination and a bad dream. You torment yourself for nothing."

If only that were so.

For there is something more, something tangible. The fact is, when I eventually got up this morning, I saw that the curator's letter wasn't on the bedside table. Instead, the pages were lying on the floor beside the bed. Now it's possible that I myself scattered them with all my paranoid exertions, but I can't assume that.

So, though I fully intended to take the chopping axe back out to the garage today, I've decided now to leave it beside my bed, at least for the next few nights—just in case a situation arises. Wouldn't any rational person do the same thing? Certainly, in view of what happened to him, I think Macbane would agree with my decision.

Not that I'll be asking anyone for advice. Some things, I always feel, you're better off keeping to yourself.

End